By Jack Gantos

Desire Lines
Joey Pigza Swallowed the Key

The Jack Henry Books

Jack on the Tracks: *Four Seasons of Fifth Grade*
Heads or Tails: *Stories from the Sixth Grade*
Jack's New Power: *Stories from a Caribbean Year*
Jack's Black Book

For Nathan!

**Jack's Black Book**

1999

Wood shop is killing me. Today I was
using the electric jigsaw so I could
carve Beau-Beau's name out of an old pine
board I found on the back of Dad's
truck. Well I was nervous using
it because I had never used one
before and I was paying real close
attention until Mr. Gilette snuck
up on me from behind and yell—
ed, "Henry you nitwit!" I turned
to look at him and the saw went
out of control and did a little
jig across my fingers. and it
hurt like having my hand
slammed in a car door and the
blood spurted out all over my
face and on Mr Gilette's hat.

and he went nutty and started yelling
at me and I got nervous and grabbed
the dancing saw but it jerked away
from me and somehow it stayed on
and I kept trying to grab the
trigger but my hands were slippery
with blood and the only thing at
that moment I could think about
was murder like a murder mystery
novel where a real demented sicko
takes a victim and cuts up his
victim. Some fingers and
toes would be difficult, but just
think how hard it would be to
saw through a leg or a neck or
a belly. But if I was writing the book
my character would be strong and cool

# JACK'S BLACK BOOK

## Jack Gantos

A Sunburst Book
Farrar, Straus and Giroux

Copyright © 1997 by Jack Gantos
Distributed in Canada by Douglas & McIntyre Ltd.
Printed in the United States of America
Designed by Caitlin Martin
First edition, 1997
Sunburst edition, 1999


Library of Congress Cataloging-in-Publication Data
Gantos, Jack.
    Jack's black book / Jack Gantos. — 1st ed.
        p.     cm.
    Summary: Comic misadventures ensue when seventh-grader
Jack tries to write the great American novel.
    ISBN 0-374-43716-5 (pbk.)
    [1. Authorship—Fiction.   2. Humorous Stories.]   I. Title.
PZ7.G15334Jab      1997
[Fic]—dc21                                    96-53107

*For Mabel Grace*

# Contents

PART ONE

Go Dog Go, or
How I Passed the Seventh Grade                    3

PART TWO

The Blind Leading the Blind, or
Fish with Feet                                    59

PART THREE

The Fall of the House of Pagoda, or
The Tattooed Toe                                 121

was the last to know that
these kind of Cocker Spaniel dogs
had their                    brains bred
out                    of them a
long                    time ago
so                    they would
                    be really
                    stupid
                    and just
                    lay

BEAU-BEAU

346.

REST IN

PEACE

Hole diggin' Dog?
around the house all day
but our Beau-Beau was like
an experiment gone bad, as if
Doctor Frankenstien had
made him from a bunch of
different dog pieces he found
at a vet's office. He had the
giant paws of a Great Dane
and the brain of a Chichuahua.
Once he was desperate to go
outside and he went out the
little cat rubber door and got
stuck half way through. Unfortunately his back half was still
inside the house so he pooped on

the rug. When we found him we
tried to pull him out but he was stuck
so dad had to get **PART ONE** he
used to pack wheel bearings and we
slathered it all over Beau-Beau's fur.
We gave ⊟⬭⬭⊟ him a tug by his
hind legs. He yelped
really loud but he
did make it through the
opening. Then I had to give
a bath that took
**Go Dog Go,** because the
greasy was so hard to
get
**or** out.
**How I Passed** ugh?
I think
**the Seventh** most
what I'll **Grade** Beau-Beau was the
about any kind
way he of bugs.
Pete
used to
feed
him any kind of
big juicy Palmetto
bug and he
would snap it

SLIM
JACK
- SPICY -
- SMOKER -
- SNACK -

I'm JACK

ingredients:
FAT, pi...
g butt...
eyes, ears + toe

JACK
SLIM

WE
LOVE
YOU

# One

It was pitch-black in my room and as I wrote I tried to imagine the size of each letter so I could keep the words in line and read what I had written in the light of morning. But no matter how carefully I wrote I knew my words would be jumbled and piled up over each other like train cars that had jumped the tracks. It didn't matter if I could read the words or not. I knew what I was thinking when I wrote them. They were the same discouraging thoughts in the light of day or in the middle of the night. I had the words memorized from saying them to myself over and over again as I walked down the street, or opened a book, or tried to write. *Moron. Idiot. Stupid.* Two weeks earlier I had received my aptitude-test scores from school and since then I had been giving myself a hard time. Now I could feel myself reaching the end of my rope.

After another restless night I rolled out of bed and held

the curtain to one side. It was just purple enough over the Teeters' roof to know it was time to get ready for school. Pete was still asleep on his side of the room. I wanted to sneak over there and strangle him. The night before, he said it was a good thing I was brain dead because if I was ever in the army and captured, the enemy could torture me all they wanted and I'd still have nothing to confess.

I looked down at the floor. My personal diary was open to the page I had last written. It looked like the scratching of a madman just moments before he did something he could never take back. If I threw myself off the Intercoastal bridge and drowned, everyone would think they knew why once they read what I'd been writing. They'd say things like, "Poor kid had low self-esteem." Or, "He didn't get enough positive reinforcement." But they'd be missing the point. Calling myself an idiot wasn't about receiving enough gold stars or pats on the head. This was about scientific proof that I was dumb. Slow. Dim. Mentally challenged. A born, biological, stone-cold *loser.*

Right next to my personal diary was my new writer's journal. It was totally blank. Not a pencil scratch. Hardly a fingerprint. I bought the plain black book with unlined pages because I had decided to write a novel. I had made up my mind to become a writer, so I figured, why wait until I'm old? Write a novel now, make some money, and move from Fort Lauderdale to Paris or New York or Dublin, where all the famous writers live interesting lives. But I didn't know how to write a novel. I didn't know what my characters were like. I didn't know the setting. I didn't have a plot, or a theme, or even a beginning, middle, or end. I didn't have a clue—yet. I was still waiting for a good idea to strike me. I had read in an old writers' magazine that authors, when they were stuck, sometimes just needed to sit around in their bathrobes and stare dreamily up at the ceiling. Until, suddenly, an angel called a writer's "muse" would descend and whisper inspirational ideas into their ears. Then bingo, their pens begin to move across the pages like the pointer on a Ouija board. But the more I stared at the cracks in my ceiling while dressed in a terry-cloth bathrobe, sucking on my lead pencil point with my ears perked up like a Chihuahua's, the only ideas that rolled around my empty head were ugly. *Give up. Throw in the towel. You don't have what it takes to write a novel.* My stupidity was stalking me like some big dumb monster with a club. Every time I thought I was smart enough to write, WHAM, I'd get smacked across the side of the head. And the more I whaled on myself, the dumber I felt, and the more it paralyzed me. I hadn't written the first word, but I hadn't given up hope.

What encouraged me to stick with writing was this one weird thing: whenever I closed my eyes, the letters of the alphabet shifted around like Scrabble pieces and formed words. Those words lined up and soon I imagined entire pages of writing so clearly that I could actually read them, sentence after sentence, as if I were reading straight from a book. A book I had written, with my name on the cover and my stories inside. I could feel the weight of that book in my open hands and inhale the clean smell of ink and paper when I stuck my nose between the pages. I could imagine looking through a bookshop window and seeing a stack of my books on display. "Yes," I'd hiss. "The idiot did it! The moron has triumphed! Those are mine." And I'd be so dizzy with pride I'd stumble down the road as weak-kneed as a drunk. But even though I could see the book with my eyes closed, as soon as I opened them the words vanished. I knew those words were in me, I just had to squeeze them out.

I preferred getting up early in the morning since it was the only time I had the house to myself. I put on my old blue private-school pants which were now too tight because I was having a growth spurt. I yanked a white T-shirt down over my head and slipped into Dad's old mud-stained loafers. Mom had given up on dressing me as a catalogue cover boy for Sears, so I dressed myself to look like a combination mental-health outpatient and day laborer so I'd blend in with the tough local kids. I ran my fingers through my hair as I walked down the hall, past Betsy's room, and into the kitchen. BeauBeau III was sleeping in front of the refrigerator door like some bridge troll trying to collect a fee each time it was opened. I gave him a little kick in the rear. "Come on," I whispered, "time to make the donuts." He hopped up and began to stretch. His fleas stretched. His worms stretched. His ticks stretched. Everything but his brain stretched. He was a mess. I figured if I were a dog I'd be just like him.

I pulled out the carton of milk, flipped open the spout, and held it to my mouth. I loved ice-cold milk and took a long drink, swallowed, and drank some more before I began to gag. I dropped to my knees and spit up a clot of sour milk onto the kitchen floor. It jiggled about like a white cube of coagulated Jell-O. Fortunately, BeauBeau III was hungry, and before I could clean the floor he lapped up what I had spit out. Who's the bigger idiot? I wondered. Me or BeauBeau III? I didn't know the answer just yet, but he was definitely my main competition, and I figured we were running neck and neck in the Bonehead Sweepstakes.

BeauBeau III was Betsy's new dog. Last year, when we all lived in Barbados, Betsy had decided she was going to go to boarding school in London. When we left the island she stayed behind, packed and ready to go. But her plans didn't work out and she grudgingly returned from Barbados to join us back in Fort Lauderdale. She called Florida "the hairy armpit of the world" and was so depressed Mom let her pick out a pet in an effort to lift her spirits. One afternoon she returned from the Animal Rescue League with an already grown cocker spaniel, and just like BoBo I, who'd been eaten by an alligator in a canal near our old house in Fort Lauderdale, and BoBo II, who we had to leave behind in Barbados, this one had no trace of a brain. Betsy was now studying French and she had named him BeauBeau III. The prissy French name didn't make him any smarter. Betsy could educate his palate with all the French food she wanted—French bread, French fries, French toast, and French dip—she could dress him up in a beret, knot a scarf around his neck, and spray him with French perfume, yet he'd still be nothing more than a common American BoBo who cuts loose with paralyzing nerve gas during dinner, pees down his own leg when excited, eats palmetto bugs, and laps up Eric's baby vomit. But I loved him. He was my soul mate, my double, and was fast becoming my mentor. I was dumb and miserable, and I looked to him to teach me how to be dumb and happy. So far, I wasn't doing too well.

As I ran a sponge over the sticky spot on the floor, BeauBeau licked at my hand. His breath almost blistered my skin. "You're revolting," I said, turning my nose away from him. "Go outside and dig a hole."

He didn't need my permission. He squeezed his way through the cat-size rubber pet-door and into the back-yard. Digging holes was his obsession. He had dug so many our yard looked like a World War I battlefield. And he dug the deepest holes of any dog I'd ever seen. He could work his entire body below the surface and as he tunneled toward the center of the earth the dirt sprayed up and formed a mound to one side. In his former life he must have been a grave robber who'd been punished when he died by being reincarnated as a dumb dog.

I brushed my teeth, washed my face, and, since I was already dressed, sprayed deodorant on the outside of my shirt. I grabbed my black book from the bedroom floor and shoved it into my backpack. I carried it with me at all times just in case my muse decided to pay a visit while I was on the bus, or trying to figure out how to open my combination lock at school. A muse could strike at any time, the old writers' magazine had stressed, "even while one was engaged in personal hygiene." I wanted to be prepared.

I had just slung the backpack over my shoulder and was tiptoeing down the hallway when Betsy cracked open her bedroom door.

"Have a nice day, BeauBeau the fourth," she sang. She had been calling me that ever since I announced the results of my school aptitude tests at the dinner table. That was a colossal mistake. Telling my family that I was dumb was even more proof that I really was dumb. If I was even a little bit smart, I would have kept my mouth shut.

I faked a lunge at Betsy and growled. I had already pulled the pins out of her door hinges—my favorite trick—and was praying she might yank the door open a little farther so it would fall back and flatten her. But she held her ground and glared at me.

"Make sure your address is sewn inside your pocket in case you get lost," Betsy advised.

I wanted to scream out, "I'm not an idiot! Leave me alone!" But if I woke the baby Mom would get involved in a bad way. So I just sucked it up, took a deep breath, and thought I'd sew some other family's address labels on me, get lost, and be sent to a home full of nice people. And I'd take BeauBeau III with me, too.

Even when my family was trying to be thoughtful toward me, it hurt. The day before, I'd found a package of alphabet flash cards that Pete hid in my backpack. After I got him in a headlock and had BeauBeau lick his face, he said he was just trying to help educate me. And for the last two weeks Mom cooked me fish sticks for dinner because she said fish was "brain food."

Dad was the only one who didn't seem to mind that I was dumb. He said that if I was going to work with my hands for the rest of my life brains would just get in the way. He had taken a new job at a concrete factory and said I could always work in the warehouse as the rat exterminator. "You just take a broom handle and pound a rusty nail through the end. And when you see a rat chewing a bag of 'crete you just stab him through the brain." The thought of rat juice squirting out of a punctured brain gave me nightmares.

I continued down the hall and slipped out the front door before anyone else woke up and gave me a hard time. As I walked down the sidewalk toward the bus stop, BeauBeau was already deep into a hole. I could just see his tail wagging and a fan of dirt overhead.

"Go, BeauBeau, go," I hollered. "Dig a hole to France and we'll visit your relatives." He hopped out of the hole and shook the dirt from his coat. I peeled the wrapper off a Slim Jim I had saved for lunch, took a bite, and threw the rest in his direction. He snapped it out of the air and swallowed it whole. "See you later, buddy," I said. He barked and went back to work.

# Two

I began to call myself insulting loser names shortly after I was sent to Sunrise Junior High. It was known as a tough school, full of kids with low potential and no plans for the future. Gary Pagoda had gone there until he failed three years in a row and dropped out. He had already been a veteran juvenile delinquent by seventh grade, and even *he* swore it was dangerous. He called it a school for the "criminally insane." So I had figured it was like a prison filled with hardened convicts with swastikas tattooed onto their foreheads and homemade knives strapped inside their motorcycle boots. That was only a guess.

What really shocked me was when I found out how true my guess had been. After I had been at Sunrise for a few weeks I'd heard all about the school's peculiar history. Before it was a school, Sunrise Junior High had been Sunrise State Detention Center. When Florida still had chain gangs working to pick up trash and cut weeds on the side of highways, the criminals had been housed in the same rooms where I now studied English, math, science, and wood shop.

This made a lot of sense when I looked at the school's architecture. The double rows of twenty-foot-high chainlink fences were topped with rusty barbed wire that over the years had snagged a lot of plastic grocery bags. When the wind picked up, the bags snapped back and forth and sounded just like the tough girls smacking their gum as they lined up outside the phone booth. There were steel gates that led into the school, two in the front and two in the back. The stone towers sticking up at every corner had been guard shacks where trained snipers could pick off any escapees. Now one tower was used as a science and weather station, another as a "Time Out" zone for hyperactive bullies, one as the DARE office, and the other as headquarters for the Latin Club. I guessed they were the only club that got a tower because the few token smart kids needed to barricade themselves in from the illiterate Huns all day.

The more I poked around the school, the more evidence I found of the old prison. About every fifty feet down each corridor, there were swinging metal doors with bullet-proof glass panels. Broken security cameras mounted on steel poles were everywhere, inside and outside. There were thick bars over all the classroom windows. But the strangest thing about Sunrise was the wood and sheet-metal machine shop where prisoners had made institutional furniture, license plates, military dog tags, and other stuff no one else would make unless they were in prison. It was the size of a football stadium. This was why Sunrise was a magnet school for vocational training in *shop*. Kids—mostly guys—from all over Fort Lauderdale were bused to our school just to make benches, picture frames, jewelry boxes, letter openers, salad sets, bedside tables, baseball bats, and other stuff they sold in a little gift store next to the Department of Social Services office, which was next to the principal's office.

There was only one way to escape from Sunrise aside from tunneling under the fences. You had to *test* your way out of the school. You had to *prove* you were smart enough to be sent to a magnet school for the arts or sciences, or a school with a college-preparatory curriculum. And so I had signed up for the tests, figuring I'd be transferred out of there in no time.

Mr. Ploof was the Guidance Counselor. One Monday, as arranged, I went into his small office, which had probably been a padded isolation cell. He had prepared a battery of tests for me.

"Are you ready to exercise your mental muscle?" he asked, and pointed to his own hydrocephalic cranium, which was as hairless and white as the belly on a watermelon.

"I can't wait," I replied. "I've been thinking about this all night long."

"Should have just got some sleep," he remarked. "'Cause you're in for a long day."

He started out by timing how fast I could stack a hundred small washers onto a thin metal rod. I didn't even turn my brain on for that one. Instead, I daydreamed about my future. I figured in about a week I'd be in a school where the teachers actually helped students to write books. All day we'd read stacks of great novels and discuss them inside and out until we knew everything about how they were written. Then we'd write and rewrite our own books until we sent them off to be published.

Afterward Mr. Ploof gave me a tray of fifty assorted nuts and bolts and I had to fit the proper nuts to the proper bolts as quickly as possible. It was a breeze.

"Pretty good manual dexterity," Mr. Ploof remarked, nodding as he jotted down some figures on a pad.

"I write a lot," I said, stretching the truth. "Keeps the fingers limber. Besides, our dog can do this stuff."

"Don't go getting a swelled noggin," he warned, as his monstrous head wobbled dangerously on his skinny neck. "The tests get harder."

"Just bring it on," I said, feeling supremely confident that I was soon going to have my ticket out of this loser school.

I did a test where I read a page of mixed-up information, then summarized it in the most logical order. That took only an ounce of common sense. Then I had a long list of sentences where I filled in the blanks about my *feelings*. That took me extra time to sort through because I always felt two or three ways about any one thing that happened to me.

After that test I was a bit run down and asked if I could take a break, stretch my legs, and eat a snack. I had a family-size Zero bar stashed in my locker.

"No," he replied. I had begun to figure out that he was one of those people who stressed every word with a gesture. He said no while at the same time slowly rotating his head back and forth. A double no. Even if you didn't understand English, you would get the universal sign language for no.

"You have to do this all in a row," he explained. "Plus, you can't be left alone. How can I tell you won't *cheat*?" To illustrate that he had asked a question his hands darted out from his sides like a puzzled Egyptian hieroglyphic.

"How can I cheat?" I asked. "The questions are a secret. Besides, you can come with me."

"Pull yourself together," he said, and narrowed his eyes. "Part of this test is endurance." He jutted out his chin, but his head began to tilt forward so he pulled it back. Then he removed the standard IQ test from its sealed envelope and placed it face-down in front of me. "Now I want you to concentrate," he instructed, and tapped a finger against his temple. "Of everything you've done today, this is the most important. The IQ results will go on your permanent record and will be with you for the rest of your life."

It was as if he was reading me my Miranda rights—*you have the right to remain silent, the right to call an attorney, the right to . . .*

He removed a stopwatch from his pocket. "On your mark. Get set." He pressed the top button. "Go!" he shouted, and pointed toward an imaginary finish line.

I was so revved up I put too much pressure on my pencil and as I wrote down the first answer my point snapped. I desperately looked up at Mr. Ploof. "Can I start over?" I asked.

He frowned down at me. "No talking. Keep going!" he instructed.

I didn't have a pencil sharpener so I began to gnaw at the wood around the lead, spitting out the pulp, until I exposed the blunt end. I felt even more like a white laboratory rat, but I pulled myself together and raced through the test. For something so important it didn't seem too difficult or take very long even though I got off to a rough start. I found it more challenging when Mom asked me to sort the laundry into lights and darks and I had to decide where to put clothes that were mauve or salmon or chartreuse. But I never thought that sorting the laundry was an indication of my future potential.

When I lowered my pencil Mr. Ploof pressed another button on the stopwatch and wrote the time down on his pad.

"You can go now, but return next week for the results," he said.

"Thanks," I replied, picking at a few splinters in my lips. I dashed out the door and down the hall. I was starving, so I got my Zero bar from my locker and went into the boys' toilet. There were a couple of scrawny guys in there smoking cigarettes and taking turns punching each other so hard in the chest that twin plumes of dragon smoke rolled out their noses. I swallowed my Zero bar too quickly and it got stuck in my throat.

A week later I was back in Mr. Ploof's office.

"Sit down," he said, and pointed to a ruggedly carved chair that was probably made by a former ax murderer. Then he patted the seat of his own matching chair so I wouldn't misunderstand him. "Take a load off."

"I'd rather stand," I said. I was pretty nervous so I jumped to the point. "What about the test results? Can I go to another school?"

He sat down and sighed. "Sorry, kid," he said, trying to sound cheerful as he opened my file. "You're just normal. Average."

"That can't be," I protested. "Just earlier this year I was better than average. In fact, I was *superior.*"

He rolled his eyes. "You may have peaked early," he suggested. "It happens." He spun my file around so I could read it for myself. "You didn't show us any reason to send you up to the next level."

I sat down. Typed out on a sheet of paper were my test results.

PHYSICAL DEXTERITY—AVERAGE

LOGIC SKILLS—AVERAGE

EMOTIONAL MATURITY—AVERAGE

IQ—LOW TO AVERAGE—85

"I don't have a low IQ," I said with my voice rising. "No way I'm this—"

He cut me off. "Be grateful it's still in the *average* zone," he stressed. "Believe me, I've seen a lot worse. If anything, this score means you should make something really spectacular in wood shop. Just so you know, before you pitch a fit and insult me, my IQ is also eighty-five." He gave himself a little congratulatory pat on the back.

I was horrified. He was the pinnacle of what I might become. This couldn't be true. It was a nightmare. I stood up and shuffled toward the door. I felt as though I had just received the worst possible sentence: Simpleton for Life Without Parole.

"Don't take it so hard," he advised, and waved at the air in front of his face. "It's not like we're going to send you to Siberia. Just join the crowd. Average guys like you and me are the majority. We're the men that make the world go around. We work in the trenches, digging ditches, unclogging toilets, mowing lawns—you know, the jobs that nobody wants to do but that *have* to be done. Who do rich people call when they need help? Guys like you and me, that's who."

"But I want to be a writer," I said quietly.

"Hey, a low IQ doesn't stop you from writing. You can do phone messages. Grocery lists. Sweetheart tattoos. Graffiti. Heck, you can pass notes back and forth in class, can't you?"

"But I want to write books," I explained.

He scratched his hairless head. "That," he replied, "could prove to be frustrating. Why defeat yourself by trying to become something you can't?"

"But I can try," I said. "Whatever happened to the idea that if at first you don't succeed, try, try again?"

"I guess nobody told you," he said matter-of-factly. "That little ditty is for losers, for old dreamers like me," and he pointed to his huge cranium, "who beat their head against the wall one too many times. Look, do yourself a favor. Pick something you can handle."

"Like a broom?"

"Now you're thinking," he said with fresh enthusiasm. "Now you're putting those brain cells to work."

"Thanks," I said in a whisper, and backed out of his office. I stumbled down to the boys' toilet and splashed water on my face. I wished those guys were in there punching each other. I would have asked them to put me out of my misery like a horse with a broken leg.

# Three

When I got off the school bus I went straight to the library. I always had a few extra minutes before wood shop started and figured the library was the most logical location for my muse to take some quiet time and visit me.

But the library was such a non-creative place it made sense that my muse never showed up. First, the few books we had were tethered on loops of braided wire to screw hooks on the shelf, just like telephone books wired to U-bolts in telephone booths. And second, we didn't have a librarian. We had a volunteer dad. He was a retired bank security guard who had been shot in the knee during an armed robbery. He ambled around with one leg pulling up the rear as if he were dragging a ball and chain. I guessed wiring the books to the shelves was his way of making sure they weren't stolen, but the result was more of a prison for books.

The first time I went to the library I asked him how I checked one out.

"This isn't a lending library," he replied. "It's a sit and read library." He pointed to one of the long locker-room-type benches running along all the shelves.

"But I can't sit here and read all day," I said.

"Then don't read so much," he suggested. "Stay busy doing other things. Besides, it's unhealthy for a young man to be cooped up in a library all day."

I changed the subject. "Do you have any books on writing?" I asked. "Such as how-to books on novels or stories? How to get in touch with your muse?"

"Kid," he said wearily, "the best how-to advice I can give you is if you want to do something, do it. Don't sit around reading about it. You want to write? Then go write. Now, why don't you take a hike. Don't you see I'm busy?"

He turned away from me and began to drill a hole through the top corner of a book so he could fit a wire through and secure it to a shelf.

"Is that a new book?" I asked.

He didn't answer. He just turned up the drill speed. Bits of paper spiraled out of the hole. I could make out a few letters where he'd drilled through a word. I hoped it wasn't a how-to book on something like first-aid. Instead of giving someone the Heimlich, you'd give them a hernia. When I didn't leave right away he looked at me and jerked his head toward the door. I wasn't that dumb. I turned and left.

This time, when I entered the library, the volunteer dad was tightening nuts on the underside of the shelves, securing his screw hooks, and examining the wire cables to make sure they were undamaged.

He turned toward me and eyed me up and down. "I've been looking for you," he said. "Come here."

"Did you get any new books on how to write novels?" I asked.

"No," he growled. Then quickly he grabbed me by the shoulders and pushed me up against a book shelf. "Stand with your arms overhead and your feet apart," he ordered as he swooped around me.

"What's this all about?" I asked.

"I'm going to search you," he explained. "Someone's been coming in here with a wrench and wire cutters and stealing my books." He patted me down from the tips of my fingers to my toes. Then he unzipped my backpack and shook everything out onto a table. "Where're you hiding them?" he asked.

"I don't know what you're talking about," I replied.

"The books!" he snapped. "The books you stole."

"I don't steal books," I said. "I borrow them."

"That's what they all say," he snarled, clearly disappointed that I wasn't the thief. "Don't you have a class to go to?"

"Yes," I said.

"Then get," he ordered.

As I left the library I looked up at the ceiling one last

time just in case my muse was getting ready to visit. Nothing was up there but a big rusty stain.

On Monday and Tuesday we had English, math, science, and history, as did any other normal school. But on Wednesday, Thursday, and Friday we did nothing but *shop*. We didn't have gym because the principal figured exercise was a waste of time for guys who were just going to grow up, do manual labor, maybe play a little softball, and retire to drink beer. Because I had gone to school in Barbados for most of seventh grade, I had missed all the metal-shop instruction and was now into the final weeks of wood shop before school ended.

After I fled the library I went down to the shop and, along with fifty other guys, stood in front of my assigned piece of heavy equipment.

"Today, men, we're going to work at making baseball bats," announced Mr. Gilette, the wood-shop instructor. He wore tan bib overalls and a hardware-store paint cap. "The bat is one of man's earliest and most essential tools, which makes it the perfect assignment for learning to operate a wood lathe."

Great, I thought, then we can beat each other's brains out during recess. Those who survive can then evolve and make spears. The next round of survivors can make bows and arrows. The winner and sole survivor can build a mahogany trophy case with the heads of all his victims on display as an example of his superior evolution.

"Each one of you should have a four-inch by four-inch by four-foot piece of pine already inserted in your lathe."

We did.

"Now, to quote Michelangelo, the secret to carving a really good bat is visualizing the finished object within the raw materials."

I raised my hand.

"Yes," said Mr. Gilette.

"I don't think Michelangelo sculpted baseball bats," I ventured.

"What's your name, young man?" he asked.

"Jack Henry," I replied.

He made a note in his green roll book. "Well, Mr. Henry," he said, and marched forward to tower over me. "Michelangelo, among other things, invented baseball bats."

"I was always under the impression it was Fred Flintstone," I said, wondering what other smart-ass things I could say in order to get kicked out of shop.

"No. It was definitely Michelangelo," he insisted.

"Are you sure David and Goliath weren't the first pitcher-batter combo?" I asked, still hoping to get the boot.

A few guys began to laugh.

"Michelangelo," Mr. Gilette persisted, then snapped his fingers overhead to cut off the laughter. "Now back to what I was saying." He spoke as if he were pounding a sixteen-penny nail through my skull. "Imagine, if you will, that Babe Ruth has come to you with the request to

make him a bat for the seventh game of the World Series.
A perfect bat. A homerun-hitting monster bat. Now, let
that be your inspiration as we begin to *visualize*. First, put
on your protective goggles."

We did. I visualized us all as annoying houseflies.

"Next, start your lathes by flipping up the toggle switch
on the lower right."

We did and the sound of the fifty electric motors picking up speed was like a jet screaming toward takeoff.

"Now," he hollered above the roar. "Take your wood
chisel and begin to press the sharp edge against the handle end of the bat, and don't be afraid to bear down on
the wood and let the chips fall where they may."

I pressed the chisel against the rotating four-by-four. A
corner of the blade dug into the wood and in an instant
the chisel was whipped out of my hand and sent hurtling
end-over-end toward the front of the shop, where it hit
the brick wall and clattered onto the floor next to Mr.
Gilette's steel-toed work boot.

"Cut! Cut!" Mr. Gilette shouted, but most everyone was
bearing down on their bats. Long ribbons of yellow pine
curled up over their heads as they dreamed of the perfect club for "the Babe." Mr. Gilette tripped a master circuit breaker and killed all the power. The lathes slowly
wound down.

"What are you, Henry?" Mr. Gilette shouted directly
into my face. "Brain dead? Or just limp-wristed?"

"I slipped," I explained.

"Have you tested high enough to be in shop?" he asked.

"I'm warm-blooded," I replied. It was beginning to dawn on me that if I was a big enough jerk they might do me a favor and suspend me indefinitely. A lot of writers got their start by being thrown out of school.

He picked up the chisel, then turned and slapped it handle first into my open hand. "If this thing had hit me just right, mister, I'd be dead and you'd be up on manslaughter charges."

"And I'd be convicted and sent right back to this school," I retorted.

He hastily removed a pad of pink slips from his nail apron. He wrote down: *Jack Henry. One hour extra shop for mouthing off.* He kept a copy for the principal and folded the other in half and shoved it down into my shirt pocket. "See you after school, motor-mouth," he said.

No you won't, I thought as I returned to my lathe.

"Let us once again imagine the unformed object within the wood," announced Mr. Gilette and switched the circuit breaker back on. The lights dimmed and flickered as if someone were being put to death in the electric chair.

By the time I finished, my bat looked more like a walking stick for a blind man. Babe Ruth could only have used it to tap his way around the bases.

At lunchtime I marched over to the cafeteria to get something to eat. Creamed chicken gizzards was the main course of the day. It had been the main course on Wednesdays since I got to the place. The cafeteria boss only allowed us plastic spoons to eat with. I guess she figured plastic knives and forks were too dangerous for us criminals in training. The slippery gizzards were pretty hard to manage with just a spoon. As I walked down a row of steel tables someone put pressure on a gizzard and it shot off the tray and onto the waxed concrete floor, where it skidded away like an escapee slug. I dodged a few more and bought a carton of milk from a tough-looking kitchen lady with a mustache. I figured she was some Mafia guy hiding in the Witness Protection Program.

I took the milk and went out to the ex-prison yard to pace back and forth and figure out a way to blow off detention. I needed an excuse to be someplace else. I thought of going to visit Mr. Ploof for more career counseling, but that was too depressing. I couldn't volunteer at the library because the library dad thought I was a book thief. Then I saw the sign on one of the guard towers. LATIN CLUB MEETING AFTER SCHOOL. ALL INVITED. I decided to check them out.

At the end of shop I raised my hand and asked Mr. Gilette if I could go to the bathroom.

"The old bathroom trick before detention," he said. "Do you think I'm going to fall for that?"

"Really," I said. "I have to go."

"I'll give you a two-minute head start," he said with a knowing smile. "Then when I find you, which I will, I'm going to teach you how to make toothpicks."

I used my two minutes to dash across the prison

grounds and over to the Latin Club tower. It will be nice to hang around with some smart kids for a change, I thought, as I pounded on the metal door.

A peek window slid open and a voice called out in Latin, *"Quis ibi est?"*

"Jack Henry," I replied, guessing that my name was the most logical answer. For about ten seconds I heard my name whispered back and forth. I looked over my shoulder. I didn't see Mr. Gilette.

"What do you want?" asked another voice, this time in English.

"I want to join your club," I said. "Hurry."

"You have to know some Latin," he replied.

*"E pluribus unum,"* I blurted out. *"Semper fi. Carpe diem."* That was all I could think of and it was as good as admitting I was a *dim bulb, non-Latin-speaking loser.* I didn't even know pig-Latin.

They swung open the door, grabbed me by the arm, and yanked me inside. As soon as I was clear of the doorway they slammed the door and lowered a wooden barricade.

It was dark and when my eyes adjusted to the candlelight I realized I was in a room with something like a handful of Shermans from the Rocky and Bullwinkle show.

"Thanks," I said.

"If you want to be a member you have to pass a Latin test," one boy said, eyeing me suspiciously. He handed me a sheet of paper and a pencil and pointed to a desk.

"Can I take this home with me?" I asked. "I don't test well under pressure."

"No," he insisted. "Now start."

I stared down at the paper. I couldn't even understand the directions. It was a fill-in-the-blanks Latin test so I knew immediately I was sunk. Here we go again, I thought. I could just picture Mr. Ploof saying, "Don't worry, kid, you'll make something really spectacular in wood shop."

"Look," I said, "I'll be honest with you. I don't know Latin. But I'm a smart kid and I'm hiding from the shop teacher, and I promise to learn it if you just let me hide out here."

"You take shop?" the president said with disgust. "That automatically disqualifies you. Nobody in the Latin club takes shop."

"Your sign said all-invited," I reminded him.

"Read between the lines," one of the Shermans shot back. "All *smart* kids invited. Not some woodblock."

"Some woodchip," said another.

"Woodpile," added a third.

"Woodrot." The fourth member opened the door and I stepped out into Mr. Gilette's shadow.

"Don't worry, kid," he said, and grabbed the collar of my shirt. "Everyone tries to escape to the Latin Club at least once while they're at Sunrise. Now come on back to the shop and I'll show you a trick on how to stack a thousand perfect toothpicks into one tiny box."

There is just no place for me here, I thought, as Mr.

Gilette steered me forward. I'm not a shop jock, or some Latin nerd, but somewhere in between. According to the old writers' magazine I read, all writers are misfits who have to make their own private place in the world. I had no idea where that private place might be, but I desperately wanted to find it.

# Four

When I finally returned home from school after detention BeauBeau was waiting for me. He had been busy all day digging holes and as I walked up the street he ran circles around the house barking and springing through the air with dumb doggy joy. Maybe he didn't have a brain, but he was having a great life.

"Be right with you," I called to him. After I changed into my work clothes I went outside through the sliding glass door and picked up my shovel. According to Mr. Ploof it was the perfect tool for me. I'd never have to work with a pen, a scalpel, a telephone, a firehose, or anything that took some brains to operate. For me it was just a good old-fashioned back-breaking round-faced shovel.

Since BeauBeau was Betsy's dog she was responsible for his deranged behavior. But she didn't want to fill in the holes he dug so she was paying me a nickel for each hole filled. It wasn't a lot of money, but it was steady work. BeauBeau and I were a team. All day he'd dig 'em, and when I returned from school I'd fill 'em. It was the kind of assembly-line work that Mr. Ploof had suggested.

One of the main differences I could find between myself and BeauBeau was that after he finished a hole he was so excited he ran about ten circles around the house. He barked and announced to all the other dogs in the neighborhood, "Hey, I dug a hole. Look at me. I dug a hole. I'm great. Hey! Come see the hole I dug." Then after he calmed down he'd dig another hole right next to the old hole. On the other hand, once I filled in a hole I'd just add one more nickel to the total, take a self-pitying deep breath, and start filling in another. I had nothing to cheer about, and that is what tipped me off that something was wrong. If I was so dumb, then why was I so unhappy? It was because the tests were wrong. If I was as dumb as they said, then I'd be like BeauBeau. Each time I'd fill in a hole I'd run around the house, waving my shovel overhead and shouting with mindless joy. But filling holes was boring, dumb, brainless work and it was a waste of my time. I didn't need to be a genius to know that.

I threw down my shovel, dropped onto one knee, and looked up into the air with my eyes closed. "Come on, muse," I whispered, "I need you now more than ever. Give me some novel-writing inspiration. I'm ready. I'm waiting. And I'm willing."

I bowed my head and waited for fresh words to flood my brain. But it was a repeat of what I'd heard before.

*Idiot. Moron. What makes you think you can write a novel?* I quickly hopped up and walked off the sting of those words. With each step I was beginning to smarten up. This muse business can't be right, I thought, as I paced back and forth. Only an idiot like me would believe that a muse might come down from the sky and whisper brilliant words into my ear.

I looked at BeauBeau. He was in a hole digging as if he had found a dinosaur bone. He may have had a dog-sized brain but he was smart enough to know exactly what he liked to do. He wasn't waiting for a dog muse to tell him to dig holes.

I didn't have to be real bright to know that if I wanted to accomplish anything I shouldn't magically expect it to just happen. Waiting for a muse was like begging for a handout, or looking for a free ride. Writing was probably nothing more than plain old hard work. And that's why more people didn't write. They took the easy way out and dug holes.

"BeauBeau, you're too dumb to know it but you're a genius. Now, hurry up and dig," I said, spurring him on. "A few more nickels and we can go to the public library for a good book on writing, and a Slim Jim."

The promise of a Slim Jim really got him going, and in ten minutes he had a huge hole so long and wide he could turn around in it without hitting the sides.

"Good dog," I cheered. "You just made me another nickel. In fact, that is a two-nickel double-thick Slim Jim crater."

He jumped out of the hole and was thrilled. He ran around me barking wildly, throwing his head back and yapping with abandon. The pre–Slim Jim saliva ran down the sides of his mouth. He stood up and pranced around his hole on his hind legs with his front paws paddling the air.

"Go, BeauBeau, go," I shouted. "Do that hole-diggin' dance."

He barked, then tore off running around the house, and with each circle he picked up speed like a tornado.

"Faster," I hollered and waved him forward. "Faster." His ears pressed back against his head. His tongue stuck out. He kicked up dirt as he sprinted past me, then turned the corner and was out of sight. But in a moment he re-appeared around the far corner.

"Do it, BeauBeau. Go for the Slim Jim gold!" I shouted.

He must have gotten a little dizzy from circling the house because he began to stumble as he adjusted his bal-ance. Then he lost his equilibrium altogether and darted full speed off to one side and plunged head-first into his double-sized hole. I heard an awful snap, and a yelp, and that was all.

I threw down my shovel and ran over to him. His head was bent back against his shoulder. "BeauBeau!" I hollered, and grabbed him under his belly and lifted him out. I laid him out on his side and straightened out his head. Somehow I knew he was dead, but I couldn't be-lieve it. Maybe he was just unconscious.

I ran into the house and pounded on Betsy's closed

door. "BeauBeau fell into a hole and I think he broke his neck," I blurted out all in one breath.

"He's French," she replied from the other side. "They faint if they have an ingrown toenail. Just tell him the Germans are invading and he'll jump up and start running."

"He's not acting," I cried. "He busted his neck. I heard it snap."

Suddenly she whipped her door open real fast and as I yelled, "Look out," it flew off its hinges and crashed to the floor.

"You are worse than stupid," she said angrily and punched me in the chest, knocking the wind out of me. "You're criminal."

She ran down the hall and out the back door.

I fought to catch my breath as I crawled down to the kitchen and grabbed a bottle of ammonia from under the sink. I unscrewed the cap and took a deep whiff and my breath came roaring right back. Good stuff, I thought. If he was just unconscious, then this would bring him around.

When I caught up to Betsy she was kneeling by BeauBeau's side with her ear pressed against his chest. Pete was leaning over her and Dad was coming around the corner. After a minute Betsy said, "No heartbeat." She held his neck just under his jaw. "No pulse. We better get him to the vet."

I threw the ammonia to one side and the plastic bottle hit Pete in the head. He fell in the hole. I thought he might have broken his neck but I didn't have time to do anything about it. BeauBeau was my main concern.

Betsy grabbed BeauBeau's chest and I grabbed his rear, and we carried him to the car.

"Don't put him on the seat," Dad hollered. "Put him over the front fender, like a deer. When you croak your bladder lets loose."

"Thanks for the real-life detail," Betsy snapped. "But we're trying to save a life here."

We lifted BeauBeau into the trunk. I climbed in and curled up next to him, then quickly ducked as Betsy slammed down the top.

Dad seemed to hit every bump, and I kept saying, "Don't worry. I'll take care of you. If you live, you can have a Slim Jim as long as the Alaska pipeline." I patted him on the neck, but then jerked my hand back. "Sorry," I said.

After Dad parked he unlocked the trunk. I hopped out and we hustled BeauBeau into the pet emergency room and laid him out on a metal table.

"He's definitely dead," the vet declared. He swung BeauBeau's head back and forth as if it were a rag doll's. "Broken neck."

Betsy sighed dramatically. "It's always the brilliant ones that die young," she said, then pointed to me. "That's why you'll live forever."

I turned away from her because I could feel the tears well up in my eyes, and I wasn't ready to fight back. I put a hand on BeauBeau's side. "Sorry, buddy," I said. "I won't forget you. I promise. You were an inspiration to me."

"What do you want me to do with him?" the vet asked.

"Whatever you do to the rest," Dad replied. "As long as it's free."

"Cremation," the vet replied.

"Can we get the ashes?" I asked. I could keep them in my piggy bank.

"Sorry," he said. "They all get mixed together—cats, dogs, squirrels, weasels, whatever."

On the way back to the car I was struck with an idea. At first I thought my muse had finally woke up, but then I realized it was just a brilliant idea that I had thought of on my own. I turned and went back into the vet's office. His assistant was struggling to slide BeauBeau into a plastic trash bag. The poor guy had already begun to stiffen up.

"Can you just freeze him?" I asked her. "You know, keep him on ice until I scrape up some money for a proper burial?"

I didn't know what a proper burial meant for a dog, but it sounded respectful.

"Sure," the nurse said. "We can keep him for a week."

"Thanks," I replied.

I went back to the car.

"What was that all about?" Dad asked.

"A private goodbye," I said. If I told him what else was on my mind he'd give *me* a proper burial.

# Five

The next day, as Mr. Gilette called roll, everyone announced what he was going to make for his final woodshop project. Mr. Gilette had been instructing us for weeks to come up with something "brilliant and useful," but not until BeauBeau died was I inspired with the perfect idea.

"Allston," hollered Mr. Gilette.

"Here," Allston replied. "Gun rack."

"Campbell?"

"Yo. Canoe."

"Henry?"

"Present. Dog coffin."

"Excuse me," Mr. Gilette said, and peered up over his roll book. "Did I hear 'dog coffin'?"

"Yes, sir," I replied.

"A dog coffin is not an acceptable project," he proclaimed. "Dogs don't need coffins. They just need a hole and some dirt." Behind me the class began to laugh.

But I stood my ground and said, "I think a dog deserves as much respect as a person."

"Look," Mr. Gilette explained, "from my point of view most humans don't deserve coffins. And the whole idea of the final project is to make something that you could actually sell. Something that you could start a business with, like gun racks or shoeshine kits, or canoes. But not dog coffins."

"Well, I think it's an exceptional business idea," I continued. "You can only use it once and then you have to buy a new one. It's the American way."

The class cracked up. I could sense they were shifting to my side and that encouraged me. Once I got it out of my mind that I was supposed to be dumb, I actually felt pretty smart.

And then Mr. Gilette did what teachers love to do when they find their power slipping. He polled the class. "Okay, wise guys," he shouted. "How many of you think a dog coffin is about the most stupid business idea ever cooked up? Raise your hand."

The hands went up as if he had pulled a machine gun on them.

I didn't even bother to count.

"Bury that idea, Mr. Henry," he concluded. "And come up with a new project tomorrow."

But I didn't. The next day he asked again, and again I replied, "Dog coffin."

The class went wild.

"If you persist in making that coffin," Mr. Gilette said, "I guarantee that you'll fail this class."

"But I'm making something worthwhile."

"Worthless is more like it," he cracked. "Why don't you just make a nice bookshelf? A pair of crutches?"

"Dog coffin," I said, standing firm.

"Then don't be surprised when you have to repeat seventh grade," he stated.

I didn't take him seriously. Nobody was stupid enough to fail shop. Even me.

For three days Mr. Gilette encouraged me to work on a different project, and each day I worked on my coffin. For once, I enjoyed the work and thought Dad was right when he said that working with your hands was a useful skill.

I hadn't measured BeauBeau, so when I drew out my plans I figured three feet was long enough. I made the coffin a foot high and made two handles, one for the front and one for the back. On the top I carved, To BeauBeau III, My Inspiration. At the end of the week I carried it home on the bus.

On Saturday morning I went down to Kmart and bought two yards of red satin.

"Taffeta," the sales lady said as she snipped it off the bolt. "Good for prom gowns. What are you going to do with it?"

"Line my dead dog's coffin," I replied.

She didn't say another word, even though I paid her one nickel at a time, which took half an hour.

When I got home I glued the middle of the taffeta to the bottom of the coffin and let the rest of the fabric drape over the sides.

When I was ready Dad took me to the vet's office to retrieve BeauBeau. We carried him out to the car in his plastic bag.

"You sure you want to go through with this?" Dad asked, as he closed the trunk.

"Of course," I replied. "I think it's about the smartest thing I've ever done."

"Well, considering your IQ," he said, "I guess this is pretty good for you. I only wish you would do this at night so the neighbors won't watch."

"Let 'em," I said. "They might learn something about being nice."

But I was glad Dad and the neighbors didn't watch what awful thing I had to do in order to prepare BeauBeau for his final resting place. Once we returned home Dad helped me carry BeauBeau into the garage. Then he left. Pete was with me when I picked BeauBeau up and tried to place him into the coffin. He didn't fit. BeauBeau had seized up solid, and frozen with his legs sticking straight out. When I put him sideways into the coffin his legs made him too wide, and when I turned him onto his back his legs stuck straight up and I couldn't lower the top. I grabbed him by the paws and tried to bend his joints but they wouldn't move. He was as stiff as an iron fence.

"There's only one thing to do," I said to Pete. I could feel the little hairs sticking up all over my body.

Pete read my mind. "No," he shouted.

"Yes!" I insisted. "Get me the three-pound hammer."

"You'll burn in you-know-where for this," he said with his face all twisted up.

"The hammer," I ordered. "Or I'll fit you in here with him."

He dragged the hammer over, then looked away and covered his eyes.

"You'd be better off plugging your ears," I advised him, took aim, and lowered the hammer with both hands. There was an awful crunching noise as I smashed BeauBeau's left front knee. Pete moaned, then started to jump up and down like a pogo stick. I folded that limb over, then hauled off and splintered the right front knee.

"Jack has lost it!" he yelled, and ran off. "He's killing BeauBeau again!"

I knew I had to hurry. If Betsy saw what I was doing she'd turn me in to the Society Against Cruelty to Animals. Who knew what Dad would say? Probably tell me I'd be better off using a band saw.

"Forgive me, BeauBeau," I muttered. I raised the hammer up over my head and brought it down again, and again, until I had busted up all his joints. Then I twisted and snapped his legs back, and tucked them up against his chest. When I finished all the gruesome work I fit him sideways into the coffin and covered him with the taffeta. Sorry, sorry, sorry, I said to BeauBeau. I didn't mean it to be this way.

Hurry, hurry, hurry, I said to myself. I set the coffin top

in place and was pounding the nails in when Mom, Dad, Betsy, and Pete scrambled into the garage. They stared down on me as if I were some serial killer chopping up another victim.

"You're just in time for the funeral," I announced as cheerfully as I could, and drove in the last nail.

"Pete," I ordered, taking control of the situation, "help me pick up the coffin." He grabbed the rear pallbearer handle with both hands. I grabbed the front and we lifted the coffin, then marched solemnly around the side of the house.

"Pick up the pace," Dad said. "The Teeters are looking out their window and I'm sure they think we're burying the baby."

"God forbid," Mom said.

"They probably think we're Satanists," Betsy speculated, and she waved to Mrs. Teeter, who had pulled the picture-window curtain to one side.

Mom made a big sign of the cross so we'd look legitimate. It probably just made us look more ghoulish.

When we arrived at the grave site Pete and I set the casket on the ground.

"Would anyone like to say a few words on BeauBeau's behalf?" I asked, and bowed my head.

Dad began to laugh. "Look," he said dryly, "I liked the dog. But keep in mind that he was so dumb he dug his own grave. What more needs to be said?"

"He barked in French," Betsy added. "So I hope he ends up on the French side of dog heaven."

"With a bunch of French poodles," Pete said.

Mom declined.

"Amen," I croaked, wrapping it up.

Pete and I bent down and lowered the coffin into BeauBeau's double-wide hole. Then I grabbed my shovel and sprinkled a load of dirt on the lid. This is the final hole he dug, I thought, and one of the last holes of his I'll ever fill in. From now on I'm going to be a writer. Not a gravedigger.

Then I made the sign of the cross and said a little prayer.

Betsy was watching me closely. "You should be institutionalized," she proclaimed. "This whole ceremony is the workings of a sick mind."

"I've already been tested," I said proudly. "And I'm not mentally ill."

"He's just really stupid," Pete said. "Leave him alone."

She left in a huff.

I gave Pete a dirty look and pointed to an open hole. "You're next," I said coldly. "You know what I did to BeauBeau. What makes you think I won't do it to you, too?"

He ran.

"Don't turn your back on me," I shouted. "I've already got you sized up for my next wood project. I'm goin' for extra credit!"

# Six

Mr. Gilette wasn't fooling.

At dinner Dad unfolded a letter and held it up over his head and waved it around as if he were trying to surrender to the enemy. "You're failing seventh grade," he announced. "It says right here," and he slapped the paper for effect, "that you're getting an F in shop."

"How?" I yelped. "Me. How?"

"Brain dead," Betsy said sadly. "Probably from sniffing too much wood glue."

"Mind yourself," Mom advised. "Jack's not challenged because of glue." She reached across the table and patted me on the head as if I were some drooling cave dweller.

Betsy reconsidered. "You're right," she said. "I'm sorry. It's not glue. He just naturally doesn't have a clue."

I kept looking back and forth at them as they insulted me. This is what BeauBeau must have felt like around this house, I thought. Everyone talking badly about him right in front of his face and all he could do was look at them with big wet doggy eyes.

"You do have a way out," Dad said somberly.

"What?"

"Shop camp," he replied. "Mr. Gilette runs a private woodworking summer camp in Kissimmee. If you attend it's like going to summer school and you'll pass into eighth grade."

"What a racket," I huffed. "What he's doing is criminal. Can't you see what he's up to? He fails me, then he charges us tuition to go to his summer camp."

"Hey," Betsy said, loving every minute of this, "don't blame your problems on someone else. *You* are the nimrod who failed *shop*."

"I have big plans this summer. I'm going to stay home and write a book." I blurted this out. I had no intention of telling anyone. Now I knew they would make even more fun of me. It was bad enough to have told them I was stupid. It was worse to tell them about my dream. "I want to be a writer," I repeated. "Not a whittler."

"Even writers have to pass seventh grade," Betsy started.

"Wait a minute," Dad said, and hushed everyone else who had lined up to take a shot at me. "You want to become a writer? Do you know what the odds are of being a successful writer? It's like becoming a pro basketball player. Millions of kids play, but only a few hundred can be pros. And what do the rest do? They end up spending all their time sitting on the couch watching the game on TV. It's the same with being a writer. What are the odds you'll ever get published? A million to one?"

"That's not the point," I said. But he wasn't listening.

"You might as well sit on your bum all day playing the lottery. No, being a writer is not a career choice. It's a hobby, something you do after work. What you need for a career is a skill, and I think woodworking is a good place to begin. So I don't want to hear any more about it. Besides, I already talked to Gilette and it's settled. He even gave us a discount because of your diminished abilities. So, next month you're going up to the Kissimmee Wood Shop Camp for Boys."

"But I want to write a book!" I said. "Can't you send me to writers' camp?"

"Don't be so lame," Betsy scoffed, and broke into a laugh. "They don't have camp for writers. People who want to write just do it. They don't wait to go to summer camp for scribblers. And they certainly don't sit around in their bathrobes all day staring toward the heavens while sucking on a piece of brain-damaging lead."

I cringed. She must have seen me waiting for my muse. But that muse business was all over with. From now on I planned to write all my ideas in my black book, and not just wait for them to appear on the ceiling. But now that I was going to wood-shop camp, where would I get the time to write? Especially around guys who carried more penknives than pens in their pockets.

I had one more chance of getting out of shop camp.

The next day after school I stayed behind and spoke with Mr. Gilette.

"Don't fail me," I pleaded. "My dream is to be a writer, not a woodworker."

"Dream on," he said. "I checked with Mr. Ploof and he gave me your test scores. Apparently, even woodworking is a stretch for you."

"Really," I insisted. "I want to be a writer and I was planning to write a book this summer. And you know I worked really hard on that coffin."

"I warned you," he said. "I humiliated you in front of the class. I distinctly said I would fail you if you made that coffin."

"I know, but give me a second chance. I think you judged me too harshly." I said this with all the sincerity I could. Then I looked him right in the eyes and added, "Besides, I'm a good kid."

It worked. "Okay," he said reluctantly. "I don't want to, but I'll give you a second chance because I'm a decent guy. Bring the coffin in tomorrow morning and if it's well made I'll think about giving you a break."

I was shocked. "But it's already in the ground," I stammered. "With a dog in it. A dead dog. My dog."

"I can't give you a grade on what I can't examine," he said matter-of-factly. Then he grinned with the total pleasure of knowing what he was about to say. "A man's gotta do what a man's gotta do. No coffin, no grade change. It's your choice."

"Okay," I said, and staggered out of school in a daze just thinking about what I had to do. When I got home I stood before BeauBeau's grave. "I have nothing but respect for you," I said quietly. "But forgive me, I have to pass seventh grade. I hope you'll understand."

That night I got up out of bed, snuck down to the garage, and got a crowbar out of the toolbox. I hoisted my shovel up over my shoulder and tiptoed around to the backyard. I kept saying to myself, You already did worse to him. Just don't dwell on it. Now dig him up, open the coffin, flip BeauBeau into the hole, cover him up, and take the coffin to school. Once you pass, you can dig him up again, put him back into the coffin, and everything will be as it was. Now just shut up, turn off your low-level brain, and dig a hole like a big dumb BeauBeau IV.

I stood on the grave and looked down at the mound of dirt. It was covered with plastic flowers, BeauBeau's dog toys, his water dish, and a little cross I had made out of Slim Jims. I bent down and carefully removed all the decorations.

When I was ready, I took a deep breath and pushed the shovel into the soft ground, then tossed the dirt to one side. I stuck the shovel in again, and again, until I heard a hollow thud. Too bad it wasn't buried treasure. I hit the top of the coffin lid again. At that moment a neighborhood dog barked and I jumped back as though I had stuck my finger in an electrical socket. I let go of my shovel and ran around to the kitchen door and dashed inside.

"I can't . . . do it," I panted, while standing in the dark. "I'd rather . . . fail seventh grade . . . than dig up the dead."

Even though I said that, I knew I didn't mean it. Deeper within me, a stronger voice roared back. "You can't go to wood-shop camp. You'll be carving ships in a bottle for the rest of your life. Now get out there and do what you have to do."

I took a deep breath, narrowed my eyes, and marched across the yard. Other writers had done what I was about to do. Once I had read about the poet Dante Gabriel Rossetti. When his wife died he put a manuscript of unpublished love poems in her hands just before they closed the coffin. No one in the world would ever read them but her spirit, he thought romantically. She was the love of his life. But a while later he wasn't feeling too romantic when he had a hard time writing any more good poems and needed money. So one dark night he went to the cemetery and dug up his wife and pulled the poems out of her bony fingers. While he had the coffin open he also took the jewels she was wearing. He later published the book and probably pawned the jewels until the checks on the new book started rolling in.

"In order to be a writer," I whispered to myself as I picked up the shovel, "you have to be tough. You have to be willing to dig up the dead for your art. I love you, BeauBeau," I said. "But a man has to do what a dog can't."

When I cleared the dirt from the top of the coffin I put down my shovel. I bent over and wiggled my hand through the damp soil until I felt the pallbearer's handle on the front. I got a grip on it and pulled. The coffin wouldn't budge. I crawled on top of it and began to scoop the dirt out around the sides. I looked over at the house to see if any lights had come on. None. So far, so good. If Betsy came out and saw me she'd call the cops and have me sent to the funny farm, where I'd be hanging out with guys who ate flies for fun.

In a few minutes I had the dirt free from around the edges. I grabbed the handle and pulled up. This time the coffin lifted out and I dragged it across the backyard to the side of the house. Already I could smell something bad.

When I had the coffin behind some bushes the most dangerous part was still to come. I had to get the top off without making so much noise that I'd wake everyone in the house. I felt around the edge of the lid until I could detect a slight opening, then I jammed my crowbar into the crack and pressed down. Then the odor of rotting BeauBeau hit me. It was worse than his breath. I could feel my face contorting as if someone were trying to rip it off, and I began to gag. Some of Mom's fish-stick supper came up into my throat. I swallowed it back down, stood up, and tottered far enough away so I could breathe some fresh air. I was this deep in it already, and I had no choice but to finish the job.

I returned to the garage. I took a rag Dad used for

gasoline spills and wrapped it around my face. "No one ever said being a writer was going to be easy," I said to myself as I knotted the rag behind my head and pulled it down just below my eyes. Then I marched back to the coffin.

Fortunately, I hadn't pounded many nails in the top because I had been in such a hurry to get the lid fastened. The gasoline rag only helped a little. I had to stand away from the coffin, take a deep breath, run back, pry up a nail, then run away from the smell and take a deep breath. Then repeat the process. When I had all the nails loose from the top, I dragged the coffin back over to the grave. I turned away, took one deep breath, then did it. I lifted the lid of the coffin, tossed it aside, and rolled BeauBeau into the hole. I peeked down at him. I shouldn't have. He was covered with a million wiggling white worms that shimmered under the moonlight. I turned away, lifted my mask, and swallowed really hard to keep the fish sticks down. I wiped my mouth across the shoulder of my shirt, lowered my mask, took another deep breath, then worked like a fiend shoveling the dirt back over him and redecorating the ground before I ran to the other side of the yard and took another breath.

I had one more thing to do. I ran back, grabbed the coffin by a handle, and dragged it to the garage. I slipped a green garbage bag on either end and taped it up around the middle. Then I yanked the gasoline rag up over my head, threw it in a corner, and snuck back into the house. I had done it. No one would believe it. But then there was only one person who would have to know—Mr. Gilette.

In the morning when I woke up I could smell something sickly sweet and disgusting. Something rotting. It was me. I sniffed my hands. I wasn't rotting, but the smell of dead BeauBeau was stuck on my skin as if it had been glued there. It was in my hair, and rising up from the pile of clothes on the floor. My pillow smelled, my sheets smelled, the air all around me smelled of dead dog.

Once we had thrown some out-of-date raw chicken in the kitchen trash and had forgotten to take the trash out before going away for the weekend. When we came home the house smelled like a dead person. We couldn't breathe. And even though we opened all the windows and aired everything out, the house reeked of rotting meat for a week. It was awful. Mom still says on really humid days she can smell the dead-chicken odor in her clothes.

And now I smelled worse than that. I threw myself out of bed and ran to the bathroom. I turned on the shower as hot as I could stand it and scrubbed my whole body, even my face, with the stiff-bristled back brush.

When I returned to the bedroom Pete was sitting up in bed.

"Oh, man," he moaned with his face wrinkled up as he sniffed the air. "What did you eat last night?"

"Lots of beans," I said, and rubbed my stomach. "I'm sorry."

"You're stupid, and you smell," he said as he rolled over and pulled the covers across his head.

I raised my fist in the air. "You'll die later," I said. "Once

I figure out a way to dispose of your body." Then I dressed as quickly as possible and went back into the bathroom. I sprayed myself from top to bottom with Bay Rum cologne. What powerful cologne did morticians use, I wondered. I'd love to get some.

When I opened the door to the garage the same gamy smell was in the air. It made the inside of my nose sting. There was nothing I could do about it. I put another layer of trash bags around my coffin and then balanced it across the seat of my bike and the handlebars. I walked it to school. If I took the bus, kids would be climbing out the windows to get away from me.

Mr. Gilette must have thought I would never do what he suggested in order to pass shop. When he saw me drag the coffin through the classroom door he seemed pretty shocked. Then when he smelled me he jumped to action.

"Take that outside," he ordered, as he marched toward me with his hand over his nose and mouth.

"Yes, sir," I replied. I took it around back where all the scrap lumber was kept and began to unwrap the tape and pull off the plastic bags.

When he caught up to me he put his hands on his hips and stared down at the coffin. "Did you actually dig up your dead dog?" he asked.

"Yes, sir," I replied. "I didn't have time to make another coffin."

"Is the dog still in there?" he asked.

"No, sir," I replied.

"Well, it smells like he is."

"It's all the worms," I explained. "And maggots."

I thought he was going to throw up so I got right to the point.

"Are you going to pass me?" I asked.

"Yes," he wailed, pulling the neck of his T-shirt up over his nose as he stepped back. "But not because of your woodwork. Because you're a sick puppy and I don't want to have to deal with you again."

I smiled. "Thank you, sir," I replied.

"Now I want you to go home and put your dog back into that coffin and rebury it," he instructed. "I'll write you a pass."

"Okay," I said. "That was my plan, anyway."

I took the long way home. I wanted to make sure everyone was gone by the time I returned. For a moment I was relieved that I wouldn't have to repeat seventh grade, or go to wood-shop camp. But then I began to imagine what it was going to be like digging BeauBeau back up in the light of day. I could make nose plugs out of Kleenex and cologne, and wear sunglasses. I was going to need rubber gloves to grab him. And I didn't think I'd ever eat a Slim Jim again.

# JACK'S TATTOO PARLOR

Abstract ART

PoRTRaits

So I was reading the news-paper and I haff to say, life is a lot more interesting then science fiction. a man was walking down the street when another man jumped out of a win-dow and landed on his head. The guy on the ground got a broken back and the

LANDSCAPE

GOTHiC

jumper walked away. also, a guy lost his ring on the beach and twenty years later he was fishing, caught a fish, cut it open and

NATURE

MODERN

found the ring in its guts. Then
some guy out west went to
catch a tr        PART TWO

foll              city one day. His dog
followed          him to the station
"Wait for me      " the man said
then got on       the train. In
the city he had        a heart attack
and died. The dog            waited and
waited. And every         day for
the next                  the dog
gr    the train. Everybody in
the town                  and
too                and when it   died
they put up a statue of the
dog by the tracks. MAN'S
BEST FRIEND, it read.
next day: Pete's in trouble
again. He found a set of house
keys on the street and he
claims he wanted to give them
back so he sneaked around
to everyone's house and       he
locks but he set off an alarm
        and the
                police came and called him a
            thief but I stuck up for him
and told the cops Pete was just insane

# The Blind Leading the Blind, or Fish with Feet

# One

My dad always said that in order to make a hard job easier you needed the proper tools, like having the perfect
three-pound hammer for cracking BeauBeau's legs into
place. So I went on a search until I found the perfect writing tool. It was an old portable Underwood manual typewriter that sounded like a Gatling gun when I really got
it going. It came in a square black carrying case with a
built-in lock and key, and I could fit it into the big front
basket of my bicycle and take it to the library, or the beach,
or any other lucky writing spot. Plus, it made me look like
a writer. A real writer. Not a scribbler. Not a dabbler. Not
some kid with a writing hobby. But a real professional with
a novel in his brain just aching to be written. That was me.
All I needed was a good story and I was ready to cash in.

　　I got the Underwood for a great price at a yard sale. I
had been riding my bike down the street when I saw it. I

pulled into the driveway of a very tidy house. Everything the lady had for sale—old photographs, pottery, kitchen utensils, and books—was marked with a little orange price tag neatly stuck to it.

"Does this still work?" I asked the lady, and pointed to the machine.

She looked at me and adjusted the black orchid she had pinned onto her hair. "Try it," she said with a sniff, then puckered her nose up as if she smelled something bad.

There was a sheet of paper in the roller and some non-writers who had only played with the typewriter had typed out a lot of misspelled nonsense. But someone had written, MOST PEOPLE ARE NOT FIT TO RUN THEIR OWN LIVES. That statement was so true it stunned me. In one sentence it summed up exactly how I felt about the world. Excellent writing, I decided. I had to read it twice so I could memorize it. Well, I'm not one of those unfit people, I thought as I rolled the paper up to a clean section. I'm taking charge of my life. This is the summer where I leave the kid Jack behind and leapfrog over high school to become Jack the man. Jack the famous writer. Otherwise, I thought gloomily, I'll have to go back to Sunrise Junior Prison Camp for eighth grade.

I spread my fingers over the keys and pounded out my name and title. JACK HENRY, WRITER. The mechanical sound of the clattering keys snapping forward to hammer the paper was a thousand times better to me than any piano music. The typewriter action was smooth beneath my fingers, and I could tell that the machine liked me. I took roll call, tapping out all the letters, numbers, and punctuation marks in a crisp line, shoulder to shoulder, across the page. They were all there, my troops, and I knew if I could position each one of them in the perfect order I would create something awesome, like when you start one of those ten-thousand-piece jigsaw puzzles. First, you find the four corners, then you link together the straight-edged border pieces, and after that you work like a fiend until you've assembled something as monumental as the entire Battle of Gettysburg. I figured a whole book was written in pretty much the same way, piece by piece.

I rubbed my fingertips on the keys, warming them up, and then I bit down on my lip and typed out my favorite writer's motto: A WRITER'S JOB IS TO TURN HIS WORST EXPERIENCES INTO MONEY. I had read it in the latest issue of a writers' magazine at the drugstore, and thought it was by far one of the most important statements ever written. A lot of small things had gone belly-up for me, but I didn't bother writing about my measly problems. I was waiting to write about something really big and bad. Something hugely disastrous, and so disgusting someone would want to pay money to read it. But so far, nothing good and juicy had come my way. Still, I wasn't panicked. The summer had just begun and there was plenty of time for pain and sorrow and *tragedy*.

I typed a silly poem I had memorized in first grade. BILLY BUILT A GUILLOTINE, TRIED IT ON HIS SISTER JEAN. SAID MOTHER WHEN SHE

BROUGHT THE MOP, THESE MESSY GAMES
HAVE GOT TO STOP. The keys didn't stick and the rib-
bon was still full of black ink. The last writer didn't get
much work done. I figured he probably had a cushy life
without a problem in the world to write about. My heart
started to pick up speed. In an instant I knew that if I
owned this typewriter I could turn my *worst experiences into
money*. I had to have it. Without it, I was like Samson without his hair—a loser.

"So what do you think, young man?" the yard-sale lady
asked me.

"It's okay," I called back to her, lifting my hands from
the keys and looking uninterested as I checked my fingertips for dirt. "How much?"

She cleared her throat so loudly the birds in the trees
flew away. "I believe the tag clearly reads ten dollars," she
replied, and sniffed again in my direction. "Do you smell
something foul?" she asked.

It was the curse of BeauBeau. No matter how many
showers I took, I still smelled like rotting dog.

"Just mothballs," I said, and curled the corner of my lip
up at an open hatbox filled with faded bras and panties
she was trying to sell.

It was Sunday afternoon. Her yard sale was almost
over. She wouldn't want to drag the typewriter back into
the garage, and there was no way I would pay ten bucks
for anything, not even to ransom Pete from deranged
kidnappers.

"Two bucks," I shot back, and tugged a Baggie with

forty nickels from my pants pocket. I shook it up and down so that the jangle of the coins might entice her.

Her eyes bugged out. "Two dollars?"

"Okay," I said calmly. "One dollar."

Her voice went up an octave, and she got all huffy. "Why don't you just steal it?" she screeched. "Just grab it and run."

I disliked people who didn't know the proper way to bargain. Especially yard-sale people who thought every piece of cruddy junk they owned belonged in a museum. She should have said seven dollars. I'd reply three. She'd say six. I'd say four and we'd agree on five. This is the universal approach to agreeing on a price.

"I don't want to steal it," I said to her. "I'm willing to give you fifty cents for it."

She flipped. "Take it!" she shouted, and began to pitch a hissy fit. "Just take it for free, if you're so cheap! But I never want to see you again!"

Free was a pretty good price, so I snapped the case shut, put it in my bike basket, and took off before she realized she was raving and saying things she didn't mean. Perhaps someday she'd find out she had done a good deed by helping a young writer start his career. Maybe then she'd crack a smile. Maybe not.

Once I had the typewriter, I needed some free time to write without someone looking over my shoulder and telling me to wash the car, cut the grass, run down to the 7-Eleven for milk, or help move furniture around the house as if it was giant pieces in a board game. Then at dinner that night, like a wish come true, my parents announced they were going to take a ten-day summer vacation without us.

"Your dad and I just need a little break from the daily grind," Mom explained, as gently as possible, since *we* were the grind.

I glanced at Dad. His lips were sealed, but I could read his mind: You kids are driving me nuts.

I beamed him my own mental message: Ditto to you, too. You can leave tonight. Take off for the whole summer. I'll become a famous writer and by the time you return you'll have to speak to my book agent before you can speak to me. You'll have to offer me a contract before I'll take out the trash, or cut the grass, or ever lift a finger again.

"We've rented a cottage on the Gulf shore. If anything goes wrong we can come right back. We hope you don't mind," Mom continued, as if reading a script.

"But nothing will go wrong," Dad predicted, and arched an eyebrow so high I thought it was going to pole-vault off his face. "Am I right?"

"You are right," we all replied in unison. No event would be disastrous enough that we couldn't survive it on our own. The house could be sucked down into a sinkhole, we could be victims of a chain-saw massacre, the baby could be carried away by an alligator, and we still wouldn't call him.

Mom put Betsy in charge of Eric, and me in charge of

Pete, which meant I owned him. This was going to be great, I thought. But there was a catch.

"Jack," Dad said, as he tapped his cigarette ashes onto his dinner plate. "What is your summer job? I don't want you just sitting around twiddling your thumbs out on the front porch. There are a lot of older boys in the neighborhood, and since you aren't too swift, they could easily lead you astray."

He caught me by surprise. Still, I knew I didn't want to make money by mowing lawns, or washing cars, or being a professional dog-walker like some of the other kids.

"I'm going to write," I said. "Be a writer."

He smirked. "Are you back on that again? Well, they say simpleminded people are really hardheaded," he said, then whistled off a little steam.

Mom gave him *the look,* and he lightened up a bit.

"Okay, while we're away you can play at writing. But when we come back, if you haven't made any money at it, then I'm going to sneak you in to work at the concrete warehouse. You can keep rats from eating holes in the bags. We had a cat, but the rats ganged up and killed it. You'll just have to lie about your age, but that's no big deal. You're smart enough to do that."

"You bet," I said. But I didn't mean it. I was scared to death of rats, but this was one fear I wouldn't have to face. I had a foolproof way to make quick money from writing. I got the idea from watching television. I was flipping through the channels when, suddenly, I saw it. There was a documentary on Mexico and it showed professional letter writers all lined up on chairs with desks and portable typewriters in a town square. People who had never learned to write would come to them and for a price would dictate letters. The writers would add fancy details, and dress the letters up with lots of adjectives. They made love letters more sexy, sad letters more tragic, and totally humdrum lives worth reading about.

I figured I could do something just like it on Fort Lauderdale beach. I had already gone down to the Salvation Army and bought a stack of old postcards for cheap. At the post office, I tried to bargain for stamps, but the postal clerk just laughed at me. I had to pay full price. But when I did all the math in my head, I calculated that, if I charged a dollar a postcard, I would make over seventy cents on each one sold. There were thousands of tourists on Fort Lauderdale beach and I figured I could write about a hundred postcards in eight hours, one every five minutes. That'd add up to better pay than any junior rat exterminator's. And it would give me perfect writing balance. Cheerful postcard writer by day, and tragedy-writing novelist by night.

The next morning we helped my parents load up the car.

"Remember," Dad grunted, as he pushed a suitcase toward the back of the trunk, "when I return, I want to see some cold hard cash. If you are going to sit on your butt all day pecking at a typewriter, you better have something to show for it, or you'll be killing rats."

"Don't worry," I replied, and handed him another suitcase. "The way my life is going, I'll have plenty to write about."

"Any moron with two brain cells to rub together can write," he said. "The problem is, getting people to read the stuff."

"I know," I replied. "You won't even read what I give you." That was a mistake.

"Well, that proves my point," he insisted, then lowered the trunk lid. "Your own father can't stand your writing."

Mom gave him *the look* again, then whispered in my ear as I kissed her goodbye. "Take care of Pete. He's been acting a bit unusual."

He is unusual, I thought to myself. So he's his normal self. "Okay," I replied. "Have a great time and don't worry about a thing."

The moment Mom closed her door, Dad tore out of the driveway and sped down the street as though he had just robbed a bank. I guess they did need a break from us.

Betsy snuck up behind me and clamped her hands around my neck. "Have you ever read the book *1984*?"

"No," I squeaked.

"At the end," she said, "the main character is captured and his enemies strap a three-sided cage to his face. Then they fill it with starving rats that chew their way into his brain."

"What do you want from me?" I gasped.

"You take care of Pete," she said. "Show up every night for dinner, do everything I say, and I'll keep rats from using your eye sockets as doorways to your brain."

"Okay," I croaked. "You're the boss." I went limp and she let me drop to the ground.

# Two

My first day out I was sitting under a palm tree like some wasted survivor on a desert island with the typewriter on my lap. Above me I had thumbtacked a big sign: POST-CARDS WRITTEN AND MAILED. ONE DOLLAR

Business was slow. In fact, I hadn't scored a customer all day. I hadn't even seen a mirage of a customer, and I was in a bad mood. Every time I looked up to make sure my sign hadn't blown away, the sun scorched my face and I thought of rats turning my brain into Swiss cheese. I had to make some money before Dad returned.

Pete was sitting next to me. He was so sluggish he looked like a snake propped up on a stick. "Give me a dollar," he moaned, and stuck out his hand. "I want to buy a Slim Jim."

He was like BeauBeau, only with a slightly larger brain. "No way," I snapped back. "Buy it yourself."

"You own me so you have to take care of me," he whined, as if it were a law.

"I own you so you have to work for me," I replied. "Now it is time for you to get your rear in gear. Because if I end up killing rats for a living, you'll be the first rat I kill."

"I just want to buy a Slim Jim, then take a swim, then fall asleep under a picnic table." He pouted.

"Wrong," I replied. "You will do none of those things. You will put your mind to a moneymaking task."

He groaned. His head drooped over to one side.

"Let me explain the number-one lesson of life," I said. "See those people all over the beach?"

"Yeah," he replied. "So what?"

"Well, millions of years ago the beach was covered with fish with feet."

"I don't get it," he said.

"Let me spell it out," I labored, and tapped him on the head. "Once upon a time we were all just single-celled dots in a pool of slimy water. Then we were fish. Then we were fish with feet. Then we were people. And now our next step is to make money. And if you can make lots of money while doing what you love to do, then it automatically means you are a genius. We didn't go from single-celled slime to people just so we could eat Slim Jims and sleep under a table."

He looked at his feet, then squinted up at me. "That's the dumbest thing I ever heard," he said. "No wonder everyone thinks you're an idiot."

I almost slugged him, but it wasn't in my best interest. "Let me spell it out even more," I said. "If fish didn't decide they wanted to walk, we wouldn't be here today."

"You've been out in the sun too long," he cracked.

I was losing patience. "We're growing up," I said.

"No kidding," he sputtered. "Nobody grows down."

"I don't mean that." I sighed. "I mean it's time to make something of ourselves. Take the next step. Make some bucks."

Pete's eyes glazed over. If I were a book, he was ready to close me.

"The point is all about you and me. Look at it this way. Some fish were dumb. They walked in the wrong direction and died. But the smart ones kept walking from one puddle to the next. The same for us. You and I are—"

"Going from puddle to puddle."

"There you go again," I moaned. "Missing the—"

"I have an idea," he said abruptly.

"That's it!" I said, encouraging him. "Evolve. Be something. Turn your idea into money."

"Dad says, 'It takes money to make money,'" he said, and held his hand out again. "I need to go home and get Dad's old Polaroid. Then I'll need ten dollars to get started."

"Started on what?" I asked. "What?"

"It's a surprise," he replied coyly.

"Well, if I'm gonna bankroll your lazy butt," I stressed, "everything you earn belongs to me."

"I'll save you from rats eating your face off," he said, and made a bucktoothed rat face.

That got me. I gave him the ten.

He jammed it into the pocket of his cutoffs, then began to half flop and half crawl across the sand like a fish with feet. After he had gone about ten yards he turned to grin at me. "When I come back, I'll have evolved," he said.

"Yeah. You'll be a newt," I muttered under my breath.

As soon as Pete left I opened my black book and began to wonder what awful things I could write about. I looked around the beach. I knew that beneath the normal surface of society lay hidden the twisted underbelly of life. That's the good stuff I wanted to write about, but everything looked pretty normal from where I was sitting. The lifeguard stood in his orange tower. The tourists were spread out on hotel towels, and after baking under the sun all morning they looked like neon-pink hors d'oeuvres on crackers. The palm readers were setting up their striped tents, and the ice-cream vendors were working the crowd. Nothing looked suspiciously abnormal. I stared at the blank pages of my book and thought, Don't panic, you've always been a magnet for weirdness. Sit tight, it will come your way.

Suddenly a bald guy with a swollen belly and a gold chain around his neck so thick you could anchor a ship on it slogged a path through the sand and stood in front of me. He had on so much suntan lotion he glowed like a freshly glazed donut.

"I want ten cards, dated the next ten days. On each one I want you to make up an excuse why I can't return to prison on time. And make it believable. You know, like my mother died and I have to attend her funeral. Or they're throwing me a parade for pulling kids out of a burning building. Stuff like that. I'm on a furlough and I have to send them to my parole officer. I'll pick 'em up after lunch."

He pulled a folded ten-dollar bill from the little mesh pocket inside the waistband of his stretchy tiger-print swimsuit.

I held out my hand, and he dropped it in. The bill was damp. I'll sterilize this later, I thought to myself as I smiled up at him.

"Make 'em good," he warned me. "You have a nice typewriter. I'd hate to see something bad happen to it."

"Don't worry about a thing," I said nervously, then smiled at him as I recited my business jingle. "You go free, and leave the writing to me."

He marched off, probably to go kick sand on little guys with cute girlfriends.

I gave him ten days of the worst bad luck I could imagine: Sun-poisoning rash on privates from day at nude beach. Stung on eyeballs by man-o'-war. One hundred stitches in foot from stepping on child's rusty sand shovel. Inner tube swept out to sea by rogue dolphins. Needed blood transfusion after wicked mosquito attack. Witness to a lifeguard mugging. Ear infection from sea monkeys. Amnesia caused by heat stroke. Buried in sand while sleeping and left for dead. Needed hip replacement after crippled by suicide surfer.

I closed the typewriter case with a snap. I figured if my postcard business didn't work out I could write headlines for the *National Enquirer* or *The Weekly World News*.

When he returned he read each one, slowly, with his lips moving. "You have a sick mind, kid," he declared.

I was thrilled. "I'm going to be a writer," I said to him. "The sicker the mind, the more money you make." I held out my hand for a tip.

"I'll give you a tip," he said, and ripped the cards in half. "If my parole officer read this junk he'd probably track me down and have me tossed in a padded cell." He flipped the pieces back over his shoulder and they blew across the sand. "Now give me back my ten-spot."

"No way," I said. "I worked really hard."

He stuck out his open hand. "I'll count to three," he growled. "One."

I stood up. "I did what you asked," I said.

"Two."

"I did the best I could. I'm not the governor. I can't write you out a pardon."

"Three!" He lunged forward and pulled the typewriter out of my hands.

"No!" I yelled as he spun around and ran down the beach with the typewriter held overhead.

"Come back with that," I shouted.

I was too late. He waded into the water and heaved the typewriter about twenty feet farther out, past the drop-off. At first the machine, in its closed case, floated and bobbed up and down on the waves. Then slowly it began to tilt to one side and sink, going down like the *Titanic*. I dove for it. The water was all sandy, and it disappeared before I could reach the spot.

I came up for air and looked back at the bully. He was a big single-celled blob that hadn't evolved.

"Let this be a lesson to you for now," he shouted. "I'll get my ten bucks later."

I hated people who tried to teach me a lesson. I was going to say something that would probably get me killed, but at that moment I spotted Pete and my mind went spinning out of control.

He was tapping his way across the beach with a fake blind man's walking stick made out of a painted cane fishing pole. On his face he had a pair of huge wrap-around sunglasses that were tinted so dark I couldn't see his eyes. Hanging from his neck was the old Polaroid camera. He tapped a few more feet, then hollered, "Get your picture taken. Two dollars. Have a lifetime souvenir of you and your loved ones on Fort Lauderdale beach for only two dollars."

No wonder Mom was concerned about his behavior. And if Dad found out about this he'd have the stick and I'd be the rat. "Over here!" I hollered, as I dog-paddled toward the shore. "Hey, blind boy, over here!"

"I'll be right there to take your picture, sir," he shouted, and waved his arms around. "Don't move."

He stirred up the sand with his cane as he clumsily

made his way toward me. I wanted to kill him. But then I thought better of punching him in the head in front of people who might really think he was blind. They'd probably beat me to a pulp, and pamper him.

"What are you up to?" I growled when I got my hands on his shoulders.

He rotated his head back and forth, and smiled widely.

"This is not what I meant by evolution," I said. "What you are doing is criminal. Mark my words," I stressed. "This is going to lead to trouble."

"It'll lead to big money," he said. "See." He reached into his pocket and pulled out a wad of bills. "I bet you don't make this from writing postcards."

I snatched the money out of his hands and began to count. "Wow," I said. "Sixteen bucks." I put it in my pocket.

"Some fish were smarter than others," he replied. "I'm already on my second box of film. Watch this."

He tapped a zigzag path through the beach crowd. I watched as he whacked a few of the sleeping sunbathers on the butt with his pole. They flipped over with a shout and he began to apologize wildly. Then he acted as if he had gotten turned around and began tapping his way directly toward the crashing waves. The people he had whacked saw him as he sloped down toward the water and they ran to catch him and turn him in the proper direction. I didn't hear what he said next, but in a moment he had them all lined up and was preparing to take their picture.

I couldn't stand still any longer. I've created a monster, I thought, a deviant fish with no shame.

I arrived in time to hear him say, "Sing out loud and I can aim for your voice." Then he held the camera up and wiggled it around. One by one they sang like opera stars and, of course, he took a perfect shot. When they saw the result they "ohhed" and "ahhed" over his ability to capture them right in the middle of the picture. He just smiled brightly and said, "It's a gift."

He had a lot of nerve. I thought I would burst their bubble and tell them about Pete's 20-20 vision. But when I saw them reach for their wallets I changed my mind.

"That will be two dollars a picture," he informed them, and stuck out his hand.

"For his operation," I pitched in, and winked.

"I take tips," Pete announced. They shelled out and drifted away. Before I could pry that money out of his hands he said, "Treat you to a Coke and a Slim Jim."

Now, that was impressive. "You've definitely evolved," I said.

"Money makes you smarter," he replied. "You should get some."

# Three

The next morning after I got Pete's camera loaded up with film and packed him off to work, I strolled along the beach to see if my typewriter had washed up. I figured if I got to it fast enough I could hose the salt and sand out of it before rust set in. But after finding a lost swim fin, an ice chest, and cracked sunglasses I gave up.

On my way back to my postcard-writing spot I passed a gypsy tent. A sign outside read: WHY SUFFER? TAKE A SHORTCUT TO THE FUTURE. LEARN YOUR MISTAKES WITHOUT HAVING TO PAY FOR THEM THE HARD WAY. FIVE BUCKS.

That was for me. If I was going to make the big money, I needed to get a head start on writing about big disasters headed my way. Little money came from little disasters, and I had plenty of those. Last night Betsy made crepes suzette, which were vile enough, but they were also hazardous. She poured a bottle of vanilla extract on a heap of ice cream and set it on fire. The bowl got so hot it cracked and the flaming ice cream melted over the table and scorched the varnish. It was really cool-looking when it happened, and we were screaming and laughing, but then the table tipped over onto the bassinet and we just managed to get the baby out before the blanket burst into flames.

This kind of thing happened all the time, it seemed, but I didn't think anybody was going to pay me to read about it. Whatever I was going to write about, it had to be worse. A lot worse, and so humiliating no one had ever thought of it before in the history of writing.

I slapped the side of Madame Ginger's tent. A cloud of patchouli incense wafted out. "Hello," I shouted, then began to cough and gag.

"Enter," she called back. "If you dare."

I dared. "Hi," I wheezed. "I want to see the future." I set my black book down on her round table, next to her crystal ball, and stuck out my palm. Madame Ginger held it between her smooth hands. She wore a gold-lamé turban and had little diamonds embedded in her long red fingernails.

"What do you want to know?" she asked fearlessly.

She wore mirrored contact lenses, which made her eyes look like polished-chrome ball-bearings. As I stared into them I saw a tiny reflection of my face. "I want to know about love and money," I said, and waved the cloud of incense away from my face so I could breathe.

"Ahh," she sighed, and threw her head back. "The two most important subjects in the world. The cause of all joy and misery."

This was perfect.

She hummed some gypsy Muzak as she charted my palm with a red fine-point marker and drew stars and half-moons and question marks. "You are a writer," she said.

I placed my free hand over my black book as if I were taking an oath. "How did you know?" I gushed, and leaned forward.

"It is written in your palm," she said, and touched a line. It made my backbone vibrate.

I didn't see what she saw, but that's what I was paying her for. "Will I write about something awful?" I asked.

"Yes," she said.

"I've already written about a criminal who threw my typewriter in the water," I said, bubbling over. "That was pretty awful."

"What I see is worse than that," she said, sounding very distressed.

"What?" I asked. "Is it something with tragic love in it?"

"Yes," she replied sadly. "Tragic, and vastly humiliating."

I was thrilled. The more misery on the page, the more money in my pocket, I recited to myself. "When will it happen to me?"

She stared even harder at my hand. "You won't have to wait too long," she said. "It's coming."

"Tell me more," I said. "I need the gory details." I opened my notebook, took out a pen, and was prepared to write down her predictions.

She began to shuffle through a deck of tarot cards, then laid them out. "Love," she murmured, as she ran her hands over the pictures. "Love, love, love." Then she brightened. "Here it is." She held up the card of an angel, then pressed it against her eyes. "I see a leg," she moaned.

"A leg. Whose?" I asked.

"I don't know," she replied. "I can't give names. Just clues." Suddenly Madame Ginger slumped down into her chair like a deflated balloon. "I'm whipped," she said, and sighed. "A leg is it for today. I need a cup of tea."

"For five bucks all I get is a leg?" I asked. "Can you tell me if it's tall, muscular, skinny, short, thick, bowed, anything?"

She closed her eyes and tried to squeeze out another vision. "I've got it," she said. "The leg you are looking for is upside down."

That confused me even more. "Is it attached to a body?" I asked. "Or has it been severed? That would be really good."

"Don't go getting psychotic on me," she snapped. "You're too young to be a sicko."

I knew that wasn't true. I changed the subject before she had a vision of what I did to BeauBeau. "Anything about money?"

"You have a lot of rodents in your financial future," she said. "Don't ask me why. Some people have a date with destiny. You have a date with vermin."

That depressed me. I could already feel the rats clawing my face. "Thanks," I said. "I'll let you know how it all turns out."

"I'll know before you do," she said, and slumped back into her chair. "If you need more advice, come see me."

"Okay," I promised.

When I stepped out of her tent I took a deep breath of fresh air. I was allergic to patchouli and coughed up a huge yellow loogie. I spit it out behind her tent. An ant walked onto the loogie and got stuck. I watched closely as it slowly drowned. I bet that's how amber is made, I thought. Then I strolled over to the Yankee Clipper Hotel to think about the upside-down leg.

The Yankee Clipper was my favorite hotel because it was shaped like a cruise ship with decks, round windows, and smokestacks. And whenever I sat at the outside patio, on a barstool, with a pair of smoky-blue sunglasses covering half my face, Coke in one hand and black notebook in the other, I felt like a famous American writer, usually F. Scott Fitzgerald, sailing from New York to Paris. He had a brilliant wife named Zelda who went insane and died in a hospital fire. That gave him plenty of tragic material to write about. I didn't have anything that horrendous in my life, but maybe the upside-down leg could lead to total humiliation. That would be awesome.

Pete came tapping by to give me the morning profits. He was a fabulous non-stop moneymaking machine. As long as he was working, I didn't have to write postcards, but could sit around all day waiting for trouble.

"I'm going to the bathroom," he said to me after I turned all his pockets inside out to make sure he had given me every cent.

"Don't aim against the wind," I advised, as he tapped across the patio and went inside the hotel lobby.

I hadn't got any writing done, as I was busy watching a squad of girls practice synchronized swimming in the pool. I figured they were on the bottom of the evolutionary scale. They were like real fish with feet. And then it struck me. Wham! There they were—eight upsidedown legs that belonged to four girls. Madame Ginger was a visionary genius. I was wondering how I might meet them when the lobby door opened and Pete came flying out. A security guard stood in the doorway and shouted, "I don't care if you're blind. Don't let me catch you going into the ladies' room again."

"Geez Louise," I muttered. "I can't let him out of my sight." I hopped up and ran over to him. "Now you're becoming a perv," I said, yanking him forward by his ear. "What would Mom say about this?"

"Don't tell her," he begged.

"As long as you just stick with being a criminal I won't say a word. Besides, you'll make more money that way."

"But it was a mistake," he cried, and slapped at my

hand. "I was practicing with my eyes closed and I went in the wrong door. I was whacking my stick around trying to find the urinal and accidentally poked a woman."

"Yeah. Tell that to the judge," I said suspiciously. "Anyway, I need your help, and you owe me."

"What do you want? I already gave you all my money."

"I want to meet those girls," I said, and pointed to the pool. "They have upside-down legs."

"I don't get it," he said.

"Madame Ginger said I'd meet someone with upside-down legs and that it would lead to devastating humiliation and shame. That's just what I need for my writing. Now, what do you see? Eight upside-down legs, right?"

"Right. But how do you know which one you're supposed to meet?"

"I'm not sure yet, but let me handle it my way," I replied. "I have a plan. Tap your way over toward the far end of the pool," I said. "The deep end. Right next to the sign that says, SWIM AT YOUR OWN RISK. I'll follow you."

We walked over there and watched. They bobbed up and down, spun around in circles, and splashed water in all directions. They looked like human lawn sprinklers doing ballet. Then they turned upside down and kicked their legs back and forth, snipping the air like scissors. They all looked dangerous to me. If you fell on top of them they'd slice you to shreds.

"How do they hold their breath so long?" Pete asked.

"Practice," I replied. "Now you take a deep breath." He

did. I ripped the stick out of his hand and pushed him into the water. He still hadn't learned to swim very well and went straight to the bottom. Forgive me, Mom, I said to myself, but he'll be okay. I figured he was good for about two minutes before I had to rescue him.

"Excuse me," I shouted toward the girls. They didn't hear me. I cupped my hands around my mouth. "Excuse me!" I shouted again. They kept spinning around, twirling their arms overhead, and spitting like fish.

They couldn't hear me because their bathing caps were pulled down over their ears. And then they turned upside down again. I looked at those upside-down legs. Which one was mine? I had to take a chance. "If my mother punched your mother," I sang, pointing from leg to leg. "What color was the blood? R . . . E . . . D." I took Pete's cane and jabbed the winner in the thigh.

That got her attention.

She stopped swimming and turned toward me. "Hey!" she shouted. "What's wrong with you?"

"My blind brother," I hollered and pointed toward him. "He's drowning!" He was. He had been under for a minute and a half and was probably blue by now.

By then the other girls had stopped, and all four of them dove underwater toward the deep end, where they grabbed Pete and brought him to the surface. I leaned forward and dragged him up over the edge and laid him out on his back.

"Quick," one of the girls said. "Give him mouth-to-mouth resuscitation."

I stared at her. "Me?" I asked.

"You're his brother," she said impatiently. "I don't want to do it."

I knew how to do it. I leaned over and opened his mouth. At the same time I whispered so that only he could hear me. "Just go along with this," I said. "I'm not kissing you." He didn't say anything back so I figured he didn't mind, or he was already dead. Then I bent over and put my lips on his and blew air into his lungs. I pulled away, sucked more air into my lungs, and started to do it again. Only this time he spewed a bellyful of water into my mouth just as I opened my lips over his.

"Ugh," I moaned and jerked my head back. There was other stuff besides water in his belly.

"Ohh, gross," I heard the girls say in perfect harmony. "That's disgusting." They were well trained.

I took another deep breath, then leaned forward and spit his spit back into his mouth. His eyes opened. "I can't see!" he shouted.

"Jerk," I said and slapped my hand down over his mouth. "I told you to fall into the water. Not drown."

He bit me on the palm and I yanked my hand back. "Goober," he said to me. "I wanted one of them to give me mouth-to-mouth."

"You disgust me," I shouted and hopped up. "I don't even know you anymore," I said, totally grossed out by him. "You've changed."

"Evolved," he said, and turned over onto his hands and knees.

"Criminal," I growled. "Sick. Perv." I turned toward the girls and smiled. "I'm sorry," I said. "He gets this way sometimes. Water on the brain."

The four of them smiled weakly, stood up together, held hands, and jumped back into the water. They didn't even say anything to me. But I wasn't concerned with all of them. When they turned upside down I noticed a red dot where I had jabbed the leg I picked. That's the one, I thought. That's my destiny.

I walked back to my chair. I pulled out my black book and started to write. This is great stuff, I thought. The weirder, the better.

"Help," Pete said again. I looked up. I still had his cane, so he crawled across the patio on all fours until he got tangled up under a table and chairs.

"Suffer," I yelled over at him. "It'll make a man out of you."

# Four

In the morning Pete and I got up extra-early and rode our bikes down to the beach before the crowds arrived. I went just in case the typewriter had finally washed up. Pete went with me because it was the only time he could take a swim and keep his eyes open.

I held his blind-boy getup and camera, and was picking through the flotsam and jetsam when in front of me a huge mound of sand was beginning to move around.

"Oh, my God," I shouted. "A monster!"

An arm emerged and wiped a wad of sand away and I saw a single giant eye blinking at me. I took Pete's stick and jabbed it right where the creature was sizing me up.

"Argh!" it growled and rose up onto all fours. Then, before I could get my feet in gear, it stood up and shivered like a dirty dog. When the sand flew off I recognized the convict who threw my typewriter in the ocean. He must have been hiding from the law disguised as a giant sand slug.

He covered his sore eye with one hand and stared out at me with his other. "You again!" he shouted. "You still owe me ten bucks, and I need it now more than ever."

"Hurry," I called to Pete as I began to back up.

Pete ran through the surf until he circled behind me and then we turned and dashed up to Atlantic Avenue. I looked for the convict but he gave up on us and was just splashing around in the surf, trying to wash the sand out of his eye. If he had used my postcards he probably wouldn't be having this problem, I thought.

I gave Pete his blind-boy supplies and camera, and a twenty-dollar bill for film. "Go get breakfast at the Cuban-Chinese restaurant and I'll meet up with you in an hour."

"Can I order a dinner?" he asked. "Betsy's cooking really stinks."

"Anything you want," I said. "Knock yourself out. Just be there when I return."

I watched as Pete safely stepped out into the oncoming traffic. Tires screeched and horns blared as he tapped his way across the street. Then I made my way down to Madame Ginger's tent.

"Good morning," she said, as she wrapped her turban in circles around her bald head. "You're a little early." The gold silk was so tight it pulled her eyes up at an angle. She looked like a plump Siamese cat. "I can wait," I said. I took a seat and examined her crystal ball. I was hoping to see where the convict went, or if Pete was spending my twenty on tourist junk. But I didn't see anything except for tiny bubbles of air trapped in the glass.

After she tucked the loose end into a seam behind her head, she leaned forward and inserted her mirrored contact lenses.

"Okay." She sighed, and poured herself a cup of coffee from a thermos. "Now, what can I do for you?"

"I need to know more about the upside-down leg," I said, and shot my palm out. "What's the next step?"

She plucked the five out from between my fingers, then held my hand. "It's not just the leg that is upside down," she said, after a minute. "It's the whole world."

"What do you mean?"

"Nothing is as it appears to be," she continued, and stirred the air above her head. "Everything has a hidden meaning."

"Like what?"

"Like your brother," she said. "He's not blind. And you are not as stupid as you seem."

Not that *stupid* label again! Mr. Ploof was right. The IQ test would dog me for the rest of my life.

"I see a young man in uniform trying to give you money," she said.

"Excellent. I love money," I murmured, as she pressed her fingers over my eyes. "What else?"

"If you need to know more about the leg, you've got to take control," she advised. "Be aggressive. You will have no tragedy, no major humiliation, no money, and no answers to life's big questions unless you go out on a limb." Then she slumped back down into her chair. She was so deflated her turban slipped down to one side.

"What about another clue?" I asked. "Something I should watch out for. Tip me off to trouble."

She thought about it. "Crushed ice," she replied.

"Is that it? That doesn't sound too tragic."

"I must warn you," she said seriously. "If you want to write about tragedy, you have to live it first. Remember, art imitates life."

I shrugged. "Well, I'm ready for anything," I replied.

"No, you aren't," she disagreed. "That's why I'm warning you."

Suddenly she sounded like Betsy. She was giving me orders on how to live my life, rather than helping me to manage it myself. "One last thing," I said, testing her powers. "Does my sister's French cooking get any better?"

She thought about it. "No," she replied. "It just gets more dangerous. Very dangerous."

"Thanks for the warning," I said. I stood up and carefully peeked between the tent flaps.

"Don't worry about that convict," she said, reading my mind. "By now he's all the way down at the other end of the beach."

I walked over to the Cuban-Chinese restaurant. Pete was sitting at a table playing checkers with some kid. "Come on," I said. "Time to make the donuts."

"One minute," he whispered. "I bet this kid a buck I could beat him even though I was blind."

I threw a buck down on the board and grabbed Pete by the shoulder. "One of these days," I said, "you're going to go too far."

By midafternoon Pete and I were sitting at a table drinking Cokes. I was chewing on the ice and feeling very suave. I had a wad of cash in my pocket that was big enough to choke a horse. I was at a cool hotel. I had my black book on my lap, pen in hand, and tragedy was only a hundred feet away and heading in my direction.

On the other side of the pool, one of the synchronized swimmers walked across the patio. She wore a sports jacket that said "Fort Lauderdale High Flying L's Swim Team." She took it off and draped it over the back of her chair before she took a seat. She was the one I was supposed to meet, since she was the one with the bruised spot on her thigh.

"Psst," I hissed at Pete, and nodded in her direction. "Check out the upside-down leg."

He lifted his dark glasses and squinted at her. "She seems too nice to be trouble," Pete said. "Shouldn't she be covered with tattoos or something?"

"Madame Ginger said nothing is as it appears," I said

knowingly. "She could be a killer. I could be her next victim. Now watch this."

I strolled up to the bartender. Earlier he had told me
he was a college kid on summer break. I figured he'd
know what to do. "See that girl over there," I said.

"That beautiful girl?" he replied.

"Shh," I whispered, and turned my back toward her.
"Not so loud." I peeled a couple singles off my wad of bills.
"I want you to give her a Coke on me."

He raised his eyebrows. "Is there something special
you'd like me to tell her?" he asked. "Something romantic?"

I couldn't say what I was thinking, which was that she
had a nice upside-down leg. "You think of something," I
replied.

He stuck out his hand. I put a dollar in it. He snapped
his fingers. I gave him another dollar. I was so entranced
with the girl that if he'd kept snapping his fingers I'd have
given him everything I had.

He plopped a couple extra cherries into the Coke, and
set it on a tin serving tray. Then in one smooth move he
lifted the tray off the bar, up over his shoulder, way above
his head, glided over to her table, then brought it down
as if he were going to behead her, but at the last second
he whipped the tray clean out from under the glass. For
one breathless instant the glass floated in midair, and then
with his free hand he snatched it and, without spilling a
drop, lowered it onto her table.

She looked up at him, smiled, and gently clapped her hands together. I read her lips. "Bravo, bravo," she mouthed.

He lowered his head, then whispered something in her ear. She giggled, then turned her eyes toward me. I gave her a slow, two-fingered salute and my shy-guy smile. It worked. She smiled back and waved her fingers at me, one at a time. Even her fingers were perfectly synchronized. Then I crisply swiveled around on my barstool and returned to my table as I pulverized a mouthful of ice.

Pete was watching me like a hawk.

"You're supposed to be blind," I reminded him.

"Watch this move," he whispered. "I'll show you why fish have feet." He stood up and slowly, painfully tapped his way over to her table. Each time he rammed his hip into a chair or kicked a table leg he let out a whimper until he had her full attention. Finally he reached her side and said, loud enough for me to hear, "Would the lady like a free picture?"

She glanced over at me. I nodded my approval, and gave her my cool, two-fingered salute and the same shy smile.

She smiled back and said something to Pete.

"Then sing loud," Pete instructed as he moved the camera around in a figure eight.

She sang, "Do you believe in magic . . ."

I nearly melted down off my chair. I believed in magic,

but this was too good to be true. I crunched down on some more ice and sent little shards of it darting through the air.

Pete took the shot, pulled it out of the camera, and then quickly took another. He gave her the first picture, then tapped his way back to me. When he sat down he whispered, "Ten dollars for the picture still in the camera."

"Three," I shot back.

"Eight."

"Four."

I got it for five. He pulled it out of the camera and as it developed before me it was as though an entire dream was shaping up into reality. I felt bliss. I felt love. This was not tragedy. Madame Ginger must have gotten her wires crossed. This wasn't about crushed ice. It was about my crush on the girl with the upside-down leg.

I got up to walk toward her. She saw me coming and, just as quickly, stood up and dove into the pool.

"I told you," Pete said when I plopped back into my seat. "Trouble. Nothing but trouble."

I had forgotten that humiliation was supposed to be literary medicine for me. "Time for you to get back to work," I snapped, feeling a bit grumpy. I checked his camera. There was one shot left. "Take my picture," I said. "And I'll change the cartridge."

As soon as Pete had tapped his way back to the beach, the young bartender came over.

"I noticed you are a writer," he remarked.

"Yes," I said, with pride. "I am." I glanced at the pool. She was still swimming.

He followed my eyes. "Would you like me to deliver a special note to her?"

"Do you have her address?" I asked.

"Can't give you that," he replied. "But for a little something extra I can see that she gets it."

"Okay," I said. "Give me a minute." I sat down and wrote on the back of the photo, "I believe in magic." I gave her my address and phone number. "Call me. Ask for Jack." I wanted to add, If my sister answers, hang up and try again. But I thought of Betsy strapping the rat cage to my face, so I didn't write anything more.

When I returned to the bar I gave him the photograph.

"That blind kid sure is talented," he said, admiring the picture. He read the back, then held out his hand for a tip. I gave him a buck. He snapped his fingers. Two bucks. He snapped again. Three bucks. He snapped again. I hesitated. Something was wrong. Madame Ginger said *he* was supposed to give *me* money.

"Just make it five," he demanded. "This is special-delivery love mail."

I blushed, and gave him the money.

"I know this girl," he said. "She's very sweet."

"Don't worry," I replied. "I only write about really sweet things." I knew that wasn't true. But there was a first time for everything.

"Would you like to know her name?" he asked coyly.

"Yes," I replied. "Absolutely."

He snapped his fingers.

I gave him a buck. He frowned. I gave him another.

"This is for her *name*," he stressed, and then he lowered his voice and leaned a little closer. "And the tragic story behind it."

That gave me goose bumps. I gave him three more bucks. Now I know why writers have to write so much. Tragedy is expensive.

"Her first name is Virginia," he said. "She's named after Virginia Woolf."

"Who's that?"

"She was a famous writer," he said. "She went insane and one day filled her pockets full of rocks and walked into the river."

"Did she drown?"

"Yes," he whispered. He turned to look at Virginia. She was still swimming. "Her parents," he said confidentially, "are very concerned about her fascination with water."

I was wrong, I thought to myself. Madame Ginger is right. This could be a tragedy. I looked over at Virginia. She had stopped doing laps and was upside down with her legs kicking back and forth. Please come up for air, I thought. Please.

She did, and I sighed with relief. I wanted her to live at least long enough to crush me like a bug.

That night Betsy continued to experiment with dangerous foods. No wonder BeauBeau committed suicide, I thought, after Betsy made me eat a butter-soaked, three-pound Monte Cristo sandwich the size of an English–French dictionary. Afterward, she served up a platter of cherries jubilee. She went into the liquor cabinet, then poured half a bottle of mint schnapps on the cherries. "Who would like the honor?" she asked, holding up a box of wooden kitchen matches.

Pete ran to the other side of the room. I grabbed the baby and ducked down behind a chair.

"Jack," she said. "Just before you came home some girl called."

"She did! What'd she say?" I asked anxiously.

She handed me the matches. "First things first," she sang.

I knew what to do. "Stand back," I shouted. "Monsieur Henri shall perform a death-defying feat." I struck a match and flicked it at the dessert. The flames shot up like the Olympic torch and melted a hole in the plastic light shade hanging over the dining-room table.

Betsy grabbed the platter with cooking mitts and whisked it over to the sink. "Don't worry," she said. "We can pick the plastic bits out."

"Well, what did Virginia say?" I asked, standing behind her and breathing down her neck.

"She said thanks for the photo, and that you are very cute."

"Yes," I hissed. "Victory is mine."

"But I worry about this girl already," Betsy said. "Because if she thinks you are cute, then she might think you are nice, and if she thinks that, then she might think you have the heart of a human when we all know you have the heart of a rat."

I didn't tell Betsy she was wrong. Really, I had the heart of a loser. Or at least I hoped so. My literary future depended upon it.

# Five

I was crossing Atlantic Avenue when I looked down the road and saw about a hundred baby sea turtles. Every one of them had been flattened by a car. When they hatched out of their nests on the beach, some of them went the wrong way and ended up on the road. Others went the right way and made it to the water. It got me thinking about the difference between real tragedy and fake tragedy. Some people think it is tragic when an innocent person crossing the street is flattened by a runaway cement truck. But that is not tragedy. That is just plain old bad luck. Real tragedy happens to people who are trying hard to do something great, like me, but through some stupid fault of their own, they screw up and everything falls to pieces. Like all the high-and-mighty heroes in Shakespeare who have a tragic flaw and end up dead, dying, or insane.

As far as I could tell, everything was going too well for me. The upside-down leg thought I was cute. Pete was making enough money to keep the rats from eating my brain. And Madame Ginger said the worst thing that could happen to me would be about crushed ice. If I didn't work a little harder to screw things up, my tragic writing was going to look like a rack of Hallmark greeting cards.

I marched over to the Yankee Clipper and took a seat at a patio table. I pulled out my black book and started making notes, when the bartender saw me and came over.

"You know, I was thinking," he said. "About what you could do to really make Virginia feel special."

"What?" I replied.

"When you aren't here and she is, I'd still deliver her a Coke on your tab."

I thought about that. "But I wouldn't be here to watch her drink it," I said.

"That's not the point," he countered. "The Coke is for her to enjoy, with or without you. Believe me, women love guys who know how to give them room to breathe."

He lost me. "How much will it cost?" I asked. I knew how to understand the bottom line.

"Give me twenty bucks," he said. "That will cover four Cokes and tips."

I winced. That was almost a whole day's work for Pete. "When can I speak with her?" I asked.

"I'll ask her," he said. "Don't worry, you're doing very well here. Every time I deliver a Coke to her, she says, 'Is it from that nice handsome young man?' And I say, 'Yes. Isn't he a prince?' She's warming up to you."

"Then let's forget the Coke thing," I said, making a bold decision. "Let's go for broke. I want a date."

"That could be difficult," he said, suddenly cooling on the idea. "Let's see what happens once she shows up."

"Okay." But already I was thinking, what could be so difficult? I'll just ask her myself. After all, Madame Ginger said I had to go out on a limb.

When she arrived I got up and walked toward her. I figured I'd ask her out, she'd say no, I'd be humiliated and have something to write about. Simple. But suddenly, as I approached her, I thought, what if she says yes? What if she's thrilled to meet me? Then I'll have nothing to write about. But then I thought about it a little more and reality set in. She was older. She was well dressed. She had manners. She was poised. She was refined. She had not said one nice word to me, ever. There was no way in ten lifetimes she'd stoop so low as to go out with a rodent like me who had done nothing but buy her a few Cokes, and poke her in the leg with a stick.

I was right. As soon as she saw me coming, the look on her face went from serene to total annoyance. She bolted across the patio and dove into the pool. It was a crushing blow, but it didn't kill me. And once my breathing evened out, and I realized I was just fine, I knew I had not suffered enough. I needed more.

I sat down and was making a few notes in my black book when the bartender arrived. "Don't take her running away from you personally," he said. "She is more shy than you are. Now, let me help you out." I gave him a five even before he could stick out his hand. He sadly shook his head back and forth. "No, no, no," he repeated. "This is a whole new level."

I gave him another five.

"I don't think you heard me," he sang.

I gave him another five.

"I can't hear you."

He was worse to me than I was to the lady with the typewriter. Well, what goes around comes around, I thought. I gave him the last of my fives.

"Okay," he said reluctantly. "I'll see what I can do."

He went over to her and said something. She shook her head and said no. He said something more. No, she said again. I couldn't hear her but I watched her mouth. I was positive she was saying no, no, no.

He walked back toward me with a big smile on his face. "Surprise," he said. "She said yes."

"Yes?" I repeated. "I thought she said no."

"You misread," he replied. "I asked if she could go out tomorrow and she said no, only tonight."

"Oh," I said. "What do I do next?"

He held out his hand.

"How much?"

"Twenty bucks for her address," he said. "But look at the bright side. After tonight you will have all the information you need and that'll be it for me."

"Okay," I replied. "But this is the last money I'll ever

give you." I dug into my pocket and thought, Which is the worse tragedy, his money-grubbing hands or her potential heartbreaking blow?

He snapped the bill out of my hand, and wrote the address down on a piece of Yankee Clipper stationery.

"Be there at six," he said. "She's a fanatic about being on time. Also, she's a vegetarian, only goes to foreign films, and is thinking of becoming a doctor."

"Wow," I replied. "I thought she had a great future as a synchronized swimmer."

He dismissed the thought with the wave of his hand. "Get real. This girl is going places."

There were people waiting for him at the bar so he left. I walked across the patio and down the beach.

I had my hand up, shading my eyes, when I heard Pete scream.

"Leave me alone!" he shouted. "Let go of me."

"You little faker," said an old woman. "My sister is non-sighted and your little charade is a cruel insult." She pulled the dark glasses off his face and hurled them into the surf.

"Help!" Pete screamed. "I'm being attacked." He gave her a couple stiff whacks on the legs with his blind-boy cane.

She snatched it out of his hands and broke it in two over the top of his head. "Criminal," she growled.

"Child abuse!" Pete hollered.

"You deserve worse," she scolded. She had an iron grip on the leather camera strap around his neck. He leaned forward and panted for air as his eyes bugged out like a Boston terrier's.

"Uh-oh," I said under my breath. "Trouble."

"Give me that money," she demanded.

"It's mine," he choked out, holding a few dollars just beyond her reach.

"You stole it from people," she snapped. "It should go to the unfortunate."

Now, when it came to money, I really got worked up. I ran across the sand, leaping over sunbathers like an Olympic hurdler until I caught up to them.

The first thing I did was snatch the cash out of Pete's hand and shove it into my pocket along with my big roll of cash. Once that was out of the way, I was ready for a fight.

"Get your hands off of him," I ordered.

"He's a juvenile delinquent," she declared. "I'm making a citizen's arrest."

"So am I," I said, grabbing her flabby arm and tugging her in the opposite direction. "Lifeguard!" I yelled.

"Let go of my arm, you awful child," she spit out. "Or I'll send both of you to a home for the depraved."

"Let go," I shot right back. "Or I'll send you to a nursing home."

Just then the leather strap around Pete's neck snapped. He shot forward and she sprung back at me. I fell and she landed with her giant butt on my lap. I thought my hipbones were crushed and my legs paralyzed for life. Then she reached into my pocket and grabbed all our money.

"Give that back," I shouted. I gave her a pinch and she hopped right up, and power-walked toward the lifeguard stand.

Every few steps she swiveled around and hollered, "Nasty boys! Don't you mess with me."

A lot of people were starting to watch, and judging by how they glared at us, they were getting the wrong idea.

"You mean old fish with feet," Pete yelled back.

"Come on," I said, and pulled him along.

"Did she get all the money?" he asked.

"The whole enchilada." I sighed.

I didn't tell him I had twenty bucks stashed at home. But that was for my date.

"I'll see you later," Pete said. "I still have some film left I can use at the other end of the beach."

"Well, be careful," I said, still limping. "If she sits on *you*, you're dead."


When I got home I checked the mailbox out of habit. There was a postcard from Mom and Dad. They said they were returning the following day. And I'll be killing rats the day after, I said to myself. I leaned down and looked into the box to make sure there was no more mail. Suddenly a hornet came shooting out and stung me on the forehead. It felt like I had been stabbed with an ice pick. I yelped and ran for the house.

Nobody was home. Betsy had taken the baby next door to swim in the Sopers' pool. They had a daughter, Christine, who had been an exchange student in Paris and Betsy was trying to figure out how to do the same thing.

I was staring at myself in the bathroom mirror. From the hornet sting my forehead looked lopsided. Like Gumby's head. A lump was forming and right at the top of it I could see the black hornet stinger where it was stuck in the skin. I opened the medicine cabinet and took out the tweezers. Then very carefully I moved the tweezers toward the stinger.

I heard Betsy open the back sliding-glass doors.

"Are you home, Jack?" she yelled. She must have seen my black book where I'd tossed it on the dining-room table.

I didn't reply because my head would move. Just when I had the stinger lined up and was about to pluck it out, she pushed open the bathroom door and it hit my elbow, which instantly drove the tweezers tips into my Gumby lump.

"Arghh!" I yelled.

"Out," she ordered. "I have to pee."

"You should have gone in the Sopers' pool," I suggested, as I closed my eyes until the throbbing pain calmed down a bit.

"They put a chemical in their water," she said. "If you pee it turns *pourpre.*"

I went out to the kitchen. In a minute Betsy joined me.

"I'm going to make some French fries for a snack," she said. "You want some?"

"Sure," I replied. I loved French fries. Plus, it was cheaper to eat at home. I figured I had money to buy Virginia a snack, but not a whole meal.

I began to set the table. Betsy had a beach towel wrapped around herself and tucked into the top of her suit like a Hawaiian dancer.

"What's the red lump on your forehead?" she asked as she cut up the potatoes.

"A hornet sting," I said, gently touching it.

"You should put some mud on it," she suggested. "That's what Indians do to make the swelling go down."

"Really?" I asked.

"Sure," she said, and poured a bottle of cooking oil into the cast-iron skillet. "Just go outside, mix a little water and dirt, and put it on."

"Okay," I said. I turned and began to walk out the sliding glass door. I thought it was open but it wasn't. I hit the glass lump first and bounced off. Luckily the glass didn't break and slice me into strips, or Betsy would have fried me up, too.

I touched my lump and winced. The pain made my eyes water.

"Let me see," Betsy said.

I turned toward her.

"You better put ice on it first," she suggested. "You can do the mud later."

I opened the freezer and pulled out an ice tray, then began to run it under some water to loosen up the cubes. I wanted to ask if she would ever go out with a younger guy with a lump on his head and near-empty pockets, but was already in too much pain.

In a minute the oil began to get hot. Betsy tested it with a piece of potato skin. The oil snapped and popped and the potato skin turned brown and crispy. She salted the potatoes, then used a wide slotted spoon to lower them into the skillet. You have to have a steady hand because if the oil splashes out of the skillet and onto the burner it can catch on fire.

As soon as she put in the first batch of potatoes there was a low whooshing sound and a giant flame, like a big red flag, snapped up above the skillet. She screamed and jumped back with the hot slotted spoon still in her hand. As I turned around to see what happened she accidentally clobbered me right on my lump.

"Oww," I hollered, and dropped down onto my knees.

Betsy grabbed a glass of water from the kitchen counter and threw it on the fire. An enormous ball of black smoke billowed up above the flaming oil. It looked like a small nuclear explosion.

"Smother it!" I yelled, and lunged forward.

Betsy unwrapped the towel from around her waist and threw it on the skillet, then turned off the burner.

I headed for the sliding glass door. In all the excitement I forgot it was still closed. Wham! It didn't break, but I hit my head in the same spot again. I staggered back. I was so dizzy I didn't know what to do next. I reached out and clutched the back of a chair to steady myself, then everything went black and I hit the floor head-first.

When I finally opened my eyes Pete was sitting on my stomach staring down at me. Betsy was washing the soot off the wall.

"What time is it!" I shouted, and looked at my watch. It was five o'clock. I pushed Pete to one side and looked into the small kitchen mirror. "Oh, my God!" I shouted. Pete had drawn a little smiley face on my lump. "I'm a freak," I cried out. I took a cloth and dipped it into a bottle of Mr. Clean, then gritted my teeth and scrubbed my lump until it was red and shiny as a drunk's nose. I was hysterical.

"What's your rush?" Betsy asked.

"I have a date," I blurted out.

I whipped open the freezer door and got some ice for my lump. I held it on my head as I ran back to my room to get dressed. I slipped the ice into my mouth in order to free my hand and push it through a shirt sleeve. I was stepping into a pair of stiff new jeans when I bit down on the ice. Crack! My right front tooth broke. Oh no, I thought, this is what Madame Ginger warned me about. I ran to the bathroom. Pete was in there with the door locked.

"You're not allowed to lock the door," I shouted, and twisted the knob back and forth. I skinned my knuckles against the jamb and blood started running down my fingers. I wiped them across my clean shirt. "Idiot," I said to myself. "Moron. Knucklehead." Immediately I noticed that anything I said was accompanied by a little whistling sound. With my tooth broken off, the air came out of my mouth funny and it sounded as though I had a very high-pitched lisp.

I ran back to my room and looked in my dresser mirror. The tooth had broken off at an angle, so that I had an empty V shape between my front teeth. I looked like a total ghoul.

I had to do something quick. I rapidly chewed up a stick of Juicy Fruit, then wadded it up behind the tooth and filled in the gap.

Betsy came into my room. "Is your date with that little girl who's been calling? Don't tell me you're dating a third-grader. Are you sick?"

I didn't say a word because I thought my gum patch might fall out. But I wanted to yell, She's not a third-grader. She's very sophisticated. She's a synchronized swimmer and probably knows more about France than you do. But I kept my mouth shut, and my feet moving. I had to get to Virginia by six o'clock.

Betsy and Pete followed me out of the house. I got on my bike and started to pedal.

"Is she meeting you on a tricycle?" Betsy hollered as I turned out of the driveway. "Or is she using training wheels now?"

I looked at my watch. It was five forty-five. I could still make it if I rode like a maniac.

By the time I got to her house my shirt was soaked with sweat all around my armpits and down my back, and my lump was so agitated I thought I could feel it twitching as it grew larger. I ditched my bike in her front hedge, ran my fingers through my hair and pulled a curl down over the lump, then pressed the doorbell. I didn't hear it ring, and no one answered. Maybe it's broken, I thought. I knocked on the door, then stepped back. Nothing. I knocked again, then pounded, and this time the cuts on my knuckles opened up. I stuck my hand in my pocket to soak up the blood. There was still no answer. I checked my watch. It was just six. I peeked in the front windows. Nothing. I checked the address on my piece of paper. I was at the right place.

She's just late, I said to calm myself. It happens. There was a small park across the street. I decided it would be more polite if I didn't wait on her doorstep. So I walked over. I saw some nice flowers a garden club had planted and realized I hadn't gotten her any. I looked around and didn't see the flower police so I picked a bunch of them. When I sniffed them my eyes began to water, and I began to sneeze. Oh great, I said to myself, my allergies have started up. I sat down against a tree and laid my flowers against my chest.

It was the first time all week that I just sat still with my hands on my lap and thought about stuff. I had been trying so hard to make everything work out so awful. It seemed like such a nutty thing to want to do, to force disasters on myself, when there were so many disasters that occurred naturally. Maybe I had plenty of trouble to write about already if I just stopped thinking there was an even bigger disaster around the corner.

I began to count up all the things that had gone wrong in just over a week. I think the fall on my head was a little worse than I thought because counting my mistakes was like counting sheep and I dozed off. When I opened my eyes about two hours later, her lights were on. By then my allergies were so bad I was sneezing, and had trouble breathing.

"Suck it up," I said to myself. "It's show time!"

I walked across the street and pressed the doorbell. Suddenly I let loose with a huge openmouthed sneeze and a great big yellow-and-green loogie shot out of my mouth and right in the middle of the flowers. Before I could shake it off the door opened. It was a girl about Pete's age. "Hi," she said, then began to laugh like a hyena. She covered her mouth, then left me standing there as she ran off and hollered, "Dan! Our friend is here."

I was squeezing the chewing gum back behind my tooth when I heard another girl say, "Darn. I thought we were gone long enough to blow him off."

Then the bartender stepped out from behind the door. "Hey, buddy," he said, "what's up?"

"I'm not sure," I stammered. "I thought I had a date with Virginia."

"You must have come to the wrong address," he replied.

For a moment I believed him. Maybe I did go to the wrong house. Maybe she was waiting for me elsewhere.

But he had only given me one address. I pulled the piece of Yankee Clipper notepaper out of my top pocket. "This is what you wrote down," I said.

He took it from my hand and looked it over. "Wow, I made a big mistake," he said, and slapped his forehead with his hand. Just watching made my forehead hurt as if I'd been hit with a tuning fork. "I gave you my address instead of hers."

Just then the young girl ran up behind him and pushed her way between him and the door. She waved my photograph in the air. "Did you write this?" she asked, then turned it over and pointed at my head. "You don't have that lump in the picture," she said.

Before she could answer, the bartender pulled her back behind the door.

"Give me that," he said.

I could hear the scuffling of feet and figured they were having a tug-of-war with the photograph.

"Ow!" she suddenly hollered. "Ow!" Then I heard her fall to the floor with a slap. "I'm telling," she howled, then ran down the hall screaming, "Virginia, Dan hit me!"

He returned looking a little sweaty and ran his hands through his hair. "For ten dollars," he said, holding the ripped photograph in his hand, "you can have this back."

I just stood there, dumfounded, trying to catch on to what was happening. Why were they all together? How did they know each other? And then everything began to clear up. "You tricked me," I said. "You must be Virginia's brother."

"I'm sorry," he said. "I didn't trick you. She changed her mind and decided not to go out with you."

"You ripped me off all along," I said, feeling all high and mighty. "You and Virginia were just using me."

"Well, who is worse?" he asked, sounding a little huffy. "Me for trying to make a little extra tip money? Or you and your *blind* brother you put to work on the beach?"

He had me there.

"Well, what about the date?" I asked, getting back to the real subject. "Were you just going to let me stand out here all night?"

He pulled his wallet out of his back pocket and removed a twenty. "Here," he said. "This should make up for some of it."

"No thanks," I replied. "I can't be bought off."

"I'm not trying to buy you off," he said. "I'm trying to make you feel better."

"I don't want to feel better, either," I said. I took a big breath and accidentally swallowed my chewing-gum tooth patch. I was horrified. "Excuse me," I said. The words whistled out of my mouth.

Just then Virginia opened the door all the way. "Sorry, kid," she said. "This was all his idea. I told my brother I wouldn't go out on a date with someone I didn't know. But he just took your money and set up the date anyway. He figured I'd go along with it, but *nobody* tells me who to date!" She gave her brother a dirty look.

"I can't blame you," I said meekly, whistling the words.

I didn't know what else to do. I just wanted to get out

of there. But since I had the flowers I held them out and said, "These are for you." They tilted forward like an ice-cream cone and my yellow-and-green loogie slid off and splattered on her shoe.

She glowered at me. "What the heck is that?"

"Whoops. Sorry," I whimpered.

"Sorry's not good enough," she said furiously, and stepped forward. "Clean that off," she said, and pointed at the loogie.

"No," I said, stepping back. "No way. It was an accident."

"You little creep," she said, pouncing at me and grabbing my shirt collar. She yanked me forward. I tripped over the front step and fell half into the house. I tried to push myself up but the little sister jumped on my back and held my head down.

"I gave you a chance," Virginia said from above. "Now lick it off." She raised her black patent-leather pump, with the shiny yellow-and-green loogie on top, to my lips. "Lick it off or I'll squish you like a bug."

It was my loogie to begin with. What goes around comes around, I thought, then stuck out my tongue and slurped it up as if eating a raw oyster out of a shell. It wasn't so bad.

"Oh, gross!" Virginia hollered. As she jerked her shoe back she kicked me on the lump.

"Arghh!" I moaned.

The little sister rolled off me. "That's sick," she said and slapped the floor. "Sick, sick, sick."

"Oh, man," the bartender said. "That is the most humiliating thing I've ever seen, and I've seen a lot of bad stuff."

I turned my head and looked up at him. My eyes were watering and it looked like I was crying. But I wasn't. It was the allergies. "Really?" I asked with a whistle. "Is this really the most humiliating thing you've ever seen?"

"Really," he confirmed. "No doubt about it."

"Then shake," I said. I stuck out my hand and he pulled me up onto my feet.

"Goodbye," I said.

I staggered toward my bike. As I pedaled away I glanced at the three of them in the doorway and remembered my writing motto: A WRITER'S JOB IS TO TURN HIS WORST EXPERIENCES INTO MONEY. I only had twenty dollars in my pocket but I felt like a millionaire.

When Mr. Adolino turned the corner he looked like he was in trouble. We had come to the French consulate's office on a field trip to look at French landscape paintings. And those are the best. But the had been paintings taken away and replaced with THE HISTORY OF FRENCH UNDERGARMENTS.

VOTE NO
PAGODA=TAX
"Pet-pad"

"Ooo La La," Johnny Greenteeth said when he turned the corner. I began to pick up my pace so I could see because already Mr. Adolino was saying, "Don't go in there boys. Don't go in there." Of course we nearly ran him over trying to get in. Johnny G. pitched a fake fainting spell and keeled over as he sighed, "I'm in heaven." I had never seen such beautiful underware before. All the underware I had seen was white. But this French stuff was all silky and colorful. And where my

underware was held up with elastic, this
stuff had all kinds of leather and silver
straps and buckles

to
glance at it for a minute because
a guard came and closed the door.
"Feel
my
pulse,"
Tommy

DEATH
ROW

said
when we
got outside
I did. It
as if
he had
just run a mile. Mr
adolino got us back on
the bus and we to Burger
king and Mr. Adolino let us order
anything we wanted one
of the paper on his head
and "I'm the King of France,
and I to dance, on Sunday's in my
undies, without my pants!" Mr. adolino
made him sit alone on the bus while
we ate free chocolate shakes and
promised him we wouldn't tell our
parents, or any other teachers what
we had seen. It was no big deal. Any
guy who has gone shopping with his mom

The Fall of
the House
of Pagoda,
or
The Tattooed
Toe

# One

It was dark. I stood in the backyard and pulled my swim mask down over my face, and slipped the snorkel mouthpiece between my teeth. I removed a handkerchief from my top pocket, poured half a bottle of English Leather cologne on it, then reached above my head and carefully poked the handkerchief into the snorkel tube. I took a deep breath and the rush of cologne fumes nearly knocked me over. But it was better than smelling the fumes of the dead and rotting.

I was doing it again. I stood above BeauBeau's grave and thrust the shovel into the dirt. I looked over both shoulders one more time just in case someone was watching. "God help me," I muttered. I lifted the shovel and threw the dirt over to one side. I pushed the shovel down again. "I didn't mean to dig you up the first time," I said to BeauBeau. I lifted the shovel, flipped the dirt onto the

pile, and pushed the blade back in. "Now I have to do it
again." I grunted as I lifted a big lump of damp soil. Suddenly it was as if I had pulled the cork stopper out of a
bottle of the worst-smelling substance known to man. A
fog of nasty-smelling BeauBeau fumes began to unfurl
and it curled up around me as I shivered. Then from the
mouth of the hole came a string of fearless, red-eyed al-
bino rats. I took a step back. I didn't want any of them
sneaking up behind me and running up my legs.

Dad had said I got off the hook from killing rats at the
concrete factory because some other dad gave his son the
job. But I was back on the hook, and I was mad. I knew
these monsters had been feasting off of BeauBeau's flesh
and they were gonna pay. I raised the shovel up over my
head and brought it down on the one closest to my shoe.
I hit it so hard I drove it into the soft earth, as if I were
pressing chocolate bits into cookie dough. "Take that, you
grave gourmet," I muttered. But then it squirmed around
and clawed its way out of the indentation. That spooked
me. It couldn't be killed. I stepped back and before I
could hit it again it ran back into its hole. When I looked
up, there were half a dozen rats crawling around the dirt,
sniffing for food and licking my shoes. "Scat," I hissed,
and kicked one cleanly into the neighbor's yard. The rest
knew I meant business and scampered back into one of
their tunnels. I dropped my shovel and ran to the side
yard and sat down under a tree. I pulled off my swim
mask and snorkel and tugged my handkerchief out of the

snorkel tube. I poured more English Leather cologne on it, then held it over my nose and mouth and took deep breaths. I was thinking about the low road, and the highroad in life. It was my plan to take the highroad and do great things. I knew it would be harder, but still it was the road less traveled and would be worth it in the end. But I had slipped, and I was stumbling along the low road with the lowest of low-minded people—the Pagoda family. When we had lived in Fort Lauderdale, before Barbados, the Pagodas were our next-door neighbors. They were definitely the most demented people in the world. Their oldest kid, Gary, had a criminal record as long as my arm. Frankie, who was my age, was psychotic ever since he dove off the roof of their house and hit his head on the edge of their swimming pool. And green-haired Susie was totally out of touch with reality.

And now I had joined the Pagodas on the road to ruin. I had bragged to Mr. Pagoda about the dog coffin. That was a mistake. Now he wanted to see it. If he liked it he thought we could make a lot of money selling them to people who bought fancy pet products. He knew a lot about selling pet products, and had made a fortune on them while we were away in Barbados the previous year, and the thought of making Pagoda gold is how I got sucked into digging BeauBeau back up.

This had all started about a month before.

We were sitting in the living room after dinner and

Mom was reading the *Fort Lauderdale News*. "Look," she said to Dad, and pointed to a section of the newspaper she had folded back. "Mr. Pagoda is running for public office."

Dad looked up from his book. "Oh, Lord," he moaned sarcastically.

"Is he running for something, or away from something?" I asked, trying to be clever.

"It says he's running for District Council on the Anti-Pet-Tax Platform," Mom replied.

"That's what happens to people who can't hold down a real job." Dad said. "They become politicians."

"What's the anti-pet-tax platform?" I asked.

"Mark Woody, the guy who is now in office, wants to tax pet owners an extra registration fee that will go to paying for animals that have no homes," Betsy explained.

"That doesn't sound too bad," I said.

"It's nonsense," Dad snapped back. "Taxes will never even out the differences between the *haves* and the *have-nots*. If it were up to the government, each time you paid to have your shoes shined, you'd be charged an extra tax for barefoot people. If you drove a car you'd have to pay a tax for people who walked. If you had a house you'd have to pay a tax for people who slept on benches. You can't tax all the hardworking people to help out all the lazy losers. That is liberal nonsense."

He had lost me. I thought we were talking about pets.

"It does say that Mr. Pagoda is a Democrat," Mom said, adding fuel to the fire.

"Figures," Dad muttered. He was a true-blue Republican. His dad had been a Republican, and had said, "If an ape ran for President, I'd still vote for him as long as he was a Republican."

One time I was writing a civics paper for school and had asked Dad what the difference was between the two political parties. He explained that if there were two starving Democrats left in the world, and only one piece of meat, they would split the meat down the middle.

"That sounds right," I said, taking notes. "Sharing is good."

"Don't fall for it," Dad objected. "They might share it, but secretly the Democrats are sneaks. As they split the meat you can bet each one is thinking, I hope you choke and die on the first bite, so I can have the rest. Democrats will stab you in the back. But the Republicans play fair and square. They'll stab you right in the chest. Instead of sharing, they'd fight it out so that the winner would get the whole hunk o' meat."

That's why he was a Republican, I figured. They were tough, and not embarrassed to be mean.

"The Democrats," he continued, "are weak. They'd rather share than fight. But believe me, neither party tries to change things for the better. They just feed on greed."

I had used his ideas in my paper and the teacher gave me a low grade and wrote a note asking where I got my nutty ideas. I was too embarrassed to tell her I got them from home, so I said I got them from a TV talk show.

Now, before he could really get worked up about gov-

ernment taxation, Mom cut him off. "Well, let's drive over
to the old neighborhood," she suggested.

"Sure," Dad said. "Maybe there is a big cage around the
Pagoda property, and they are all under house arrest
along with all their stinking show dogs." He smiled at the
thought.

We got in the car and drove a few miles from one side
of Wilton Manors to the other. It didn't take long to reach
our old neighborhood. We cruised up the streets, past the
Metrics' house, the Peabos', the Gibbonses', and the Veluc-
cis'. They all looked the same. Nothing had changed. It
didn't even seem as if the grass had grown, or new flowers had bloomed. It wasn't that I expected something
dramatic to have happened, like everyone building a second story, or painting their houses plaid or polka-dot, but
I thought there would be some noticeable improvements.
Maybe that was because I was always changing, hopefully
growing up and getting better, and I guess I expected the
same from the rest of the world. But when I looked out
at the neighborhood, it was the same old shabby place,
and it wasn't getting any better.

And then we stopped in front of the Pagodas' house.
Nobody said a word. There was no cage around their
house as Dad had wished. But something had definitely
changed for the better. Their house was beautiful. Their
scruffy old lawn had been replaced with new sod so that
it looked like a perfect hair transplant. All the dead tree
stumps had been yanked out and smoothed over. The
house was freshly painted in a soft peach. The shrubs

and boxwood hedges were crisply trimmed. There was no broken glass in the windows. And there were a gold Mercedes and a huge SilverStream Motor Home parked in the new double-wide driveway.

"Are you sure this is the right house?" Pete asked.

"Check out the roof," Dad said, and pointed. "You can still see the shadow of the red atom-bomb target they painted up there."

"The question should be," Betsy said, "do the Pagodas still live in this house?"

Just then the front door to the silver trailer opened and Gary Pagoda stepped out, yawned, and rubbed the sleep from his eyes.

"Oh, my God," Mom cried out. "Look at him."

All of us leaned to one side to stare out the windows, so that the car tilted. He was dressed only in skimpy French underwear and the tattoos of women and birds and bumper-sticker sayings all over his chest and arms made it look as if he had fallen asleep on the Sunday comics.

"Cool," Pete said. "I want tattoos like that!"

I hope he didn't mean the naked lady on Gary's shoulder.

"The only tattoo you'll get will be from my right hand on your backside," Dad cracked.

"It's not polite to stare," Mom said, and slipped her hand across his eyes.

I also thought the tattoos were *cool*, but after what Dad had said to Pete I just kept the thought of getting one to myself. Dad had an anchor tattooed on his arm, but he had been in the Navy and excused it by saying he was drunk and stupid and young when he did it, and afterward it was too late to change. I wasn't drunk, but I was young and I did worry that I was stupid. But I still wanted one. In fact, I wanted a couple hundred. I had this idea once of getting the world's greatest art tattooed across my back. I'd have the *Mona Lisa, Whistler's Mother, Washington Crossing the Delaware*—all the classics. Except the paintings would be the size of postage stamps, so I could travel around the world as a one-man museum and make a fortune by taking off my shirt and selling people magnifying glasses. When I first got this idea I was so thrilled I told it to Betsy. She replied that if I tattooed a line between all the freckles on my face it would spell out "bonehead from another planet."

"I wonder where they got the money to fix the place up?" Dad asked, rubbing his chin.

"Maybe they sold a couple of those brain-damaged kids to a medical lab," Betsy replied.

"Or just won the lottery," Mom guessed.

"Maybe Mr. Pagoda finally invented something really important," I suggested. "Something that has changed the whole world." Everyone looked at me as if I was out of my mind.

"Well, *maybe*," I repeated.

"Yeah," Dad said sarcastically. "And maybe one day you'll change from a knucklehead to a rocket scientist."

Here we go, I thought. It was bad enough having to worry myself on the subject, but my family only made it

worse. I had just started eighth grade and it was open sea-
son again for jokes about my IQ level. And Mom was back
to feeding me fish sticks. Now as I gaped slack-jawed at
the rich-looking Pagoda house, I felt really dumb. I had
always thought I was smarter than all of them rolled into
one. But how smart could I be if I was just sitting there
in a rust-bucket of a car while thinking, I wish I were a
*Pagoda*.

"We better get going," Mom said. "If they see us they
might invite us in."

"Yeah," Pete said, and wrinkled up his nose. "And if you
breathe the stinky dog-poop Pagoda air in their house
you'll be paralyzed for life."

Dad put the car in gear and we slowly cruised down the
street and around the corner. When we got to Wilton
Manors Boulevard there was a billboard with Mr.
Pagoda's giant painted face beaming down on us. VOTE
PAGODA! NO PET TAX! it read.

"Hey, Dad," I said, joking around. "For once you and
Mr. Pagoda are on the same side."

"That just goes to show you how bad my luck is in this
town," he muttered.

No one said another word. The Pagodas had passed us
by and we were all depressed. Mom tried to cheer us up
by having Dad stop at the Dairy Queen and treat us all to
a strawberry dip. But it only reminded me of the time Mr.
Pagoda poured a gallon of his experimental cherry-
colored sun-block into the swimming pool and made us
all dive in about a hundred times. Each time we climbed

out, we were recoated with a waxy, pinkish oil which floated on the surface and was supposed to "automatically safeguard the skin," according to Mr. Pagoda. Unfortunately, it made our feet so slick the only way to reach the end of the diving board was to crawl out on our hands and knees.

# Two

Two days later Pete burst into my room. "You won't believe this," he shouted, waving a shiny brochure above his head. "You aren't as dumb as you look. You were right. Mr. Pagoda invented something and now they are rich! Look!"

I snatched the brochure out of his hand and threw myself across the bed. THE PAGODA PET PAD was printed in bright red letters across the top. Below was a picture of a dog cautiously staring at a little rug that was blocking its way into a living room which had been prissily decorated with white furniture. It looked like God's living room. Below the picture was an explanation: "Vet Approved. The PAGODA PET PAD is a safe and painless way to correct bad pet habits! Keep pets from entering rooms and off of furniture. Just plug in the PAGODA PET PAD and once your pet receives a few uncomfortable shocks, it will soon alter its problem behavior. GUARANTEED."

I looked at the price. "Eighty bucks!" I shouted. "No wonder they're rich."

I could have thought of the Pet Pad, I said to myself. But I hadn't. I hadn't thought of Kleenex, or toilet paper on a roll, or toothpaste, or tiny screwdrivers to fix your glasses, or back scratchers on a long stick, or Pet Rocks, or any of that stuff. I wished I were one of those people who had just one brilliant idea and turned it into a fortune. Mr. Pagoda had, and now I felt more stupid than ever before.

While Pete was busy telling everyone what he had discovered, I rode my bike over and looked at their house from across the street. Someone had stuck a hand-drawn sign in his yard. PAGODA for District Council—NO PET TAXI! I read it twice before I realized there was a mistake—NO PET TAXI! Then I thought, well, maybe he was against pets riding in taxis, too. After all, he was now a politician so he was obligated to keep saying stuff. And who was I to second-guess him? He was the one with the brains and money.

No matter how nutty they are, I thought, they are my friends. I took a deep breath and threw my arms up into the air as I crossed the street. "Let the Pagoda games begin," I declared, as if I were announcing the opening of the Olympics.

Gary Pagoda was sitting on the front lawn next to a

bucket. I crept up behind him and just stood there. The bucket was filled with gasoline. A small tape recorder was at his side. A woman's breathy voice kept saying over and over, "Breathe deep, exhale. Breathe deep, exhale."

I was a little nervous because the last time I had seen him he'd threatened to stab me to death with his Kentucky Toothpick. Now I was worried that if he was breathing gasoline fumes he'd be really nasty. "Hi," I said, as friendly as I could.

He ripped a match out of a matchbook, lit it, then quickly dunked it into the gasoline.

I took a step back. "Hi," I said again.

"I heard you the first time," he snarled. "I'm concentrating."

He lit another match, then quick-as-a-cat put it out in the gas.

"Is this a good idea?" I asked, just as the silky voice on the tape recorder said, "Now let's make a list of positive images. Kittens . . . clean underwear . . . fresh snow . . ."

Gary made a face and snapped off the tape player. "Don't get all weak in the knees," he said with that bully tone of his. "The trick is to drown the match before you can ignite the fumes. You gotta be quick. If you can dunk ten in a row I'll give you ten bucks. If I do ten in a row you give me five. What do you say?"

That was a pretty good deal. "Can you give me a few warmups?"

"Sure," he said, and tossed me the matchbook.

I ripped one off, lit it, then quickly plunged it head-first into the gas. It went out. I did another, and another, without going up in flames. "Ready," I said, figuring I'd have ten bucks in a few minutes.

"Okay," he said. "You're on."

I lit the first one and dunked it. The second. The third. The fourth. The fifth. I had total concentration. I held the matches two feet above the gas, paused to let the flame grow, then stuck them straight down into the gas. Six. Seven. Eight. Nine. Ten. "Finished," I said smoothly, and tossed him the matches. "You're up."

He took a step forward and stood about two inches from my face. "How much will you give me if I set the entire matchbook on fire and dunk the whole thing?"

He still scared me. "Ten bucks," I said, knowing that if he did it I would still break even.

"Watch this," he ordered. He lit a match, then used it to light the corner of the matchbook. He held it upside down until the remaining match heads went up in a ball of flame, and then quickly he plunged it into the gas.

The explosion was awesome. There was a loud whoosh followed by a wall of red flames and heat. I threw myself back onto the lawn and began to roll over and over. I didn't actually see that I was on fire but I wasn't taking any chances. When I stopped, I saw Gary still rolling. Smoke was coming off his pants. He was laughing wildly when he jumped up and ran around the corner of the house. I smelled burning hair, and touched my eyebrows. They were singed down to a stubble. Great, I thought, now I'll have to draw my eyebrows on like those old movie stars. And if I have to explain to Dad how this happened he'll burst into flames and scorch the rest of my hair off.

I stood there for a minute, spitting on my fingertips and swabbing down my eyebrows while waiting for Gary to come back. But he didn't. The gas was burning a black patch on the new front lawn. The tape recorder had melted down into a blob of molten plastic, and the NO PET TAXI sign had caught fire. A trail of thick smoke lifted up into the sky. I smiled. This was just like old times. The people next door, who now lived in the house we used to live in, were staring out their window and shaking their heads back and forth. I waved to them. "Up your nose with a rubber hose," I sang. "I'm a Pagoda wannabe and proud of it!" They closed the curtains. That used to be us, I thought. When we first moved in next to the Pagodas we, too, thought they were insane. But now I felt really happy to be back with them. And the only reason why, I figured, was that I was just as stupid as they were. The Pagodas were my kind of people.

I took a deep breath and pressed the doorbell. A little speaker over my head blared out, "Whatever you're selling we don't want none!" Probably another Pagoda invention, I thought. An automatic anti-salesman device.

Then it sounded like half a dozen little dogs were barking and scratching the inside of the door.

Frankie Pagoda answered. He had a black patch over one eye, like a pirate.

"Yo ho ho," I sang. "It's your old pal Jack Henry. What happened to you?"

I should have been more polite and said hello first, but I was overexcited.

He stared down at the dogs and kicked them out of the way. "I hurt it," he said quietly.

"How?"

"I was prying open a gallon of paint with a screwdriver when the tip slipped and I drove it up through my eye."

All I could think of was Robin Hood shooting an arrow into the center of a bull's-eye. It made me squint. "Are you blind?" I asked.

"One eye only," he replied.

"Do you have a glass eye?"

"I did," he said. "But Gary borrowed it last Halloween and I haven't seen it since."

"How's Susie?" I asked, taking roll.

"Oh, she's still got all her pieces," he said. "But she's started to do gymnastics so you can bet she'll break her neck or something."

"We saw an ad for the Pet Pad," I said, wanting to change the subject. "Is that thing for real?"

"Amazing, isn't it?" he replied, instantly cheering up. "Can you believe we've made a fortune on Pet Pads?"

I couldn't even bear to think about it. They'd made a

bundle on an idea any toddler with a hairpin and an electrical outlet could put together. I figured that made me about the stupidest kid on the planet. Maybe my IQ *was* low, way low, below the Pagoda line.

"Come in," he said. "I'll show you how it works."

"Cool," I said.

We went inside the house. Everything might have been new, but it all still smelled like old dog poop, and pee, and pine-scent spray. That much hadn't changed.

"We have a Pet Pad on the couch," he said, and pointed at it. "It keeps the dogs from jumping up."

I looked over at one of their yappy Pomeranians. Its hair was standing straight out like a scared porcupine's.

"What happened to the poodles?" I asked.

"Couldn't take the heat."

Frankie bent down and removed a small transformer from behind the couch. It was wired up to the Pet Pad. "Dad customized this pad," he said. "The Pomeranians need a little extra zap because of them already being so high-strung." He turned a dial to a setting that read TEN POUNDS. "Touch it," he instructed. "You'll only feel a tingle."

I placed my hand on the pad. It wasn't very strong, kind of a light shock, like when you hold a nine-volt battery on your tongue.

"Isn't this thing dangerous with kids around the house?" I asked.

"Nay," Frankie replied. "Dad says most people probably buy them to keep the rug rats and crumb-catchers from crawling on the good stuff anyway. Besides, we tested it on a lot of kids and not one of them got hurt. If anything, the kids also figured out pretty quick not to sit on the couch."

"You touch it," I said.

"Okay, but turn it up to the setting marked TWENTY POUNDS. Gary and I made up a game called Death Row, where we take turns giving each other a blast."

I did.

"I'll be the Boston Strangler," he yelled out, and touched the pad. He didn't even blink.

"Your turn," he said.

"I'll be Jack the Ripper," I declared.

He turned up the dial to FIFTY POUNDS. When I touched it my eyelids fluttered and I shook uncontrollably. "Ha!" I shouted when I lifted my hands. "You can't kill the Ripper!"

"Yeah. Now turn it up to a HUNDRED POUNDS."

I did and he touched it. Wham! His whole body jerked back as if he'd been hit with an invisible baseball bat. "The Strangler survives to kill again," he said gruesomely, and lunged toward the Pomeranians. They fled down the hallway. Then he took the transformer and turned the dial up to the last notch, marked with a skull and crossbones. "Your turn, Mr. Ripper," he said gleefully.

I leaned forward and waved my hand over the pad. It seemed to hum, and the little hairs on my arms stood up.

"Don't be a wuss," Frankie said. "It won't hurt you."

I gritted my teeth, turned, and sat on it. Wham! The next thing I knew I was on the other side of the room. I had hit the coffee table, bounced off, and knocked over a bunch of dog-show trophies.

When I opened my eyes, Mr. Pagoda was staring down at me. "Hey, welcome back, Jack," he said. "You okay?"

I lifted my arm and he jerked me up off the floor. "Frankie," he said, "don't overzap your old buddy. We could use him to help us hand out leaflets."

"For Pet Pads?" I asked. I was still a little woozy.

"No," he said. "To get out the vote. Didn't you see the sign on the front lawn?"

"Yeah," I said. "And the billboard, too." Just then I glanced out the back glass doors. Gary climbed up the pool ladder and was shaking his head back and forth to get the water out of his ears. He was stark naked. When he saw me looking at him he grinned and pointed to a red burn spot on his butt. I thought it was a bad time to remind him that he owed me ten bucks. I looked back at Mr. Pagoda. He was dressed as if he were going fox hunting in Ye Olde England. He wore tight red pants, with a little black velvet jacket, knee-high black leather boots, a riding crop, and a black leather hunting cap.

He caught me staring at his outfit. "You like it?" he asked, and struck a fashion pose. "I'm giving an anti-pet-tax speech at the Las Olas Kennel Club. Very upscale voters, so I have to look the part."

Just then Mrs. Pagoda entered the room and blew a few

ear-piercing notes on a little brass horn. "Let the voter hunt begin," she shouted.

Gary opened the sliding glass door. "Did you call me?" he asked.

"Go put some clothes on," she said. "Or get a tattoo on your privates—one or the other."

"Will do," he said with a smile, and closed the door.

Mrs. Pagoda turned to me. "He's doing so much better since the therapy," she whispered. "He doesn't hurt other people anymore. And he hasn't stolen a car for three months."

I was relieved to hear that.

"Knock on wood," said Mr. Pagoda. "Now let's get going. I've got an election to win. We're going to take this anti-pet-tax issue all the way to the White House."

"That's right," said Mrs. Pagoda. "It's taxation without representation for pets."

I looked down at the nervous Pomeranian. I could just imagine it yapping, "Give me liberty or give me death!" ready to make the ultimate sacrifice for its species.

Before I left I asked Frankie, "How come I don't see you at school?"

"Are you at Sunrise?" he asked.

"Yeah."

"I took some tests and they said I was too smart and sent me to Nova," he said. "Did big-headed Mr. Ploof give you the tests?"

"Yeah," I said. I was embarrassed to tell him my scores

but I did anyway. "They said I was average and kept me."

"Don't sweat it," he said. "The same thing happened to Gary. They said he was just average, too."

Great, I thought. Gary Pagoda and I are on the same level. "One more thing," I said to Frankie. "What's Gary listening to on his little tape recorder?"

"That's his self-help therapy," he replied. "Whenever he gets wired up and angry he has to listen to a therapy tape to calm him down."

"Well, it didn't work," I said.

At dinner that night I told everyone I had gone over to visit the Pagodas. "I'm going to be part of the democratic process," I said. "Mr. Pagoda wants me to help him beat Mr. Woody."

"He needs more than help," Dad said. "He needs a miracle."

"Well, he's pretty confident," I said. "He said he's going to take the anti-pet-tax issue all the way to the White House."

"Yeah," Betsy chimed in. "And they'll rename it the doghouse."

"I wish you all wouldn't be so cynical," I said. "I'm working for positive change, and you all are so negative."

"A Pagoda in the White House is *not* positive change," Dad said.

"Yeah," said Betsy. "If you want positive change, you should just stop hanging around them."

"Or get plastic surgery," Pete added.

I stood up. "Just wait," I said. "You'll all want to visit me when I'm living next to the White House."

"Sure," said Betsy. "There's always a line in front of the outhouse."

I turned and walked back to my room. Every time I try to do something positive, I thought, my family tries to run me down. Well, I'll show them. I'm going to be on the Pagodas' winning team.

# Three

On my first day back at Sunrise I had seen Gary in my shop class. He was so much bigger than the other kids he looked like a second teacher. I had successfully avoided him for a month, but after he had seen me at his house he came over to my shop bench.

"Aren't you three years older than me?" I asked.

"Yeah, but back when I was a juvenile delinquent I failed a few years in a row, so now I'm making up for it. Let's be shop buddies," he said. "My hypnotherapist said I should stop hanging around *bad influences*"—he nodded toward the guys I had seen him with earlier—"and should be with nicer guys."

"What's a hypnotherapist?" I asked.

"It's a lady who hypnotizes me, then when I'm zonked out she plugs thoughts into my brain with a tape that repeats positive ideas like 'Never hurt people' and 'Play by the rules' and 'Cheaters never prosper'—soft stuff like that. And then when I pop out of my trance I behave better."

I was certain that if I had a therapist she would want me to stay away from guys like Gary Pagoda.

"Come on," Gary said. "Lighten up. I know I've been a psychopath in the past but everyone deserves a second chance."

"Okay," I said. I figured if I really believed in positive change, then it was possible that Gary Pagoda was no longer a killer just looking for a victim.

He stuck out his giant calloused hand. "Buddies," he said. "Now shake on it."

I looked him in the eye. He needed a shave. He had a gold tooth. I glanced down at his outstretched hand. L-O-V-E was tattooed across his knuckles. His left hand spelled out H-A-T-E.

"Okay," I said. I took a deep breath and shook his LOVE hand.

"Awesome," he said. "This is really a breakthrough for me. You're the first non-criminal friend I've ever had."

"Didn't you have nice friends when you were in kinder-garten?" I asked.

He thought about it, then replied. "That's one thing I've never been able to figure out. Did I turn them into bad kids, or did they turn me into a bad kid?"

"I guess if I turn into a criminal we'll know," I ventured to say. I was still afraid to say something too funny around him in case he lost his sense of humor and took offense.

"You know what you're going to be doing later?" he asked.

"No," I said.

"Passing out voter leaflets with me."

"I have some other things to catch up on," I replied.

He gave me a stern look and aimed his chin toward me as if lining me up for a punch. "We're buddies now," he said. "Blood brothers." Then he punched me in the shoulder. "My therapist said she wanted me to spend more time with nice kids. And you're *it*!"

Why didn't the therapist just tell him to get a nice pet? Or maybe he'd already gone through that stage and the pet didn't survive.

"Okay," I said. "I'll be over once I do my homework."

"Skip the homework," he said.

"I'm trying to be a good influence," I stressed, and slowly stepped back. I didn't want to make any sudden moves and get him riled up. He might have needed a few more sessions with the hypnotherapist. I was thinking that I needed to get an old pocket watch and if he started to lose it I could wave it in front of his eyes and calm him down.

"You can do homework tomorrow," he insisted. "Today I'm in charge."

I felt as if I had been kidnapped by a lunatic stalker.

"As soon as I get home I'll ride my bike over," I said. "I promise."

"Forget the bike," he replied. "I'll pick you up in the motor home."

"That giant thing?"

He nodded. "Hey, I've had that motor home up to a hundred and twenty," he said. "If it had wings I'd fly it around like a bomber."

I gave him the address. He read it. "You guys sure have gone downhill since moving away from us," he remarked.

Not far enough, I thought.

By the time I got home from school I forgot all about my fear of Gary Pagoda, and instead felt proud that he had chosen me to be a good influence on him. Dad had always said I led Pete astray and gave him a lot of really bad advice as an older brother. And Betsy claimed I was so lousy at running my own life that I should be legally prevented from making any decisions for myself. So when Gary picked me to be his buddy and help him be a better person I felt as though *I* was a better person. And I felt smart. Maybe I'll become a therapist, I thought. I could go around helping people be nicer to themselves and each other, kind of like a Johnny Appleseed of positive change.

I'd just been home for a minute and was standing in front of the open refrigerator drinking out of the milk carton when Betsy yelled out from the living room, "Hey! Does anyone here have a friend who drives the Goodyear blimp?"

"That's for me," I yelled back. "It's Gary Pagoda."

Betsy was so shocked she put her book down and ran into the kitchen. "*You* are hanging around with Gary Pagoda?" she asked.

"Yeah," I said. "He's a pretty mellow guy since he got some therapy."

"Right!" she scoffed. "Therapy for him is eating puppies like you for breakfast."

"No way," I said. "I'm killing him with kindness."

"Well, watch he just doesn't kill you the old-fashioned way—with a knife through your neck."

I wiped my mouth on my sleeve and dashed out the front door before she started to make sense to me. After all, if his hypnotherapy wore off, I'd be his first victim.

The motor home couldn't even fit in the driveway so he was parked on the street.

"Hurry up," he yelled from the driver's-side window when he caught sight of me. "Dad gave me a list of things to do as long as your arm."

I opened the door and climbed into the passenger seat. It was so high up I felt as if I were sitting on top our house. "What's our first stop?" I asked.

"Old-age homes," he replied, and pointed to a list on the console between us. "Dad's political consultant says if we get the retirement vote we'll kick butt. On election day I'll drive all those ancient wrinkle rats down to the polls and make 'em vote Pagoda, or else I'll threaten to drop 'em off out in the Everglades." He laughed a cruel laugh.

"Now, is that nice?" I asked, sounding a lot like my mom.

"You're right," he said, and popped me one on the shoulder. "I won't threaten any of 'em. I was just fooling around."

"Well, that's how trouble begins," I said, again sounding just like my mom. I took a deep breath, and figured it was time to change the subject before I drove him crazy. When I saw a tattoo of a rattlesnake around his wrist, I said, "I'd love a tattoo." That was a mistake.

"Yeah," he said, and took another bite of his teriyaki-flavored Slim Jim. "Let's screw the leaflets until later. I know the best tattoo artist in the South." He pulled a U-turn and we almost tipped over. When he straightened out the wheel he clipped the fender of a parked car. Then he just kept going.

"You know what my favorite show is on TV?" he asked, while picking up speed.

I tightened my seat belt as I thought of the most violent show. "Roller derby?"

"Nay," he said. "Demolition derby. I love watching those cars smash into each other like bumper cars. When we used to steal cars we'd play demolition derby where we'd drive down the street and sideswipe parked cars. It was awesome."

"Did the police ever catch you?" I asked.

"Sure they did," he said. "Heck, they knew it was us. I mean, how many guys do you know that are as crazy as I am?"

No one came to mind. No one even got close.

"See what I mean," he said. "The police knew there were no other nuts like me in this town."

"Where are we going?" I asked.

"Dania," he replied. "All the bikers go to this one awesome guy, Savage Sam."

"I don't have any money," I said. "We can do this some other time."

He waved me off. "Don't sweat it," he said. "I owe you ten bucks for starters, and you can pay me the difference later."

When we arrived at the tattoo parlor Gary pulled up onto the front yard, which was nothing but packed dirt and weeds. A big motorcycle with a skull and crossbones painted on the gas tank was chained to a dead palm tree. We climbed down and stood before the black door of a little tilted house.

Before we could ring the doorbell a tall, nasty-looking guy in black leather pants, no shirt, a handlebar mustache, and a bald head stepped out onto the porch. "Hey, Pagoda, you loser!" he yelled. "They finally let you out of the can. Come on in. You're in luck. One of my appointments canceled, so I have time for a job. Now, what is it you are after?"

Gary pointed at me. "Here's your next victim," he said.

"Well, kid," Savage Sam the Tattoo Man asked. "You got any ideas?" He stood in front of me as if he were some kind of tattoo menu.

I was stunned. He had the strangest tattoos. Over his

heart, he had a tattoo of a heart with a nail driven into it. Over his lungs, he had a tattoo of lungs filled with green smoke. Over his liver, he had a liver inside a large martini glass. He reminded me of one of those plastic anatomy models in school. The kind where you can see through their clear skin and examine all the organs. Only Sam was a model of organs gone bad. He even had a brain tattooed on his bald head, with a little turned-off light bulb in the middle.

"Well," Sam said again. "What's your big idea?"

I'd rather have gone home and cleaned the toilet, or washed dishes, or pulled weeds. That was my idea. Anything but what I was doing. I kept thinking that it was my job to be a good influence on Gary. And if I was doing my job I'd just take a deep breath and say, "I changed my mind." But I knew Gary would just groan and get all grumpy, and Savage Sam would roll his eyes like I was some dumb kid and say, "Wuss. Chicken. Loser. Don't waste my time." Then he'd throw me out the front door.

So I said, "Yeah, I have an idea. In memory of my dead dog, I want a little dog tattooed on the tip of my big toe. The smallest dog ever, like a dog so small it could fit next to Abraham Lincoln's feet on the back of a penny. A dog about the size of a flea, so that if my dad saw it he would think it was a piece of dirt."

Savage looked back at Gary. "So you brought me a challenge," he said, grinning and nodding his dead-brained head.

"I told you I had smart friends," Gary replied, giving me the double thumbs-up.

"Awesome," Savage said as he picked up his high-speed drill and revved it a few times. "I'm up for it, dude." He turned to me. "Take off your shoe and sock."

I did. He studied my toe for a minute. "I'll do my best to keep it small," he said. But judging by the giant teeth tattooed on the outside of his face, the thick arteries climbing up his neck, and a full-size 3-D backbone over his backbone, I didn't think the word "small" was in Sam's vocabulary.

First, he washed my toe with one of those hand wipes you get in restaurants after you eat a lobster. Then he put on a rubber glove. When he turned on the tattoo gun the needle whined like a dental drill, and when he pressed it against my toe it felt the same way, only worse. There was no novocaine. Gary held my foot down on the mat and I bit down on a rawhide dog-chew toy as Savage Sam drew on me. I didn't dare wiggle my toe, for otherwise I figured BeauBeau's face would have a scratch line across it like when you just goof around with an Etch-A-Sketch.

About an hour later I moaned, "Can't you hurry?"

"I'm an artist," Savage replied, somewhat insulted. "If you want something quick, go buy one of those sissy stick-on tattoos that your mom can wash off at bath time." Then he continued to drill me with that needle at a hundred pinpricks per second.

When he finished the dog he asked, "Any name you want underneath?"

"BeauBeau," I mumbled. I was half delirious from the pain.

He snickered. "What? Did you ever have a girl suck on your toes?" he asked.

I spit the dog toy out of my mouth. "No," I said. I couldn't see the connection. I couldn't even imagine it. Why would anyone suck on a toe? Suddenly I thought I had gone insane. Gary Pagoda was now my best friend, we were driving around in the Goodyear blimp on wheels, I was in a section of town that was a hangout for America's most-wanted criminals, I was getting a tattoo from a human-anatomy model who was asking if I ever had my toes sucked on by a girl, and I was chewing on a dog toy. I wasn't a good influence. *I* was under the influence, and I wanted out.

"Can I suggest something like, 'I'm your puppy love,' " Sam asked, trying to be helpful.

"No, just BeauBeau," I replied. "And in cursive."

"Okay," he said. "You're the boss."

Finally, when it was all over he took a step back and admired his work. "There, it's now on forever. The only way you can get that off is with a hatchet."

I was sure Dad had one.

I hopped off the table and hobbled over to a chair. Savage gave me a hand mirror so I could examine the work. Instead of BeauBeau, he had written YO-YO. I didn't say anything—besides, YO-YO was sort of BeauBeau's nickname, and would probably be my name, too, once Dad or Mom or Betsy got one look at my toe.

Then he turned to Gary. "Anything for you?" he asked. "I'm on a roll."

Gary unbuttoned his shirt. "Yeah," he replied. "I been thinking. How about writing in big letters DAD FOR PRESIDENT just below the TAKE NO PRISONERS—KILL 'EM ALL AND LET GOD SORT 'EM OUT! and above the fightin' Irish Leprechaun."

"You want it in American-flag colors?" Savage asked.

"Cool," Gary replied. "He'll really dig this when I whip off my shirt at dinner."

I knew I would never take off my shoe again in front of anyone in my family. That is, if I could ever get my shoe back on. My toe had swollen up so much I could only get my foot into my sneaker about three-fourths of the way. I just crunched down the back of the heel as if I were wearing a bedroom slipper.

As the tattoo drill whirred, Gary and Sam kept up a conversation about old pals, and old criminal times. I just closed my eyes and dropped my head into my hands.

What have I gotten myself into? I thought. This isn't what I'd call taking the highroad.

# Four

I was sitting in the bathroom soaking my toe in a jar of warm water. I knew I couldn't get rid of the tattoo, but I was trying to get the swelling to go down and keep it from being infected. Another day with Gary Pagoda, I thought, and I'll be checked into a mental institution. I balanced my diary on my lap and wrote, "Maybe I am really as dumb as Mr. Ploof said I was. I can no longer deny the facts. I haven't written the blockbuster novel I set out to write. I haven't made a fortune and moved to Paris. And even Frankie Pagoda is smart enough to test out of Sunrise. Dad was right. Brains will only get in the way for me. I should build a career based on physical labor."

Just then Betsy yelled my name. "Jack, Jack! Come here quick!"

I hopped up and knocked over the jar of water. I

yanked on my sock and ran into the living room. Betsy pointed at the TV. It was a Mr. Woody commercial. He was holding a Pagoda Pet Pad and saying, ". . . my opponent claims he is anti–pet tax, and pro-pet. But you be the judge." He set the pad on the ground, plugged it in, and a lab technician set a dog on it. Mr. Woody turned the pad on and the dog yapped out in pain, did a little dance, and jumped off. "A vote for Pagoda is a vote for pet abuse," said Mr. Woody, as the dog licked its tender paws.

"Pagoda is finished," Betsy announced. "The Pet Pad is his Achilles' heel."

"Maybe not," I said. "People know that dogs need negative reinforcement. It's no worse than a little tap on the butt with a newspaper."

Betsy scoffed. "If you want to see negative reinforcement," she said, "you should see Mr. Woody's other commercial. He has a senior citizen testifying that he accidentally stepped on a Pet Pad and it zapped the pacemaker in his heart and he almost died."

She was right. Mr. Pagoda was finished unless he had a secret weapon I didn't know about. Maybe he had one more invention to help him fight off Mr. Woody's ads.

That night Gary Pagoda tapped on my window.

I pulled back the curtain. I could barely see him because he had covered his face with black shoe polish like some kind of Marine commando. But the streetlight reflected off his gold tooth and I recognized him.

"Come out," he said. "I need to talk with you."

"About what?" I whispered.

"Just get out here," he ordered. "Dad has sent us on a mission."

Suddenly I was getting a very bad feeling that Gary was Mr. Pagoda's secret weapon. As I got dressed in dark clothes, I wondered what we might do. Maybe we could take undercover photographs of Mr. Woody selling dogs and cats to medical researchers where their hair would be shaved and their heads drilled and filled with wires. Maybe Mr. Woody had a mansion built with the tax money he had collected to help cats and dogs. Now, if we could get those kinds of pictures, Mr. Pagoda would have a fighting chance. Otherwise, he was doomed.

I slipped out the front door, trotted across our front yard, and climbed into the mobile home.

"What's our mission?" I asked, as we pulled away. "Where are we going?"

He removed a cassette tape from his top pocket and pushed it into the tape deck. I expected to hear our top-secret orders from Mr. Pagoda. Instead, a woman's voice came on. It was Gary's therapist. "Gary," she said very calmly. "Close your eyes and breathe deeply. Relax and breathe deeply."

I glanced at him. His eyes were closed, and he was still driving.

"Gary," she said. "Remember to *center* yourself." I wasn't sure what she meant but we were driving down the middle of the street.

When we began to drift toward the curb I reached forward and pressed the button to eject the tape.

"Hey," he snapped and grabbed my hand. "That was helping me focus."

"Focus on the road," I suggested, and pointed to a telephone pole lined up in our headlights.

He steered to miss it, then snatched the tape and tossed it out the window.

"Now, why did you do that?" I asked.

"It wasn't helping," he said, like some weary zombie warrior. "Nothing is going to help anymore."

I didn't like the way he said that. "I was thinking that your dad needs an invention, like a secret weapon that can turn negative publicity into positive publicity," I said.

Gary leered at me. "I'm his invention," he said, confirming my fear. "I know how to wipe out Mr. Woody's lead."

"I mean, is there a button you can push and Mr. Woody's lead evaporates? Something like that?" I said. "Something scientific and brilliant, like a pro-Pagoda brain wave?"

"I'm the button," Gary said. "And I've just been pushed."

I hoped he hadn't been pushed over the edge. But he had.

Now he was driving the mobile home through the streets with the lights off. Then he cut the engine and we began to coast down Wilton Manors Boulevard.

"Where are we going?" I asked.

"Hunting," he whispered.

"For what?"

"Signs," he replied. "When we reach the corner I want you to jump out and grab all of the Mr. Woody signs and throw them in the back."

"Isn't this against the law?" I asked, knowing that it was. But I was trying to remind him.

"This is war," he replied. "You saw those Mr. Woody commercials. A guy like me can't just stand back and take this kind of abuse."

"Don't you think you are taking this too far?" I asked. "We could be arrested and they could send you away for a long time."

"It doesn't matter," Gary said. "I've tried to go by the straight and narrow, but nobody plays fair." He dodged a dog that had wandered into the street.

"That's not the point," I said. "We all know that politicians don't play fair."

"Then why play? I'd rather just do what I want. I'd rather be a political assassin, or a flaming kamikaze."

"I think you're losing it," I said, taking a chance that he might get even more angry. "Maybe we should turn around and try to find your tape."

"Just do what I tell you to do," he said like the old Gary, the one who loved to sharpen knives all day and throw bowling balls off highway overpasses. "Or else."

I could just imagine the evening news with a policeman saying, "We are searching for a suspect who killed a young man late last night. The body has not yet been identified. But there is a tattoo on one of his big toes of a dog named Yo-Yo." Eventually Savage Sam would identify me, and my parents would bury me in BeauBeau's coffin.

Gary tossed me a flashlight. "Now get going," he said.

"I'm supposed to be a good influence on you," I replied, trying one last time to reason with him. "Not your partner in crime."

"Hey," he said menacingly. "If I wasn't here with you, I might set this thing on fire and run it right through Mr. Woody's picture window. So see, you have been a good influence. I'm only pulling up a few signs."

I jumped out of the mobile home and ran into the field where a bunch of signs were nailed to wooden stakes pounded into the ground. I flicked on the flashlight and looked for Mr. Woody's face. I felt as if I were burglarizing a home. When I spotted a sign I grabbed it and pulled it out of the sandy soil. This is all wrong, I thought. Dad might be cynical about politics, but what I was doing was criminal. Then I thought, if I don't do it Gary will take one of the wooden stakes and drive it through my heart.

"Come on," he yelled. "Hurry up. We got a million more of them to pull up by sunrise."

I grabbed a bunch of signs and carried them to the big side door of the mobile home. Gary opened the door and I threw them in.

"We'll burn these later," he said.

We drove to the next corner and I pulled up a few more. When we got to a billboard Gary jumped out of the mobile home with a can of spray paint. He went around to the back of the billboard and climbed up the ladder. When he stood on the platform he wrote MR. WOODY SUCKS.

"Can't you be more clever than that?" I yelled up at him.

"What's wrong with what I wrote?" Gary barked back. "He sucks! That means don't vote for him."

"It does not," I said. "It sounds so immature." I knew the moment I said the word "immature" that I was dead meat. When he climbed down the ladder he ran and lunged at me. I fell over backward and he sat on my chest with both his huge hands around my neck.

"I didn't mean it," I choked out, thinking, Here comes my death.

"I won't kill you 'cause you been nice to me," he said. "But if you say one word to the cops I'll have Savage Sam tattoo 'Jack sucks' on your forehead. So just keep your mouth shut."

"Okay," I croaked.

Then he jumped up and ran back to the mobile home.

I hopped up onto my feet and watched as he coasted down the road like a silent ballistic missile searching out a target.

That was the last anyone ever saw of him for forty-eight hours, until election day.

# Five

Mr. Pagoda had another secret weapon. Sympathy. For the last two days before the election he went on television pleading for his son to come back. He even suggested that Mr. Woody had something to do with his disappearance. And somehow he managed to ask for people's votes while the Pomeranians sat on his lap like electrocuted wigs.

"I told you," Dad said. "Politicians will say anything to get elected."

Mr. Pagoda's sympathy request couldn't counter Mr. Woody's commercials. He'd shown an infant crawling across the Pagoda Pet Pad when zap! the tot flew backward like a fish being jerked out of water.

The next day everyone went to the polls. And that evening I went over to the Pagoda house for the election party.

Mr. and Mrs. Pagoda, Frankie, Susie, and I were all

squeezed onto the Pagoda couch watching the TV and waiting for the final ballot results. Right from the beginning it didn't look good for Mr. Pagoda. And an hour later he called Mr. Woody and conceded. In a few minutes all the local news stations announced that Mr. Woody would declare his victory.

As Mr. Woody stood out on his front yard answering questions from the press someone suddenly yelled, "Look out!" Mr. Woody and everyone dove for cover as Gary drove across the lawn in his mobile home, which had flames streaming from the windows. It looked like the explosion of the *Hindenburg* zeppelin we had seen in a history-class movie. The TV cameraman caught it all, even the flaming SilverStream roaring away down the street.

We just sat there. Stunned.

"I hope he didn't hurt himself," said Mrs. Pagoda.

"And he was doing so well," said Mr. Pagoda. "This is really depressing. But I'm glad that thing was a rental."

Frankie looked at me and winked. Then he reached down under the skirt of the couch and removed the Pet Pad transformer, and before I could stand up he gave it a full blast. Wham! All of us were suddenly jolted off the couch and onto the floor. We knocked over the coffee table, the dog trophies, the framed dog photos, and their collection of Avon dog-shaped cologne bottles.

"Mercy me," said Mr. Pagoda. We all crawled away in a daze on our hands and knees as if leaving a car wreck.

Suddenly Mr. Pagoda jumped to his feet. "That's just

the kick in the butt I needed," he hollered. "I'm not finished yet. I'm going to mount a comeback!"

"With what?" Mrs. Pagoda asked wearily. "We're broke from the election, and the remodeling, and the cars, and can't sell any more Pet Pads after Mr. Woody did us in, and God only knows what trouble Gary has caused."

Mr. Pagoda scratched his head. "I need a new pet product to sell. Something new to market." He looked out at all of us who were standing around him. "Now, which one of you has a good idea?" he asked.

And that's where I stepped in like the bigmouthed idiot I am. "I've got an idea," I said. "How about a dog coffin?"

Mr. Pagoda looked at me with wide eyes. "Brilliant!" he shouted. "Sensational! That's a million-dollar idea, son. Why didn't I think of that?"

I was so caught up by his enthusiasm I said, "I have one at home already designed and everything."

"Great," he said, and clapped his hands together. "Bring it over and we'll work on the details."

"We've got to split the profits fifty-fifty," I insisted, striking a deal while it was hot.

He stuck out his hand and we shook. I was grinning from ear to ear. I'm going to be a millionaire, I sang to myself. Then I danced a little dance as if I were doing a jig around a pot of gold.

"Now you've got the Pagoda spirit," said Mr. Pagoda.

About ten minutes later, as I rode my bike home, a police car drove by with Gary in the back seat. I wasn't much help to him after all, I thought. Neither was his therapy tape. He was going to have to straighten up all by himself.

Now, as I sat in the dark backyard, breathing English Leather cologne through a handkerchief, I knew I couldn't dig BeauBeau back up, not for any amount of money. BeauBeau was dead and buried. It was time for me to leave him rest in peace. And time for me to move on.

The weird thing about the Pagodas, I thought, is that our family was like theirs. Not in the small ways, but in the big ways. There they were, having *made it,* having some money and some chance to do something different. Something better. But they didn't. Just like us, they could figure out how to make money, but they couldn't figure out how to use that money to change their lives. Not just by buying a bigger house or fancier car, but changing who they were, how they behaved, what they wanted to become. That was our problem, too. Dad could sometimes figure out a way to make money, but it never really changed us, or solved our problems. And so somehow, just as he figured how to make it, he also lost it. Just like the Pagodas. Maybe it wasn't about money at all. It was all about ideas. About who you were, and what you wanted to do with your life, what you wanted to become, and how much you love being yourself.

I stood up, held my breath, and quickly spread the dirt back over the grave. I tamped it down with my foot, my foot with the dog-tattooed toe. "I've changed my mind," I whispered.

I returned to the garage, stripped down naked, and threw my smelly clothes in the trash. I tiptoed through the house and into the bathroom, where I took a long hot shower to wash everything away. Tomorrow, I said to myself, I'm going to wake up and everything is going to be exactly the same, except for me.

# WESTWIND

# Also by Ian Rankin

**The Inspector Malcolm Fox Series**

The Complaints

The Impossible Dead

**The Detective Inspector Rebus Series**

Knots & Crosses

Hide & Seek

Tooth & Nail
(*previously published as* Wolfman)

A Good Hanging and Other Stories

Strip Jack

The Black Book

Mortal Causes

Let It Bleed

Black & Blue

The Hanging Garden

Death Is Not the End
(*a novella*)

Dead Souls

Set in Darkness

The Falls

Resurrection Men

A Question of Blood

Fleshmarket Alley

The Naming of the Dead

Exit Music

Standing in Another Man's Grave

Saints of the Shadow Bible

The Beat Goes On: The Complete
Rebus Stories (*a story collection*)

Even Dogs in the Wild

Rather Be the Devil

In a House of Lies

A Song for the Dark Times

**Other Novels**

Witch Hunt

Blood Hunt

Bleeding Hearts

Watchman

Doors Open

Dark Entries (*graphic novel*)

# IAN
# RANKIN

# WESTWIND

BACK BAY BOOKS
Little, Brown and Company
*New York   Boston   London*

Copyright © 1990, 2019 by John Rebus Ltd.

Back Bay Books / Little, Brown and Company
Hachette Book Group
1290 Avenue of the Americas, New York, NY 10104
littlebrown.com

Originally published in Great Britain in 1990 by Barrie & Jenkins Ltd.
First published in hardcover in the United States by
Little, Brown and Company, January 2020
First Back Bay trade paperback edition, January 2021

Back Bay Books is an imprint of Little, Brown and Company,
a division of Hachette Book Group, Inc.
The Back Bay Books name and logo are trademarks of Hachette Book Group, Inc.

The publisher is not responsible for websites (or their content)
that are not owned by the publisher.

The Hachette Speakers Bureau provides a wide range of authors for speaking events. To find out more, go to hachettespeakersbureau.com or call (866) 376-6591.

ISBN 978-0-316-49792-3 (hc) / 978-0-316-49793-0 (pb)

Cataloging-in-publication data is available at the Library of Congress

Printing 1, 2020

LSC-C

Printed in the United States of America

*For my sisters,*
*Maureen and Linda*

# WESTWIND

West wind, wanton wind, wilful wind, womanish wind, false wind from over the water.

— George Bernard Shaw, *St Joan*

# INTRODUCTION
# BY THE AUTHOR

*Westwind* was originally published on Thursday March 1 1990. My diary entry for that day announces the fact thus: 'Yes, *Westwind* was published to ONE review (in the *Guardian* and very small). Jesus. A flop from the word go.'

As you can see, I was not in what is these days referred to as 'a good place' in the early months of 1990, as my diary of the time regularly records. Here's Wednesday February 28: 'I was wondering today, when will *Westwind* be published? I knew it was scheduled for March and books are always published on a Thursday. But it *can't* be tomorrow surely – Barrie & Jenkins (my publisher at the time) would have been in touch re possible sources of publicity. Surely my author's copies should have arrived? But on returning home a gift bottle of whisky greeted me. Must be tomorrow then – with so little ceremony!'

It's easy to be sanguine as I look back at my younger self, but I was demonstrably starting to lose belief in my abilities, doubting my future as a publishable writer. I was also slogging my guts out, working a day job in London and trying to find space to write in what free time remained to me. My first Rebus novel, *Knots & Crosses*, had been published without fanfare in 1987. On May 12 of that year I record in my trusty diary that 'I should be doing the satellite novel (*Westwind* in other words). I'm doing nothing.' Well, not *nothing* exactly because at the same time I was also polishing the spy thriller which would appear the following year as *Watchman*. I was living in Tottenham and working as an assistant at the National Folktale Centre, based at what was then Middlesex Polytechnic.

Unusually for London, this meant I could walk to work. It also gave me access to a computer, while at home I still hammered away on a noisy electric typewriter. Not that the computer, with its large floppy disks, was much use to me – I didn't know anyone else (my publisher included) who used one. My first Amstrad word processor was still a ways off, while the fax machine in my workplace remained as mysterious to me as the Sphinx.

I'm not sure what gave me the idea that a techno-thriller would be my next project.

*Knots & Crosses* had been a fairly traditional whodunit. *Watchman* was a spy novel influenced by Graham Greene's *The Human Factor. Westwind*, on the other hand, would start with a space shuttle plummeting to earth and a malfunctioning satellite. It seems to me now that I was feeling my way towards what kind of writer I wanted to be. High on the list was: successful enough to give up the day job. I'd tried the crime novel and the spy novel and now I was going to attempt to write the sort of high-tech thriller that sold by the pallet-load in airports and railway stations. So it was that I visited my local library on Tottenham High Road and asked the librarian for anything they could give me to do with space shuttles and how satellites work. Many of the resulting books proved too technical for me – my degree was in English literature rather than mathematics and physics – but a few proved useful. (I'll admit now that one of them was a children's book.) Then there was the trusty Rand McNally *Road Atlas of the USA*, since part of the book was going to be set there (international sales ahoy!) and I'd yet to visit that country outside of novels, movies and TV shows.

As you can see, I was young, hungry, naïve – and driven.

Turning to my diaries again to help me with this introduction, I was surprised at the long gestation of *Westwind*. The first mention I can find is May 1987, and by June I was happily at work on it. At this time it was called *Coffin Burial*, and my one issue was that my typewriter needed repairing. In July 1987 I was chipping away at it while also editing *Watchman*. By August, I was having doubts, but in September, I was finding some of the writing 'v exciting' and 'heart-pounding'. By December, the first draft of the book was finished and the title had been changed to *Westwind*. (I'm not sure where *Coffin Burial* came from – I did think it was a poem, but I can't find it on the internet. My memory was, it might have been John Masefield, but again I can't find it in a list of his works – though I did come across a poem of his called 'The West Wind'. Coincidence?)

My agent read the book over the festive period and got back to me in January 1988. He was not enthusiastic and wanted major revisions before submitting it to a publisher. Okay, so by March I'd tweaked the book, but then everything seemed to go quiet. There was TV interest in *Knots & Crosses* and I was also working on a script for a potential film of my first novel *The Flood*. I was also getting ready for publication of *Watchman* and applying for jobs with a bit more pay than I was getting at Middlesex Poly. By May, I was at work on a new Rebus novel (which would eventually see the light of day as *Hide and Seek*) and by the summer I'd secured work as a journalist on a monthly magazine called *Hi-Fi Review. Watchman* was out and receiving some good reviews (if decidedly sluggish sales) and *Westwind* was languishing. By September, my agent was apologising that he still had no takers for the revised book. I was almost too busy to notice. My new job came with a ninety-minute each-way commute, during which I was devouring novels which I'd started reviewing for the newspaper *Scotland on Sunday*. I'd also been approached to pitch script ideas to ITV's *The Bill*, and I was working away between times on the Rebus book . . .

Then, praise be, my agent phoned with news. My old editor from Bodley Head (who had taken both *Knots & Crosses* and *Watchman*) had switched publishers and was now at Barrie & Jenkins. He wanted to revitalise their meagre fiction list. In short, he wanted *Westwind*. By January 1989 I was discussing further edits to the book and by March I'd signed a contract. Nineteen eighty-nine saw me continuing to write *Hide and Seek* (at this point titled *Dead Beat*) while revising *Westwind*, and still working as a hi-fi reviewer. *Westwind* was eventually finished by July. I had a new editor by then, however, and she disliked some of the book's tone, finding it too humorous for a thriller. She wanted a tougher book and I did my best to comply, meaning a further edit. Which brings us to March 1 1990 and publication.

Not that anyone noticed. There was one hardcover printing, one paperback, and one in large format for readers with limited sight. It didn't sell to the USA and no foreign-language publisher wanted it. What's more, the book had taken so long to get into print, and been through so many permutations and revisions, that I could muster very little enthusiasm for it myself. Every time my agent or editor had asked me to rework it, I had acquiesced, until it felt like it wasn't really my book at all – certainly not the one I'd set out to write.

So I decided that it would rest in a dark corner of my consciousness, never to see the light of day again.

Until Twitter changed my mind.

There had been the odd occasion where a fan at a signing would tell me they'd read it and liked it. Those fans had either got lucky in charity shops or else had shelled out a lot of money to a book dealer. Yes, the book had its fans, but I wasn't among them until someone on Twitter persuaded me to give the book another look. 'It's better than you think it is, Ian.' It had been so long since I'd read it that it felt like reading another writer's work. This proved to be a good thing – I could be objective as I raced through the pages. Yes, it had a few faults and some of the sentence construction was overwrought. It also felt a little bit dated, but on the other hand it also seemed prescient. I had set it in an alternative 1990 where American troops are being pulled out of Europe. International tensions are high. The US is retrenching and the military is worried about the future direction Europe will take. Satellites circle Earth, being used potentially to spy on everyone and everything. No one knows who to trust, or what's about to happen.

Yes, I saw plenty of parallels with the current geopolitical situation, but I also enjoyed reading it. The characters came to life, the plot was pacy, the villains were scary and the heroes believable. And oh the nostalgia! Central locking for cars was obviously a fairly new thing (not *remote* central locking, mind), since I mentioned it more than once. Then there were the Filofaxes, floppy disks and cassette tapes. People smoked on aeroplanes, Tower Records had arrived at Piccadilly Circus, and Germany was still divided into East and West.

I'd forgotten that the listening base where Martin Hepton works was sited at Binbrook, Lincolnshire – a location I'd chosen because my sister Maureen (married to an RAF technician) had lived there for several years and I'd stayed with her as a teenager over the course of one or two long, hot school-holiday summers, back in the days when I was convinced I was going to be either a rock star or a poet. This is partly why I have the notion that 'Coffin Burial' must have been a poem. But during the course of writing the book, I started disliking that title. My British spy satellite was called *Zephyr*, and a zephyr is a light breeze or 'the west wind'. Bearing in mind that (influenced by Alan Moore's comic *Watchmen*) I was calling my spy novel *Watchman*, maybe I had the idea that my novels could all start with the letter 'w'. The third Rebus novel, after all, would be titled *Wolfman* (before an astute editor in the US asked me to alter it to *Tooth and Nail* so as not to deter non-horror book buyers). The George Bernard Shaw quote at the start of the book was probably another piece of serendipity – the 'false wind from over the water' might refer to either the US or Russia. It certainly hints that those you think of as your friends may actually have hidden intentions and ulterior motives.

I've given the original printed text a polish, hopefully ridding it of those flawed sentences and scenes. A few words have been added here and there, while others have been removed or altered, but it is essentially the same book that it always was, just thirty years older and a little wiser . . .

Ian Rankin, 2019

# Part I

Today may mark the end of a great alliance as hundreds of US forces personnel await the transport planes which will take them home, away from the country they have for so long helped defend. Many were tearful last night as they said their farewells to the friends made in this country. They are sorry to go, and we are sorry to see them go. But Britain is a part of Europe now, and it was a democratic decision to part from our erstwhile allies. Let us hope to God it will not prove a foolhardy decision to boot. Already, there are whispered doubts about the efficacy of European defences, and as an island we should be doubly worried about our reduced defensive capability, robbed as we now are of much of our protective power. The mortar may have been removed from the bricks, and who knows when the wolf from the East may come, demanding entry?

Editorial in *London Herald*, 15 July 1990

# 1

He watched the planet earth on his monitor. It was quite a sight. Around him, others were doing the same thing, though not perhaps with an equal sense of astonishment. Some had grown blasé over the years: when you'd seen one earth, you'd seen them all. But not Martin Hepton. He still felt awe, reverence, emotion, whatever. If he had called it a spiritual feeling, the others might have laughed, so he kept his thoughts to himself. And watched.

They all watched, recording their separate data on the computer, keeping an eye on earth from the heavens while their feet never left the ground. Hepton felt giddy sometimes, thinking to himself: this is the only earth there is, and we're all stuck with it, every last one of us. At such moments, the thought of war seemed impossible.

The ground station at Binbrook was small by most standards, but quite large enough for its purpose, and it was sited in the midst of the greenest countryside Hepton had ever seen. He had been born here in Lincolnshire, but had grown up in 1960s London; 'swinging' London. It had swung right past him. With his head stuck in this or that textbook he had never quite noticed the bright clothes, the casual attitudes, the whole hippy shake. Too often, when his head wasn't in a book, it had been raised to the sky, naming a litany of stars and constellations. And it had led to this, as though by some predetermined scheme. He had reached for the skies and had touched them. Thanks to *Zephyr*.

*Zephyr* was the reason behind all this activity, all these monitors and busy voices. *Zephyr* was a British satellite. *The* British satellite. It wasn't the only one they had, but it was the best. The best by a long shot. It could be used for just about anything: weather-watching, communications, surveillance. It could drop from its orbit to within a hundred kilometres of earth, take a pristine picture, then boost back into the higher orbit again before relaying the information back to the ground station. It was a clever little sod all right, and here were its nursemaids, keeping a close eye on it while it kept a close eye on the British Isles. Nobody seemed quite sure why Britain was *Zephyr*'s present target. Word had gone around that the brass – meaning the military and the MoD – wanted to survey this sceptred land, which was fine by Hepton. He would never tire of staring at the various screens, seeing what his satellite saw, making sure that everything was recorded, filed, double-checked. And then viewed by the generals and the men in the pinstripe suits.

He had his own ideas about the present surveillance. The United States was pulling its troops out of Europe. It all looked amicable and agreed, but rumours had started in the press, rumours to the effect that there had been a good amount of shove on the part of the mainland European countries, and that the American generals weren't entirely happy about leaving. The rumours had led to some demonstrations by right-wing parties, asking that the 'USA stay! USA stay!', and an organisation of that name had quickly been formed. More demos were now taking place, and vigils outside the embassies of Britain's partners in Europe. Not exactly powder-keg stuff, but Hepton could imagine that the government wanted to keep things nailed down. And who better than *Zephyr* to follow a convoy of protesters or keep tabs on rallies in different parts of the country?

All at the touch of a button.

'Coffee, Martin?' A cup appeared beside his console. Hepton slipped his headphones down around his neck.

'Thanks, Nick.'

Nick Christopher nodded towards the screen. 'Anything good on the telly?' he asked.

'Just a lot of old repeats,' answered Hepton.

'Isn't that just typical of summer? Honestly, though, I'll go mad if we don't get some new schedules soon.'

'Maybe we're due for a little excitement.'

'What do you mean?' asked Christopher.

'Well,' said Hepton, cradling the plastic beaker, 'I've heard that the brass are around today. Maybe Fagin will put on a simulation for them, show them we're on our toes.'

'Anything for a shot of adrenaline.'

Hepton stared at Nick Christopher. Rumour had it that at one time he'd shot more than just adrenaline. But that was the base for you: when nothing was happening, the rumours seemed to start. Christopher was reaching into his back pocket. He brought out a folded, dog-eared newspaper, its crossword nearly completed. Hepton was already shaking his head.

'You know I'm never any good at those,' he said. Nick Christopher was a crossword addict. He'd buy anything from a kiddies' puzzle book to *The Times* to feed his habit, and over by his desk he had weighty tomes dedicated to his pursuit: dictionaries, collections of synonyms and antonyms and anagrams. He often asked Hepton's help, if only to show how close he had come to solving the day's most difficult puzzle. Now he shrugged his shoulders.

'Well, see you at break time,' he said, heading back towards his own console.

'Biccies are on me,' Hepton said.

There was a sudden wrenching of the air as an alarm began to sound, and Christopher turned back to smile at him, as if to congratulate him on his hunch. Hepton put down his coffee untouched and checked the screen. It was filled with flickering white dots, static. The other screens nearby were showing the same electronic snow.

'Lost visual contact,' someone felt it necessary to say.

'We've lost *all* contact,' called out another voice.

It looked as though Fagin had set them up after all. There was immediate activity, chairs swivelling as consoles were compared, buttons clacked and calls made over the intercom system. Despite themselves, they all relished the occasional emergency, contrived or not. It was a chance to show how prepared they were, how efficient, how quickly they could react and repair.

'Switching to backup system.'

'Coding in channel two.'

'I'm getting a very sluggish response.'

'So stop talking to snails.'

An arm snaked past Hepton's shoulder and punched numbers out on his keyboard, trying to elicit a response from their own. Nothing. It was as if some television station had packed up for the night. All contact had been lost. How the hell had Fagin rigged this?

Hepton lifted his coffee to his lips, gulped at it, then squirmed. Nick Christopher must have dropped a bag of sugar into it.

'Sweet Jesus,' he muttered, the fingers of one hand still busy on his keyboard.

'Coded through.'

'No response here.'

'I'm getting nothing at all.'

A voice came over the speaker system, replacing the electronic alarm.

'This is not a test. Repeat, this is not a test.'

They paused to look at each other, reading a fresh panic in eyes reflecting their own. *Not a test!* It had to be a test. Otherwise they'd just lost a thousand million pounds' worth of tin and plastic. Lost it for how long? Hepton checked his watch. The system had been inoperative for over two minutes. That meant it really was serious. Another minute or so could spell disaster.

Fagin, the operations manager, had appeared from nowhere and was sprinting from console to console as though taking part in some kind of party game. Two of the brass were in evidence too, looking as though they'd just stepped out of a meeting. They carried files under their arms and stood by the far door, knowing nothing of the system or how to be of help. That was typical. The people who held the purse strings and gave the orders knew nothing about anything. That was why the budgeting on *Zephyr* was so tight. Hepton glanced at the pair again. Grey, puzzled faces, trying to look interested and concerned, unsure what to be concerned about.

Suddenly Fagin was at his shoulder.

'Anything, Martin?'

'Nothing, sir.'

'What happened?' Fagin trusted Hepton, and knew him to be fastidious.

Hepton shrugged his shoulders, feeling more impotent than he could say. 'It just started snowing,' he said, gesturing towards the screen. 'That's all.'

Fagin nodded and was gone, his reputation for competence on the edge of being wiped out. Like sticking a magnet on a floppy disk: it was *that* easy to lose it all in a moment.

Then:

'Wait a minute!' It was Nick Christopher's voice.

'Yes,' someone else called from further off. 'I'm getting something now. We've regained radio contact.' There was a pause. 'No, lost it again.'

The brass exchanged glances at this news, and both checked their watches. Hepton couldn't believe what he was seeing. They seemed to be worrying about the time. All the while, a billion pounds' worth of high-tech was whizzing about blindly, or crashing towards earth, and they were worrying about the time.

'Are you sure you had it?' yelled Fagin.

'Yes, sir.'

'Well then, get it back!'

'Trying.'

Despite the adrenaline gnawing at him, Hepton felt a sudden inner calm. All would be well. It was just a matter of trusting to fate and pushing the right buttons. Who was he kidding? *Zephyr* was lost for good.

Someone was standing behind him. He glanced back and saw Paul Vincent watching intently over his shoulder. Vincent was the youngest of the controllers, and the least confident.

'Come to see how the professional does it, Paul?' Hepton said, grinning nervously at the screen. He saw Vincent's reflection smile wanly back. Then he began pushing buttons again, trying every combination possible. He had used up all the rational choices. Now he was trying the irrational, asking the computer to do the impossible.

Paul Vincent's face was suddenly at his ear, though the young man's eyes still appeared to be studying the monitor.

'Listen, Martin, there's something I want to show you.'

'What?'

Vincent's gaze remained fixed to the screen. His voice was low, just audible over the noise all around.

'I can't be sure,' he said, 'not a hundred per cent, at any rate. But I think there's something happening up there. Either that or I've been doing something wrong. I had it on my screen a little while back.'

'What do you mean, "something happening"?'

'I'm not sure yet. Foreign data.'

'Have you reported it?'

'Of course.'

Perhaps that was why the brass were on the scene, and why they had looked momentarily scared.

'Are we talking about interference?' Hepton's voice was low too.

'I don't know. I could make a wild guess, but I'm not sure it would help. I'd like you to confirm the data.'

'When did it start?'

'About half an hour ago.'

'Coincidence?'

There was a sudden whoop, then cheers and some applause.

'We've got her back!'

Hepton's eyes went to his screen. They had indeed got her back. He was staring at a fuzzy but identifiable picture of Britain, taken from all that unbelievable distance. The image was out of focus, but they could soon put that right. What mattered was that *Zephyr* was working again.

'Panic over,' he said, turning now to face Paul Vincent. 'So what about this foreign data?'

'I've saved the readout on disk. Come and see.'

Paul spoke without blinking, and still softly, though the clamour around had grown. He was young but, Hepton knew, not an idiot. A first in astrophysics from Edinburgh, then research in Australia. No idiot, but not a hands-on expert either. It was his job – his sole responsibility and specialism – to monitor the space around *Zephyr*, seeking space trash, debris, meteorites, waves of interference. He'd never made a mistake when it had counted. Never.

'Okay, Paul,' Hepton said. 'Give me a couple of minutes to put things right and I'll come take a look.'

'Thanks.' Vincent looked relieved, like a man who needs reassuring that those pink elephants he can see really are there. Maybe they were, at that. He left Hepton's side and returned to his distant console. Then again, maybe the kid was losing his touch. There had been a bout of sulking a week ago to do with some girlfriend or other. Hazard of the job. Shift work, odd hours, occasional days on end cooped up in the base. Sleeping four to a room in two sets of bunk beds. Hepton wasn't sure he could take much more of it himself, despite the pleasures of earth-watching. Who ever thought to ask him if *he* were lonely? Nobody. He thought of Jilly, and wondered what she was doing while he sat here. He didn't want to think what she was doing.

The brass were looking pleased about something. Well, they'd got *Zephyr* back, hadn't they? One said something to the other, and Hepton, watching the man's lips move, caught the words 'three minutes forty'. The other nodded and smiled again. So they were discussing the length of time the satellite had been lost to its ground base. Three minutes and forty seconds. Longer than ever before. Almost too long.

Things were calming down all around. Fagin had gone to speak with the brass. They were in a huddle now, their eyes glinting. Hepton couldn't see their lips any more. Well, it was none of his concern.

He busied himself with putting his console right. He had pushed a few too many of the wrong buttons in the wrong sequences. Adjustments were needed. And then he would visit Paul Vincent on the other side of the room.

'More coffee?' It was Nick Christopher.

'You put sugar in the first.'

'An honest mistake. I'll fetch you another.'

'Don't bother. What do you think went wrong back there?'

'Put it down to a hiccup. Everything malfunctions from time to time. Between the two of us, I think *Zephyr* was cobbled together like its namesake, the old car. We'll be lucky if it stays the course.'

'It was out for three minutes forty seconds.'

'What?'

'The brass were timing it.'

'Then maybe it was an exercise.'

'I don't think Paul Vincent would agree.'

'Martin, you're talking in riddles.'

'Sorry.'

'Now what about that coffee?'

'No sugar this time?'

'Promise, no sugar.'

'Okay then.'

The brass had disappeared, and Fagin with them. Waving them off, probably. Hepton wondered what the weather was like outside. He could check by using the computer, but wouldn't it be so much nicer just to walk outside and take a look? Sunny, showery, cool, breezy. Inside, the air conditioning kept things temperate, and the lighting was designed specially so as to be bright without giving glare. Same went for the screens. You could stare at them all day without getting a headache, which didn't stop him succumbing to the occasional migraine. He pushed back into his chair. It, too, had been designed for maximum comfort and minimum stress. He stuck a thumb either side of his spine and pressed, feeling vertebrae click into place.

'No sugar,' said Nick Christopher, handing him the beaker.

'Thanks.'

'Only another twenty minutes till break.'

'Thank God.'

'So what were you saying about Paul?'

'Oh, just that he's got some data he wants me to check.'

'Data?' Christopher sipped his own coffee. 'What sort of data?'

'I don't know till I've looked. Probably nothing important. You know what Paul's like.'

Christopher smiled. 'He's like a kid with a train set.'

'Exactly,' said Hepton.

But by the time he wandered across to Paul Vincent's console, Vincent himself had vanished. Hepton looked at the computer screen. It was blank. He tried coding in, but it remained blank.

'Temporary fault,' said Fagin from behind him. 'Was there something you wanted?'

'Just checking.'

'Checking what?'

'Oh, you know . . .'

'Well you won't get much joy. Part of the disk's been wiped.'

'You mean the hard disk?'

'Yes.'

'Because of the malfunction?'

'Or more likely Vincent's panicking.' Fagin had it in for Paul Vincent, everybody knew that. It was whispered that Paul reminded him too much of his own son, who had left home at seventeen and never returned.

'Where is Vincent, by the way?'

Fagin shrugged. 'I don't know. The little boys' room perhaps.'

'What happened back there?'

Fagin seemed to think about this. 'I'm just glad we got her back,' he said at last. 'We'll find out eventually.'

'It wasn't a test then, to impress our friends?'

'Friends?'

'Those two generals.'

'Not at all. What makes you say that?'

'Oh, they just seemed to be timing our response, that's all. And they looked fairly happy with the outcome.'

'Nobody likes to lose a satellite, Martin.'

'Of course not, sir. If you'll excuse me, it's almost my break. I think I'll try to find Paul.'

'Fine.' Fagin was picking up the internal telephone, pushing buttons. The panic was over; things had to go on.

Three minutes and forty seconds. Usually a malfunction could be located and corrected within sixty seconds. There were backup systems, a computer locked into every function of the satellite, ready to pinpoint the failure and repair it. After sixty seconds, you could assume that the computers had failed to find the fault, and you began to worry. So you went to manual, checking everything yourself. At the two-minute mark, you panicked.

Three minutes and forty seconds. The brass had seemed satisfied. Fagin seemed satisfied. Paul Vincent had reported his findings, but nobody seemed to want to know. *What the hell was going on?*

Hepton went to the toilets, then checked the canteen, the recreation area and the TV room: nothing. The table tennis players hadn't seen Paul Vincent, the guys watching a porn film hadn't seen Paul Vincent, nobody had seen Paul Vincent. He had disappeared. Hepton sat down in the TV room to think. The porn film was in German, not that a degree in languages was necessary to understand the plot. The film was being beamed via satellite, probably from a mainland European station. One bored weekend they'd spent several hours using the base's sophisticated communications technology to home in on a couple of television satellites. Now they could pick up just about any station they liked and decode any scrambled signal. The picture today wasn't the sharpest, but the cameraman was in close enough so that this didn't really matter . . .

*Zephyr.* What did Paul Vincent know about *Zephyr?*

Hepton caught up with Nick Christopher in the canteen, where he was scooping up chips and beans with a fork and holding open a book with his free hand.

'What are you reading?' Hepton asked.

Christopher showed him the cover, 'Albert Camus, *The Fall.* I found it in the library.'

'What's it like?'

'I don't know. Nothing's happened yet. What's wrong?'

Hepton realised that he was sitting with head in hands, elbows propped on the table.

'I can't find Paul,' he said.

'Perhaps he doesn't want to be found,' said Christopher, scooping up another mouthful of beans.

'Maybe you're right at that,' said Hepton, stealing a limp lukewarm chip from the plate.

The afternoon drifted back into ordinariness. After the break, it was back to the consoles. The system, though, was failing to yield the source of the malfunction. Fagin walked from monitor to monitor, for all the world like a factory-line foreman. He stopped at Hepton's desk.

'It seems Paul Vincent has been taken ill,' he said, scribbling something on his clipboard.

'Ill? Can I go see him?'

'He's not in the rest room. They've had to take him to hospital.'

'Christ, that was a bit sudden.'

'The doctor thinks it might be simple exhaustion.'

Exhaustion. Paul was not only the youngest of the crew, he was the fittest too. Twice a day he jogged around the perimeter fence, a haul of two and a half miles. He was the only one of them who used the multigym. He had the stamina of an athlete. Hepton sat at the console, his mind whirling. The nearest hospital was twenty miles away. He had to go there.

Fagin had walked away now and was examining another monitor. Hepton looked across to where Paul Vincent's monitor sat untended, the chair pushed in beneath the desk with the finality of a coffin lid being nailed down. He shivered. There was something very odd about this whole thing. A curious mind had brought him into the world of astronomy and astronautics, and that same mind was now needling him to look a little further into things. And yes, he would.

# 2

He tasted smoke in his nostrils and felt blood gouge its way along the creases in his spacesuit. The vibration in the shuttle intensified still further, becoming more than a roller coaster. A roller coaster had once terrified him as a child, and he had determined never to be afraid of anything again in his whole life, a decision that was ending here and now with the most complete terror he had ever felt.

Through the glass he caught a quick glimpse of the ground crew; already the fire engines were racing forwards, but too late. Sparks flew from the seared undercarriage, and a final all-encompassing ball of flame sent him veering towards pale darkness.

But then suddenly Adams was at his side, his head bloodied, and Adams' hands slid around his throat, growing tight, and all the time he was shouting:

'You sonofabitch! You sonofabitch! I won't forget! Not ever! The burial's what matters! Coffin's got to be buried!'

It was all so unnecessary, Dreyfuss thought. We're dying anyway; why don't you let me die in peace? The tarmac below was churning like the sea, as unsteady as a fairground ride. Adams' hands were still there. Blood pounded in Dreyfuss' ears, tortured metal, the whine of the uncontrollable engines. How could it have happened? Total malfunction. Absolute and total, just as they were starting the descent. *How could it have happened?* It was typical of his life that he should die with a question unanswered in his mind.

And then, finally, he blacked out.

The emergency team were ready. They'd been ready since the first warning that something was wrong on the space shuttle *Argos*. Now they started to jet, engulfing white foam over the stricken craft, snuffing out flames until the whole thing looked like a children's toy in a bubble bath. The crew had come from the ground station to watch. There had been six men on board: five Americans and one Briton. Most of them were praying that the Americans, at least, would still be alive. They didn't really give much thought to the only Briton, Major Michael Dreyfuss. These days, it was strictly a case of looking after number one.

The few small fires were quickly put out. Thankfully, the *Argos* had little fuel left in its tanks to burn. Nevertheless, the surface metal of the shuttle was too hot to touch, even with asbestos gloves. But they managed at last to wrench open the doors. Inside, they could smell smoke, singed rubber and something less pleasant still. They expected to find corpses, but the last thing anyone expected to find was five of them, one of which had its hands embedded in the neck of the single crew member left alive . . .

# 3

General Ben Esterhazy sat in the back of his chauffeur-driven limo and wondered why there was no bourbon left in the drinks cabinet. He hoped there'd be some at the airbase. Not that there was much left of the base. They were dismantling and moving, shipping the boys back to the States. Lousy damned country anyway. He'd spent a few years in Germany just after the war. People starving. A mother really would lie down and open her legs for a tin of beef and some powdered whatever.

The country didn't seem to have changed that much. But now Europe had forgotten all about World War Two, had gotten eyes bigger than its belly. All the talk now was of Europe, a Europe that saw no place for the US forces lined up in a thin defensive wall against the East.

'Well, fuck them.'

'Sorry, General?' Esterhazy's aide, Lieutenant Jerry Bosio, sitting in front beside the driver, had turned his head to catch the words.

'Never mind,' growled Esterhazy. He picked up a bottle of Glenfiddich whisky and poured himself an inch. Esterhazy had a jutting, aggressive face ending in a nose like that of Punch. He'd put on weight since they'd given him a desk job, but not much weight. His tits didn't sag the way some middle-aged men's did, and he could wrestle marines half his age.

'Where the hell's the soda?' he muttered. The streets of Bonn were in a mid-evening hiatus. Nobody seemed much bothered about the official car or its cargo – there had been so many such cars in Bonn of late – and this suited Esterhazy fine. The last thing he needed was either cheers or jeers. If they cheered, were they cheering because they were glad to see the back of the American forces? Or because they were glad of those forces and wanted them to stay? God alone knew. Ben Esterhazy didn't. The talks had dragged today. The interpreters seemed to be in some kind of stupor, and the delegates likewise. It was winding down, the pull-out already being implemented. All they were really talking about now was the dotting of a few i's. That had never been Esterhazy's way.

But now his part in the comedy was over, and tonight he was flying back to the States. He relaxed, sipped his drink, rested his head on the seat-back. He was going home. The work was done. He'd put in an appearance for the sake of appearances, he'd signed this and that piece of paper. Now he could go back to the men in Washington and tell them it was done. Not that they really cared. If Europe wanted to go it alone, let them. That was democracy's attitude. But if there were to be a war, the men in suits would be the first to take cover, and the first to order the troops straight back into the kill zone.

'Well, fuck them.'

'Sir?'

'Never mind.'

'Sir . . .'

Esterhazy realised that the aide's hand had reached into an attaché case and come out with an envelope, towards which he was trying to attract the general's attention.

'What the hell is it?' said Esterhazy, snatching at the paper.

'Message came through for you, sir,' said Bosio. 'Sorry, I forgot to give it to you earlier.'

'Idiot.' Esterhazy tore open the envelope and unfolded the note inside.

*SORRY YOU COULDN'T MAKE IT TO THE BURIAL.*

For the first time that day, General Ben Esterhazy smiled.

# 4

Martin Hepton put down the telephone. At the third attempt, he had found out something concrete about Paul Vincent. He had found out that Paul was no longer in the hospital. He had been sent on to a rest home for a period of 'recovery', as the hospital doctor had termed it. Exhaustion, that was all it was. That was all.

Hepton walked along the corridor, paused outside the gym, then pushed open the door. It was a well-equipped gym. Healthy bodies meant healthy minds. Not that anyone ever used the gym. No one except Paul Vincent. Hepton went to the multi-gym, the so-called 'torture machine', and hoisted himself up on the arm-lift bar. He brought his chin up to touch the bar, then relaxed his arms until his toes touched the floor.

'That's one,' said the voice behind him. It was Nick Christopher, smiling, letting the gym door swing shut behind him.

Hepton smiled and pulled himself off the floor again, straining this time, coming down heavily.

'Two,' counted Christopher.

'Enough for today,' said Hepton, feeling the blood pound in his chest.

'Is this man out of condition? I ask myself.'

'Okay, let's see you do some.'

'Stand aside, shrimp.' Christopher pulled a crossword book out of his back trouser-pocket and handed it to Hepton, then gripped the bar and heaved himself aloft. He managed fifteen pulls, then rested, breathing hard.

'I'm impressed,' said Hepton.

'If there's one thing regular sex does for you,' explained

Christopher, taking the book back, 'it gives you a strong pair of arms.' They both laughed.

'I wouldn't know sex if it hit me in the face,' Hepton said.

'That's your problem then,' Christopher said. 'You can't tell the difference between sex and a slap in the face.' He paused. 'How are things with Jilly?'

'What things? I haven't heard from her since she went to London.'

'Have you tried calling her?'

'Only every day.'

'So do you get the feeling it's all over?'

'Just a little.'

'Sorry to hear that, Martin.'

Hepton shrugged. He gripped the bar again and managed two more hoists.

'What about Paul?' Nick Christopher asked.

'What about him?'

'Have you managed to find out anything?'

'Apparently he's gone off to some rest home.'

'Jesus, it must be bad then. I thought those places were for the dying and the dead.'

Hepton tried a third hoist, failed, and dropped to the ground. 'Better book me a room in one then,' he said. 'After you've bought me a drink.'

They sat down in the cafeteria, drinking cans of cola and eating crisps.

'Is this supposed to be brain food?' Christopher asked. Then: 'What do you think of that shuttle, the *Argos*, crashing like that?'

'I think our man was lucky to get out in one piece.'

It was front-page news, of course. Tomorrow it would be relegated, but for today, Major Mike Dreyfuss was famous, which was, Hepton supposed, what the bastard had always wanted. Hepton had two very good reasons for being jealous of Mike Dreyfuss. For one thing, the man had actually touched the skies, while all he, Hepton, could do was watch them.

For another, Dreyfuss and Jilly went back a long way. They had never been lovers, perhaps – though he had her word alone on that – but they had been friends, very close friends, and while she had allowed Hepton into her bed and her body, her mind had stayed closed to him. Yet she had spoken of Dreyfuss with such tenderness . . .

'Well,' Nick Christopher was saying, 'I can't see him having an easy time of it. I mean, there he is in America, the sole survivor of a disaster in which all the Americans on board perished, and here we are kicking the Yanks out of Europe, making us not very popular over there.'

'I see what you mean,' said Hepton. It was all he could do to stop himself from smiling. He stuffed his mouth with crisps instead. Yes, front-page news Dreyfuss might be, but for all the wrong reasons.

# 5

The light was diffuse and coloured the burnished gold of . . . The description ended there. His mind wasn't up to it. He decided to open one eye, just a little, and saw an underwater blur of greys and blues and whites, bathed in the same golden light. He blinked, opened both eyes and saw that he was lying in a hospital bed. A private room. Lavender paint on the walls, machines standing beside the bed, a drip feeding his left arm. Through the slats of the blinds streamed the day's raw sunshine. Golden light.

He was alive then.

A nurse sat dozing in the heat, a paperback novel on her lap. Where was this? Why was he so sore? His mouth was raw. Then he remembered – the shuttle had crash-landed. Couldn't get the undercarriage down. Couldn't get anything to work. Total shutdown of the onboard computer. Now how the hell could that have happened?

And what about Heinemann, O'Grady, Marshall, Wilson, Adams? Were they alive or dead? The fate of Hes Adams especially interested him. He let out a little whistle of air, as much as he could manage without feeling pain. It was enough. The nurse stirred, opened her eyes and smiled at him. Then closed them again as she stretched. A good big early-morning yawn, and then another smile, as though they were waking up in bed together; lovers.

'Good afternoon, Mr Dreyfuss. How do you feel?'

Dreyfuss. That was his name. It was as good a name as any. He tried answering her question, but his throat was dry and sore. He swallowed painfully, and she seemed to understand. Rose from her chair and poured some water from a jug into a glass. There were flowers on his bedside cabinet. Not many of them, a couple of small bunches.

The water was tepid. He had trouble swallowing.

'Thanks,' he rasped. 'Needed that.' Speaking was like rubbing something raw against sandpaper.

'You've been asleep a long time.'

'How long?'

'Several days, I think. I've only been on shift a couple of hours.'

'Where am I?'

'Sacramento General.'

It sounded like the title of a bad western. He supposed it was a hospital in Sacramento. He'd never been to Sacramento before. One of his reasons for wanting the shuttle mission was so he could see a little more of the States. He'd only been three times previously, and then never for long. As a child, growing up in the rapidly disappearing slums of east Edinburgh, he had dreamed of all this, of spacemen and of America, playing out the dream with toy spaceships that he would send hurtling to their doom.

'The others . . .' he began, but already the nurse had pushed at a buzzer above his bed. God, her body looked good, wrapped in the flimsiest layer of white cotton. He could almost taste . . . What was it he could taste in his mouth, right there behind the caked dryness and the lees of water?

It was smoke, blood, fear. And hands tearing at him. Why were hands tearing at him?

'Good afternoon, Major Dreyfuss.'

A man in a white coat, stethoscope swinging reassuringly around his neck, had pushed open the door. Behind him came two others, one in a general's uniform, the other looking like a worrier from the State Department. They stood slightly to left and right of the doctor, like tumours growing out of his sides. Good, thought Dreyfuss: his powers of description were coming back.

'Hello,' he said, but the doctor was studying his chart, and then studying the nurse. He smiled at her.

'I don't think I've seen you before, have I?'

She smiled back. 'No, Doctor. The name's Carraway.'

'Well, Nurse Carraway, has the patient been behaving?'

'Yes, Doctor.' Now she was looking towards Dreyfuss, and there was that smile again. The doctor turned towards him too.

'How do you feel?'

'One hundred per cent, Doctor. When can I get up?'

The doctor laughed. 'Not for a while yet, I'm afraid.'

'What's the rush?' snapped the general. It was a serious question.

Dreyfuss closed his eyes.

'I've had a relapse, Doc,' he said. 'I'm allergic to goons.'

'Why, you sonofabitch—' started the general, only to be stopped by the civilian's upraised hand.

Dreyfuss opened his eyes and stared at the slats of the blind, trying to recall where he had seen that colour before, that golden colour, and heard those words before, too.

A ball of flame. Fuel igniting. And the voice of Hes Adams in his ear: *you sonofabitch.*

'Leave him be, Ben,' the civilian was saying. 'He's traumatised, probably doesn't know what he's saying.'

'He knows all right.'

'Come on,' the civilian insisted, leading the general towards the door. 'I'll buy you a drink and you can bore me with the story of Bonn.'

The doctor watched them go and seemed to relax a little. He approached the bed.

'Nice chaps,' Dreyfuss commented. The doctor seemed not to understand, then smiled.

'You mean General Esterhazy and Mr Stewart.'

'If that's who they were.'

'That's who they were.' The doctor watched Dreyfuss sip more water. 'Throat sore?'

'A little,' said Dreyfuss. 'Listen, I meant what I said back there. When can I get up?'

'Just hang on in there.' A pencil-fine beam of light shone into Dreyfuss' left eye, then his right. 'What do you remember about the accident, Major?'

'What accident?' Dreyfuss smiled at the doctor's look of alarm. 'Only joking,' he said. 'I remember a ball of flame; it really did look like a ball, too. I felt like I could have given it a kick. I didn't, though. It kicked me instead. Then I suppose I must have passed out.'

'And where were you when this happened?'

'On the shuttle, of course. The shuttle was called *Argos*, and we were coming in to land, and there were six of us.'

'And what had the shuttle been doing?'

Dreyfuss made a show of trying to think.

'Major?'

'I . . . don't seem to remember that,' he lied, though why his instincts told him to conceal his returning memory was a mystery.

'Well, don't worry about it.' Dreyfuss caught Nurse Carraway staring at him fixedly. But when his eyes met hers, she slapped a smile onto her face again. 'Do you remember the names of the other crew members?' the doctor was asking.

'Let's see.' Dreyfuss tried to look as though he was thinking hard. He wondered why Nurse Carraway was so intent on his answer. 'Heinemann,' he said at last, 'Adams, Marshall, O'Grady, Wilson.'

'Good, Major Dreyfuss. Now think back.' The doctor began to check his pulse. Dreyfuss had the idea that this was less even than a routine check; that it was a cover under which the doctor could ask his questions. Without knowing exactly why, he had the feeling that there was a good reason why he shouldn't tell him everything he knew. 'What,' the doctor was saying, 'is the next thing back that you remember *before* the fire?'

This was perfect: they expected – *wanted* – him to have amnesia.

'Major?'

'Well . . .' Dreyfuss started, licking his lips. He stared at the lavender walls, at a concerned Nurse Carraway, at anything that might appear to be jogging his memory. 'I remember taking off, the whole thing with ground control, with Cam Devereux – he was my contact on the ground. Everything was going according to schedule. But . . . I'm not sure why we were up there in the first place. No, wait, we were launching a satellite, right?'

The doctor smiled.

'That's right, Major. Launching one of our communications satellites. Don't worry.' He patted Dreyfuss' shoulder. 'It'll come back to you in time. This sort of thing is quite usual in cases of trauma. And you took a few nasty bumps when you landed.'

'Nothing serious, though?'

'No, nothing serious. You just need to rest. Does your head hurt?'

No, his head didn't hurt. He put his right hand to his forehead and felt a plaster there.

'Yes,' he said, 'a bit of a headache.'

'We'll get you something for that. I'll be back to see you shortly. Meantime, if there's anything you need, just ask Nurse . . .?' The doctor had forgotten her name.

'Carraway,' she said. She smiled at Dreyfuss again, her hair the colour of honey. And he smiled back. By which time the doctor had left the room and the door was swinging shut. A voice was raised somewhere in the corridor. The goon, thought Dreyfuss, the one called General Ben Esterhazy.

'Can I see a newspaper?' he asked Nurse Carraway. She was

sitting down with her book again, legs crossed. Were those silk stockings she was wearing? Since when were silk stockings regulation issue for nurses?

'I'll have to check on that, Mr Dreyfuss.'

'Didn't you hear? It's *Major*.'

'Of course it is. I'm sorry.'

'That's okay.'

She had risen to her feet, but instead of leaving to fetch a paper, she approached the bed.

'Can I just ask one thing?' she said.

He smiled. 'How can I stop you?'

'I was just wondering . . .' Her fingers stretched towards him, stopping just short of his throat. 'I was wondering how you got those bruises on your neck.'

*Hes Adams' fingers trying to wrench the life from him, when they were both already dead.*

'What bruises?' he said, his eyes clear and honest.

She smiled, but uncertainly. Then walked to the door and opened it, turning back to look at him before leaving. Dreyfuss checked that there were no cameras trained on him from the corners of the room, no holes drilled in the wall. Seeing none, he allowed himself the luxury of a smile.

# 6

Parfit stared at the security room's various screens as they relayed the passing parade outside the embassy. Most days now there was a demonstration of some kind. It might be the French embassy or the German embassy. But mostly, as today, it was the British embassy. Today's crowd was small. Thank the unseasonal Washington drizzle for that perhaps. They were yelling something, but the cameras hadn't been wired for sound, not outside the perimeter wall at any rate. It didn't matter. He knew the gist of their chants. You don't want us, we don't want you – that sort of thing. And he took their point. Whether he agreed with it or not was irrelevant.

There had been some ugliness in other parts of the country. It was tempting to say the less civilised parts. A section of the USA would forever stay frontier country, and God help any unwary English tourist straying too far from the safety of their metropolitan hotel. So far this week, Parfit had had reports of two firebomb attacks on British businesses in Boston and New York, several broken windows, threats, casual violence, and sixteen muggings, one of which had taken place in a picnic area of Yosemite National Park.

Then there were those who were merely annoyed: the British businessmen who were losing contracts, the British immigrants who were being harassed at work. And all of it filtered back via the great brown fan to the Washington embassy, where some of it landed squarely on Parfit's too-small desk.

'Looks peaceable enough, Mr Parfit,' said Tom Banks, one of the security team whose job it was to watch the screens, seeking breaches in the line of defence.

'The rain will cool their tempers, Tom,' said Parfit. 'See you later.'

'Bye, Mr Parfit.'

He was headed for Johnnie Gilchrist's office, the inner sanctum. Towards Gilchrist's door, the carpet pile seemed to grow discernibly deeper. It was said that this was because so few people dared disturb Gilchrist in his lair. Like many myths, there was a core of truth to it. But Parfit knocked anyway, his distinctive three short raps and one long.

'Come in, Parfit.' Seated behind his desk, half-moon glasses resting precariously on his aquiline nose, Gilchrist could look tame enough, more the retiring scholar than the shrewd – and vicious – career diplomat. He and Parfit had sharpened claws on one another in the past, but at least each understood the other's territory. Gilchrist's job was to get things done, no matter what. Parfit's job was damage limitation. There could never be one without the other.

'Sit down.'

Parfit sat, crossing his legs. The chair was as uncomfortable as it needed to be. It was not designed for long-stay visitors.

'Another demo outside.' It was a statement of fact.

Gilchrist removed his glasses and rubbed at the red indentations either side of his nose.

'It seems quiet enough today,' Parfit commented.

'Thank Christ for that at least then.' Gilchrist slipped the glasses on again, pushing them down firmly onto the bridge of his nose. 'Now, what about Dreyfuss?'

'What about him?'

'Come on, Parfit. What's your game?'

'I don't know what you're talking about.'

Gilchrist waved the comment aside. 'You should be there in Sacramento. *Somebody* should be there at least. Has he regained consciousness yet?'

'We think so.'

'*Think?*'

'It's not easy getting straight answers just at the moment. You should know that, or haven't you noticed that our dealings with the cousins have become rather frosty? We keep in contact with the hospital authorities, who pass us on to somebody else, and that somebody else tries to sell us a call-back-tomorrow or an I'll-check-and-call-you-back.'

'All the more reason why somebody from the embassy should be there.'

'I'm going.'

'Yes, but when?'

'Maybe tomorrow.'

Gilchrist stared hard at Parfit, who didn't flinch. 'Is that a maybe-maybe or a maybe-definitely?'

'It's a maybe-probably.'

Gilchrist smiled in defeat, then took off his glasses again to rub at his nose. He had been doing this ever since Parfit had known him, and it irritated him more than he could say.

'So,' Parfit began, 'is there anything I should know about the state of play on the pull-out?'

'No. NATO's making its usual balls-up of the whole thing. Nobody seems able to agree with anybody else. Fallings-out left and right. If only we had the right bloody government in power . . .'

'But we don't.'

'Quite. So instead it's complete chaos, and what are the Soviets doing? Have you noticed?'

'I wasn't aware they were doing anything.'

'Exactly. They're just sitting back enjoying the bloody show. Oh, and speaking of bears, Ben Esterhazy's back from Bonn. Not the happiest of soldiers, by all accounts. There's talk that he'll be heading for Sacramento.'

'Oh?'

'Well, most of that shuttle crew were his men after all.' Gilchrist sighed. 'We really could have done without this on top of everything else.' He pulled a newspaper from the drawer of his desk and began to read aloud. '"The Jonah Factor. Major Michael Dreyfuss, the Briton they did not want on the tragic shuttle mission, was still seriously ill in Sacramento General Hospital today. Ground observers report that the shuttle's undercarriage appeared not to operate during its descent towards Edwards Air Force Base."' He looked up at Parfit. 'Et cetera,' he said, 'until this at the end: "Whatever happened, one thing is clear. The people of the United States will long remember the dealings of the past few weeks with the British government, the British people, and one British subject in particular."' He threw the paper back into the drawer. 'They're talking about Dreyfuss, and yet you're letting him lie there—'

'I have a good reason.' Parfit snapped his mouth shut, but too late. He had already said it. Gilchrist smiled again, nodding.

'I thought there must be a reason. So come on, what is it?'

Parfit sighed. 'Not here.'

'Very well then, let's stretch our legs as far as the secure room. I'm all ears, I'm sure.'

# 7

At last, Hepton had two clear days free from the base, and could take a drive into the country. Ripening fields, the sun beating down as it had no right to do in the course of an English summer. An occasional splash of garish yellow where rape – vegetable cash to the farmers – had been sown. But mostly the fields were green, or were delivering up golden buds of wheat and barley. A beautiful country. He so seldom noticed it, but it was the truth. He had become blind through living his life underground, but like a mole, he had burrowed his way to the surface and was now scenting the air anew. He checked in the Renault's rear-view mirror. The Ford Sierra was still with him, a hundred yards back but quite noticeable, there being so little traffic on these winding roads.

Twenty minutes ago, he had slowed behind a tractor, though overtaking would have been easy, and had watched the car behind him edge forward until the face of the driver – female – was clear in his mirror. The face of a businesswoman, but she didn't appear to be in any rush. So that when he had waved her past, she had flashed her lights once in acknowledgement, but shaken her head too. And stayed behind him.

She was still behind him, sometimes gaining, sometimes losing. He thought of pulling in to a café, to see whether she would follow him. After all, this might be innocence itself, a chance encounter that might lead . . . well, anywhere. Except that he had to press on. Paul Vincent was in the Alfred de Lyon Hospital, and the Alfred de Lyon Hospital was an inconvenient forty or so miles away yet. So he drove on.

He thought of *Zephyr*, of the miracles satellites could perform. He stuck an arm out of his window and waved towards the sky, wondering if he could be seen. There was no doubt that *Zephyr* could see him if it wanted to. It could give close-ups of his car, of his number plate. But *Zephyr* wasn't trained on him. It was trained on a series of air force bases, where the US personnel were preparing for their flights back home. Or at least that was what it had been watching yesterday evening, on Hepton's last shift.

Something niggled, though, something he had noticed and mentioned in passing to Nick Christopher. It was to do with Buchan Air Force Base in the north of Scotland, just outside the town of Peterhead. Buchan had been an RAF radar station, but then the American forces had moved in for a time. Hepton had watched it before. He liked the quality of light in northern Scotland. That was what niggled: the sun was setting early in Buchan.

'Cloud cover,' Christopher had explained. 'I've seen the weather reports. Overcast skies.'

'Yes,' Hepton had said, 'but they're not overcast.'

And Christopher had shrugged his shoulders, then placed a hand on Hepton's own.

'Maybe when you go to visit Paul, you and he should swap places. What do you say?'

Then they had both laughed and gone to watch the night's television.

Was something wrong with the weather, then? Or had the *Zephyr* malfunction caused some tinting of the lens, some aberration to appear on the glass? What the hell. He'd think about it some other time. For today, he had forty-eight hours' worth of off-base permission, and he intended to use the time well. He switched on the radio and found a station broadcasting a phone-in about the Geneva arms talks. The Soviets were offering yet more deals. Jesus, what were they going to do with all those redundant guns and tanks and missiles? Better yet, what would they do with all that redundant manpower?

On another station, two critics discussed the latest high-grossing American film, *Gun Law*. They'd had a bootleg tape of that on the base last week. Usual vigilante stuff, all about how the USA should pull up the drawbridge and let everyone outside the moat rot. Laughable really, yet some of the men on the base had started acting tough the very next morning, and come in wearing black T-shirts and white jeans, the way the hero did.

'Strange times,' Hepton said out loud, flicking to another

channel. Mahler. Radio 3, he supposed; some lunchtime concert. He didn't know which Mahler it was, but he knew it was Mahler. Jilly had listened to Mahler before, during and after each session of love-making. Which had seemed weird to him at first. In fact, it had seemed weird *all* the time. She would push his prone body away from her so that she could go and change the cassette tape and then would come to him again and give him a hug, just to show that she liked him a little bit too.

But not enough to stop her taking the newspaper job in London, not enough to stop her zipping a bag and throwing it into the back of her MG, giving him a brief embrace while her eyes glazed over with thoughts of leader columns and front-page scoops. A peck on the cheek, and then into the driving seat where she belonged, no seat belt necessary, though he had warned her before.

'Phone me!' he had called, but she never had. And now it was over. He had toyed with the idea of using *Zephyr* to track her down, to peek through some bedroom window as she pushed away another prone body and went to change the tape.

It was a nice dream.

After the Mahler, there was the one o'clock news, including a small item on Major Mike Dreyfuss and the American reaction to the shuttle disaster. Predictable stuff. He had watched the TV pictures. Orange flame, the nose of the craft crumpling, turning in on itself, more explosions. It was a funny thing about Dreyfuss, though. He was in his late thirties, a few years older than Hepton, not exactly his physical prime. Hepton had read about the other candidates who'd been in the running for the UK's only place on the mission. They'd been young, strong. So why Dreyfuss? Not that it was any big deal. Not the big deal it was when the first Briton in space had gone up on that Soviet mission, or when the second one had gone up soon afterwards, courtesy of the Americans. No, to be Britain's third man in space: well, there was something pathetic about that, wasn't there? He allowed himself a guilty smile.


The Alfred de Lyon Hospital was, for the most part, a rest home, and had been chosen not because it was so far away from the base but, in Fagin's words, 'because Paul is suffering from some kind of nervous exhaustion, and they specialise in that'. Now that Hepton re-ran that statement in his head, he saw an ominous ambiguity to it. He checked in his mirror but couldn't see the Sierra. He signalled and came to a halt by the side of the road, where he waited for three minutes. But there was still no sign of the car. Somehow, he felt disappointed. Maybe he should double back. The woman might be in trouble, her car might have gone off the road . . .

Or, more likely, she had taken a turning and was heading towards her destination.

Maybe Nick was right, Hepton said to himself. Maybe I do need to book myself into this place. He started the car again, and within quarter of an hour was turning the Renault through an imposing main gateway and up a country house driveway of gravel so clean it might have been polished that very morning. Therapy for the patients, perhaps?

As he rounded a bend, a rabbit leapt into his path and he nearly hit it. He braked hard and watched it flee across an expanse of manicured lawn and into some shrubbery. Skin tingling, he opened the car door and stepped out. He could hear a car approaching the gateway. When he turned, he saw the same Ford Sierra driving past. He listened as its engine faded into the distance. Smiling, he got back into the Renault and drove up to the imposing entrance of the Alfred de Lyon Hospital itself.


'I must have made a mistake then, it's as simple as that.'

They were sitting in the morning room, a modern extension to the main building fitted with patio doors and filled with pot plants. It was like a hothouse, and Hepton, who had already taken off his jacket, now dragged his tie loose from his neck. Paul Vincent, dressed in slippers, thick dressing gown and sunglasses, didn't exactly look ill. He looked rested and a little tanned. In fact, he looked a good deal healthier than Hepton felt.

'Still,' Vincent continued, 'it's good to see you, Martin. Thanks for coming. So tell me, what's happening back at the base?'

Hepton shook his head. He hadn't driven all this way for gossip. 'What makes you so sure you made a mistake?'

'Well,' Vincent opened his arms in supplication, 'like you say, nothing's been done about it. And Fagin doesn't seem to think anything's amiss.'

'Fagin can make mistakes.'

'Not while I've been working for him he hasn't.'

'So how come we lost *Zephyr* for over three minutes?'

'You can't blame that on him.'

'Why not? He's in charge, isn't he?'

'Martin, what's wrong?' Vincent seemed genuinely concerned.

Hepton rubbed sweat from his forehead. It was a good question. What *was* wrong? Why was he so keen to see mysteries where there might be none? Paul Vincent didn't seem anxious. Nick Christopher didn't seem anxious. Fagin didn't seem anxious. So why was he bothering?

'I don't know, Paul. It's just . . .' He sighed. 'I really don't know.'

Vincent smiled. 'It really was nice of you to come. I haven't seen anybody since I came in here.'

'What happened to you? I mean, back at the base?'

He shrugged. 'I'm not exactly sure. One minute I was fine, the next I was in hospital.'

'And what did the hospital say?'

'You know what they're like. The patient always gets to know the least.'

'Who was your doctor?' Hepton had asked the question in a rush. It seemed almost to catch Vincent out; he stared at Hepton before replying.

'McGill, I think. Yes, a Dr McGill.'

Hepton sat back in the chair and looked around. A few elderly men were seated in wicker chairs. Two were playing a game of chess so delicately they looked to be moving in slow motion. The heat was prickling Hepton's neck and back. He rubbed a finger beneath his shirt collar and glanced towards the doorway, where two muscular male orderlies stood, their jaws fixed. Like soldiers on parade, he thought, rather than nurses caring for the sick.

'So what's it like here?' he asked.

'The food's good,' said Vincent. 'Mind you, the sex isn't up to much.'

They laughed, but Hepton was beginning to catch something behind his friend's eyes, something trapped behind that dead, unfocused look.

'Are they giving you any drugs, Paul?'

'No more than I usually take.' Vincent laughed again, but Hepton managed only a smile, listening to that laughter, to its nervy hollow centre.

'Know what I think, Paul?' he said. Then he leaned towards his friend and lowered his voice. 'I think you're in trouble. I think you're frightened. I think this is all bullshit.' He nodded in the general direction of everything around them. 'And I think you need a friend like me. Maybe I'm wrong.' He rose to his feet. 'Give me a call if you feel like talking.'

'Martin!'

But Hepton knew that the only way to end the scene effectively was for him to walk and keep on walking. So he did. He wasn't going to learn anything here, not unless he could scare Paul enough to make him say something.

He was practically at the car when he heard footsteps hurrying across the gravel behind him.

'Martin, wait!' Paul Vincent caught up with him, looking paler now after the exertion. 'Martin.' He paused for breath. 'At least stay for afternoon tea.'

It wasn't the answer Hepton wanted. He opened the driver's-side door. Vincent's hand came down onto his own level.

'Look,' he said. He glanced around him. 'I'm going to say this just the once, but that should be enough. You always were a good listener, weren't you?'

'I still am, Paul.'

'Well, listen now. Stay out of it. Take a holiday. Suggest it to Fagin. He'll approve it. Go off somewhere warm.' He laughed at this, the sweat gleaming on his face. 'I mean somewhere exotic, somewhere quiet.'

'That's friendly advice, is it?'

Vincent shrugged. Hepton could see the two orderlies in their white uniforms watching them from the main building. Could he bundle Paul into the car and make a getaway? Not against the fitter and younger man's will. He climbed into the Renault and closed the door.

'Tell me,' he said through the open window. 'Really, just between us, what did you think you'd discovered?'

Vincent sighed. His voice when he spoke was no more than a whisper. 'There was something up there, Martin. Something big.' He glanced over his shoulder towards the orderlies. 'But that doesn't seem to be the point.'

'How do you mean?'

'The point seems to be that no one *cares*. One name, Martin.'

'Yes?'

'A man called Villiers. He came to see me, to ask a few questions. He didn't give his name, but I asked at the desk afterwards and they told me. I didn't like him much. Steer around him if you meet him.'

'What questions did he ask?'

'Oh, I don't know, routine stuff. What happened at the base? What happened with my computer? That sort of thing.' Vincent paused. 'The disk got wiped, didn't it? The hard disk?' Hepton nodded, and Vincent sighed. 'They're being pretty thorough.'

'You're saying the disk wasn't wiped accidentally?'

'I'm not sure, but I never was a great believer in coincidence.'

'No, me neither. But then someone in the control room must have wiped it.'

'I suppose so, yes. I got the impression Villiers wanted everything kept as quiet as possible.'

Which, Hepton thought, seems to mean keeping you out of the way.

'Thanks, Paul,' he said.

'Remember what I said about taking a holiday.'

'Goodbye, Paul. Look after yourself.'

'You too, Martin. And I mean that. You too.'

Driving off, Hepton checked in his rear-view mirror and saw the two orderlies approach Vincent. Vincent had the look of a lonely man, of a man unfairly imprisoned. Hepton felt his hands harden around the steering wheel. He pressed down a little on the accelerator and enjoyed the momentary feeling of complete control.

# 8

The Palladio Bookshop was sited not far from Holborn Underground station, and every weekday morning the shop's proprietor, Mr Vitalis, would take the Piccadilly Line Tube from his home in Arnos Grove. He always walked up the escalators rather than standing, but this was due not so much to impatience or any need to be getting on as it was a keen desire to keep himself fit. After all, Mr Vitalis was nearing fifty, though he looked older. Some said his background, to judge from his voice, was east European, and that he had come to England at the outbreak of World War Two. Others, examining his olive skin, proclaimed him Greek, while a few guessed at Italian and fewer still north African. In a sense, they were all correct, since Mr Vitalis liked to think of himself, in the truest sense of the phrase, as a man of the world.

The Palladio was fairly quiet in the mornings, busying at lunchtime with customers from the offices and shops, browsing as they munched on a sandwich or sipped from a carton or can. In the afternoon, a few of the regulars usually dropped in either to buy or to sell. Mr Vitalis had a good reputation with the city's book reviewers, who would offer him the latest titles, once they had been finished with, for one third of the cover price. These books Mr Vitalis sold on to libraries and, it must be said, other bookshops. And in this way he made his money.

He kept few friends, but those he did keep, when entertained for the first time at his home, could not help but comment on its size, and on the superb works of art he had collected over the years. He would smile, and then move the conversation along to literary gossip or some commentary on current affairs. For Mr Vitalis loved conversation.

Today, however, the few regulars who called at the Palladio for an afternoon's tea and chatter found the usual pavement stall locked up inside the shop, and the shop itself deserted, with a neatly written note sellotaped to the inside of the glass door: *Apologies, friends, but Palladio closes early today. Business as usual tomorrow.*

They'd never heard the like: Mr Vitalis shutting up shop early? Perhaps there was a woman behind it. After all, he *was* a man of the world. They were sure there would be *some* story in it, and surer still that Mr Vitalis would be telling the story tomorrow afternoon over tea.

Not many would have looked for Mr Vitalis in the back of a black cab, for he was known to abhor the things, always choosing to travel by Tube or bus or foot.

'I'm a social animal at heart, you see,' he would explain.

And while he was considered something of an aesthete, his tastes could not be said to be expensive in most areas, so some might have been more surprised still to see the taxi drop him outside a Park Lane hotel called the Achilles, where, having paid the driver, he talked animatedly for several minutes with the uniformed doorman. He then entered the hotel lobby, while the doorman stared evenly at the traffic roaring past the entrance.

Mr Vitalis looked as though such hotels were part of his everyday existence, walking up to the reception desk with a polite smile on his face and his eyes as dark as the shiniest black olives.

'Good afternoon,' he said. 'I'm expecting a friend. I wonder, has he arrived yet? His name is Mr Devereux, an American.'

The clerk checked the register, then remembered.

'Oh yes, sir,' he said. 'No, Mr Devereux hasn't arrived yet. We have some mail waiting for him. That's why I recall the name.'

Mr Vitalis looked surprised.

'But I am right, am I not? I mean, he *is* due today?'

The clerk flipped over a page of the register. 'No, sir,' he said. 'We have Mr Devereux's name in for tomorrow.'

'Ah.' Mr Vitalis nodded. 'I must have a crossed line then. Well, tomorrow it is. Thank you.'

And with that he turned and walked back through the lobby, pushing his way out of the main door, which he held open courteously for an elderly lady and the fruits of her shopping trip. On the hotel steps, he paused again to exchange some words with the door-man. Not many words this time, but they seemed to leave their impression, for the doorman's cheeks were crimson with shame as Mr Vitalis walked towards the taxi rank, where he opened the door of a waiting cab, heaved himself in and slammed it shut behind him.

# 9

Hepton had been thinking about it all the way back to the base. So much so that when he glanced in the rear-view mirror and saw no sign of any car following him, he merely shrugged and kept on driving.

They were surprised to see him at the gate.

'Thought you'd got a couple of days' leave,' one guard said.

'Can't keep away,' Hepton replied, starting the car forward as the barrier rose to let him into the compound.

He parked, then went straight to Fagin's office, a small white-washed room next to the female toilets on the second level. There was always a faint aroma of urine and disinfectant in the room, which nobody mentioned and everyone put down to its location. But Fagin seemed happy there; some might have said disturbingly so.

Fagin, too, was surprised to see him, but admitted as much only by the raising of his thin eyebrows when Hepton walked in through the door.

'Sit down, Martin, please.' Hepton sat. 'Have you seen Paul?'

'Yes.'

'And how is he?'

Hepton looked around the room before answering. There were photographs of satellites, spaceships and aircraft covering the walls, and three pinboards filled with postcards and other memorabilia. Then he looked towards Fagin.

'He's fine,' he said.

'Good,' said Fagin, returning the look. 'So what can I do for you?'

That was the question, thought Hepton: what *could* Fagin do for him? What was it Paul Vincent had said . . .?

'Actually,' he began, 'it's about Paul. He looks so fit, he reminded me it's a while since I've had a break. I mean a proper break. I was wondering if I could be spared for a week or two.'

Fagin seemed to consider this. 'Well . . .'

'I know I'm not due any additional leave right now,' Hepton continued. He was waiting for a shake of the head. Fagin hated to see people go off on holiday. Work was what he lived for, and he didn't see why others shouldn't be the same. So Hepton waited. He knew he wasn't owed any holiday time, and Fagin knew it, too. Besides which, there was a strict routine to be obeyed, which meant giving four weeks' notice of intended vacations.

Fagin's face wrinkled.

'I'm not sure we *can* spare you just at the moment, Martin. I take it you'd want your leave to start immediately?'

'If possible, yes.'

Fagin was shaking his head, but slowly. 'I'm not sure,' he said again.

'Nick Christopher could stand in for me,' Hepton said, thinking fast. 'He knows the set-up on my console as well as I know it myself. And Curtees could take over from him.'

'I'll have to think about it, Martin. I'll try to give you an answer one way or the other as soon as I can, but no promises.'

'Well, thanks anyway.' Hepton made to rise, but paused. 'Oh, one more thing, sir.'

'Yes, Martin?'

'Have you discovered what went wrong with *Zephyr*?'

'Not yet. I'm just thankful we didn't lose her altogether.'

'Yes, so you keep saying.' Hepton rose from the chair. 'It couldn't have anything to do with whatever else was up there, could it?'

Fagin smiled quizzically. 'How do you mean, Martin?'

Hepton shook his head. 'No, maybe not. I just thought that whatever it was that was up there interfering with *Zephyr*'s airspace might have caused the satellite to malfunction temporarily.'

'There wasn't anything else up there.' Fagin seemed bemused. 'What made you think there was?'

'Oh, just Paul's data. Have you checked it yet?'

'I told you, the disk—'

'Oh yes, the disk malfunctioned too, didn't it?' Hepton shook his head. 'Well, these things happen, don't they, sir?' he commented archly.

'Yes, they do, Martin,' said Fagin coolly, watching as Hepton walked to the door and made his exit.

Hepton descended the metal stairs to the ground-floor level and walked along the corridor towards where two telephone booths were situated. As usual, one of these had a notice taped to it saying *OUT OF ORDER*, to which some wag had prefixed the single word *BANG*. But the other telephone was working. Hepton dialled directory enquiries. His call was answered immediately.

'Hello,' he began. 'I'd like the number of a hospital in Grimsby. It may be the only hospital, I'm not sure.'

A few moments later, he had several numbers in the back of his diary. He drew lines beneath them all with his pen, thanked the operator and rang off. Then, finding more change in his pocket, he dialled the first number.

'Hello,' he repeated, when the call was finally answered. 'Could you put me through to Dr McGill, please?'

It took the receptionist a little time. 'I'm sorry,' she said at last, 'there's no Dr McGill working here.'

'Thank you,' Hepton said, ringing off. He felt actual relief: it would be something of an anticlimax if Vincent's Dr McGill were to exist outside of the young man's imagination. He called the other two numbers with the same negative result.

So there was no Dr McGill. Had Paul Vincent ever even been taken to hospital in the first place? Or had he been at the Alfred de Lyon all the time? It was a question Hepton couldn't yet answer. He took his pen and wrote the name *VILLIERS* in his diary. Another figment of Vincent's imagination? A second visit to the nursing home was becoming absolutely necessary.

Two hours later, Hepton was playing pool with Nick Christopher when the internal note arrived. He read it out aloud.

'"Leave can begin at once. Send us a postcard. Henry."'

Christopher came to see. 'Jesus,' he said, 'he really signed himself Henry. Fagin *never* uses his Christian name. Never.'

Hepton wafted the note in Christopher's face. 'Now will you believe that something's going on?' he said.

He had spent the past half-hour trying to make sense of his suspicions to Nick Christopher, but it seemed that the more he talked, the flimsier everything became. But now this. The granting of an immediate holiday, courtesy of Fagin.

Courtesy of Henry.

Christopher returned to the table and played a shot, but it went wide of the pocket and he sighed, putting down his cue.

'Okay,' he said. 'Run through it again for me, starting at the beginning.' And this time he was concentrating as Hepton told his story.

# 10

Hepton went to his dorm, pulled a suitcase out from beneath one of the bunks and started packing. Nine months ago, he'd taken out a year's rental on a small flat in the market town of Louth, plumb in the middle of the town's market area and not far from Binbrook. He'd reckoned it would make a little love nest for Jilly and him, whenever they could find a couple of days or more free to spend together. But then she'd taken the London job, forsaking her own local paper, where she had been something of a star. There had been a murder, made to look like suicide, and Jilly had investigated. She hadn't exactly been able to prove anything substantial, but she had goaded the police into taking another look, and from there they had pronounced the suicide a murder. From where it was a short step to declaring the murderer (the dead woman's son) found and guilty (twelve years).

Jilly's story had found its way into the national press, and then the *London Herald* had jumped in with the offer of a job. Of course she'd been right to take it. It was the perfect career move at the right time. So the flat had gone unused and unloved, but Hepton had kept it on, using it for the occasional tryst, more or less unsatisfactorily.

He didn't pack much, just enough to make people think he really was going to take a holiday. Then he waved farewell to Nick Christopher, who waved back, and made for his car.

At the security barrier, the guard came out of his hut.

'Off again, are you?'

'That's right, Bert,' said Hepton, smiling.

'I don't know, some people . . .' Bert went back to his post.

Hepton waved at him, too, as he drove underneath the rising barrier and took a right turn onto the main road. Louth was less than twenty minutes away.

There had been a market that day, but the only signs in the town centre were scraps of vegetables in the gutter outside the entrance to Hepton's flat. He lifted his suitcase out of the car and unlocked the main door. There were three flats in the house: one on the ground floor, one on the first floor and another in the attic. His was the first-floor flat, and he took the winding stairwell with accustomed awkwardness, manoeuvring the suitcase around the twists of the climb.

There was no mail waiting for him on the matting that covered his hall floor. The neighbour downstairs, Mrs Kennedy-Hall, had a key to the flat and sent the mail – bills always – on to him at the base. He unlocked the door. The flat smelt musty. He hadn't been here in over a fortnight, and then only to play the gigolo in a failed seduction.

The place looked tidier than he remembered it. They had drunk a lot of wine that night, and rather a lot of neat gin (there being no tonic water to hand). None of it had helped. He couldn't remember clearing up afterwards, though. Perhaps Mrs Kennedy-Hall . . . But no, it would be more her style to hire someone to tidy.

Then he heard the sounds, at first placing them in the street below. The sounds of running water, of things being moved, breakable things. There was someone in his kitchen . . .

He ran towards the source of the noise and stood in the kitchen doorway, dumbstruck. At the sink stood a tall, attractive woman, perhaps a year or two younger than him. She had rolled up the sleeves of her white blouse and was up to her elbows in soapy water. Clean dishes stood on the draining board, the worktops shone, the whole place was sparkling. The woman turned, saw him and smiled.

'Hello,' she said. 'You must be Martin.'

'That's right,' Hepton said at last. 'And who the hell are you?'

'Harriet,' she answered, letting the water out of the sink. 'My friends usually just call me Harry.' She dried her hands on a dish towel, then held out the left one towards him. There were no rings on her water-reddened fingers. 'How do you do?'

Hepton shook her hand awkwardly, right-handed himself, and she noticed his hesitation.

'Oh dear,' she said, 'I'm always doing that – shaking with the wrong hand, I mean. Sorry.'

'Not at all,' said Hepton. The shock of finding a stranger in his flat, a breaking-and-entering charlady, was ebbing. Questions filled the space. 'But who are you?' he asked. 'How did you get in?'

'Care for some tea?' Harry had turned her back on him and begun to fuss with the kettle.

Hepton stared down at her legs, supple, slim legs wrapped in thin black stockings. She wore a blue pinstripe skirt to just below the knee. It was half of a suit, the jacket of which he now saw was hanging over one of the chairs beneath the freshly wiped foldaway table.

'There's today's milk in your fridge,' she was saying, 'and some Assam tea in the cupboard. The place was quite barren. I hope you don't mind. I went to that little shop on the corner.' She turned to smile at him, and despite himself, he smiled back.

'I think you should know—' he started.

'Oh,' she interrupted, sniffing the interior of the teapot speculatively, 'but there's very little I *don't* know, Martin. Very little indeed. That's why I've been sent along here. Do you take milk?'

'Who sent you here?'

She smiled again, with her unblemished English rose of a face, then waved an expansive arm around the kitchen.

'All neat and tidy,' she said. 'That's how I like things. I can't remember, did you say you took milk?'

'Yes,' he said, beginning to feel distinctly uneasy. It was difficult to find an order for all the questions welling up within him. 'How did you get in?'

'Didn't I say?' She began pouring water from the kettle into the teapot. 'Your door was open.'

'Open?'

'Wide open. No breaking and entering necessary. Well, no breaking at any rate. So I suppose the worst I can be accused of is cleaning with intent.' She had placed everything on a tray, which she now double-checked. Satisfied, she lifted it. 'Shall we go through to the living room?'

There was little Hepton could do but follow her, knowing that he needed answers but knowing also that she seemed determined to give them in her own way and in her own time. Well, he had lots of time, didn't he? He was on holiday. All he needed was patience.

They sat down and she poured, handing him a cup.

God, he hadn't used this tea set in living memory, preferring a chipped red mug. It had come with the flat, the tea set. But then so had the mug.

'I thought it was odd,' Harry continued, 'your door being open like that, so I called in to report it. I'll pay for the call, of course.'

'Called in to whom?'

'To my employers,' she said, 'who are, ultimately, *your* employers. It'll be useful to keep that in mind.'

'Why?'

She chose to ignore this, lowering her fine eyelashes as she sipped from her cup. Hepton drank too, playing her at her own game. The tea was strong and aromatic. Harry put down her cup and crossed her legs.

'You saw your friend this morning. Paul Vincent. And now your little holiday begins.'

'That's right.' Then it hit him. 'And you,' he said, 'drive a black Ford Sierra.'

She smiled, but did not reply.

'You were following me?' he said.

'Why were you so anxious about Mr Vincent?'

Hepton shrugged. 'It's no secret. Paul was taken ill. He's a friend of mine, as you yourself said. So, naturally, I was worried.'

'But there's more to it than that, isn't there?' Her voice had taken on a hard, professional edge. He stood up.

'Look,' he said, 'I'm sorry, but I've got no proof that you are who you say you are – not that you've said very much.' He walked to the window and stared down into the street. An old man was stooping to pick up a discarded piece of fruit from the side of the road.

'Very good, Martin. I was beginning to wonder if you'd ever get round to asking. I thought you'd forgotten procedures. Take this.' She produced a slip of paper from her skirt pocket and rose from her chair to hand it to him.

From close up, he could smell the subtle soap she used. She wasn't wearing perfume, though; either that or his nose wasn't attuned to it. He stared at the numbers on the paper.

'It's a telephone number,' she said. 'Ex-directory; you won't have come across it before. If you dial it, you will find yourself speaking to your superior, Mr Fagin. It's a direct line. He'll give you clearance to speak to me, and he'll promise also to give that permission in writing. Don't worry, nothing you might say to me will get back to him.'

'You don't have any identification on you?'

'Nothing formal,' said Harry. 'It's against the rules. I can let you have a library ticket or my credit card, but that's about it.'

Hepton smiled but was already picking up the telephone. The receiver at the other end was answered after the very first ring.

'I suppose that's you, Martin. I was told to expect a call. Listen, I want you to tell them *everything*, do you understand? It may be more important than you think. Don't let it spoil your holiday, though; just get it all off your chest and then you can enjoy yourself.'

As Hepton listened to Fagin's unmistakable voice, saying little himself, he watched Harry picking invisible hairs off the arms of her chair. His head was spinning. *What is all this about?* A little while ago, Fagin hadn't seemed interested in anything he or Paul Vincent might have to say. Yet now he was ordering Martin to tell all. He wrenched his thoughts back to the here and now in time to catch Fagin's final statement:

'If you keep anything from them, you could get into serious trouble, and they'll *know* if you're hiding something. That's their job. I must go now. Goodbye.'

As though she had heard everything, Harry raised her head at this, staring towards him with a righteous look on her face. Hepton put down the telephone and sank into his chair, feeling not at all comfortable in his own home. He pinched the bridge of his nose, then straightened up.

'So what do you want to know?' he said.

'What I really want, Martin,' Harry began, 'is not so much to be told as to do the telling. As I said before, there probably isn't much you could tell me that I don't know already. You should be aware, however, that this is a matter of national security. It sounds like a cliché these days, but I'm in absolute earnest. It is in everyone's interest for you to forget whatever Paul Vincent told you.'

'Told me about what?'

Her look was that of a disappointed schoolmistress, some favoured pupil having let her down. Hepton stared at her evenly.

'Told you,' she said, 'that he had noticed something on his monitor.'

'Then there *was* something up there?'

'Certainly there was . . . interference. We're looking into it.'

'But who's "we"?'

'You could say that I do PR work for the armed forces.'

'Public relations?' Hepton sounded doubtful. Harry shrugged. 'But I don't understand,' he persisted. 'What have the army got to do with it?' Then he remembered. *Zephyr* was watching for civil unrest during the US pull-out. The army must be on standby, of course.

'As a matter of interest, Martin, what do *you* think happened?'

'Me?' Hepton seemed genuinely surprised. 'Why should anyone be interested in what *I* think?' He remembered his final sighting of Paul Vincent, looking scared and beaten. For some reason, the memory stirred him to anger. 'I'll tell you what I think,' he said. 'I think you know *less* than you're saying, not more.' He was out of his seat now, standing over her. 'I think you should get out and leave me alone. That's what I think. And if I want to tell anybody about all of this, then I'll damned well tell them.'

She stood too, her eyes on a level with his. Her face had tightened, and there were spots of red on either cheek. Her voice when she spoke was as cold and lifeless as a deep freeze.

'Of course you must do whatever you see fit. I'll get my jacket.' He followed her to the kitchen and watched her put the jacket on. She surveyed the newly cleaned work surfaces. 'Neat and tidy,' she said, 'that's how I like things, Martin.'

'Is that a threat?'

She smiled at this, but not pleasantly, and moved past him into the hall, opening the front door. She paused on the threshold, reached into her jacket pocket and brought out a laminated business card. Well, it looked like a business card, but in fact all there was on it was a printed telephone number. 'You can contact me at that number,' she said.

Hepton stared at the card. 'What did you mean when you said we work for the same bosses?'

She chose not to reply, but reached again into her pocket and held out a ten-pence piece towards him. 'For the call,' she said. He accepted the money. She was leaving now, but she turned one last time. 'You know Major Dreyfuss, don't you?'

'How do you know that?'

'It's my job,' she said.

He watched her descend the stairwell, then listened as she walked along the passage to the main door. He closed his front door and walked briskly to the living room window, but there was no sign of her in the street outside, no sound of her shoes moving away. His head was spinning. His flat, his private life, everything had been suddenly whisked away from him, reshuffled and brought back altered beyond repair. The old man was still examining stray scraps left by the market stalls. Dispossessed, but no more so than Hepton was himself. As Hepton watched, the man arched his back, straightening it, and in that moment looked up at the window. Hepton flinched, shrank back into the room. Was he being watched? Who was watching him? He realised that he wasn't just confused. He was afraid. Terribly afraid, and yet without knowing quite why.

Harry used a small infrared device to disconnect her car alarm as she walked towards the black Sierra, then unlocked the boot and took from it a large attaché case, which she carried with her to the driver's-side door. Sliding into the seat, she quickly opened the case and studied the telephone equipment inside. She should check in, but she still wasn't sure how much of a threat Hepton was. He seemed at the same time quite innocent and quite devious. Of course, as she knew from experience, even the innocent could be dangerous. She had to be sure. She closed the case again, unlocked the glove compartment and removed from it a small black plastic module. Switching it on, she was rewarded with a high-pitched bleep and a strong green light at the centre of a series of radiating LEDs. It wasn't the world's most sophisticated tracking device, but it would do. She placed the tracker on the passenger seat and sat back, hands on the steering wheel, eyes staring straight ahead, waiting . . .

# Part II

*Independent*, 21 September 1987

Part II

# 11

Days were passing. Dreyfuss felt sure of that, though he slept mostly. Probably because of the drugs they were giving him: the ones he could see, the ones they asked him politely to swallow; and perhaps the ones he couldn't see, concealed in his drinking water, his meals.

But after his latest bout of unconsciousness, he awoke not to the restorative sight of Nurse Carraway, but to two stern figures, the same men as before, the ones the doctor had named as General Esterhazy and Mr Stewart.

The general was examining the cards attached to the few flowers that had been sent to the invalid.

'Who's Jilly, for Christ's sake?' he asked the other man, unaware as yet that Dreyfuss' eyes were opening.

'Just some woman he knows. They used to date in school apparently.'

*God, they know so much about me . . .*

'He was married, though?'

'Divorced now. The ex-wife lives somewhere in Australia.'

'I notice *she* didn't send any flowers,' the general commented, taking pleasure in the fact.

Dreyfuss noted that Stewart seemed subdued, while the general himself was as abrasive in his speech as a grinding tool. Now Stewart had noticed that Dreyfuss' eyes were opened to slits.

'General,' he warned, and both men came to the bed. Dreyfuss could smell salt and something sweeter, an aftershave perhaps. 'My name's Frank Stewart,' said the civilian. 'I'm from the State Department.'

He's CIA, Dreyfuss thought. Either that or NSA.

'And this is—'

'Jesus Christ, Frank,' snapped the general, 'I can make my own introductions, can't I?' He turned his eyes to Dreyfuss. The pupils were inky, like staring down the barrel of a pistol. 'The name's General Ben Esterhazy.'

Esterhazy, one of the biggest of the cheeses. He had been on a mission to Europe and hadn't been able to meet with the *Argos* crew to offer them good luck. Instead, an aide had come to give them the general's best wishes.

'Pleased to meet you,' said Dreyfuss in a voice weak from sleep. In fact, he didn't feel at all bad, but he didn't want the hospital thinking he could be moved. He felt safe here, safe from choking hands. And he still had to find out a few things. 'They're all dead, aren't they?' he asked.

'Every goddamned one of them,' Esterhazy said bitterly, while Stewart threw him a look that said he shouldn't have told Dreyfuss that. Dreyfuss had the feeling there was no love lost between these two men, or between their respective organisations.

Stewart dragged the nurse's chair closer to the bed and sat down. He was a heavyset man in his early fifties. Dreyfuss thought his hair had probably been grey for quite a few years. In build, however, he was Joe Frazier to Esterhazy's Ali. The general was tall, and as broad as Americans liked their heroes to be. Esterhazy had been publicly and vociferously opposed to the European pull-out, and had received a polite but stinging slap on the wrist from the White House as a result.

Which hadn't stopped them sending him to Europe to negotiate the terms of the pull-out itself.

'So,' Frank Stewart was saying, 'how are you doing?'

Stewart had slipped out of his jacket, which he was now hanging over the back of the chair. Dreyfuss noticed the gold armbands on his shirtsleeves. He had never seen anyone wear bands before, outside of old movies. Maybe a snooker player or two, but only of the old school. Perhaps they were there to cut off the supply of blood to Stewart's fists, so he wouldn't sling a punch at General Esterhazy. Stewart's eyes were as murky as prunes swimming in semolina, and the cracks on his face weren't there from laughing. He reached into his pocket for a crisp white handkerchief with which to mop his forehead. Dreyfuss knew who he was now: he was Spencer Tracy playing the tired, put-upon father in some film.

'I'm doing okay,' Dreyfuss answered, pouring himself a little water. He saw for the first time that the drip by his bed had been taken away. There was a fresh sticking plaster on his arm where the syringe had been removed.

'Better than some,' spat Esterhazy.

'Ben, for Christ's sake—'

'Well, what do you want from me?' Esterhazy exploded. 'Tears and flowers?' He slapped at the bunch of flowers nearest him and sent some petals spinning floorwards. 'Five good men died up there.'

'Do we know what happened yet?' asked Dreyfuss.

'*We* don't, no,' said Esterhazy. His eyes drilled into Dreyfuss'. 'Do you?'

Dreyfuss took his time, sipping the water, thinking over his reply. But Stewart was ready with another question.

'The doc says you've got a case of partial amnesia. Is that right?'

'Yes.'

'So what *do* you remember?'

Dreyfuss rested his head against the pillow. 'I was chosen as the British member of the *Argos* mission. We were launching a communications satellite. Everything went fine . . .' He stared at the ceiling, seeing the control panel again, the computer screen, the readouts, which had stopped making sense. Heinemann had been watching the screen, too, but hadn't said anything. He didn't seem to think there was anything wrong.

But there was.

And at first Dreyfuss hadn't said anything, in case the answer was simple and they all sneered at him again, thinking him underqualified to be on the flight, thinking him stupid. But then he had mentioned it to Hes Adams . . .

'Yes?' Stewart prompted.

'Everything went fine, like I said. But when we were coming in to land, the onboard system failed.'

'Christ, we *know* that!' shouted Esterhazy. 'Tell us something we don't know.'

'Ben, please.' Stewart's voice was pleading. He smiled at Dreyfuss.

*Techniques for the survival of interrogation, number one: trust no one, and especially not anyone who appears to be your friend.* That was what they had taught him. He would have to be careful of this man Stewart.

He had a question to ask for himself.

'How far is Sacramento from Edwards Air Force Base?'

'Maybe three hundred miles,' Stewart said.

'Why was I brought here then? Why not a hospital closer to Edwards?'

Stewart turned to Esterhazy. 'Yes,' he said, 'why was that, Ben?'

'I told you, Frank, we were trying to throw off the press. They've been round this thing like vultures. We were also trying to avoid any ugly scenes, public demonstrations, folks wanting him strung up.' Esterhazy was relishing this. 'So instead of taking him to Bakersfield or LA, which would have been obvious choices, we landed him at McClellan and brought him here. And what do we get by way of thanks? Squat!'

Stewart ignored this, his attention still on Dreyfuss. 'Those bruises on your throat aren't love bites, are they, Major?'

'I suppose we all panicked when the shuttle was coming down.' Dreyfuss had had time to prepare this story. 'We all got a bit crazy.'

'Bullshit,' hissed Esterhazy. 'They were the best. They wouldn't panic. They'd take it like men. I *know* they would.'

'If you say so,' Dreyfuss said.

'Sonofabitch,' Esterhazy growled.

There was that word again. *Sonofabitch! The burial's what matters. Coffin's got to be buried!* But what coffin? Whose? Had Hes Adams meant the shuttle itself?

Esterhazy was coming towards the bed. He looked massive, and not a little dangerous. 'What the hell is it with you, Dreyfuss? Just what is it you're trying to hide? I *know* you know something. Damn you, I want to know what it is.' He turned to Stewart. 'Get out, Frank. Give me ten minutes with this bastard.'

'Ben, don't be stupid. You're a general, not some damned sergeant in the marines. And this isn't Vietnam. This is the United States. That's not the way we work.'

Esterhazy's voice had become almost neutral. 'Yes it is, Frank,' he said. 'You should know that. Now either you get out of here, or I'll have a couple of my men drag you out.'

'Ben . . .' Stewart's face was purple with blood. Nobody had talked to him like this for quite some time, which, Dreyfuss supposed, meant he was fairly high up in his organisation. But he held his rage and got slowly to his feet. 'You're making a mistake,' he said. Esterhazy was smiling now.

'Hell, Frank, what do you think I'm going to do? Wire electrodes to his nuts? Your gang might have stooped to that once upon a time. But all we're going to do is talk. Just a one-to-one. Because the major is holding back on me, and I don't like that.'

Stewart was at the door now, hesitant, but ready to leave.

*Techniques for the survival of interrogation, number two: when a team of two is involved, everything they do is calculated, everything is a trick. Don't be fooled.*

'Tell me something,' Esterhazy was saying, his breath close to Dreyfuss' ear, 'how come nobody from your own embassy has even bothered to come see you? Huh? Answer me that.'

Esterhazy's hands were leaning on the edge of the bed, and Stewart was turning the handle, opening the door, making to leave.

But there was someone outside the door, and as Stewart opened it, they walked in, as though they had been standing there for some time listening, awaiting the moment to make the most effective entrance.

'Good day to you, gentlemen,' the intruder said by way of introduction. 'The name's Parfit, British embassy.'


What was he, some kind of child? To be ignored like that, to be left here in his room while the three of them went off for a meeting. Parfit, British embassy. Just like that.

'Well, Jesus, it's about time one of you guys turned up,' Esterhazy had sneered. 'If this' – jerking his head in Dreyfuss' direction – 'if this had been one of ours in your country, we'd have been at his bedside before the goddamned shuttle had stopped smoking! We look after our own, and I'll tell you—'

'I'm sure you will, General.' Parfit's voice was as clean as a polished window. 'Is there a room where we can sit down and discuss things?'

'There's the administrator's office,' offered Frank Stewart.

'Excellent,' said Parfit. He came to the bed and touched Dreyfuss' shoulder. 'I'm glad to see you looking so well, Major. We'll talk soon.'

And then they'd walked out of the room and left him. Dreyfuss fumed for a couple of minutes, his heart racing, angrier than he'd been since the crash. Then he pulled at the bedcover and swung his legs off the mattress and onto the floor. The floor itself was warm to the touch, yet the room was cool. He stood up, feeling his legs wobble from inaction. He locked them at the knees and drew himself to his full height. A few hesitant steps took him to the washbasin, where he splashed cold water onto his face. He looked in the mirror, and saw a pale face, a gaunt face, the hair cloying and in need of shampoo. The skin was singed from the shuttle blaze, and cream had been smeared onto his cheeks and forehead. And yes, those bruises on his neck were prominent. He looked a mess.

He dried himself with a towel, feeling sweat trickling down his back from the effort thus far. Then he shuffled over to where the flowers sat. There were two cards: one from Jilly, and one from Cam Devereux.

*Cam!* He held a snapshot in his head of Cam's beaming face, that air-hostess-style voice: 'Hi, I'm Cameron Devereux. Call me Cam, everyone does. I'll be your contact down here while you're up there.' The day they'd gone to visit the *Argos* ground station, meeting with the men who would be their eyes and ears on earth while they were circling in space. The controllers, with their crew cuts and striped shirts, seated in front of screens that could show anything from the height and trajectory of the shuttle to the pressurisation of the cabin and the heartbeats of the men inside it.

Cam, too, had a striped shirt and a crew cut. He also had a smile. God, that assured smile, a fortune in dental work. Even the mechanics in this country smiled like movie stars. But he had a weak handshake, and would melt like wax if a hand grabbed at his smooth lapel or threatened to tweak his WASP nose. However, there was every chance that he would know something about what had gone wrong, or at least would have his suspicions.

I shouldn't have been up there in the first place, Dreyfuss said to himself now. He had been chosen over younger men and better men, men more computer-literate, men fitter, more intelligent. He had told the selection panel at his third and final interview: 'I'm just an airman who wants to be an astronaut.' Hoping that candour would stand up where his credentials had faltered. It had: the Americans wanted him. Everyone had wondered why . . .

'Major!' It was Nurse Carraway, entering the room on her silent rubber heels. 'What are you doing?'

'Just taking a look at my flowers.'

'I didn't think you were strong enough to walk.'

'Willpower, that's all.' He shuffled back to his bed and sat down on its edge, where General Esterhazy's heavy knuckles had recently rested.

'Well, anyway, it's time for your medication.' She was holding a tiny paper cup filled with liquid in one hand, and a yet smaller cup containing a mixture of tablets in the other. Dreyfuss accepted both. He put the liquid down on his bedside cabinet and picked one of the tablets out at random, holding it between forefinger and thumb. It was oval-shaped and purple in colour.

'What's this?' he asked. He felt bolder now that Parfit had arrived.

'What do you mean? It's just medication.'

'No, come on, you're a nurse. What *kind* of medication? What's its purpose? What's its medical name?'

She seemed flustered. Dreyfuss had not seen her flustered before. 'Well?' he goaded.

She smiled. 'Major Dreyfuss, if you don't want to take the tablets, that is your concern. But I should warn you that I'll have to report—'

Dreyfuss laughed, shaking his head. 'Get out of here,' he said. 'Go on, shove off.' His grin was purposeful. 'You're not a nurse. A nurse on the wards would know what the drugs were called, nicknames, medical names, Christian names. A real nurse would know that. But you, Nurse Carraway, you don't know anything. As General Esterhazy might put it, you don't know squat! Incidentally,' he was on his feet again, shuffling forwards, 'which one of them do you work for, Stewart or Esterhazy?'

'Major Dreyfuss,' she spluttered, 'I . . . I don't know what you're talking about.'

'What's more,' he went on, enjoying this, 'the doctor who came to see me that first time had never seen you before. Plus,' he said, staring at her legs, 'I can't see too many nurses wearing silk hosiery, can you?'

She was staring at her legs too now, as though unable to believe their treachery.

'Go on,' he said tiredly, 'go and make your report.' And with this he fell back onto the bed and lay there shading his face with his arms. There was a pause of several seconds before he heard her shoes squeak. She had turned round and was going to the door, which opened silently. Dreyfuss felt tired and tricked and used. His head was thumping, and he wondered if any of the tablets in the cup would ease it.

'Bravo.'

It was Parfit's voice. Dreyfuss took his arms from his face and jerked his head up. Parfit was standing in the doorway, holding the door open with the tip of a polished black leather brogue. He came into the room, letting the door close softly. His shoes made a solid clacking noise on the flooring as he approached the bed.

'Do you always eavesdrop on people's conversations?' asked Dreyfuss.

'Goes with the territory, I'm afraid. So how are you?'

'Fine.'

'Yes, for the moment perhaps. But everyone around you seems ever so slightly agitated. I shouldn't think your safety here could be guaranteed for much longer. What do you say?'

'You mean I can leave?'

'Well of course you can leave. Nobody's been forcing you to stay.'

Dreyfuss groaned.

'Unless, of course,' Parfit said, 'they got you to sign any papers.'

'What kind of papers?'

'Papers committing yourself to their care?'

'I haven't signed anything.'

'You're sure?'

'Positive.'

'Very well then. I'll just make a few arrangements, and then we'll have you out of here.'

'Have you told them I'm leaving?'

'Who?' Parfit seemed amused. 'Esterhazy and Stewart? Good Lord, it's not up to them, is it? It's up to the doctors and the hospital administrator. I foresee no problem.'

'They won't be very happy.'

If anything, Parfit's smile broadened. 'No,' he said, 'no, they won't, will they?'

He was about to leave, but Dreyfuss stopped him.

'One question, Parfit,' he said.

'Yes?'

'What took you so long to get here?'

'We'll talk about that elsewhere,' Parfit said, looking around the room. His meaning was clear: walls really do have ears. Dreyfuss nodded. Parfit again turned to leave.

'Parfit?'

'Yes, Major Dreyfuss?'

Dreyfuss was smiling too. 'It's nice to see you again,' he said.

# 12

Cam Devereux arrived at London's Heathrow Airport desperately tired and in need of the vacation this was supposed to be. His cotton sports shirt was sticking to him, and his scalp tingled as he ran his hands over his thinning hair. He was so tired. But how could he rest? His mind felt inflamed. How could he stop himself replaying events, seeing that stranger arrive at the ground base control room? Seeing the stranger given an office of his own and a console, ignoring the curious looks of the other controllers? Seeing *Argos* itself gliding erratically towards earth, flailing across the runway . . .?

Yes, he needed a vacation. They'd told him that. He needed a complete break; everybody did, everybody connected with *Argos*. They had *ordered* him to take a break. So he had chosen to come to London, despite their protests about leaving Europe well alone. London was a city he could happily get lost in, and wander through all day from district to district. He liked almost everything about it, including the things the Londoners themselves seemed to loathe, such as the subway system. So, having waited for his baggage, he headed downwards, beneath the ground, far away from the sunlight and the sky, and bought a ticket to Green Park station, from where it would be only a short walk to his hotel. The other people who got into his compartment of the Tube train were travellers like himself, hauling too much baggage behind them. He himself was travelling light by comparison. You could always buy what you hadn't brought, especially with the thick wallet of travellers' cheques they had given him.

'Look on it as a bonus,' they had said. A bonus for what? he was tempted to ask. But he had never questioned anything in his life . . .

until now. Now, his head was full of unanswered questions and fears. He again examined his fellow passengers, and saw that they looked every bit as nervous as he felt. First-timers in London, he supposed, and wary of every step.

Maybe at last he could stop looking over his shoulder. Maybe he could stop worrying about what he had seen, what they seemed to *know* he had seen. And had paid him to forget about, paid him by way of a holiday, a swanky hotel, a plastic wallet full of paper money. Maybe they'd leave him alone. And maybe when he stopped worrying, he'd stop thinking about it too.

Maybe, but he doubted it.

Still, he had to make it look like a holiday. He would visit a few of the sights, do a little shopping. All the time waiting for his new controller to make contact. He had asked for one, and they had agreed to his request, though reluctantly. But he had negotiated from a position of strength. He had information after all, didn't he? He had something to tell. If only he knew what it was . . .

# 13

The morning was bright, despite Martin Hepton's mood. He awakened to his clock radio, just in time to catch a studio debate between someone from the Pentagon and the Minister for Defence turning into a full-scale shouting match. The radio presenter sounded genuinely alarmed as accusations were hurled across the table. Lack of co-operation, distinct misunderstanding of the mood of the European Community, defenders not terrorists, never asked to be here in the first place. Et cetera.

Hepton smiled to himself as he listened. If intelligence and communications were good enough, he reasoned, there would be no arms race: everyone would *know* what everyone else had. That was why he felt no jab of conscience at his job, even when attacked at parties by people who could not understand why he did what he did. Not that he did very much. There would be the occasional full-scale surveillance operation, covering the movements of a suspected spy or some military attaché. Someone in a car might just notice that another car was following, but they couldn't suspect that they were being watched from space. Mostly these jobs were for the security services. Now and again they were for the military. There had been illicit peeks at what this or that US listening post was up to; the one at Menwith Hill, for example. Against the rules, of course. Snooping on the enemy was all well and good, but spying on your allies . . .

Maybe that was why NATO was in such a shambles. European countries were squabbling with each other. America was pulling its defences out and retrenching back in its homeland. A ring of steel was going up around the USA: not just missiles and tanks and manpower, but economic steel and the steel of mistrust. The USA could be self-sufficient if it wished, and that was the way things were headed. Companies were finding it harder to export their goods to the States. Diplomacy had about it the air of the refrigerator. What had gone wrong? Just over a year ago, Hepton had been delighted with the way the world was going. The EuroGreens were keeping things sane as far as the environment went, the left wing of the European Parliament was pushing through some worthwhile legislation. The mood was distinctly upbeat. Even Britain was becoming more . . . well, European.

So what had happened? Hepton had blinked and the edifice had started to crumble: squabbles, economic downturns, the troubles in Pakistan and Turkey . . . And now the pull-out. He fumbled for the radio's off-switch and made for the shower. Standing beneath the spray, he thought of the dream he'd had in the night. Mike Dreyfuss had been in it. So had Jilly. They'd been seeking each other, finding each other, but then losing each other again.

When he came out of the shower, he heard the telephone ringing. He ran, naked, to the living room and picked up the receiver.

'Hello?'

'Martin? Is that you? Thank Christ I've found you. I tried at the base but they said you were on leave.'

It was Paul Vincent, sounding edgy. No, more than that, sounding frightened.

'Where are you?'

'I'm still at the nursing home. I've been trying to reach you.'

'What's wrong, Paul?'

'They've got guards watching me, Martin. I mean, they watch me *all* the time. I can't stand it. They said I could leave soon, but I think they're planning something, God knows what. Please, come and get me, Martin. I want out of here.'

'Okay, Paul, just hang on. I'm coming. It'll take an hour, maybe a bit longer. Just keep calm. Okay?'

'Okay. But hurry, please.'

'Paul, I know there isn't any Dr McGill. They never did take you to hospital, did they? And you didn't become ill. Isn't that right?'

Vincent sighed loudly. 'Yes. They said they were security. I was on my break. They asked me to go with them. They brought me straight here. I drank some tea and the next thing I knew I'd crashed out for a solid day.'

'Drugs?'

'They wouldn't admit it, but I get the feeling they'd been questioning me during that time. The bastards won't admit *anything*.'

'You mean the staff?'

'Not all of them. No, these were other people. People brought in by Villiers.'

'With Fagin's knowledge?'

'I don't know.'

'Okay, Paul. Hang in there. I'm on my way.'

'Thanks, Martin.'

Hepton pulled on a pair of denims and a T-shirt, hardly aware of what he was doing. He slipped on his shoes, grabbed his jacket, then took a last quick look around and left the flat, pausing to check that the lock had connected and to turn the key in the mortise. He didn't believe Harry's story of finding the door ajar. He had spent over an hour checking for bugging devices that she might have left behind. He hadn't found any, but that didn't mean anything. There were many other possible points of entry into a closed environment or a telephone line: no one knew better than he what technology was capable of.

Shit, if they were listening in on his telephone, they would already know about Paul. He had to hurry.

Outside, he glanced around as he unlocked the door to his Renault. He crouched beside each wheel arch and peered beneath the vehicle, running a hand around the body in search of a tracking device. Nothing. No black Sierra parked in sight. No tramps picking fruit off the ground. He got into the car, fired it up and sped down the cobblestoned street. He started to think about Paul Vincent, and the line of thought led him back to *Zephyr*. How often did Fagin entertain bigwigs? Three, maybe four times in a year? A large coincidence then that he should have one such party in tow on the day *Zephyr* chose to blow a fuse. Hepton smiled grimly at this, remembering how he had once used the phrase 'blow a fuse' when talking with Jilly about the satellite.

'You mean those things actually have fuses?' she had said, and he'd had to explain that he was using layman's language. She had bristled at this, and insisted that he explain things to her in more technical terms. So for over an hour he'd spoken of SIGINTs and COMINTs and geostationary orbits, while she had listened intently, asking occasional questions. At the end of his explanation, she had smiled.

'You really are a clever little sod, aren't you?' she had said, and he'd nodded. What else could he do?

Clever, Martin, but perhaps not clever enough. He was used to being given orders, used to doing what he was told, to being nothing more than an operative. He seemed a long way from that now. Those uniformed high-ups were still in his mind. Three minutes and forty seconds, and they'd looked pleased. What was it about *Zephyr*? What was it that was so classified even the control personnel couldn't be told of it? For he was sure now that the malfunction had been a test of sorts, that it had been being put through its paces, with the brass there to watch, and that it had passed the test.

But what *was* the bloody test?

If anyone was following him, they were good. He didn't catch sight of a single suspicious car or person on the drive to the Alfred de Lyon Hospital. Everyone was doing his or her bit to seem genuine, from the lady driver who nearly hit him at a junction to the man whose dog ran into the road, causing him to brake hard.

So far so good. Paul Vincent had sounded on the verge of a breakdown. Hepton didn't feel too good himself. His body seemed extraordinarily tired and sluggish, his brain befuddled. He was hoping that Vincent knew more than he had been saying to date. It seemed the only way to unlock the hoard of answers to this whole thing.

He made good time on the drive, steered the car through the gates of the Alfred de Lyon and sped up the gravel drive. He didn't bother with the small car park, leaving his Renault outside the main doors to the building. In the reception hall, he went straight to the admissions desk, where the white-coated lady on duty smiled, recognising him from the previous day.

'I've come to see Mr Vincent,' he said.

'This must be his lucky day,' she said. 'Two visitors—'

'Two?' Hepton interrupted.

'Yes, a young lady arrived half an hour ago to see him.'

'A young lady? Short fair hair?'

The woman nodded thoughtfully. 'Yes, that sounds like her.'

'Is she still here?' snapped Hepton. He was growing afraid now. What if he had missed them? What if Harry had already whisked Paul Vincent away somewhere . . . somewhere Hepton couldn't find him?

'Well, I haven't seen her leave. I'll try Mr Vincent's room.' She picked up the telephone, pressed two digits and waited while the extension rang. Then she frowned. 'There's no answer. Perhaps they've gone to the sun lounge.' An attendant was coming from that direction. 'Oh, Roddy,' she called. 'Have you seen Mr Vincent?'

'I thought he was in his room,' the attendant called back. Hepton felt the hairs bristle on the back of his neck.

'Where's his room?' he said.

'The end of the corridor on the first floor, but you can't just—'

He couldn't just, but he already was: he ran to the sweeping staircase, took it two steps at a time, stumbling at the top, and ran along the first-floor corridor. He pushed open the last door he came to and looked in. It was a large, airy room, the walls cream-coloured and the bed a double. Some of Paul's things were lying about, but not untidily. There was an en suite bathroom, and Hepton paused at this door before turning the handle, expecting the worst.

'Paul?' he called. Then he pushed the door and let it sweep open on its silent hinges. But the bathroom was empty. He felt momentary relief, though he couldn't say exactly what he had thought he would find. Then his neck prickled again. Paul wouldn't have left knowing that Hepton was on his way. He would have stayed close to his room. He wouldn't have let Harry take him away without a struggle. Not unless he'd been drugged . . .

The woman from the front desk was standing at the bedroom door, with the attendant peering over her shoulder.

'He's not here,' she said.

'So where is he?' Hepton's voice was loud, and the woman recoiled a little.

'The stool from beside the bed's not there either,' she said. 'Maybe he's taken it into the garden . . .'

'I'll go and look,' said the attendant, skipping away, glad perhaps of a little bit of action. Hepton was back in the corridor again. He examined the other doors. Three, like Vincent's, were unmarked. Other bedrooms, he supposed. And one was marked *Stores*.

'Where else might they have gone to talk?' Hepton asked the woman.

'Well, there's the television room, of course, but it's not ideal for conversation. Some of our patients are slightly deaf, and they like the volume turned up. Then there's the morning room and the library.'

'Library?'

'Downstairs. It's usually empty. But I'm sure I would have seen them go in there. They'd have had to go through reception to get to it.'

'Would you check anyway?' The woman seemed doubtful. Hepton tried a smile. 'Please?' he said. 'It's very urgent that I talk to Mr Vincent.'

She hesitated. 'Very well then,' she said, and turned and walked back along the corridor.

Hepton stared into Vincent's room. Where the hell could they be? Wait, though: a building like this would need a fire escape, wouldn't it? He walked back along the corridor and continued past the staircase. Just around the next corner was a door marked *EMERGENCY STAIRS*. He smiled and pushed it open.

He was standing at the top of an enclosed stairwell, its steps winding and made of concrete. There was a window looking out onto the hospital's rear car park. He glanced at the dozen or so cars and saw the black Sierra parked there. He smiled again. Then he heard a sound from below him. Heels scuffing on stairs.

'Harry?' he called. He started to descend, then stopped. There was no sound now from below. 'Harry?' he repeated. He listened and heard the sound again. Footsteps, not descending now but climbing. Coming towards him. He was about to approach them, but something about the sound stopped him, something distinctly ominous. The steps were slow and even, and he could hear only one pair of feet. No Paul, then. Only a woman's heels. Silently he retreated a few steps until he was back beside the door and staring down the twelve or so steps to where the staircase turned a corner. There was a shadow on the wall below him. Then a figure appeared on the lower landing.

Harry.

And she was holding a gun.

Her face was devoid of emotion as she saw him and angled the gun up towards his head. Hepton dived towards the door and yanked it open. He threw himself through it and into the corridor, looking to left and right. He heard Harry's feet quickening on the stairs behind him and ran back along the corridor. The receptionist was standing at the top of the main staircase.

'There you are,' she said. 'I've looked, but there's no sign—'

'Get back downstairs!' yelled Hepton, startling her. Then he was past her, running towards Paul Vincent's room. He realised that he should have pushed past her and down the stairs, well away from Harry and her gun. But there were people downstairs, lots of them. He couldn't endanger all those lives. Very noble, Martin, he thought. But now what could he do? He stared at the door marked *Stores*. Beneath this sign was a smaller one indicating that a fire extinguisher was located within. Well, any weapon was better than none.

He saw as he approached that the door was ever so slightly ajar.

Behind him, he could hear the receptionist. She hadn't gone downstairs; instead, she had followed him along the corridor. Any second now, Harry would round the corner and be upon them. Hepton pulled open the cupboard door.

His eyes met a pair of legs. They were hanging a couple of feet above the ground, and on the floor lay an overturned stool. Hepton's eyes started to move upwards, his teeth gritted in growing horror. The body's arms hung limply; the head lolled at a tight angle. A thin metal tube, almost certainly carrying electrical wires for the building's lighting, ran the breadth of the large cupboard's ceiling, and this was what the green garden twine had been tied to.

The green garden twine that was cutting into Paul Vincent's neck.

His face was purple, eyes and tongue bulging obscenely. Somewhere behind Hepton the receptionist shrieked. He leapt forward and wrapped his arms around Vincent's legs, lifting them a little higher, then reached up with a finger to pull the twine out from where it had cut into the neck.

'Get me scissors!' he hissed. 'Or a knife – anything that'll cut this.'

The woman had a small pair of nail scissors in her pocket and handed these to him. After that initial shriek, she had quickly calmed. Hepton supposed she had seen this sort of thing before, working here. He cut the twine and eased Paul Vincent's body down, bringing it out into the hall and laying it on the carpeted floor.

'I didn't know,' the woman was saying. 'I never realised the poor man might—'

'He wouldn't!' Hepton snapped back at her. 'He wouldn't do this.'

He looked past the receptionist, along to the end of the corridor, and saw Harry standing there. Their eyes met, then she turned swiftly and was gone, back towards the emergency stairs.

'Wait!' he shouted.

The receptionist saw him staring and glanced back along the corridor too, but saw nothing. No doubt she thought him emotional and in shock.

Hepton stared at Paul Vincent, then at where Harry had been standing. He made his decision and bent over his friend, pushing Paul's swollen tongue out of the way and sticking two fingers into the young man's mouth, searching down towards the throat, checking if there was a clear flow for air. Then he pinched Paul's nose and gave mouth-to-mouth resuscitation.

'Come on, Paul,' he said. He pushed down with both hands on Vincent's chest, once, twice, three times. Pause. Once, twice, three times again. He checked for a pulse. There wasn't one – but then there was! Faint, but there.

'Is he . . .?'

Hepton turned to the woman. 'Go get a doctor,' he hissed.

'Yes, of course.' She hurried away.

Hepton kept trying the mishmash of life-saving techniques, remembering bits of each of them from the training sessions he had attended more than a year ago. He pushed down hard again on Vincent's chest with the heels of his hands. There was a palpable groan from the inert body. He crawled back to Vincent's head, his mouth close to the deep-red ear.

'Paul? Paul, it's Martin. Come on, Paul. You're going to be fine. Paul?'

The opaque eyes seemed to clear, the mouth trying to form words. But the voice box was shattered, the windpipe raw. Hepton brought his own ear close to Vincent's mouth. There were white threads of saliva at the edges, hanging from swollen lips. The word was hoarse, barely recognisable as speech. But Hepton heard it, where others might have thought it mere babble.

'Arrus . . . Arrus . . . Arrosss . . .'

And then the breath seemed to rattle within, the eyes became filmy, and Hepton could only crouch there, staring at his friend. The doctor was rushing along the corridor now, and would do what he could. It was already too late, Hepton knew. His own ministrations had served only to extend the waning life by a moment. But in that precious moment, Paul Vincent had given him something. A word.

*Argos.*

He left the body, rising slowly to his feet. Then he remembered Harry, and turned on his heel. He ran along the corridor, swung round the corner, pushed open the door to the stairs. He didn't mind now, didn't care if he ran straight into her and her gun. All he held in his mind was burning rage. But a glance through the window showed him that the black Sierra had gone. He leaned his forehead against the glass and closed his eyes.

'Paul,' he whispered. Then he began to cry.

# 14

They sat him on a sagging chesterfield sofa in the musty library, declared the room off-limits to the inquisitive patients and gave him sweet tea to drink. Meanwhile, Paul Vincent's body was being laid out on the bed in his room, his possessions gathered together, his family informed. A tragic suicide: that was what it would become. But Hepton, sipping his tea, knew this was not the truth. A policeman came to see him, a detective in plain clothes. Hepton told him about Harry.

'Yes,' the detective said. 'Mrs Collins on reception said Mr Vincent had had a visitor.'

'She killed him.'

The detective raised one eyebrow. He had already been informed that Hepton was in shock.

'She killed him,' Hepton repeated. 'She had a gun. I saw her.'

'But Mr Vincent wasn't killed with a gun,' the detective said slowly, as though explaining something difficult to a child. 'He hanged himself.'

'No, she did it. She hung him up there.'

The detective decided to ignore all this. He referred to his note-book. 'The name we have for the visitor is a Miss Victoria Simmons.'

Hepton shook his head. 'Her name's Harry.'

'Harry?' The detective sounded doubtful.

'Short for Harriet.'

'And her second name?'

Hepton shrugged. 'I don't know. She's something to do with the military. That's what she told me, anyway. You can ask my boss, Mr Henry Fagin. I'll give you his number . . .'

'Yes, well, meantime just you rest, Mr Hepton. You've had a bit of a shock.'

'I'm fine. But I'm telling you . . .' He looked up at the policeman. A simple-looking face, disguising a simple-working mind. He shook his head. 'Never mind,' he said. 'Never mind.'

The duty doctor gave him a couple of tablets, but Hepton refused them. He didn't need calming down, or cheering up. He didn't require the proffered lift home. He was quite capable of driving himself.

Paul had given him a name: *Argos*. Perhaps the truth had been too obvious, too glaring, too outrageous. But now that he thought it over, it was quite true that the United States space shuttle *Argos* had been in space at the time *Zephyr* had malfunctioned. But *Argos* wasn't supposed to be anywhere near *Zephyr*'s orbit. It had been a thousand or more miles away, launching another satellite. With Dreyfuss on board, now its only survivor. A coincidence? Paul had given him that one word because he had suspected *Argos* of interfering with *Zephyr* in some way. One person would know for sure.

Dreyfuss.

But how the hell could Hepton get to him? There had to be some way. The Foreign Office, perhaps. Their people in the United States would have access to him, surely? That might mean a trip to London . . .

London.

Of course! Jilly would have been keeping in touch with him. Hepton just *knew* she would. Partly from friendship – mostly from friendship, even – but partly because she had a nose for a story, and Dreyfuss was news. That was that then: he'd pack a bag and head for London. But first there were more questions to be asked of him, more tea to be served up and drunk. Why garden twine? Why suicide? Why by hanging? Why in a cupboard? He kept his answers to himself. Garden twine was strong. It wasn't suicide, but murder. Hanging to make it *look* like suicide. A cupboard to prevent the body being found too quickly.

Because Harry had known Hepton was on his way, and there hadn't been much time. Not enough time for an overdose, and not enough time for an abduction. No one, of course, had seen anything. No one had heard anything No chair falling. No choking or kicking. It was a neat operation. Neat and tidy. Hepton couldn't get Harry's face out of his mind.

Eventually they had to let him go. He gave his address in Louth, got into his car and drove off at a steady pace, picking up speed only when he was out of the nursing home's gates, picking up more and more speed until he caught himself doing seventy. Too fast on these roads. Braking, slowing. He didn't want there to be any other accidents.

Parking outside the flat, though, locking the car door, he felt a fresh wave of foreboding wash over him. Harry had killed Paul to stop him saying anything about *Zephyr* and, more especially, about *Argos*. Hepton thought of Harry again: *I like things neat and tidy.* With Paul gone, he knew he himself had become a target. Perhaps the only target left.

He stood at the bottom of the stairwell for a long time, listening. Then he climbed quietly to the first floor. He slowly pushed open his letter box and listened for sounds in the flat. There were none. Then he unlocked the mortise and the Yale lock and opened the door. There was a piece of paper lying on the floor of the hallway. He unfolded it and read: *Need to speak with you. Please come to the Coach and Four, 7.30. Nick.*

Hepton looked at his watch. It was 7.25. He'd have to hurry; the Coach and Four was a good seven or eight minutes' walk away. He'd never been to it before, there being two other pubs nearer the flat. He wondered why Nick wanted to meet him. Perhaps he had discovered something. Well, Hepton had things to tell him too, didn't he? Things about *Zephyr* and *Argos*. Things about Paul Vincent. Things about his death.

It hit him then, standing in the hall with the note in his hand. A huge tremor ran through him, and the strength left his body. He leaned against the wall for support and thought he was going to be sick. Was this what delayed shock felt like? He stumbled into the bathroom and ran cold water into the basin, splashing his face and neck. He wasn't going to be sick; the feeling was passing. He had to be strong, for his own sake. And he wouldn't be late for his appointment.

There was only one real route to the Coach and Four. It took him up a narrow, cottage-lined street, a street he'd always admired. But the people who lived there these days weren't farmhands or labourers or even small merchants. They were estate agents and accountants, most of them working in London during the week, coming here only at weekends. And as this wasn't yet the weekend, the street was deserted. At the end of what might seem to some a cul-de-sac, he turned right into a narrower lane yet, which would bring him out across from the pub. It too was quiet; one side being workshops and garaging, the other the backs of some houses, high fencing protecting the privacy of the gardens. A few brave motorists used this lane as a shortcut, though its surface was rutted and booby-trapped with potholes. He could hear a car now, slowing in the street behind him, turning into the lane. But there was plenty of room for it to pass him.

He turned to look at the car and saw the nose of the black Sierra as it started to speed towards him. Harry, clearly visible behind the windscreen, seemed to be enjoying the look of terror on his face. She gunned the vehicle forwards just as Hepton turned and ran.

He was no judge of distance but reckoned that he couldn't make the end of the lane before the car caught him. He quickly sought an open door to one of the workshops, some garage that hadn't been locked up. But it was useless. The Sierra was only a few yards from him when he made up his mind. He braced himself against the metal door of one of the garages, then pushed off from it and sprinted across the line of the oncoming vehicle. Harry accelerated harder yet, but Hepton had judged it right, and he leapt at the high wall of one of the gardens, his fingers seeking the top edge of the brickwork. They found it, and he pulled himself upwards as the Sierra curved towards him, its front wing searing against the wall. He swung his legs upwards so that the roof of the car just missed them, and hung there, teeth gritted, thinking suddenly and absurdly of the multigym's chinning bar.

The Sierra screeched to a stop at the end of the lane, just as Hepton was about to drop back to the ground. Then its wheels spun and it started to reverse hard towards him. Christ, he couldn't hang on much longer, and he hadn't the strength to pull himself over the wall. But then the car stopped, idled for a moment.

'What's going on?'

Hepton turned his head and saw that a man had appeared from a gate in one of the garden fences. He was in his shirtsleeves and carried a folded newspaper, obviously having just been disturbed from an evening's reading in his garden. Hepton dropped to the ground and watched the Sierra start forwards slowly, turning out of the lane and speeding away.

Of course: there couldn't be any witnesses, could there? It had to look like an accident. Hepton saw it all clearly. The note from Nick was a fake. *She* had chosen the pub because she'd known he had to walk along this lane to get to it. And in the lane there would be no escape, and no one to see the car hit him. But it wouldn't have been hit-and-run. That might have looked too suspicious. No, she would have stopped and played the innocent. She would say he had jumped in front of the car, perhaps, and everyone would come to believe her, because it would be shown that Hepton was distraught, unstable after watching his friend die earlier in the day.

Just another suicide.

'I said, what's going on?'

Hepton snapped out of his reverie, went to the man and shook his hand.

'Thank you,' he said, then began to jog back the way he had come, leaving the man standing there uncomprehending.

He arrived at his car without further incident. They wouldn't want his death to look suspicious, so he didn't bother to check for bombs under the chassis or snipers on the rooftops. He just got in and drove, trembling throughout his body, heading south towards Boston and further on to Peterborough, and beyond that London.

He stopped once for petrol and asked the attendant where he might find a telephone. There was a payphone on the wall outside the gents'. A man was coming out of the toilets, his face wet. Hepton had noticed a car parked beside the pumps. The man smiled.

'Never any bloody paper in these places,' he said, explaining the wet face. Hepton nodded. 'Needed a bit of a splash, though,' the man went on. 'Driving to Leeds tonight. Bloody long way, but the roads are quieter at night than through the day. I'm a rep, you see. You get to know these tricks.'

Hepton smiled again, but offered no reply. The last thing he needed was a lengthy conversation with a professional traveller. The man seemed to take the hint and moved past him, towards the station shop. Hepton turned his attention back to the telephone. He lifted the receiver, slipped a ten-pence piece into the slot and dialled the number of the base.

'Hello,' he said. 'I'd like to speak to Nick Christopher if he's around.'

It took a minute or so, then Nick's voice came over loud and clear.

'Nick here.'

'Nick? It's Martin.'

'Hello, Martin. What can I do for you?'

'I just wanted to check something. You didn't leave a note at my flat, did you?'

'A note?'

No, of course he hadn't. Because he was in Binbrook, not Louth. Because the note had been written by Harry. Which meant she knew Nick Christopher was Hepton's best friend . . .

'Nick,' Hepton said. 'There hasn't been someone there asking questions about me, has there? A woman in her late twenties, short blonde hair, attractive?'

'No, can't say there . . . Hang on, yes, there was somebody here like that. Saw her go into Fagin's office. Tasty piece.'

That was it then. All she'd had to do was ask Fagin who Hepton's closest friend on the base was. Then she'd used his name to lure Hepton into the trap. Not the cleverest of traps, but then it had probably been devised in haste, now that she saw him for the threat he really was.

He rang off and found another ten-pence piece, then took from his pocket the card Harry had given him. He had begun to feel a kind of strange elation at having cheated death. In fact, he felt more alive than he had done in months, perhaps even years. He dialled the number, ready to taunt whoever answered, but heard only a continuous whine from the receiver. He tried again, with the same result. Disconnected.

Had they cleared out then? Or changed the number when they had decided Hepton must die? There didn't seem any other explanation as to why Harry would have given him the card. Unless . . . He studied it more closely. Thick card, inflexible, covered in a plastic coating. Quite a robust thing, really, given that all it contained was a telephone number, and a discontinued one at that. He asked the attendant if he possessed such a thing as a knife. The man looked dubious, but they went to the shop, where he found a Swiss Army knife. The rep was whistling cheerily, selecting a dozen or so chocolate bars before moving on to the sparse display of music cassettes. Hepton chose the thinnest blade on the knife and began to cut along the edge of the card, the attendant watching, unsure what to expect. The rep came over too, his selections made.

The plastic was tough, but once he was through it, Hepton noticed that the card itself was very thin, more like paper. He began to peel it off, revealing a thin piece of metal studded with solder.

'What is it?' asked the rep, intrigued now.

'It's a PCB,' Hepton answered, quite calmly.

'A what?' asked the attendant.

'A printed circuit board. Smallest one I think I've seen.'

There could be no doubting that it was a transmitter of sorts. Crude, as something this size needed to be, but probably effective. Hepton smiled, shaking his head. No need to check your car's wheel arches these days for an unwieldy magnetised box; something the size of a business card would do the job every bit as well.

'Can I pay for these?' the rep asked the attendant and, show over, the attendant nodded, taking back his knife and going behind the counter. Hepton stood beside the rep, waiting his turn to pay for petrol.

'I'd like a receipt too, please,' the rep said to the attendant as Hepton held the transmitter between forefinger and thumb and gently, surreptitiously, slipped it into the man's jacket pocket. He held his breath, then stepped away. But the rep hadn't noticed anything, and with any luck he would continue all the way to Leeds still in blissful ignorance.

'Have a good trip,' Hepton called to him as the man went out to his car. Then, having paid for the tankful of petrol, he went out to his own vehicle, started it and headed off in the opposite direction, whistling.

As he drove, he remembered something and reached into his pocket, bringing out the note Harry had left for him, the one that had led him by the nose towards his intended death. He rolled down the window and threw it out. Was there anything else she had given him? No, nothing, not unless she had planted something on him without his knowledge. He would have to check his clothing.

Wait a minute, though . . . she *had* given him something else: a ten-pence piece to pay for the call she said she had made yesterday evening. He angled a hand into his trouser pocket and brought out all his loose change, scattering it on the passenger seat. Then he picked out the three ten-pence pieces that lay there and threw them out of the window too. He hoped someone would pick them up. If one of them contained a backup transmitter, Harry might have another long, hard and fruitless journey ahead of her.

Something else was niggling him. Several things really. For one, Fagin had ordered him to talk to Harry, to tell her everything he knew. So was Fagin in on it too? Or was he merely obeying orders? And who the hell was Villiers? What was it Harry had said? Something about 'my employers, who are, ultimately, your employers': but who – ultimately – was Hepton's employer? The Home Secretary? The head of the MoD? Someone in London, he'd bet on that. But it might take a journalist's nose to discover the final answer. A good journalist. Someone he could trust.

Supposing, that were, Jilly would even want to speak to him again.

# 15

In fact, the smooth-dressed, smooth-spoken Parfit did not return, and Dreyfuss, who had been keening like a young whelp, grew first agitated and then worried and then frustrated. Parfit had said he was coming back to take him away from Sacramento General, away from the vicious General Esterhazy and the cunning Frank Stewart, away from nurses who weren't real nurses and drugs that did more than merely put a man to sleep. So where the hell was he? What was he doing?

The evening stretched into night, and the night saw Dreyfuss sleepless, pounding the floor of his room on aching feet. A night-duty nurse looked in on him, but he growled at her and she quickly fled. A male attendant, black, uncertain, asked him if he wanted anything.

'Nothing,' he snarled, and paced the cage again.

When breakfast arrived, he found himself waking on top of the bed, still wearing slippers and a dressing gown, his forehead damp with sweat.

'Hot in here,' said the nurse, a teenager who certainly looked more like a nurse than Carraway had.

'Yes, it is,' Dreyfuss answered, sitting up with his back against the mound of pillows. She placed the tray on a trolley and wheeled the trolley over until it was positioned in front of him.

'Ham and eggs,' she said, removing the cover from the plate. Dreyfuss nodded hungrily and started to tuck in. Three or four chews later, he remembered about Parfit, and the hunger left him. He sipped at the coffee, still chewing the food in his mouth, desperate to swallow it but somehow unable to. Eventually he spat it back into his paper serviette.

The nurse returned after twenty minutes and took the tray away. She didn't say anything about the untouched food.

'How are we this morning?' the doctor asked brightly, pushing open the door.

'We're fine,' said Dreyfuss glumly. 'When can we get up?'

'I did hear,' the doctor said mock-conspiratorially, checking Dreyfuss' pulse at the same time, 'that we *had* been getting up. Pacing the floor at all hours of the night.' He stared at Dreyfuss with soulful eyes. 'Hmm?'

'I'd like to leave today.'

'Fine.' The doctor had stopped checking the pulse. He now peered into Dreyfuss' eyes. 'Where will you go?'

'I don't know; a bit of sightseeing, maybe. Book into a hotel, see a few shows . . .'

'In Sacramento?' The doctor laughed. 'No, I think you'd be better staying just here, Major Dreyfuss.'

And that was what he did. Though he willed himself to move, to just open the door, walk down the corridor and leave by the hospital's front door, he had no idea what he might be stepping out into. A demonstration, perhaps; an angry mob; some lone gunman looking to make the news?

He sat tight, his gut quivering whenever someone walked noisily past the door of his room. But Parfit didn't come. Someone else came instead.

Frank Stewart.

'Can I speak to you for a minute?'

'Can I stop you?' Dreyfuss' voice had bite, but he waved for Stewart to sit down. Secretly he was glad of some company.

'How do you feel?'

How *did* he feel? He felt strange, staring into Spencer Tracy's eyes like this.

'I know what you're thinking,' Stewart continued.

Dreyfuss doubted it. 'Go on,' he prompted.

'You're thinking that somehow you're to blame for what happened to *Argos*. Forget it; you couldn't have done anything.'

'I couldn't?'

'Well, could you?'

Dreyfuss thought about this. What was Stewart trying to get him to say? 'I don't know,' he said at last.

Stewart seemed pleased with this reply and drew his chair closer to the bed.

'I know there's something wrong,' he said, his voice almost a whisper. 'I know there's something cooking.'

'Are you CIA or NSA?'

Stewart seemed surprised by the question. 'I'm State Department,' he said.

'Right,' Dreyfuss said, sounding as unconvinced as he felt.

'Okay, okay. I'm on secondment to the NSA.'

Dreyfuss nodded. 'And what,' he said, 'makes you so sure something's "cooking", as you put it?'

'Just a feeling. When you reach my age, you get a nose for these sorts of things.'

Now if that wasn't a line from a Spencer Tracy film, what was? 'What sorts of things?' Dreyfuss asked, enjoying throwing Stewart's statements back at him as questions. This way, he gave himself a little room for manoeuvre.

Stewart's voice grew quieter yet. 'When General Esterhazy was in Europe, another of our staff generals, William Colt, very high up at the Pentagon, sent him a message. It said, and I quote, "Sorry you couldn't make it to the burial." That message was sent at almost exactly the time your shuttle was crashing.'

The burial! Hes Adams' face swam into view amidst the smoke and sparks and heat.

Stewart could see his words having an effect. 'What is it?' he hissed. 'That means something to you, doesn't it? Has it jogged your memory, Major? Not that I believe for one moment that you really *have* got partial amnesia. I've got to hand it to you, though. You've got the doctors fooled.'

'Nurse Carraway wasn't a real nurse.'

Stewart nodded. 'So I understand. Ben Esterhazy had her planted here. I didn't know anything about it.' His voice fell again. 'It's him you've got to be careful of, not me.' Dreyfuss stared at him stonily. Stewart shrugged his shoulders. Then he changed tack. 'I hear tell,' he said, 'that when you landed, the ground crew had to prise Major Adams' fingers from off your throat. Adams was one of Esterhazy's men too. He was his golden boy at one time, but then he screwed up on a mission. Got himself compromised. Then suddenly he ends up on *Argos*. That made me a little curious. What was going on up there?'

Dreyfuss was thinking. Yes, it was true: Esterhazy and Adams had the same words at their disposal – "coffin's got to be buried"; "sorry you couldn't make it to the burial" – and it meant something to both of them, something worth dying for, worth killing for. He *had* to tell someone. His brain was feverish. He felt he would burst if he didn't speak. Where was Parfit? Parfit should be here, not this American secret serviceman. The confessor was wrong, but still the need to confess was strong. Too strong.

He cleared his throat as a prelude. 'We were up there to launch a communications satellite,' he said. 'That's what *I* thought. But it was like some joke was being played on me, like I wasn't being let in on something. They were grinning . . . I think the rest of the crew knew. Hes Adams definitely knew what was going on. We launched the satellite okay. Then I saw some figures on the screen, co-ordinates I thought at the time. And a series of numbers. There was one sequence that kept repeating itself. I tried to memorise it, but it was way too long. I remember how it started, though: Ze/446. I wondered about that, but nobody seemed too bothered. Then I asked Hes – Major Adams – about it, and he laughed.' Stewart's face was so intent at this point that Dreyfuss felt nothing would tear the older man's eyes off him. 'I knew then that something was wrong. And I felt that I wasn't intended to get off the shuttle alive, because I'd been stupid enough to tell what I'd seen to the one man aboard who knew what it all meant. Then later,' he continued, swallowing, 'when we were dying and everything went haywire, Adams started choking me. He was mad, screaming at me, "Coffin's got to be buried!"'

Stewart looked startled at this, then sat back in his chair, as though he were thinking hard. He folded his arms and seemed to require no more from Dreyfuss for the moment. Dreyfuss was thinking too, thinking how hungry he suddenly felt.

'Now hold on,' Stewart said at last. 'Let me see if I've got this straight . . .'

'Got what straight, Mr Stewart?' asked Parfit, stepping into the room.

Stewart looked embarrassed, but recovered quickly. 'Just asking the major here some questions about the flight.'

Parfit looked towards Dreyfuss. 'And does the major want to be questioned?' he asked.

'The major wants to be told he can get out of here,' Dreyfuss said, remembering now that he was angry with Parfit, who had left him here for so long.

Parfit made a sweeping gesture with his arm. 'Your carriage awaits,' he said.

Stewart was rising to his feet. 'Wait a minute. Major Dreyfuss can't just walk out of here. He's under medical care.'

'Nonsense,' Parfit replied. He went back to the doorway, leaned out into the corridor and picked up a large paper carrier bag. 'I hope these fit,' he said, bringing the bag to the bed.

Dreyfuss was already on his feet. He opened the bag and brought out trousers, underwear, a cotton shirt, socks and a pair of canvas shoes.

Stewart watched him dress, but his words when he spoke were directed at Parfit.

'You know this is crazy, don't you? Esterhazy will blow all his fuses when he finds out.' But he sounded as though this was not a wholly unpleasant thought.

'I'm hoping he does just that,' Parfit returned.

Dreyfuss knew there was some undercurrent to this exchange, something they were managing to say to one another without his understanding. He slipped on the shoes. The clothes were a near-perfect fit.

'Ready?' said Parfit.

'Ready,' answered Dreyfuss.

'I'm glad we managed to have some time together, Major,' Stewart was saying. Dreyfuss smiled but did not reply. Parfit had already turned in the doorway, and held the door open as Dreyfuss took his first steps out of the room, into the bright, disinfected corridor.

Parfit kept a couple of steps ahead of him as they walked. Dreyfuss felt elated at first, light-headed, but then started sweating. He had paced his room, but that had called for little real exertion. Now, after sixty or so strides, his hair was prickling and his back began to feel damp. The corridor was quiet: no staff, and all the doors except his own looked to be locked tight. They came to a set of swing doors and opened them. Now they were in a larger, noisier, busier corridor, one of the hospital's main arteries. Dreyfuss looked back at the doors they had just come through and saw that a large *NO ADMITTANCE* sign and a radiation symbol warned the unwary against entering his own silent corridor.

He had been expecting to see an armed guard at least. What had been stopping journalists from trying to visit him? Not just that sign, surely. Then he noticed an orderly sitting on a chair by the door, pretending to be on his break and browsing through a newspaper. His eyes were toughened glass as they fixed on Dreyfuss and

Parfit, and Dreyfuss knew he was a guard of some kind, but an unobtrusive one.

'Does he know who we are?' he said to Parfit as they walked on.

Parfit glanced back towards the orderly. 'Well, he knows who *I* am. I've had to get past him to see you, yesterday and today. But he's here to stop people getting in, not coming out.'

'What took you so long to come back?'

But Parfit was flurrying on again, and it took all of Dreyfuss' energy and concentration to keep up with his pace. The question lapsed.

'How much did you tell Stewart?' Parfit asked.

'Quite a bit.'

'Mmm. That's all right then.'

'What do you mean?' But Parfit wasn't about to answer this question either.

Everybody was too busy being sick or being a comforter of the sick to pay them much attention, but at the main door, Dreyfuss hesitated. Something would happen. They'd be stopped. He'd be dragged back to his room and questioned again. They wouldn't get away with it. As Parfit approached the glass doors, they opened on a motorised hush, and then both men were outside.

Outside, it was warm, but with a strong breeze. And there was cloud cover. A storm was coming. Dreyfuss began to shiver as the sweat on his body cooled. A large sedan pulled up to the kerb, and Parfit opened the back door, ushering him inside. The driver was a thickset man with the face of a well-used hammer. He stared at Dreyfuss in the rear-view mirror. Parfit closed the door after him and they drove off.

'This is Ronald,' Parfit said to Dreyfuss.

Ronald nodded, unsmiling, then concentrated on his driving.

'Where are we going?' asked Dreyfuss.

'Washington. There's a private jet waiting for us at the airport.'

'A private jet? Is that standard Foreign Office issue?'

Parfit smiled. 'It's not ours, I just borrowed it from someone who happened to owe me a large favour.'

Dreyfuss nodded.

'So,' Parfit was saying, 'I think you'd better start at the beginning, hadn't you?'

'I nearly died up there.' Dreyfuss turned towards him. 'Why didn't you warn me?'

'But if you'll remember, I did warn you. That's why we're sitting here today.'

Yes, Dreyfuss remembered all right. The telephone call telling him he'd been picked for the *Argos* flight, and then the arrival at his home of a man in a pinstripe suit, introducing himself as 'Parfit, Foreign Office'. He had come, so he said, to give Dreyfuss a pre-briefing briefing. In fact, he had come with a warning.

The first thing he had done was go through Dreyfuss' curriculum vitae, but in much more detail than the interview panel had done. He had cited Dreyfuss' age as a point against him. Other minus points included lack of experience and slight problems of stamina. Dreyfuss, who had been elated at the news of his selection, began to feel distinctly uncomfortable at this.

'Yes, but they still chose me,' he had said.

'Exactly, Major Dreyfuss,' Parfit had replied. 'Exactly.'

So there had to be a good reason, and Parfit was intrigued to know what it was. Dreyfuss had been bottom of the British list of candidates – no disrespect intended – and they couldn't figure out how he could come top of the American list. But there *would* be a reason, and it was judged worth warning Dreyfuss to be on his guard, and to give him a few tips, a few lessons in the art of survival in a hostile environment.

'You were right about that,' Dreyfuss said now. He had just been telling Parfit what he had told Stewart, but in a little more detail this time. 'I didn't get into a space shuttle, I got into a coffin.'

'So you think the shuttle itself is the coffin that had to be buried?'

'Don't you?'

Parfit rested his head against the seat-back, thinking things through. 'No,' he answered at last. 'No, I don't, not entirely.'

'So what *do* you think was being buried?'

'I don't know. Perhaps we should just ask General Esterhazy. He seems to be involved after all, doesn't he?'

'But you don't think Frank Stewart is?'

'If he were, he wouldn't have been asking you questions the way he did. He wasn't questioning you to find out how much *you* knew. He was doing it because *he* doesn't know much of anything himself.'

'It's a military thing then?'

'Perhaps. Whatever it is, someone's going to a lot of trouble over it, which would seem to indicate that it is fairly special and not very small in scale.'

'Such as?'

'I could only posit a few guesses.'

'Posit away.'

Parfit sighed. 'Anything between an assassination and a war.' He paused. 'They're not mutually exclusive.'

'A *war*?'

'Why not? Look at the way things are going.'

'Christ . . . a war.' Dreyfuss felt weak again. 'But wait, if it's such a big thing, why did they keep me alive?'

'Well, that's easy enough. Five men had already died, and yet you had been pulled alive and in surprisingly good health from the wreckage. The TV cameras and newspapers caught all that. So your sudden death in hospital would have looked a mite suspicious.'

'We were all supposed to die, though, weren't we? All the crew?'

'It looks that way. A kamikaze mission to launch a communications satellite. An unlikely scenario, you'll admit.'

'But it wasn't just a comms satellite, was it?'

Parfit turned towards Dreyfuss and smiled, seeming pleased that he had worked this out. 'The question is,' he said, 'what was it?'

'I know one way we might find out.'

Parfit seemed interested now.

'How?'

'My controller on the ground, Cam Devereux. He might know.'

Parfit nodded. 'It's an idea. But even supposing he knows anything, why would he tell us?'

Dreyfuss seemed not to understand the question.

'I mean,' Parfit said, 'why should he be friendly towards us? Can we assume he's not in on it – whatever "it" is?'

'Well,' said Dreyfuss, 'can you think of anyone else who might have the answers?'

Parfit considered this. 'Off the top of my head, no.'

'Besides which,' Dreyfuss continued, 'I got on well with Cam. He sent flowers to the hospital. We struck up what you might call a special relationship.'

Parfit raised an eyebrow. 'Any particular reason why?'

'We had something in common,' said Dreyfuss. 'As kids, we were both scared to death of roller coasters.'

Parfit stared at him. Dreyfuss smiled back.

'Well,' Parfit said, 'I suppose we've nothing to lose by talking to Mr Devereux. Best wait until we're safely back in the embassy compound, though. We'll try and contact him from there. All we need to do now is find someone who would know what that readout meant. Ze/446 – you've really no idea?'

'No, but if Cam Devereux can't help, I might know someone who can.'

Now Parfit looked genuinely impressed.

'A friend of a good friend of mine,' he continued. 'He works with satellites in the UK.'

'And what is his name?'

'His name's Hepton,' said Dreyfuss. 'Martin Hepton.'

# 16

Hepton took his car to the long-term car park at Heathrow and slept the night there. He awoke cramped and stiff, locked the car and wandered off towards the terminal building in search of breakfast. He hadn't been to Heathrow in what seemed like years. The place was huge, a city almost in itself. Eventually he found what he was looking for, and drank two cups of coffee before buying an over-priced croissant, then another, then a third, chewing each one slowly as he considered his options. His first plan still seemed the best: get in touch with Dreyfuss.

It was early, but the cafeteria section was busy with business executives and security men. Hepton felt scruffy and a little too obvious. He went to the toilets and washed, tidying his hair as best he could. At the sky shop, he bought a comb and a toothbrush. He also bought two newspapers, neither of which carried any mention of Paul Vincent's death. Not that he had expected them to.

He found a cashpoint machine, and was about to empty it of his day's maximum allowance when he hesitated. Would they have access to his bank account? By 'they', he meant Villiers and Harry. If so, they could track him as far as Heathrow just by tapping into the present transaction. On the other hand, he had to have money, and if he took it out now at least they wouldn't be able to pinpoint him to London itself. He might even be about to get on a plane, mightn't he? Running scared and flying for cover. So he pushed the card home, tapped in his identity number and withdrew ten crisp ten-pound notes.

He had decided to leave the car here. For one thing, they had his licence plate number and the car's description, so he didn't want to drive it around London. Besides, he had the feeling that in London a car might actually slow him down. It wasn't a series of roads out there; it was a jungle. Which was all to the good. He wanted to lose himself there, and hope the big-game hunter in the black Sierra went home without a kill.

He took the uncrowded Tube train towards town. It filled up as it hit west London, then became claustrophobic as it neared the centre. South Kensington came as merciful release. But all he was doing here was changing platforms to the District and Circle Line, and the train that eventually arrived was again crowded. How could people live like this? He thought of green fields, of Louth. Of hangings and cars trying to crush him . . . Safety in numbers: that was what a city provided.

So he stopped hating the packed carriage, and rubbed shoulders with an extraordinarily pretty young woman until Westminster, where, despite the temptation to keep travelling, he finally alighted. Tourists were already busying themselves with the day's chores, cameras and video cameras trained on the Houses of Parliament and Big Ben. Hepton headed up Whitehall and realised suddenly that he didn't know which of the large, anonymous buildings he needed. Understated signs beside the impressive doors were the only indication as to their identity. A man was striding purposefully towards him, black briefcase in hand. Hepton recognised the style of the briefcase: soft leather, more a school bag than a business case. There was a small crown above the nameplate. He had seen visitors from the MoD carrying such bags when they came to the base. He stopped the man.

'I wonder if you can help me,' he said. 'I'm looking for the Foreign Office.'

The man said nothing; merely indicated with his head before walking on. Hepton stared at the building towards which he had nodded, then started towards its arched main door.

*ALL PASSES MUST BE SHOWN* declared the sign just inside the doors. Below it, another notice advised that security alert was condition Amber. Security alert was normally at Black. Hepton knew this from his own dealings with the MoD, though Binbrook had its own, different grading system. Above Black came Black Special, which meant there was cause for caution, and after Black Special came Amber. Amber was what government departments had

gone to after the Libyan bombing. Amber was serious, only margin-
ally less serious than Red. Hepton had never seen a Red alert, and,
knowing what it meant, hoped he never would.

The uniformed guard was eyeing him suspiciously.

'Can I help you, sir?'

'I hope so,' Hepton said. 'I'd like to speak with someone about a
friend of mine. This friend is in the United States, and it's vital that
I contact him. Is there anyone here who might help?'

'Why not just phone your friend, sir?'

It was a fair question. Remembering Paul Vincent and Harry,
however, Hepton knew that speed was of the essence. He hadn't
time to muck around, to engage in little games of 'let's pretend'. He
needed to get past this first obstacle quickly, and he knew of only
one sure way to do it.

'Well,' he said, 'it's not quite that simple. You see, he's Major
Michael Dreyfuss, the man from the shuttle crash.'


Eventually he was given a visitor's pass to fill in, which he did, using
the name Martin Harris. Then he was shown to an office along a
sweeping, red-carpeted corridor. There were many doors, bearing
room numbers and sometimes the name of an individual or a section. The room Hepton eventually entered, however, had neither. A
young man sat behind a desk. He stood as Hepton entered, leaned
across the table to shake his hand and gestured for him to take a
seat.

'Would you like some coffee, Mr Harris?' There was a percolator
standing on a table beside the small window.

'Please,' said Hepton.

As the man poured, Hepton studied the room. It had bookshelves,
but no books, and the desk looked to be unused. Though it boasted
some papers and a box of biro pens, there was a layer of dust covering its surface, evidence that this room wasn't often occupied. He
wondered if he had walked into some kind of trap.

'Milk?'

'Please, no sugar.'

He was handed a cup and saucer. The young man sat down again,
sipped, then looked up.

'So then, Mr Harris, what can we do for you?'

'Well, I'm a friend of Major Michael Dreyfuss . . .'

'Yes, so you said.'

'And I really would like to get in touch with him.'

'Any particular reason why?'

'To wish him a speedy recovery, of course.'

The man nodded. 'It's taken you a while to get round to that, hasn't it?'

Hepton reminded himself that he had no time to play games. 'Look,' he said firmly, 'there's just something I need to speak with him about. Something personal, but very important.'

'Oh?' The civil servant had picked up one of the new biros and was examining it. It struck Hepton that he didn't know who this man was.

'I'm sorry,' he said, 'I didn't catch your name.'

'Sanders,' the civil servant said. 'And you said yours was Harris.'

'That's right.'

'Well, Mr Harris, it's just that we have to be careful. A lot of people would like to speak to Major Dreyfuss. I'm sure you understand. Reporters from the less scrupulous newspapers, and other people. So, if there's some way we can establish your identity . . .?'

Hepton cursed silently. Sanders was shrewder than he had anticipated. He shook his head. Sanders appeared to have been expecting this.

'Or,' he said, 'if you can prove your relationship with Major Dreyfuss . . .?'

Hepton thought this over. 'We have a mutual friend,' he said at last. 'Miss Jill Watson. She's a reporter on the *Herald*.'

The civil servant looked up from his pen. 'And she sent you here?'

Hepton saw the implication and shook his head. 'No, no, of course not. She doesn't even know I'm in London, for Christ's sake.'

'No need to lose your temper, Mr Harris.' Sanders was writing Jilly's name on a sheet of paper. 'But you've no proof of identity on you?'

Oh, what the hell, thought Hepton. If they're going to check on Jilly, they'll get my name eventually.

'My name's Hepton, not Harris,' he said.

Sanders seemed satisfied. 'But you signed the visitor's pass Harris. That could get you into trouble, you know. Why the deception?'

'Look, I just want to get in touch with Major Dreyfuss. If you could help me contact him . . .'

Sanders rose to his feet. 'Wait here a moment, would you, please?' He walked smartly to the door. 'Help yourself to more coffee,' he said, making an exit.

Hepton stayed seated, but couldn't relax. This had seemed such a good idea at the time. There was bound to be someone from the FO in contact with Dreyfuss. It had seemed so simple . . . But now he had given them so much, and they had given him nothing. He got up and went to the window, pushing aside the net curtain to look out. All he saw was other windows in another building. They too had net curtains, making it impossible to see into the rooms.

He crossed to Sanders' desk and examined it. The papers, as expected, were just blank sheets. The drawers of the desk were locked. Over at the bookcase, he wiped a finger along one surface and it came away carrying a bud of dust, which he blew into the air. There was another door, a cupboard perhaps, but it too was locked. He went to the percolator and refilled his cup, drinking slowly. What was happening? Where had Sanders gone? Would Harry walk in through the door? Had he delivered himself to her on a plate?

When the door did finally open, Sanders himself stood there, looking composed.

'If you'd like to follow me, Mr Hepton,' he commanded, and they set off together back along the silent corridor and up an imposing staircase. There weren't so many rooms on this second level. A large and busy reception area was the hub of the activity as people walked briskly in and out of the various offices. Telephones rang, and a few visitors sat on modern upholstered chairs, flicking through magazines.

Sanders approached the reception desk and said something to the prim woman seated there. She filled in another pass, which was torn from its pad and handed to Sanders, who in turn gave it to Hepton.

'Sign it, please,' he ordered, and Hepton accepted the proffered pen. 'Best stick to calling yourself Harris,' Sanders advised. 'That way it doesn't get complicated when you've handed back both passes and somebody tries to collate the day's visitors in and out.'

'Right.' Hepton signed himself as Martin Harris and followed Sanders towards one of the doors. This led into a smaller reception, where a young black secretary tapped away at a computer.

'Morning, Sarah,' said Sanders, passing her and pausing at yet another door. Sarah smiled at Hepton, and he smiled back. He was thinking now that everything was going to be all right.

Sanders had knocked at the door. There was a command from within, and he opened it, ushering Hepton into the room before him.

It was a decent-sized office, its furniture a mixture of the antique and the up-to-date. Books lined one wall, while another contained paintings and prints. The fourth and last was taken up for the most part by a large window, again net-curtained. At the window stood a middle-aged man, an important-looking man. The cut of his clothes was expensive, and where his cheeks had been shaved there was a bright ruddiness that bespoke health and wealth. Hepton had the feeling that he had seen this man before somewhere, on television perhaps.

'Ah, Mr Hepton. Do come in, please. I'm George Villiers.'

*Villiers!* Hepton's heart shrank to the size of a peach stone. But he kept his face neutral, betraying no emotion, and finally shook the proffered hand. It struck him that Villiers wouldn't – couldn't – know that Hepton knew about him. He had to stay calm, not give anything away. He breathed deeply to stop himself from hyperventilating. His heart was racing, but he kept his posture stiff.

Villiers motioned for him to sit, and Hepton did so. Then Villiers seated himself and drew his chair in towards the table. Something about his actions – a clipped, rehearsed quality, a feeling that each movement of the body possessed its own cause and effect – told Hepton that he was ex-military. And not all that ex either.

Villiers lifted a sheet of paper from his desk. It was a typed sheet, not the one Sanders had taken with him from that first room. 'Can you tell us why you wish to contact Major Dreyfuss?'

'No,' said Hepton briskly. 'If you could just pass a message on to him that I'm trying to reach him, perhaps—'

'You're on holiday at the moment, aren't you?'

'Yes, but how could you—'

'These things aren't difficult. All right, Mr Hepton. We'll see what we can do. Where will you be staying while you're here?'

'I haven't decided yet.'

'With Miss Watson, perhaps?'

'No, I don't think so.'

'Oh?' Villiers stared past Hepton's shoulder, towards where Sanders stood. 'I was under the impression the two of you were friends?'

'We are. That is, we were.' Hepton's thoughts were quicksilver now. This was a man he'd been told to avoid, told by Paul Vincent, who was now dead. He couldn't afford to let Villiers know anything, and already the man knew too much . . . 'We broke up. We haven't seen one another in months.' Hepton sounded bitter, and made his face look the same. They had to be made to think that he wouldn't be contacting Jilly.

'Ah.' Villiers went back to studying the typed sheet of paper. Hepton noticed that there was a buff-coloured file on the desk, down the edge of which was written a name: *Dreyfuss, Major M.* The paper had undoubtedly come from the file. Villiers seemed to know who Hepton was, and didn't seem overcurious about Jilly. Therefore he already knew as much as he needed to know. Had he gleaned the information from the typed sheet? Hepton doubted it. No, there was another reason why Villiers knew about him.

Villiers looked up suddenly and caught Hepton staring at him. He smiled, as if to say: I know what you're thinking. Then he read through the sheet again, and Hepton relaxed. Villiers *couldn't* know he knew.

'So how will we contact you, Mr Hepton, should we get through to Major Dreyfuss?'

'As soon as I know where I'm going to be, I'll let you know.'

'Yes.' Villiers sounded sceptical. 'That would probably be best.' He seemed preoccupied.

'Is there anything wrong?'

'Wrong?' Villiers looked up.

'I mean, wrong with Major Dreyfuss. Any reason why I shouldn't be allowed to speak to him.'

Villiers smiled. 'Oh no, nothing like that. Nothing like that at all. But procedures, you know . . .'

'Red tape?'

'Exactly. A bore, but it's what we're paid for.' He smiled again, and Sanders laughed quietly.

'Is there someone from our embassy with Major Dreyfuss?'

Villiers' smile vanished. 'Why do you ask?'

'Well, I would have thought it usual to have someone there beside him. To make sure everything's all right.'

'There's someone with him,' Villiers said in a cool voice. 'Don't worry on that score, Mr Hepton. Now, if you'll excuse me . . .'

'Of course.' Hepton stood up.

Villiers reached out a dry, cold hand for Hepton to shake.

'Just tell us when you get settled in somewhere, and then when we get through to Major Dreyfuss, well, we'll take it from there. All right?'

Not really. Hepton felt that he had failed badly. But at least the mood in this office had alerted him to the fact that something was going on out in the States. Perhaps Dreyfuss was in danger from the rednecks who had nicknamed him 'Jonah' after the crash. Perhaps, though, there was another kind of danger altogether. On the other hand, he had walked into the lion's den, and here he was walking out again. He decided to classify this fact a minor victory.

'Thank you,' he said, following Sanders out of the door.

As soon as Hepton had gone, Villiers took a fountain pen from his pocket and scribbled down a brief summary of the meeting. Then he amended the information about Hepton and Miss Watson on the typed sheet of paper, initialled the summary and slipped it into the Dreyfuss file. From the top drawer of his desk, he took out another folder. This one was unlabelled, and into it he slipped the single typed sheet to which he had been referring throughout the meeting. This was the file on Martin Hepton.

He locked his drawer and picked up one of the two telephones on his desk, punching in three digits.

'Sanders is seeing someone to the front door,' he said in a monotone. 'Have them followed. But keep it low-key. A one-man job, if you can.' He listened for a moment. 'No, no forms to fill in on this one. I want it kept strictly off the books.' He listened again, his cheekbones showing red with suppressed anger. 'Yes, I know,' he hissed. 'I'll assume full responsibility, just bloody well do it!' Then he slammed down the receiver and stared at it, thinking hard. Hepton wanted to speak to Major Dreyfuss. If he did so in Villiers' presence, then Villiers would find out all he needed about what both men knew. So why keep two old acquaintances apart? He picked up the other receiver.

'Sarah?' he said. 'Put through a call to Washington, will you? I want to speak to Johnnie Gilchrist.'

# 17

The city was swarming, and there was no shade to be found. Hepton tried to keep to the backstreets, the narrower passages that neither sun nor tourists could penetrate. The tourists were predominantly European and Japanese. The Americans were staying closer to home this summer. He went into a café for a cold drink, but found the heat indoors unbearable, so came away thirsty. The man who had been a dozen paces behind him walking in was still a dozen paces behind him when he walked out. Hepton smiled.

Where was he heading? In all honesty, he did not know. He stepped into a few shops, browsed, then came out again empty-handed. He crossed the expanse of Green Park with the man still behind him, and in Piccadilly he visited two large stores, taking lifts up, stairs down and back-door exits where possible.

He didn't know where he was headed, but he knew where he was avoiding going: the offices of the *London Herald*. Could he face Jilly? What would she say? Would she help him? He tried to rehearse various lines as he walked the streets. They all sounded false. They all *were* false. What was more important, however, was that he should shake this tail before he tried to contact her. Otherwise he would be drawing her into the nasty little web, and that was the last thing he wanted to do.

Lunchtime approached, and he felt hungry again. Breakfast at Heathrow seemed an eternity ago. He touched the roll of banknotes in his pocket and decided to treat himself to something at Fortnum's. But the queue for the Fountain restaurant was disheartening, so he left again. Besides, his clothes were looking decidedly shabby and slept in: definitely not the stuff of a Fortnum's luncheon.

One of the floorwalkers had kept a beady eye on him all the way around the ground floor.

He had been expecting a tail, of course. Now that Villiers had found him, he would want to keep tabs on him. But who *was* Villiers? He appeared to be some not-very-minor official at the Foreign Office. What was all or any of this to him? Hepton didn't know. But he did know one thing. Like a dog offered a bone, it was time for him to shake his tail.

At Piccadilly Circus there was a large record shop – new since his last visit to London and exactly what he was looking for. He entered the noise and the confusion of aisles. At the main door he had spotted a uniformed security guard, and had passed the alarm system with its warning to potential shoplifters. The place was well protected. He walked up and down the aisles, squeezing past this and that browser. He paused by a display of compact discs and saw, from the corner of his eye, the tail browsing a few aisles further along. He smiled and picked up a disc enclosed in a protective clear plastic sheath. On the back of the packaging was a price label and a barcode. Through the barcode ran a strip of silver. Pleased, he examined the disc again. *Barbed Wire Kisses* by The Jesus and Mary Chain. Yes, this would do.

He walked casually back along the aisle, towards where the tail was now enthusiastically reading the sleeve notes to an offering by The Dead Milkmen. As he was about to pass the man, he paused and put a hand on his shoulder. The tail flinched, but kept his eyes on the record. Hepton kept his hand where it was and brought his face close to the man's ear.

'I'm starving,' he said. 'I think I'm going to go to lunch now. Okay?' Then he moved quickly away towards the main doors. The man hesitated, then put the record back into its rack and followed.

Hepton was already on the pavement and hailing a taxi. Damn: the tail would have to hurry. He'd have to find a taxi too, in order to follow Hepton's taxi. As he was about to push open the heavy glass door, a sudden high-pitched whine came from behind him. The security guard was upon him immediately, hands on his shoulders, turning him around. The tail protested, but the guard's hands were patting his jacket, and one of them slipped into the left pocket, bringing out a compact disc.

The tail glared through the glass at Hepton, who was bending to get into his taxi. Hepton waved at him and grinned. Then the door slammed shut and the taxi moved off into the line of traffic.

'Where to, guv?' the driver asked.

'First, a clothes shop,' ordered Hepton. 'Nothing too flashy. And somewhere between here and the Isle of Dogs.'

He reckoned he would need a shirt, jacket and casual trousers. He reasoned that he would be less conspicuous dressed smartly, and also that he needed a change of clothes in any event, otherwise his description could be circulated too easily. It was tempting to relax a little, to forget that somewhere out there Harry was waiting, ready to kill him if she must. He would use his credit card to buy the clothes: even if Villiers had access to his credit card record, it would take a little time for the transaction to come to light. Villiers knew he was in London. The least Hepton could do was make it difficult for the man to circulate a description of him. That necessitated a change of clothes. A change of hair colouring would be an idea, too. And, while he was at it, why not a change of height and weight and sex?

Despite the terrors of the past twenty-four hours – or perhaps because of them – Hepton threw back his head and laughed. The cab driver glanced into his rear-view mirror.

'Glad somebody's happy,' he said. 'Journalist, are you?'

'What makes you say that?'

'We get a lot of journalists come into town at twelve o'clock for a drink, then have to get a taxi back half an hour later so they can start work again. Mad, those journalists are. You know the ones I mean, down at that new place in the Isle, where the *Herald*'s printed.'

'Oh yes, the *Herald*,' said Hepton casually. 'That's where I'm headed to, as it happens.'

'Thought you were,' the driver called, chuckling. 'I've got a nose for that sort of thing, you see. A real nose. But first off, let's see about getting you that clobber, eh?'

# Part III

The result is a complex network of intelligence-gathering and communications installations throughout Britain ... There are two main reasons why there are so many such installations in Britain. First, geography. Britain may be a peripheral country on the north-west fringe of Europe, but to a military planner, things look different. Britain sits astride the shortest route from the US to Europe. American policy is 'forward defence' to prevent war on US soil. This involves monitoring Soviet activities as far forward as possible ... Second, there is the 'special relationship'. While some of the installations are purely British, most are either part of the US military system or linked directly to it.

Ian Mather, *Observer Magazine*, 19 April 1987

# 18

The Isle of Dogs was everything Hepton had been expecting. It was, in fact, a building site, a hotchpotch of half-completed monoliths and half-demolished houses. The headquarters of the *Herald*, however, if not what he had hoped to find (he had fond memories of *The Front Page* and *Citizen Kane*) was certainly what he had thought he might find. The metal and glass cube that was home to the newspaper was protected by a high security fence. A barrier lay across the road at the entrance to the site, and two security men watched from their little prefabricated building there, while video cameras scanned the perimeter.

'Checkpoint Charlie, they call it,' said Hepton's taxi driver, accepting the fifteen pounds' fare and a small tip. 'Cheers then.' And with that he wheeled the taxi around and away.

Hepton stared again at the construction before him, trying to find some hint of a soul. There was none. He walked towards the barrier. One of the security guards donned a cap and came to meet him.

'Can I help you, sir?'

'I'm here to see one of the journalists, a Miss Jilly Watson.'

'Watson, did you say?' The guard was already turning back towards his office. 'Follow me, sir. Expecting you, is she?'

'No, not really. I'm a friend of hers.'

'I see, sir.'

The other guard lazily watched several screens, each one showing a corner of the compound. There was a mug of dark brown tea in front of him, proclaiming its owner to be the *World's Best Dad*. Another bank of screens showed the interior of the large building behind them, where the workers moved like ants. The first guard looked through a sheaf of A4 printed paper on his desk.

'Watson, J. Extension three-five-five,' he said to himself. He punched several numbers into his telephone receiver, and, looking up, saw that Hepton was watching the screens. 'Good, aren't they?'

'Yes,' Hepton responded. It seemed everyone was a spy these days. And everyone had a camera trained on them.

The guard's call had been connected. 'Hello, it's the gate here. Got someone to see Miss Watson.' He listened to a voice speaking at the other end, then put his hand over the mouthpiece. 'What's the name, sir?'

This was the moment Hepton had dreaded. 'Martin Hepton,' he said.

'Martin Hepton,' the guard repeated into the mouthpiece. There was a pause while he listened again, then he motioned with the telephone towards Hepton. 'Wants a word, Mr Hepton,' he said.

Hepton took the receiver cautiously. 'Hello?' he said.

'Martin? Is that you?' Jilly Watson's voice sounded vibrant.

'Yes,' he said.

'What are you doing here?' But it wasn't a sniping question; rather, it was filled with honest and welcome surprise. Hepton lightened: she was *pleased* that he had come.

'I wanted to see you,' he said.

'Great! But they won't let you in here. You need passes and all that kind of stuff. We're not allowed visitors; a bit like a prison.' She laughed. 'If nobody gets in, nobody can steal our scoops, that's what they reckon. What time is it?' She checked her watch. 'One thirty already! Christ, I haven't eaten yet, have you?'

'No.'

'Well, that's settled then. You can take me to lunch. There isn't much around here, but there's a wine bar not too far. Do you have a car?'

'No, I came by taxi.'

'Well, wait at the gate and I'll bring my car round. Okay?'

'Fine.'

'Martin . . .?'

'Yes?'

'It's good to hear your voice.'

Click. The connection went dead.

'Coming down, is she, sir?' asked the first guard. Hepton nodded. 'Nobody's allowed in, you see,' the guard went on. 'Security.'

'Bloody daft if you ask me,' rejoined the second guard, cupping his hands around his mug. The first guard now took off his cap and sat down.

'Ours not to reason why,' he said.

Hepton nodded agreement, but he wasn't about to complete the couplet.


The guard operated the barrier from inside the gatehouse, while Hepton slid into the reassuringly familiar seat of Jilly's red MG sports car. She leaned across to peck him on the cheek, then waved towards the gatehouse and revved the car out onto the main road.

'You look great!' Hepton shouted above the wind and the sound of the engine.

'So do you,' Jilly replied. 'You never used to dress like that.'

Hepton examined his newly purchased clothes. 'I'm on holiday.'

'In London?'

'Yes.'

'And you thought you'd surprise me. How lovely.' The smile left her face. 'I did mean to get in touch, Martin. I didn't want to lose you as a friend. But . . .'

'Forget it.' He tried to steel himself; this wasn't the time to become emotional. 'So how's the job?'

'Oh, fine.' But her voice had taken on a false edge.

'Really?' he prompted.

'Well, no . . . not really. In fact, it's awful. I seem to get all the shitty jobs to do, all the really boring things. I think the editor likes the idea of me, he just doesn't like *me*. If that makes any sense.'

Hepton nodded. 'It makes sense.' He could no longer contain his next question, his first real question. 'Have you heard anything from Mike Dreyfuss?'

'No, nothing, I sent some flowers to the hospital in Sacramento, but I don't know if they arrived. Did you know they'd taken him to Sacramento? They tried to keep it a secret, but our sister paper in the States found out.' She sighed. 'Poor Mickey.'

'Yes. I'm trying to get in touch with him.'

'With Mickey? But why?'

So he told her.


They sat at a corner table in the wine bar. The waitress had cleared away their plates and brought them coffee. There was an inch of wine left in the bottom of the bottle, and Hepton poured it into Jilly's glass. She had sat quietly and attentively all through lunch, while he had continued his story. Now and then she would ask a question, in order to clarify some point, but other than that she was silent. Hepton remembered the day she had ordered him to teach her about satellites. She had been the same then.

Occasionally she jotted a few notes into a clean page of her Filofax, and when Hepton had finished talking, she drew a thick line beneath what she had written so far, then numbered the individual points.

'Well?' he asked. 'Do you think I'm going mad, or is something happening out there?'

She gave her answer some thought. 'I don't think you're mad, no. But at the moment you don't really know what's going on, you don't have any proof that anything's going on, and you'll have a hard job convincing anyone that anything's going on. Despite which, I believe you. But then I'm a reporter, we'll believe anything.' She saw that Hepton was looking dispirited and squeezed his hand. 'You're safe now, Martin. You've got me to look after you.' He smiled at this, but knew she could see he was tired; more than that, he was drained. He needed rest and sleep and to forget about the past few days for a little while.

'Come on,' she said. 'I'll put lunch on expenses, then give the office a ring.'

'Why?'

'To tell them I'm not coming in this afternoon. I'm going to be working on something, and you're going to be resting.'

'I am?'

'My flat's not far from here. You can stay there while I go into town.'

'What are you going to do?' Hepton did feel drowsy, but then he'd had the larger share of the wine. He could feel the effort in each word he spoke aloud.

'I'm going to see what I can find out about this George Villiers character, among other things.'

'Jilly . . .'

'What?'

'You're sure it's okay for me to go to your place? I mean . . .'

'It's all right, Martin. There's no other man around just at the moment. Christ, I wish I had time for one.' She paused, then tapped the Filofax. 'I want to take a look at this. God knows, it'll make a nice change for me to do some sleuthing again. Who can say, there may even be a story in it.'


Hepton was asleep on his feet by the time they reached Jilly's apartment block by the river. He had been expecting, if anything, an old converted warehouse, but in fact the block was of recent design.

'Mock warehouse,' Jilly explained.

There was a security system at the main entrance, and each flat had its own little video screen so that callers could be identified before being let in. That might come in handy, Hepton thought to himself.

The flat itself wasn't huge, though Jilly stated that by London standards it was more spacious than most. The living area was open-plan, with a bedroom and bathroom off it. There was a narrow veranda – not for the nervous – outside the French doors that took up the far wall. And yes, there were views of the Thames, though fairly unsavoury ones. The river itself was a mottled grey colour, and across the water there were gasometers, a stretch of wasteland and not much else.

'You can see for miles,' Jilly said. 'Make yourself at home. I'll try not to be too long, though parking can be hell itself in town.'

'Where exactly are you going?'

She tapped the side of her nose. 'Journalists never reveal their sources, especially before they've visited them. It's bad luck.' She bent down to give him a peck on the cheek, then closed the door behind her and was gone.

Hepton was surprised. He really didn't feel anything more than friendship towards her now. When she'd been far away and inaccessible, he had longed for her, but now that they were together again, there wasn't the same spark. Perhaps Jilly had been right to come to London. Their affair would have fizzled out in any case, wouldn't it? Better to make a clean break. He lay along the sofa and closed his eyes, not intending to sleep. He just wanted to rest . . .

He awoke to the sound of a purring telephone. He hadn't been asleep long, and felt light-headed, disoriented. He reached for the receiver and picked it up.

'Hello?' he said.

There was a silence on the other end, a crackling of wires, and perhaps, in the background, someone's fluttering breath.

'Hello?' he said again. Still nothing. Then a short laugh.

'You've been a very bad boy, Martin.'

Hepton felt his fingers tighten around the receiver.

'Hello, Harry,' he said. The light-headedness left him. He was wide awake now. 'How was Leeds?'

There was that laugh again, laughter lacking humour but filled instead with cruelty. 'Leeds was a clever idea, Martin. I couldn't think why you'd be going there. Then I realised you'd found my little device.'

'How did you track me down?' Not that he was really interested, but he needed time to think.

'I spoke to your employer. He told me how depressed you'd been when your girlfriend moved to London. I thought it was worth a try.'

Hepton's mind was working now. There was no point mentioning to her that he knew about Villiers. It would be a cheap point to score, like throwing an ace onto a low card. No, he'd keep his ace for the moment. But he needed to knock her off balance. She was sounding a little too confident, and this, married to her thoughts of revenge – he could hear how bitter she was about Leeds – made her doubly dangerous.

'You should have killed me back at the nursing home,' he said. 'Don't think you're going to get a second chance.'

'What are you going to do? Run for it?'

'No, I'm going to wait right here.' For Paul, he was thinking. 'And when I see you, I'm going to kill you.'

The laughter this time had a hysterical edge to it. Good: his words were having their effect.

'That's fine, Martin,' she said at last. 'I'll see you soon then. I'm calling from just outside your building.'

And with that the telephone went dead. Hepton paused, put the receiver down and got to work.

# 19

Three short knocks followed by one long.

'Come in, Parfit.'

Parfit entered Johnnie Gilchrist's office. Gilchrist was pouring himself a drink.

'Want one?' he asked.

'Why not?' said Parfit. 'I'll have a small brandy, thanks.'

Gilchrist poured half an inch of Martell into a crystal glass and handed it to Parfit.

'Cheers,' he said. They chinked glasses.

Gilchrist took a mouthful of his own whisky, then smiled, shaking his head.

'I have to hand it to you, Parfit. Getting hold of a private jet like that. I won't ask what favour the owner owed you.' He paused, inviting Parfit to tell him anyway, but Parfit merely savoured his drink. 'How is the patient?'

'He's fine,' said Parfit. 'I don't think he was overly pleased about being brought in from the airport in a crate, but he'll get over it.'

Gilchrist smiled again, then sat down, gesturing for Parfit to do the same.

'How was the City of Trees?'

Parfit looked quizzical.

'That's what they call Sacramento,' Gilchrist explained, pleased that Parfit hadn't known. 'Home of the Pony Express.'

'More relevant, it's also the home of McClellan Air Force Base, which is where they landed Dreyfuss once they'd decided he shouldn't stick around Edwards. To answer your question, the City of Trees was . . . interesting.'

'So your gambit paid off?'

'What gambit, Johnnie?'

Gilchrist rubbed a finger around the rim of his glass. 'Leaving your man there so damned long on his own. You wanted to see what they'd try to get out of him, didn't you?'

'That's your interpretation. I was hoping for . . . a reaction.'

'I take it you got one?'

'Oh yes. You know a man called Frank Stewart?'

'*The* Frank Stewart? National Security Agency?'

'Yes, that's the one.'

'What about him?'

'He was there.'

'Good God. I wonder why?'

'I got the feeling it wasn't so much to do with Dreyfuss as it was to do with General Ben Esterhazy.'

'So Esterhazy was there too?'

'Yes, you were right about that. What's more, he was looking fairly rattled.'

'Oh? Any particular reason?'

'Several, I shouldn't wonder.' Parfit finished his drink and took the empty glass back to the drinks cabinet. He left it there and walked to the window, from where he watched the remnants of another demo as they chanted something incoherent, their fingers pointing towards where he was standing. He gave them a wave, which seemed to anger them further. 'Esterhazy's up to no good, Johnnie. I can't say yet quite what, but I'm getting closer.' He returned to his seat.

'Don't tell me about it, Parfit. It would only make me an accessory. Just tell me what you need.'

'Two things. Two names, to be precise. One is Cameron Devereux. He was a member of the ground control crew on *Argos*. I'd like to talk to him, face to face if possible.'

'And the other?'

'Is someone called Martin Hepton. He works on one of our own tracking stations back in England, somewhere in Lincolnshire.'

Gilchrist considered this. 'Must be Binbrook then. What of it?'

'Dreyfuss knows him vaguely, and wants to ask him about something.'

'Martin Hepton, you say?'

'Yes, why?'

'I had a message from George Villiers in London. He phoned

while I was asleep.' Gilchrist picked up some sheets of paper from the tray on the corner of his desk, finding the one he needed. 'Yes, here it is. It seems Hepton paid Villiers a visit, wanted to know how to reach Major Dreyfuss.'

Parfit sat back in his chair. 'Now that *is* interesting.'

'More than mere coincidence, you think?'

'So Hepton's in London?'

'It would seem so. Right, I'll get on to this Devereux character. Shouldn't take long.'

Parfit was already standing, ready to leave. 'Thanks, Johnnie.'

'Parfit?'

'Yes?'

'How big is this thing? Should I be starting to make noises in the direction of our masters?'

'I'd leave it for now,' said Parfit confidently. 'It might all blow over.'

Not that he believed it would. He just didn't want more people than absolutely necessary knowing he was on to something. It was all down to trust in the end, and Parfit didn't trust anyone. Not even Johnnie Gilchrist, not entirely.

# 20

Dreyfuss had been given a room containing a foldaway bed and not much else.

'Not so different from the crate,' he had commented on arrival. Not that he had minded the crate too much. He didn't want anyone knowing he was in Washington with the climate the way it was right now.

Parfit explained that most of the embassy staff were sleeping on the premises these days, so beds and furnishings were scarce. However, he did return a couple of hours later with a portable television, a radio and some books.

'If anyone asks where they came from,' he said, 'say they were here when you arrived.'

Dreyfuss nodded at this. He didn't want to know where these items had come from, and he didn't care where they had come from; he was just glad that *he* had them now, and not someone else. His room, such as it was, must have been a storeroom. At least he could think of no other use for a space measuring twelve feet by ten and tucked away in the furthest, highest corner of the building. There wasn't even a window, but there was a small skylight, desperately in need of a clean.

'I'd have been better off back at Sacramento General,' he commented.

'I really do doubt that,' said Parfit.

There was a knock at the door, and it was pushed open by a feisty individual wearing half-moon glasses. He was breathing hard, obviously unused to climbing the stairs to this attic level.

'Ah, Parfit,' he said.

Parfit introduced the two men.

'Major Michael Dreyfuss, this is Johnnie Gilchrist, a colleague of mine.'

'How do you do?' said Gilchrist, shaking Dreyfuss' hand. Then he noticed the portable TV. 'Nice-looking model. I've one just like it in my own room.'

Dreyfuss tried to avoid Parfit's eyes.

'So,' Parfit said, 'what brings you so far out of your lair, Johnnie?'

'I'll tell you. I've been trying to make contact with this man Devereux.' Dreyfuss and Parfit both looked interested, and there was nothing Gilchrist liked more than an attentive audience. 'Devil of a job I had, too.' He turned to Dreyfuss. 'These days, Major, the international situation being what it is, a diplomat's life is not easy. Not that it ever was.' He looked around the room. 'Don't believe I've been this far north in the building before. But I do recall some story – before my time – of some of the secretaries squeezing out of that skylight to sunbathe nude on the roof. One of them's supposed to have gotten herself stuck, and—'

'What about Devereux, Johnnie?' interrupted Parfit.

Gilchrist hated to have his stories ruined. His eyes blazed away at Parfit for several seconds, then he said simply: 'He's gone.'

'Gone? You mean disappeared?'

'Not in so many words. Apparently he was a bit shell-shocked when the shuttle crashed. So now he's on extended leave.'

'Do we know where?'

'You won't believe it, Parfit, but it seems he's gone to London.'

'London?'

Now Parfit and Dreyfuss exchanged glances.

'I'm not sure,' Parfit said, 'whether that's to our advantage or not. What do you think, Johnnie?'

'Well, we can have him traced and picked up easily enough.'

'Yes, but can he give us the information we need by telephone? I was rather hoping to speak to him in person. Any explanation he can give might be a bit technical, mightn't it?'

'Why don't we get someone who knows about satellites to talk to him for us?' Dreyfuss asked.

'Someone like Martin Hepton,' said Parfit.

'Hepton?' Dreyfuss sounded uncertain.

'He'd be perfect. For one thing, he knows about satellites, and for another, he's in London.' Parfit turned to Gilchrist. 'Get your man Villiers to find out where Hepton's staying. We need to speak to him.'

'I've just had a word with Villiers, actually,' said Gilchrist. 'He said Hepton had mentioned the name of a friend in London. Jill Watson. Villiers didn't reckon Hepton was headed there, but there's always a chance . . .'

Parfit noticed the numb look on Dreyfuss' face. 'What's wrong, Major?'

'I don't want Jilly getting mixed up in this,' Dreyfuss hissed. 'Anything but that. Keep her out of it, Parfit.' He grabbed at Parfit's wrist and held it tight. 'Keep her out of it!'

# 21

Hepton went to the door and studied the tiny surveillance screen. It showed the main door of the block, and, at the touch of a button, the interior hallway as well. There was nobody about. It was five o'clock. People would still be at work. More importantly, there was no sign of Harry.

He went back to his exploration of the flat. He found a chef's knife in the kitchen drawer and slipped it into his pocket. In another drawer he found a large box of matches. He shook it to convince himself of its contents, then slipped it into his pocket too. From the living room's waste-paper bin he took a copy of the previous day's *Herald*, then, so armed, returned to the front door of the flat and opened it.

He looked left and right along the corridor. All clear. Then he stared up towards where the smoke detector sat, a neat little unit flush-mounted into the ceiling. He had noticed it upon arriving. He always noticed ceilings.

That, Martin, he said to himself, is what comes of an adolescence spent staring upwards.

The rolled-up newspaper took a little encouragement, the first three matches failing to catch. He tore a few strips down the sides, then tried again. These strips caught and ignited the rest of the paper. The ceiling was high, and he stood on tiptoe beneath the smoke alarm, holding the newspaper as close to it as he could.

It took forever. His arm ached, and he wondered what he would say if someone happened to emerge from one of the other five apartments along the corridor. But no one did. The paper started to smoulder, the smoke rose, and finally the detector began to whine, setting off alarm bells all around the building.

Elated, Hepton darted back into the flat, stubbed out the flaming newspaper in the sink and poured some water on it. He went back to the video screen at the front door and saw that people were already emerging from their apartments, milling in the main hallway downstairs. He went out onto the veranda and waited. There was a stiff breeze and he breathed hard, staying calm. The Thames was smelling like a sick old pet, but he didn't mind that. He leaned out over the balcony and peered down onto the veranda of the flat beneath, then pulled himself back. There was no need to be rash. He could take the stairs to ground level, the same as the other inhabitants. He already had the evidence of his own eyes and his continuing life to the fact that Harry did not like a crowd. She enjoyed doing her slaying in private.

Suddenly he heard what he had been waiting for: approaching sirens. He rushed back inside and out into the corridor. A couple of people, looking as though they had been disturbed in the act of coitus, were standing by the lift, their clothes disarranged. The man was frantically pressing at the button beside the doors.

'I shouldn't think you'll get much joy,' Hepton informed him. 'These things shut off when there's an alarm. It's much safer to use the stairs.'

'Is there a fire?' the man asked.

'Yes, upstairs,' said Hepton. 'We'd better hurry.'

The three of them set off downstairs together. At the third landing, they joined a slightly larger group.

'*Is* there a fire?' someone asked.

'Yes,' the man with Hepton said, mimicking him. 'It's upstairs.'

Between the third and second landings, Hepton, to the rear of the small party, saw that someone was pushing their way back up through the descending group. There was always someone, someone who'd forgotten a treasured memento or the pet cat. He was about to remonstrate when he realised it was Harry. She was pushing hard now, her anger showing. And in her eyes he saw a kind of madness. There could be no doubting: she was out to kill him, witnesses or no.

Then she glanced upwards and, separated from him by only a handful of bodies now, saw Hepton. Her eyebrows rose in victory, and she dug a hand into the pocket of the checked jacket she was wearing. But the hand stuck there as somebody tried to squeeze past her downstairs.

'You should go back, love,' someone warned her. 'Save yourself. Never mind what's up there.'

Hepton turned on his heel and started up the carpeted steps two at a time, pushing hard as though his knees were mechanical pistons. The banisters were new. Dark polished wood with brass supports. His arms pulled hard on them, heaving his body upwards. He didn't pause at the third floor – he needed territory he could recognise. Instead he left the stairs at the fourth floor and ran back to Jilly's flat. Once inside, he closed the door quietly, then locked it. He realised that his right hand was gripping the kitchen knife. The video screen showed him the main lobby on the ground floor. People were beginning to move outside, some of them explaining to a fireman where the blaze was situated. Hepton could no longer hear the sirens and supposed they had been turned off. Well, he couldn't give them a fire . . . but fire was useful in other ways.

He walked quickly to the kitchen and filled the largest pot he could find with water from the hot tap. Then he manoeuvred it onto a ring of the gas cooker and turned the flame on full blast. It was Dark Ages stuff, but potentially effective. He pondered the contents of the food cupboard. The only pepper, though, seemed to be in the form of peppercorns. Useless. He cursed Jilly's yuppie lifestyle. Where were the tools? The saws, electric drills? The screwdrivers and spanners? What use was the broken edge of an empty champagne bottle against a killer toting a gun?

Then it struck him: Harry knew that Hepton had come to Jilly's flat. Therefore she would know Jilly's name . . .

*And Jilly's name was engraved on the front door's silver nameplate!*

Cautiously, Hepton took a few paces towards the door. He could hear no sounds. Maybe Harry had taken a wrong turn. He pressed his ear to the door. Still no sound. Then the world exploded.

The solid wood of the door splintered just a few inches to his right, beside where the battery of indoor locks was placed. There was a roaring in his ears, the result of the explosion. Another gunshot splintered more wood and severed the first lock's mechanism.

Hepton walked backwards into the kitchen. The pot was bubbling on the hob, and he lifted it with both hands grasped around the handle, walking back into the hallway just as a third shot severed the final locks and Harry's foot kicked the door open. She saw Hepton directly in front of her and raised the pistol, but then saw what he was holding . . .

Some of the water sloshed out onto Hepton's hands and wrists, scalding him, but he felt no pain as he held the pot out to one side like a tennis player preparing a double-handed return. He swung it forward, then jerked it back again. Harry was already half turning away from the water, and it caught her sideways on, spraying her clothes and her hair, splashing across one cheek, one ear, one tightly shut eye. She gasped, and Hepton threw the pot down, starting towards her. But her survival instinct was as strong as his, and blindly she brought the gun up and started firing. Firing wildly, but even a wild bullet was lethal.

Hepton dodged back into the flat, slammed the door shut again and ran. His eyes were focused on the open French doors. Then he was out on the veranda, and there was only one route possible. He swung one leg over the edge of the balcony, then the other. Crouched, gripping the steel rail, he let his feet slide off into space. He gained momentum, swinging his legs, the edge of the veranda hard against his stomach, then took one last swing outwards, started in again and released his hands. Like a high jumper, he felt his backbone graze the rail of the balcony below. Then his feet touched its solid floor and he pulled himself upright. Only to stare at the French doors, identical to Jilly's in every way except one.

They were firmly locked. He cursed. Somewhere above him, Harry had stopped shooting and was screaming instead.

'I'm going to kill you, Hepton! Going to shoot you to hell, you bastard!'

He looked left and right and saw with relief that the next apartment along had its windows open to the elements. There was no time to waste. He climbed nimbly onto the rail and leapt across the four-foot gap, landing safely and darting inside just as Harry arrived at the veranda diagonally above and, her sight restored, but still hurting, fired two shots into the balcony floor behind him.

He ran through the living room and pulled open the door into the hallway, taking the stairs down three at a time until he arrived in the lobby.

'Look, there he is now,' the man who had been standing at the lift said to a fire officer. He was pointing at Hepton.

'Excuse me, sir, I believe you know—' the fireman started, but Hepton simply pushed him aside and walked quickly from the building.

There were two fire engines parked outside, their blue lights flashing but the firemen themselves looking relaxed: just another false alarm. A bright red MG turned the far corner and began speeding towards the block. It was Jilly. He waited until she had almost pulled up next to the fire engines, then leapt forward from the crowd. She saw him and stopped the car, rising from her seat.

'Martin! What's happened?'

'I'll tell you later.' He heaved himself into the passenger seat. 'Just get us out of here.'

She hesitated, wanting to know what was going on.

'Let's go!' he shouted, and his voice frightened her. She started the car off, did a three-point turn and, watched by the huddle of neighbours, drove back the way she had come. Hepton tried scanning the rear of the car, both sides and the front all at the same time.

'Martin?'

'What?'

'What the hell are you up to?'

'Just keep driving. I'm looking for a black Sierra.'

'You mean that woman Harry?'

'Yes. She came to the flat. She's just tried to kill me.'

'Christ.' Jilly's face lost a little of its colour. 'Did she start the fire?'

'What?' He looked at her, then grinned. 'Oh, no, I did that. Don't worry, all I did was set the smoke alarm off.'

'So you could make a getaway?' Jilly seemed impressed. 'That's brilliant, Martin.'

'It might not have been if you hadn't shown up.' He noticed that his hands were stinging, and examined them. White blisters were appearing where the water had scalded him. Jilly grimaced.

'Those look sore.'

'They're nothing,' said Hepton, meaning it. He hoped Harry was in agony.

'So where to now?' asked Jilly.

'A hotel, I suppose.' He was still checking for a tail. 'I can't believe there isn't someone on to us. Drive into town, Jilly. That way maybe we can throw them off.' Looking out of the side window, he saw a red Vauxhall Cavalier driving very fast in the direction from which they were coming. Detectives, he guessed. On their way to a fire that never was. With any luck, they'd pick up Harry. But he doubted it.

'Well I must say, Martin,' said Jilly, attempting levity, 'this isn't the way I usually end my working day. Normally it's a gin and tonic at the wine bar.'

Hepton turned to her again. His look was contrite. 'I'm sorry you had to get mixed up in this, Jilly.'

'I'm not.' She was smiling. 'Besides, I haven't told you yet what I found out about your civil servant.'

'You mean Villiers?'

'Who else? Martin, you're not going to believe it.'

'Try me.'

'Well, your description of him was spot on. You know you said you thought he had some kind of military background? He was in the Royal Marines until not too long ago. A major, to boot. Pretty high up. There was a fight on Brown Mountain – at least I think that's what it was called. Anyway, somewhere on South Georgia. Villiers led his men into what turned out to be a trap. A lot of them were killed. It was hushed up here, of course. Bad for morale.' Jilly was warming to her story, and as she continued, she pushed a little harder on the accelerator. 'Villiers seems to have snapped. He'd seen plenty of action. Oman in the fifties, Belfast in the sixties and seventies. But something happened to him in the Falklands. After he saw his men die, he just couldn't stop killing the enemy, and when the enemy were dead, he turned on his own men. Kill crazy, they call it. Apparently it happens sometimes.'

'Christ,' said Hepton quietly.

'He was a good soldier, too.' Jilly slammed her foot on the brake as a red light loomed. She idled the car and turned towards Hepton. 'They had psychiatrists on him from the minute he landed back home. He seemed normal enough by then, but nobody was taking any chances. Bad for public relations, having a killer in your midst.'

'So they pensioned him off?'

'One of the disabled. They even gave him a medal, I forget which. It's in my notes.'

The car started off again, turning left at the lights.

'And the government hired him?'

'Well, yes, in a way. The Foreign Office gave him a job. His actual title is pretty vague, but he knows his stuff: countries, political climate, that sort of thing. God only knows why it had to be him you saw when you visited the FO.'

'Because,' said Hepton, 'he'd been expecting me.' His voice was level. 'He'd figured out, you see, that I was curious and that my curiosity would probably lead to Mike Dreyfuss.'

'But how could he know?'

'He's a cunning little bastard. Cunning enough to string us along, because he doesn't know we know about him. *That's* our big card. Meantime, he'll probably want to know just *how* much *I* know.'

'What about this Harry, though? She just wants you dead, period. Isn't she working for Villiers then?'

'I'm not sure.' Hepton thought it over. 'No, I'm sure she *is* working for him. Or, at least, they are both working for the same ultimate employer.' Harry's words were coming back to him: *my
employers, who are, ultimately, your employers.* But what did it
mean? 'In any case,' he said, 'I think Harry's become . . . what was
that phrase you used? Kill crazy? Yes, that's what she is. Kill crazy.'
He examined the cars moving past them. Then he turned to Jilly
again. 'How did you find all this out anyway?' He was both
impressed and curious to know.

'A guy I met at a party,' Jilly explained. 'One of the old guard of
Fleet Street hacks. He's been around a bit, reported from Afghani-
stan, Belfast, Beirut, that sort of thing. It's a passion with him, the
military. He's written a couple of books. He was able to tell me some
of it off the top of his head. The rest he got by making a few phone
calls. That's what you call a network. Every good journalist needs
one.'

Hepton's mind was still trained on Villiers. 'Yes,' he said vacantly.
A network . . . 'Anything else?'

'Isn't it enough?' Jilly sounded slighted. She was checking in her
rear-view mirror.

'Yes, yes, I suppose so. Thanks for . . .' She was still staring in the
mirror. 'What is it?' He turned and caught a glance, three cars back,
of a dark-coloured Sierra. 'Shit,' he hissed, gripping the seat with
his hands.

'Is that her car?' Jilly asked, her voice level.

'I think so.' Hepton looked back again. The dark car was in the
process of overtaking one of the vehicles between them. He let out a
sigh of relief. 'No, it's okay. It's not a Sierra. It's a bloody Cavalier.'

Jilly's shoulders relaxed too. She was nearing another set of
lights. 'I think there's a shortcut here, unless they've blocked it off.'
She signalled left and squeezed the MG into an alleyway. The high
buildings either side seemed purpose-built to hem them in. There
was a screech of tyres behind them. The Cavalier was following,
speeding up. Hepton remembered the night Harry had tried to run
him down in an alley almost as narrow as this, and every bit as
deserted. Then he recalled that he had seen the red Cavalier before:
hurrying towards Jilly's flat as they were making their getaway.

'They're chasing us!' he called.

Jilly responded to the Cavalier, pushing the MG down a gear and
hitting the accelerator. They were running now, careering past
parked cars, braking hard to take an almost impossibly tight

turning into a two-way street. Hepton held on, teeth clamped together. Jilly was a good driver, but not good enough. They weren't going to shake the Cavalier. It was mere yards behind them now, and he peered through its black-tinted windscreen. Two men. Definitely men, though he couldn't have said more than that. Not Harry, then.

The extended blaring of a car horn brought his head round to the view to the front of the MG. It took him a moment to realise that the horn was their own, and that the heel of Jilly's left hand was hard against it. She had turned the headlights on full-beam, too. The traffic was becoming clogged. She scraped past a bus, paintwork peeling like confetti, but ahead the lights were at red, and the traffic was at a standstill in both directions.

'Hang on!' Jilly yelled, throwing the MG to the right, braking hard as she did so and spinning a full one hundred and eighty degrees. On the other side of the road now, the Cavalier roared past them, braking hard itself. There was a squeal as the driver threw his wheel round, bumping onto some central bollards. These stopped him, and he reversed, the traffic cursing angrily all around him. Jilly glanced back to see that the Cavalier had lost a lot of ground, and let out a whoop.

'Where did you learn a stunt like that?' Hepton gasped. His heart felt like a bird in a cage too small for it, fluttering against the bars. The breath came from him in short bursts.

'I didn't,' Jilly answered, clearly enjoying every moment of this. 'Put it down to instinct.'

'Fine. But every traffic cop in the area's going to have our description and registration in about five seconds flat.'

'Five seconds? Don't talk daft.'

'Haven't you heard of car phones?' Hepton yelled. 'Half those BMWs you just nearly totalled will be on them right now.'

'What are you saying, Martin? That we ditch the car and *walk*?'

'Just get us away from here,' he said, looking back again. 'And fast.'

Jilly looked in her mirror and saw that the Cavalier was not about to give up the chase. In fact, it was gaining at a steady rate.

'Bastards!' she yelled. The lights ahead were turning red. She held the horn down again and pulled the car into the middle of the road, passing the waiting line of traffic. There was a no-right-turn sign, so she threw the car to the right just as the other traffic was responding to the green light. Hepton looked out of his side window and saw a motorbike messenger heading straight for him. On Jilly's side, a white van was already braking, but too late. The front of the van hit Jilly's door, sending the sports car scudding sideways, where it collided with the bike. The driver was thrown clear, rolling like a pro. Another day in the city. Jilly tried to keep the MG moving, but her front driver-side wheel had buckled. The car protested, growling meanly.

'Last stop,' she said, face pale. The Cavalier was manoeuvring slowly, gingerly past the stalled traffic. Drivers were opening their doors to take a look at the mad bastards who had caused the accident.

'You ought to be fucking well locked up!' the van driver screeched. The bike courier, however, was casually examining some scuffs to his leathers, uninjured himself. Jilly got out of the car. So did Hepton. The Cavalier stopped beside them. Hepton's hand went into his pocket and found the knife he had taken from the kitchen.

'We could run for it,' Jilly said, but her legs were shaking wildly.

The doors of the Cavalier opened and the two men got out. Hepton recognised one of them. It was Sanders, the man from the Foreign Office. Sanders turned to his partner.

'You better stay here, Clive.' He surveyed the chaos. 'Try to clear this up with the police when they arrive.' Then he nodded in Hepton's direction. 'I'll take these two back with me in the car.'

The other man nodded slowly, not looking at all happy with his allotted task, but unable or unwilling to protest.

'Where are we going?' Hepton asked as he and Jilly walked to the car. His grip on the knife relaxed.

'I'm getting you out of this,' Sanders said, indicating the scene around them. He was shaking too, obviously not used to car chases and crashes. 'I would have thought that was reason enough for you to be grateful.'

'It is,' said Jilly. Even her lips had gone white with shock.

'How did you find us?' Hepton asked.

Sanders shrugged. 'I used a bit of initiative. Besides, what other leads did I have? All I knew about you, Mr Hepton, was that you had a friend in London called Jilly Watson who worked on the *Herald*. It wasn't too difficult to find out where Miss Watson lived. Then when I saw you racing away from the scene like that . . .'

'Someone tried to kill me back there,' commented Hepton, seeking a reaction. Sanders raised an eyebrow, nothing more. Hepton decided to try another tack. 'I lost your first tail, though, didn't I?'

'First tail?' Sanders seemed genuinely puzzled. Hepton beamed. He'd been right: Villiers was using the department for his own ends, without everyone knowing about it. Sanders, for one, didn't seem to be aware of the tail. He would bear that in mind.

'I'd still like to know where we're going,' he persisted.

'There's an old friend who wants to speak to you,' Sanders answered, his irritation showing.

'Who? Villiers?'

'Mr Villiers, yes. Indirectly. But someone else.'

'Who?' Jilly asked, wondering herself now; the mention of Villiers bringing with it a renewed sense of menace.

'A Major Michael Dreyfuss,' said Sanders, sliding into the driver's seat. 'Now come on . . .'

# 22

George Villiers was frowning when they arrived at his office. One hand rested on the telephone in a manner suggesting his frown had something to do with a recent call. He looked up as Hepton and Jilly entered. Sanders stayed outside, closing the door on them. The evening light was a deepening orange, casting long shadows in the room and creating a nimbus around Villiers' head.

'You really have caused us a great deal of trouble,' he stated. 'God knows whether we can keep it out of tomorrow's papers.'

'Blame your henchmen,' said Jilly, sitting down without being asked. She had regained her composure during the drive to Whitehall. Indeed, having realised that she was about to get away with breaking every traffic regulation in the book, she was on something of a high. She crossed her legs and folded her arms. 'They were like maniacs,' she explained, studying Villiers. 'Martin's life is in danger, and then they came racing after us. What were we supposed to do?'

Villiers' face showed no emotion. He turned to Hepton, who was about to sit down.

'*Is* your life in danger, Mr Hepton?'

'Oh yes,' Hepton said quietly.

Villiers appeared to ponder this, then picked up his telephone and waited.

'A pot of tea,' he ordered when the line was picked up. Then he replaced the receiver.

'What's this about Mickey?' Jilly asked.

'Mickey?'

'Major Dreyfuss,' Hepton explained.

'Ah.' Villiers paused. 'Sanders told you then.'

'He wouldn't say anything other than that.' Jilly was up on her feet again. She was nervy still; that much was more than obvious. Hepton hoped she could keep in control. It was a kind of madness to have come here, and yet it felt like the right course of action. The questions still needed answering, and who better than Villiers to do it?

'Right.' Villiers leaned forward, resting his arms on the desk. 'Well, it's true enough. After Mr Hepton called here, I was able to contact our embassy in Washington. Major Dreyfuss is there at the moment, though that must remain strictly between us. Ah . . .'

Sanders pushed open the door and brought in a tray, the cups chinking together as he moved.

'I hope you're a better tea-maker than you are a driver,' Jilly commented, the hint of a sneer on her face.

Sanders paused, but chose to ignore her. He left the tray on the desk in front of Villiers, then exited again. There was something else on the tray beside tea. It was a sheet of paper. Villiers slid it towards himself, glanced at it, then turned it so that the writing was facing away from him. His right hand went to his inside pocket and came out with a fountain pen, the top of which he removed to reveal a gold nib.

'Miss Watson?'

'Yes?' Jilly stopped pacing and came to the desk. 'What's this?'

'Routine, I'm afraid. I know Mr Hepton has already signed, as was required of him when he started work. If you would just . . .'

Jilly picked up the form and studied it. It was simple and to the point. It was the catch-all.

'The Official Secrets Act?' she said, smiling. 'Well, why not?' She snatched the pen from him and scratched her name on the paper, then handed back both paper and pen. Villiers looked satisfied, and slid the sheet into the top drawer of his desk. 'I don't mind signing something I'm quite willing to break,' Jilly said with finality. Villiers' satisfaction took the slightest of jolts. Jilly had picked up the teapot. 'Shall I be mother?'

Villiers accepted his cup with what grace he could muster. He was still playing the senior civil servant.

'So what's this about Dreyfuss?' asked Hepton, growing impatient.

'Ah yes, Major Dreyfuss. Well, he'd like a word with you.'

'With me?' Jilly said, hopefully.

'Alas, no, with Mr Hepton.'

'*Me?*' Hepton could not hide his surprise. 'Whatever for? He hardly knows me.'

'Yes, but he knows you by reputation, apparently. The embassy will be calling in another five minutes or so.'

'But what does he want?'

'I really can't say.' Villiers sat back, lips tightly closed, as though prepared to sit out the time before the phone call in silence.

'Tell us about the Falklands,' Jilly said nonchalantly.

Villiers twitched and leaned back in his chair, as though he had just been given a mild but unpleasant electric shock.

*No*, thought Hepton. This wasn't the time to give away secrets. He saw why Jilly had done it. She was a journalist, a journalist who knew something about the man before her. Her professional instinct was to go for the jugular, startle him into some kind of revelation, get him worried . . . but this wasn't a newspaper story. This was entirely more serious.

'Jilly,' he warned, 'not now.'

'Why not?' she snarled. 'Why not now?'

'Because I say so.' His voice was cold and hard, but his eyes were ablaze. She read his thoughts and seemed to understand them. Villiers had a bemused smile on his face.

'I'm sorry,' he said to Jilly, 'what was it you were about to say?'

Her cheeks were red. 'Nothing,' she said.

Villiers turned to Hepton. 'You know I served in the Royal Marines then?' Hepton stayed silent. 'You both seem to know a lot about me, Mr Hepton. Now why should that be? Why should a lowly civil servant interest you so much? Hmm?'

But now it was Hepton's lips that stayed tight shut. Villiers rose from his chair and turned to stare out of his window. Hepton glanced at Jilly, whose face looked pained. She mouthed, 'I'm sorry,' at him. He merely winked in reassurance. Villiers turned back to face them.

'I'm not sure speaking with Major Dreyfuss would be such a wise move,' he stated. 'I'd like you both to leave now.'

Hepton hadn't been expecting this. But he saw that it made sense. He had been brought here to speak to Dreyfuss so that Villiers could ascertain how much he knew about *Zephyr*. But now Villiers had discovered that Hepton knew about *him*, making the telephone call hazardous. Indeed, Hepton now saw, it was imperative to Villiers that Hepton and Jilly leave, since their call to Dreyfuss would doubtless include their suspicions of Villiers himself . . .

'We're staying,' he said. Jilly looked at him, uncomprehending.

'Not if I want you to leave,' Villiers said quietly.

'Nevertheless, we're staying.'

Villiers stared at him, then smiled, coming back towards the desk. 'You're a clever man, Mr Hepton. But you're also incredibly stupid.'

He reached out a hand to pick up the receiver of the internal telephone, but just at that moment the other telephone started ringing. Hepton leapt from his seat, grabbing Villiers by the shoulders and propelling him away from the desk, pinning him against the wall. Villiers was strong, and he struggled.

'Jilly,' Hepton hissed between gritted teeth. 'Answer the bloody phone!'

She did so. 'Hello?'

Villiers had stopped struggling. Hepton relaxed a little, then remembered the man's Marine training. A heel crushed down onto the toes of his left foot, and he gasped. Then two hands chopped into his ribs. Villiers crooked his index fingers and pressed hard against them with his thumbs. He jabbed the second knuckle of each rigid forefinger into Hepton's neck. Hepton's grip on him fell away. But when Villiers made to push him aside, Hepton clutched at him again, and the two men fell sprawling to the floor.

Jilly was shouting into the receiver. 'It's Villiers! He's trying to kill Martin! It's George Villiers!' She wasn't calling for help; she was just letting the facts be known.

Villiers, hearing her words, let out a growl. His hands went to Hepton's throat again. Hepton drew back a fist and punched him deep in his stomach. Villiers had been Royal Marines, yes, but not for some years, years spent behind a desk. His gut was soft, and the blow winded him, giving Hepton time to climb back to his feet. He swung a foot at Villiers' head, but Villiers' reactions were still fast. He dodged the swing and grabbed Hepton's leg, tugging him off balance and down onto the floor again, clambering atop him.

The older, heavier man's weight was enough to pin Hepton down. A hand scrabbled at the desktop and came away again clutching a paperknife. Too late, Hepton remembered the kitchen knife in his own pocket. He caught Villiers' wrist, but Villiers had found new strength. The knife pushed downwards against Hepton's resistance. Villiers was smiling now, a look of tranquillity on his face. Close combat was his true calling; killing was his destiny . . .

The office door opened and Sanders looked in. His mouth fell open at the sight of his superior kneeling on top of Hepton with a knife poised above his throat.

'Christ almighty!' he gasped.

He loped towards the two men, and as Hepton watched, he seemed to turn his body sideways, raising one leg. The leg flexed, shot out, and a well-shod foot slapped into Villiers' jaw, cracking his head to one side and throwing him off Hepton. Hepton scrambled to his knees, but Villiers was already on his feet. He seemed to take in the whole situation – Hepton, Sanders, Jilly still talking on the telephone – at a single glance, and started for the door.

'Sir . . .' Sanders laid a restraining hand on his shoulder, but Villiers pushed him aside and ran out.

'Get after him,' Hepton ordered.

'What?'

'You saw him. He was going to cut my fucking head off. Get after him!'

Sanders hesitated, then crossed to the other telephone, dialled two digits and spoke.

'Security,' he said. 'Sanders here. I want George Villiers apprehended. Yes, that's right. No, it's not a joke. He's trying to leave the building. I want him stopped.' He slammed the receiver down again and looked to Hepton, who nodded at him in thanks.

'Martin?' Jilly was saying. She was holding the receiver out towards him. 'Martin, they want to speak with you . . .'


The problem with the secure line, a line unlikely to be tapped into by prying ears, was that it made voices sound as though they were trapped somewhere between an anechoic chamber and a sardine tin. There was a flat, dull lifelessness to the sound, with occasional bursts of jangling metallic tone.

Was it any wonder then that Dreyfuss did not sound like the man Hepton had met one day for lunch with Jilly? But Hepton was intrigued by the secure line, too. Did it use a satellite link? And if so, how secure could it ever be? He took several deep breaths as he took the receiver from Jilly. She was shaking, and he placed a hand on her shoulder to let her know he was all right.

'Is that you, Martin?'

'Yes.'

'Mike Dreyfuss here. What the hell's going on?'

'A man just tried to kill me. Lots of people seem to be trying to kill me of late. This one was a civil servant.'

'Is Jilly okay?'

'She's fine.' Hepton glanced across towards where Jilly, her arms folded in front of her, leaned against the wall. She nodded and smiled, confirming his opinion.

'What?' Dreyfuss seemed to be conferring with someone at his end of the line. 'Hold on, Martin,' he said. Then his voice was replaced by another.

'Mr Hepton?'

'Yes.'

'My name's Parfit. We haven't spoken before.'

'Parfit?' Hepton repeated, his eyes on Sanders.

The young man, who had been pacing the room as though still unable to believe the scene he had just witnessed, drew himself upright at the sound of the name. His eyes turned to Hepton.

'I work at the embassy here in Washington,' Parfit was saying. 'What's all this about George Villiers?'

'He wants me dead.'

'But why, in God's name?'

'That's a good question, Mr Parfit. It has something to do with the reason I've been trying to get in touch with Major Dreyfuss.' There was a knock at the door. A uniformed guard opened it and had a short whispered conversation with Sanders.

'Oh?' Parfit sounded intrigued. 'And what reason is that, Mr Hepton?'

The guard had gone. Sanders looked towards Hepton and shook his head: there was no sign of Villiers. Hepton couldn't help wondering how hard the guards had tried. He also wasn't entirely sure that he could trust Sanders himself. Yet here he was, having the conversation he wanted with the people he needed to speak with. He took another breath, his heartbeat slowing a little, the roaring in his ears more of a gentle breeze now.

'The day the shuttle crashed—' he began. But Parfit interrupted.

'Wait one moment, would you, Mr Hepton? I'm going to put you on our conference facility, so that Major Dreyfuss can participate.'

Hepton waited impatiently.

'Okay, go ahead now.'

He began again. 'The day the shuttle crashed, about the time *Argos* was launching a satellite or whatever it was doing up there, *our* satellite went haywire. A friend of mine had an idea what had happened, but he ended up dead. Before he died, he gave me one word. That word was *Argos*.'

There was silence at the other end. Hepton glanced towards Sanders, who was listening intently.

'Martin?' It was Dreyfuss' voice. 'What do *you* think happened?'

'I'm not sure. But people are getting killed because of it.'

'All right then,' said Dreyfuss. 'Listen, I've got part of a sequence. I wonder if you know what it means. The whole sequence was much longer, but all I have are the first few letters and numbers.' He paused. 'Ze/446.'

Hepton smiled. He could have completed the sequence for them if they wanted.

'That's an easy one,' he said. 'It's *Zephyr*, of course. It's part of *Zephyr*'s identification code.' His smile vanished. 'How did you get hold of it?'

'One of the crew on the shuttle had it on his screen. It kept flashing up.'

Hepton's blood went a few degrees colder. 'Then you were trying to lock onto *Zephyr*.' It was a statement.

'That's just what I was thinking.'

Parfit's voice came on the line. 'Tell me about *Zephyr*, Mr Hepton.'

'What do you want to know?'

'What exactly does it do?'

'It's an all-purpose satellite, as versatile as we want it to be.'

'What was it doing the day it went haywire?'

'Not a lot. We'd been running some regular checks on it.'

'Well, what might it be doing now? Any specific jobs it was supposed to carry out?'

'A few. The big one, I suppose, is monitoring the troop pull-outs.'

'The pull-outs?'

'Nobody's supposed to know. But we've been keeping an eye on the US bases in Britain.'

'But why?'

'To make sure it all runs smoothly. There are some protest groups, including one pretty big one called USA Stay. They said they intended to stage some kind of resistance. You know, linking hands around a camp, or putting a padlock and chain on the gate. Symbolic stuff mainly. But the brass wanted to know what they were up to.'

'The brass?'

'Yes, the military. They've been keeping an eye open. A couple of high-rankers were on site when *Zephyr* malfunctioned.'

Hepton was trying not to be melodramatic. He wanted to state facts rather than his own suppositions, just to see what Dreyfuss and Parfit might make of it. This was the first time he had told anyone the story – Jilly excepted – and it felt good. Almost like the confessional.

'Then,' he continued, 'a friend of mine who works beside me thought he had something on his computer, some data showing interference with *Zephyr*. Next thing I know he's been rushed to hospital, and soon after that he's supposedly hanged himself in a closet. Then a woman called Harry tried to shoot me, run me over, and shoot me again.'

'Harry?' Parfit sounded almost excited.

'Yes. Do you know her?'

'I think so. We had a run-in with her four or five years ago. I thought she'd retired.'

'She tried to kill me.'

'Surprised you're still alive then. Killing is her job. But how in hell is she mixed up in this?'

Hepton stared fixedly at Sanders. 'My friend, the one who died. He told me to watch for someone called Villiers. I think Villiers and Harry are working together.'

'But working on *what*?' asked Parfit. 'That's the question. What does this satellite . . .'

'*Zephyr*,' said Hepton.

'Yes, *Zephyr*. What does it *do* exactly when it's hovering over its target?'

'It takes photographs and sends them back to control.'

'Control being where?'

'Binbrook.'

'Are these still photographs or videos?'

'Stills, mostly. The data is beamed down to us, and the pictures develop on a machine almost instantaneously.'

'Ingenious,' Parfit said, as though he meant it. 'A little like a fax then?'

Hepton smiled again. 'A little, yes.'

'But clear?'

'Clear enough. In focus, if that's what you mean.'

'Ingenious,' Parfit said again. Then: 'Sorry, hold on a second, will you?' There were muffled sounds at the Washington end, the sounds of a conversation. Hepton thought he heard the name 'Johnnie' mentioned at one point. Then Parfit's voice came back, loud and more or less clear. 'Sorry about that. Right, so are we any further forward, do you think?'

'Well, we know that *Argos* locked onto *Zephyr*,' said Hepton. 'Probably using the satellite it was launching. What we don't know is why. I had the idea it was all some kind of secret test, trying out some capability of the satellite that the powers-that-be wanted to keep hidden from even the ground controllers.'

Parfit seemed to consider this. 'Hmm,' he said at last. Hepton wasn't sure whether it was an interested 'hmm' or a sceptical 'hmm'; the scrambler was still robbing the voices of any emotion. Then Parfit cleared his throat, and Hepton thought he could hear Dreyfuss whispering something, a name . . .

'As Major Dreyfuss has just reminded me,' Parfit said, 'there is a man who might help us. His name is Cameron Devereux. He's the other reason we called. Devereux was Major Dreyfuss' contact at mission control. What you need to realise is that *Argos* was meant to crash, and with no survivors.'

'A suicide mission?'

'I doubt whether the crew knew that, though they must have known why they were up there in the first place. One of them tried to strangle Major Dreyfuss.'

'Strangle Dreyfuss?' Hepton saw the effect of his words on the room. Sanders, who was starting to sit, now stood up again, and Jilly looked aghast.

'This man said something about needing to bury a coffin. Does that mean anything to you?'

'No, nothing. So what about this Devereux?'

'He might well know something about the sabotage. And if so, he *may* also know what the mission was.'

'So talk to him.'

'Yes, but he's gone on vacation to London.'

Hepton rested against the edge of the table. 'Has he now? And you'd like me to talk to him?'

'Well, you might understand him better than we amateurs could.'

'Okay, Mr Parfit. Where is he staying?'

'A hotel on Park Lane, I believe. The Achilles. Our intelligence sources have just come up with it. He booked in yesterday.'

'I'll go there this evening.'

'Good man. Take care, won't you? If Harry's supposed to have—'

'Yes, I know.'

'Who's there in the room with you? I mean, besides Miss Watson. I've already spoken with her. Or rather, I've already had her screaming at me that you were being murdered before her eyes.'

Hepton's smile returned. Yes, ten minutes ago, Villiers had held a knife to his throat. Yet now he could smile about it, could brush it aside and get on with whatever action was necessary. He felt changed inside, in some profound way. He felt stronger.

'Sanders is here.'

'Sanders?' Parfit recognised the name. 'He's a good man. Take him with you when you go to see Devereux. Any sign of Villiers?'

'I think he's escaped.'

'Hmm. Well, he can't get far. Put Sanders on, would you?'

'Sure.' Hepton held the receiver out. 'Parfit wants a word,' he said.

Sanders looked at the telephone as though it might be about to bite him. Hepton didn't know who or what Parfit was, but he knew he was important enough for the mere mention of his name to scare Sanders half to death. He jabbed the receiver towards the young man, who licked his lips and stepped forward to take it from him. Gingerly, the way someone might handle a snake for the very first time.

'Hello?' Sanders said.

Hepton went over to Jilly and quietly filled her in on the details of his conversation with both Dreyfuss and Parfit. She listened sporadically, still shocked from the earlier struggle.

'I should have clouted him,' she said, replaying the moment over and over again in her head. 'I should have helped you, Martin. But instead I just stood there, yelling into the bloody telephone. Asking someone in *America* to help. Isn't that crazy?' And she gave a tiny, nervous laugh.

He hugged her, and felt her arms pull him inwards, and the feel of her brought back such memories . . .

'Er . . .?' The voice was Sanders'. 'Miss Watson?' She relaxed her hold on Hepton. 'Major Dreyfuss would like a word.'

Hepton couldn't help but feel a twinge of jealousy at Jilly's reaction. She let go of him, a schoolgirl grin appearing on her face, and almost skipped to the telephone.

'Mickey? Hello there. How are you? Did you get my flowers? You did! I tried telephoning the hospital but I could never get through.'

Sanders seemed embarrassed as he approached Hepton, his eyes everywhere but on Hepton's own. His voice when he spoke was muted.

'Look, about Mr Villiers . . .'

'Villiers is a maniac,' hissed Hepton. 'You people have known that all along, but he was useful to you so you conveniently ignored the fact. What's more, he's working with another bloody maniac called Harry.'

'But I don't understand. What has he done?'

Hepton considered this. There was no way of knowing, not without apprehending Villiers himself, or perhaps talking to the American, Devereux. He shrugged.

'What was Parfit saying?'

'You're to be given twenty-four-hour protection. Meantime, we'll put out a full-scale search for Mr Villiers. Well, not exactly *we*, since it'll have to be handled by the other lot.'

'The other lot?'

'You'd probably call them MI5.'

'What about Parfit?'

'He's MI6.' Sanders was perking up now. 'That's who I work for.'

'And presumably who Villiers works for too?'

Sanders stared at him. 'Yes, well . . .'

Hepton heard Jilly laugh, and glanced across to where she was sitting, perched on the edge of the desk, looking relaxed and with the telephone cord playfully twisted around one finger. Funny how people could change from moment to moment . . . She was ending her conversation. She dropped the receiver back into its cradle and hugged herself, looking radiant.

'He sounds fine,' she said.

'Yes,' Hepton agreed.

'I just wish . . .' But she didn't finish the sentence. Hepton was looking sad, and right now she felt like cheering up the whole world. She came to him and hugged him to her. Then pulled away to examine his face. 'We're going to be all right too, aren't we, Martin?'

'Of course we are,' he said, sounding more confident than he felt. He reached into his pocket and brought out the kitchen knife. 'As long as we've got this,' he said. Jilly recognised it.

'That's from my kitchen!' she cried. Then she laughed and hugged him again. 'What were you going to do with it? It's as blunt as my editor's sense of humour.'

'I don't know,' Hepton said. He was still studying the knife, trying to answer her question. 'I think I was going to kill Villiers with it.'

'Ugh!' said Jilly, giving a little shiver. 'What happened to him anyway?'

'He can't be found in the building,' Sanders explained, his voice taking on a tone of apology. 'We're still looking.'

'But how hard?' asked Hepton. 'How hard are you looking? Who else is in on this thing besides Villiers and Harry? It seems to stretch halfway around the world as it is!'

Sanders' voice became a monotone. 'You can trust me,' he said. 'Now if you'll excuse me, I'll be back in a few minutes. Would you like anything? More tea? Something stronger?'

'I could murder a gin,' said Jilly.

Hepton realised that his own throat was dry. He nodded.

'Two G and Ts then,' said Sanders, opening the door. 'I'll see what I can do.'

True to his word, two dusty glasses were delivered by a bemused security man a few minutes later. Hepton sank his in two gulps, then sucked on the tiny slice of lemon. Jilly savoured hers, reclining in Villiers' chair, her feet on the desk.

'Cheers,' she said.

'And don't we deserve it,' observed Hepton.

The door opened again and Sanders re-entered, looking pleased with himself.

'Right,' he said. 'It's about that knife of yours.'

'The Sabatier?' Jilly's face was quizzical.

'That's right,' said Sanders. He was unbuttoning his jacket. 'Anyway, you won't be needing it now.' He tugged the left side of his jacket open. Strapped beneath his shoulder was a brown leather holster, from the top of which peeped the butt of a small, fat handgun. '*This*,' he said, 'is what we need. Especially when dealing with Harry. Now, shall we go?'

# 23

On the way to the Park Lane Achilles Hotel, Sanders told them about Harry.

'It was four or five years ago. I'd just joined the department . . .'

What department? Hepton was tempted to ask.

'I remember meeting Mr Parfit for the first time. He struck the fear of God into me.'

Sanders seemed excited. Hepton decided that the secret agent hadn't seen much action in his musty set of offices. He didn't appear to be over-experienced either, driving a little too fast, potentially attracting attention. And now that he had been assigned to protect Hepton and Jilly, he was much less reticent, much more talkative, much more like a human being.

Hepton wondered why it was, then, that he liked him less this way.

'Mr Parfit had spent months on the case. There was going to be an assassination attempt.' He turned to them. 'I won't say on whom. But the identity of the assassin was what we couldn't uncover. We were looking for a regular, you see, a Carlos the Jackal or whatever. But it turned out to be a woman, a young and good-looking one at that.'

Hepton could feel Jilly bristling at this.

'The beautiful Harriet, in other words,' Sanders continued, unaware of Jilly's glowering face. 'She was the assassin.'

'So what happened?'

'Oh, Parfit tracked her down, or at least his team did. She did a runner and was never heard from again. Until now.'

'What about Villiers?' Hepton asked, his voice as neutral as an idling engine. Not that the Cavalier's engine *was* idling. Sanders pulled past some evening traffic and cut into the stream again just ahead of a purring Jaguar.

'I've worked with Mr Villiers for two years. When I started with him, I was told he was a bit . . . well, that he might be prone to . . . outbursts.'

'What did his job entail?'

'Nothing very much. He just waited. When advice was needed on one of his specialities, he'd be called for.'

'That must have been tedious.'

Sanders nodded. 'He hated it. Desk-bound after years of combat training. God knows, I'd hate it too in his position. They say he was a great soldier.'

'You mean good at killing people?' Jilly asked. Sanders reddened, but didn't answer.

'Did you ever suspect he might be involved in something?' Hepton asked him. 'Something you weren't allowed to know about?'

Sanders shook his head. 'Mr Parfit asked me a similar question on the telephone back there. I'll tell you what I told him: I didn't suspect anything. I'm still not sure that I do . . . I mean, it could all be some ghastly mistake, couldn't it?'

'No,' said Hepton flatly. 'No mistake.'

The car had reached the top of the Mall. Buckingham Palace lay directly in front of them. Hepton watched intently as a slow-moving line of army trucks approached from the other direction and drove past, heading in the direction of Trafalgar Square.

'There's a lot of troop movement at the moment,' said Sanders, attempting a change of subject. 'To do with the pull-out, I suppose. I'm against it myself. The pull-out, I mean. I think most people are.'

'Not me,' said Jilly. 'I'm glad they're going.'

Sanders stared at her in his rear-view mirror but kept his thoughts on her politics to himself.

'What about Harry?' asked Jilly. 'What else do you know about her?'

'We don't know much,' Sanders admitted. 'But there was plenty of speculation at the time. Fifteen years ago, a brigadier general's unruly daughter went missing in Germany. She left a note saying she was running away. She was fifteen, rebellious. A lot of anarchist literature was found in her bedroom.'

'And her name was Harriet?' Jilly suggested.

'No,' said Sanders. 'Her name wasn't Harriet. But her mother's name had been. Her mother was dead. The story went that the general used to get roaring drunk and hit his wife, made her life hell. She committed suicide when the daughter was eight or nine.'

'Well, well,' said Hepton, very quietly, filing this information away.

Hyde Park Corner came next, and then they were sweeping into Park Lane itself. Sanders entered the right-hand-turning lane and cut across the oncoming traffic, bringing the car to a stop outside a flat-fronted hotel of marble and smoked glass, which seemed very similar to the other hotels clustered around it. Three steps led to a line of six glass doors, behind which lay tantalising glances of a marble reception hall lit by sparkling chandeliers. In front of the steps stood a liveried doorman, and above him was a large canopy proclaiming the single word *Achilles*.

Sanders got out of the car and locked his door. When Hepton closed his own door, he watched the button on the inside of the window slide neatly into place of its own accord.

'A wonderful thing, central locking,' he mused.

Jilly was staring at the hotel's frontage. 'The things I'd do for a long, hot bath,' she said.

The doorman was coming towards them. 'You can't leave it there, sir,' he called, gesturing towards the Cavalier.

Sanders reached into his inside pocket and brought out a wallet, which he flipped open.

'A security matter,' he said. 'We shouldn't be too long.'

The doorman studied the ID carefully. 'Well,' he said at last, 'I suppose that'll be all right then. Want the manager, do you?'

'That's quite all right.' Sanders beamed back at him. 'We'll manage.' He moved past the doorman and up the steps.

'I thought he was supposed to be our bodyguard?' Jilly whispered as they followed, leaving the bemused doorman staring at their backs.

'He is.'

'Well he's not doing a very good job then, is he?'

'He's a bit too keen on playing the spy,' Hepton agreed. 'We can't afford to relax, Jilly. I think we're going to have to cover our own backs, rather than depending on Mr Sanders to do it for us.'

'Well, as long as we've got the kitchen knife, we should be safe,' said Jilly.

They entered the hotel lobby. The doorman was looking at the car now, checking colour, make and registration. Then he walked briskly up the steps and pushed open the doors. The car's occupants were at the reception desk, their backs turned to him. He went to a bank of public telephones along the wall nearest the door, picked up a receiver, inserted a ten-pence piece and dialled seven digits. He had to wait seconds only for a response.

'Achilles,' he said, identifying himself. 'I need to speak to Mr Vitalis.'


'Mr Devereux, please,' Sanders said to the woman behind the reception desk. She was wearing an identity badge and a well-worn smile.

'Room two-two-seven,' she said. 'Can I call him for you?'

'No thanks. That's floor two, room twenty-seven?' Sanders checked. The woman nodded, not about to waste a spoken answer. 'Thank you,' he said, turning from her. He stood for a moment, seeming to be deciding between the lift and the stairs. 'Stairs,' he said finally.

'You take the stairs,' Jilly objected. 'I'll take the lift. It's been a long day.'

Sanders stared at her. 'A lift is a trap, remember that. Once you're inside, there's no way out.' He started walking towards the pink-carpeted staircase. 'I'll see you up there,' he called.

Jilly looked to Hepton for a decision. Hepton shrugged his shoulders. Wearily they began to follow Sanders. He was right, though, that was the annoying part. He had obviously had some training in this sort of thing, while they were amateurs.

They climbed, counting the seventy-two steps to the second floor. The corridor was vacant, little noise coming from the rooms themselves. This was a hotel for the wealthy – businessmen as well as holidaymakers. And the wealthy had gone out to play in the London evening. Two things struck Hepton at the same time. The first was that Devereux might not be in; the second was that someone of his standing shouldn't be able to afford the Achilles. Hepton had seen the three-figure room charges displayed beside the desk.

They passed an ice machine, a drinks dispenser and an electrically operated shoeshine, then stopped outside a door.

Room 227. Sanders paused, listened, then knocked. There was silence. He knocked again. Nothing. He rested his hand on the door handle and checked that the corridor was still empty. As he was about to turn the handle, the door was opened from within. A man in shirt and trousers stood there, hair unkempt, the shirt rumpled, socks but no shoes on his feet. He had obviously been awakened from a nap, and was trying to stifle a yawn. When he saw that the three figures outside his door were not members of the hotel staff, he widened his eyes a little, trying to rouse himself.

'Yeah?' he said.

'Mr Devereux?' Sanders had fixed a sympathetic smile to his face.

'That's right.' His voice was American. There was an innocence to it that Hepton had noted before with American accents.

'Mr Devereux, my name's Sanders, I'm from the Foreign Office. We've come to talk to you about Major Michael Dreyfuss.'

'About Mike?' Devereux was wide awake now. A note of anxiety crept into his voice. 'What's wrong? Jesus, don't tell me he's up and died?'

'Oh no, he's quite fine. But he did telephone from America. He wanted us to talk with you.'

Devereux took in all three faces individually, wary still. Then he threw out an arm and pulled the door open to its fullest extent. 'You'd better come in,' he said. But looking into his room, at the sprawl and untidiness there, he seemed to change his mind. 'No, wait, on second thoughts, let me meet you in the bar in five minutes.'

Sanders seemed disapproving, but managed to keep the smile more or less intact. 'Right you are,' he said.

The door closed, leaving the three of them out in the corridor, much as they had been before.

'Sounds good to me,' Jilly said. 'One of you men can buy me a very large drink.' She was already heading back towards the stairs. Hepton began to follow, but saw that Sanders was staring at Devereux's door, his bottom lip clasped between upper and lower teeth.

'What's wrong?' he asked.

'How do we know he'll come to the bar?' Sanders whispered. 'I mean, he could do a runner.'

'He didn't look the running type,' Hepton offered, turning to follow Jilly.

Sanders watched him go, in an agony of sorts: should he stay and wait for Devereux, or follow his charges? A low growl left him, and he stalked back down the corridor after them.


It took Jilly less than a minute to finish her first gin. She examined the tall glass, still half full of unmelted ice.

'Better make it a double next time,' she said. She caught the waiter's attention and he walked smilingly towards her, knowing a potentially good customer when he saw one. Jilly ordered her double, but Hepton and Sanders shook their heads. Hepton was nursing a half-pint of lager, Sanders a tomato juice. They were seated at a corner table – at Sanders' insistence – from which they could watch the door to the hotel lobby and still have a view of the other occupants of the cocktail lounge. Not that there were many occupants to watch. The resident pianist was playing to a table of four well-dressed women, their clothes younger than their years. They applauded every tune, but quietly, politely, and he bowed his head each time, accepting gracefully, as he hoped to accept their drinks and their tips.

Two businessmen stood at the bar, slowly smoking cigars, sipping whiskies. They glanced around the room occasionally, looking first at the table of women and then over towards Jilly. They weren't hopeful; just looking.

'This is nice,' Jilly said without much attempt at sincerity.

Then Sanders, who had been the most subdued of the three, almost leapt from his seat, waving frantically towards the door, where Cam Devereux was standing. Devereux saw him and approached the table. Sanders sat down again, looking relieved and more animated again. Devereux squeezed into the booth beside Hepton. He had washed, changed his clothes and combed his hair. He had also had time to think, and was more wary than ever, as his first question showed.

'Who did you say you were?'

But the waiter was walking briskly in their direction, awaiting Devereux's order.

'Glenlivet, plenty of ice,' Devereux said, just as briskly. When the waiter had gone, he repeated his question. Sanders was about to respond, but Hepton beat him to it.

'I'm Martin Hepton. This is Jill Watson.'

'And you both work for the Foreign Office, too?'

'No,' said Jilly. 'We're friends of Mickey.'

'Mickey? You mean Mike Dreyfuss? How long have you known him?'

'Since school,' Jilly answered.

Devereux nodded slowly. 'I haven't known him more than six months,' he said. 'But he seemed like a great guy.'

'No need for the past tense,' Sanders said. 'He's still alive, remember.'

'Yeah.' Devereux's voice was like melting ice. His drink arrived and he gulped at it.

'This is a nice hotel,' Sanders noted aloud. 'It must be costing you a fortune.'

Devereux smiled and looked straight at Sanders as if to say: I know what your game is. 'I'm not paying for it,' he admitted. 'My employers are picking up the tab. Necessary R and R.'

Sanders was relentless. '*Is* it necessary?'

'Hell, yes,' Devereux said loudly. 'You ever see guys you'd gotten to know torched in the blink of an eye? Guys you respected suddenly dead, and all the time they're dying you think maybe you can do something to help, but you can't? Jesus!' His face was red now, and his voice had grown deeper. There was a silence at the table while they waited for him to calm down.

'Another drink?' asked Hepton, whose own glass was empty.

'Look,' Devereux said, 'let's just cut the shit, okay? What do you want?'

Hepton didn't know quite where to start, but both Jilly and Sanders had turned to him, expecting him to speak. 'Major Dreyfuss telephoned us,' he began. 'He was wondering what you know about the crash.'

'What's it to you anyway?'

'Our lives are in danger,' Jilly said quickly, 'and we want to know why. We're scared.'

Devereux seemed confused. '*Your* lives?'

'And that of Mike Dreyfuss,' Hepton continued. 'You see, I work at the control base for the *Zephyr* satellite, and somehow that satellite is tied up with the *Argos* shuttle. It looks as though the shuttle was trying to tap into *Zephyr*. We don't know why. Maybe *Zephyr* was doing something – something secret and something somebody wanted to know about.'

'Send a satellite to trap a satellite, huh?'

Hepton smiled. 'Maybe. But then the shuttle crashed, making the whole thing look like a suicide mission.'

'Not suicide,' Devereux said sharply, examining his empty glass. 'Murder. Sabotage, if you like.' He took a deep breath. 'Hell, I don't know why I'm telling you this . . . or maybe I do.'

He paused again, as if thinking things through. Then he began to speak.

'The day of the launch,' he said, 'some new guy turned up in the control room. He had a console tucked away in a far corner. A console they'd brought in the previous week. Well, he told me his name, but not much else. I can't even remember now what he said his name was. He knew what he was doing, though; I mean, he knew how to operate the computer, but he wasn't like one of us. I took a look at his screen that day, and he was in touch with the onboard computer. It was as if he knew something we didn't.'

'Such as?' asked Hepton.

'Such as that the whole onboard computer program had been fixed before the shuttle went up, and all it needed was the touch of the right buttons in the right order to bring a doomsday code into operation.'

'A doomsday code?' The question was Jilly's.

'Self-destruct,' Hepton explained. '*Zephyr* has one too, in case it falls into the wrong hands.'

Sanders was enthralled. 'So this man caused the shuttle to malfunction?'

Devereux was staring into his glass still. He'd played these scenes out a hundred times before in his head. 'You should have seen his monitor. It was like a Christmas tree, all these lights . . .'

There was a pause. Hepton broke it. 'Did you tell anyone about this?' He was thinking how closely Devereux's story followed his own, or even Paul Vincent's.

'Yes,' Devereux said. 'That was when they *strongly* suggested that I take a holiday.'

Hepton nodded. 'So what's it all about, Cam?'

'Hell, I don't know. I don't *want* to know.' Devereux looked up from his glass at last. 'No, that's a lie. I *do* want to know. I can tell you this: that wasn't a comms satellite *Argos* was launching. It was something else, something secret. Something for the military. There were a couple of the chiefs on site to watch the launch . . .'

Hepton remembered the brass who had watched over his own side of things. It couldn't be a coincidence.

'. . . and I figured the satellite must be some kind of intelligence-gatherer. Maybe a communications intercept.'

'Did the rest of the crew know?'

'The ground staff knew, or at least we guessed.'

'But what about the shuttle crew?'

'Well, Mike Dreyfuss didn't know. But as for the rest of them . . .' Devereux shrugged his shoulders. 'What does it matter, they're dead now.' He turned suddenly and held his glass aloft, yelling

towards the waiter, 'Another one of these!' Then he looked back at
Hepton. 'Have I told you anything you didn't know?'

'Oh yes,' Hepton answered thoughtfully. 'Quite a lot.' There was
one thing, one innocuous thing Devereux had said, that kept echo-
ing in his head. *A communications intercept.* Something didn't ring
true, but he couldn't think just what.

# 24

As Sanders drove them to the safe house in St John's Wood, Jilly dozed drunkenly in the back seat, her head resting in Hepton's lap. Hepton himself felt wide awake and stone-cold sober. He saw Devereux's face again as they took their leave of him at the Achilles Hotel. The American's eyes had looked dull and unfocused, a man tired of living; or at least of living with lies. A man haunted by his own fears.

From time to time, Hepton glanced back to see if any cars were following them, and each time he did so, Sanders would offer a confident 'I'd have spotted them by now.' Which didn't make Hepton feel any easier. The late-evening traffic was dense, and as they stopped at lights alongside a black cab, Hepton studied the foreign-looking male passenger, who, catching his eye, bowed his head slightly as though in acknowledgement before the lights turned green and both vehicles moved off.

'Why St John's Wood?' he asked Sanders.

'Because that's where the nearest Security Service safe house is.'

'But you're not MI5, are you?' Hepton didn't know much about spies, but he did know that MI5 – the Security Service – handled intelligence work at home, while MI6 – the Secret Intelligence Service – covered foreign operations.

'Yes,' Sanders agreed, 'but unfortunately the Security Service has to be in on this too. After all, we're *in* Britain. This is their territory. But since the United States is involved also . . .'

'It's a joint operation, then?'

'I believe there have been a couple of meetings today to clarify the situation. Not that we enjoy working together, you understand. It's a matter of trust.' Sanders glanced round at Hepton. 'You're lucky, actually. Their safe houses are a bit nicer than ours.' He smiled.

They passed Lord's Cricket Ground and continued up Wellington Road. Hepton had vague memories of a student party he had attended twenty years ago at a flat somewhere near Grove End Road. The hostess' parents had bought the place for her. The night of the party, her friends had done their level best to wreck it. So much for peace and love.

Sanders turned left off Wellington Road and drove slowly down a narrower street of detached and semi-detached houses, some of them compact, others rising to three and four storeys. He stopped beside one of the smaller detached houses and flashed his lights once. A man appeared from nowhere and opened the garage attached to the side of the house. Sanders negotiated the car into the space and switched off the engine. Behind them, the garage doors were being pulled shut again, though the man operating them remained outside.

'Home sweet home,' Sanders said. 'You lucky swine can get some rest now. I've still to write my report and meet with my bosses.'

The garage lights came on, and Hepton eased Jilly out of the back of the car. Sanders had opened another door, connecting with the house itself. Together they helped Jilly through it, along a carpeted hall and into a small, well-furnished living room, where she collapsed onto the sofa. Sanders pushed his hair back into place and straightened his tie.

'Journalists,' he said, staring at Jilly. 'Right, I'd better be off. There are two bedrooms upstairs. Kitchen on the other side of the hall. Toilet next to the door to the garage, and bathroom upstairs. I think one of the bedrooms even has an en suite.'

'All mod cons,' said Hepton. 'Is there a telephone?'

'Yes, but I shouldn't try using it. It just routes you straight through to a watcher team.'

'Watcher?'

'Surveillance.'

Hepton glanced around the room. 'Bugged?' he asked.

Sanders shrugged his shoulders. 'Oh,' he said, remembering something. 'And if you need anything, either pick up the phone or tap on the kitchen window. There are a couple of security men front and back. Otherwise, sleep tight.' He made to leave.

'See you in the morning,' said Hepton.

A few minutes later, he heard the car start up and reverse out of the garage. He went to the living room window to peer out. A tiny front garden separated the house from the pavement and the street beyond. Sanders' Cavalier backed noisily into the road and started off, gathering speed. Hepton could see no sign of the security man, who presumably was closing the garage doors again. In the lamplight on the other side of the road, an overdressed woman stopped to let the tiny dog she was walking do its business in the gutter. She looked middle-aged, her face heavily made up. Hepton stared hard through the window at her, trying to find Harry's features beneath the make-up. But he couldn't. And the woman didn't even glance across the street. She just watched her dog, cooing at it, and then walked on again, her heels noisy in the silence of the night.

Hepton turned towards Jilly. Her eyes were open and she looked around in bemused fashion, studying this new environment.

'Where are we?' she asked, her voice slurred.

'Come on,' he said, feeling himself relax for what seemed the first time in days, 'I'll show you to your room.'


Hepton's sleep was dreamless, and he awoke early, refreshed. He ran a bath and lay in it until the water turned from hot to tepid. There was a portable radio on the windowsill, and he switched it on, letting the morning's news programme wash over him like so much water. There were traffic reports, relaying stories of five- and six-mile tailbacks on some of the roads into London. The world, it seemed, kept on going as though it were just another day, and in London that meant millions of people setting off to work.

The thought was too much. He sank beneath the water, then surfaced again. Drying himself, he switched off the radio so he could concentrate. There was an idea in his head, an idea about what was going on. But what could he do with it? That was the problem: apart from Jilly, there was no one he could trust, not completely. So he mulled over his idea and tried to fit together the remaining pieces of the puzzle.

In the kitchen, he found all he needed to make breakfast. There was bacon in the fridge, and eggs, butter and milk. A fresh loaf of bread sat on the breakfast bar, along with a new carton of orange juice, a jar of coffee and a pack of tea bags. There were pots of honey and marmalade in the cupboard, and a bowl of sugar, too. Everything had the look of having been put there only the day before.

He set to work, and even found a tray to put everything on before climbing the stairs. Outside Jilly's room he paused, wondering whether it was necessary to knock. It wasn't. The door opened suddenly from inside, and there stood Jilly, already dressed and looking fit and well. There were no signs of the night before, other than dark patches beneath her eyes.

'Good morning,' she said, opening the door wide to let him in. 'Is that for me?'

She sat on the edge of the bed and accepted the tray, draining the glass of orange juice before starting on the food.

'Aren't you having any?' she asked, chewing on a triangle of toast.

'Not hungry,' Hepton said. He sat on the padded stool beside the dressing table. Then he noticed that her hair, though drying, was wet. 'How long have you been awake?' he asked.

'Not long,' she answered. 'I heard you in the bathroom, so I got up and took a shower.'

Yes, he had forgotten she was in the room with the en suite. 'So how are you feeling?'

'My head's a bit groggy. I suppose I drank too much. But then we didn't have anything to eat last night, did we?'

'No, we didn't,' said Hepton, recalling that this was true. Neither of them had professed much of an appetite after the events of the afternoon.

Suddenly he heard a noise on the staircase, feet moving upstairs. He turned his head towards the open doorway just as Sanders appeared there. If anything, the young man was more smartly dressed than ever. He wore a stiff-looking pinstripe suit, with polished black shoes, white shirt and plum-coloured silk tie. Hepton wondered if perhaps he had been promoted overnight.

'Ah, good,' Sanders said. 'You've eaten.' This was plainly not true: Jilly had not yet touched the plate of bacon and egg. 'Sorry to rush you,' he continued, 'but there's a meeting in forty minutes at HQ. They'd like you to be there.'

'Who would?' Jilly asked through a mouthful of toast.

'Wait and see,' said Sanders, obviously flustered. 'Now come on, will you, please. The traffic's diabolical out there.'


They headed back towards the West End, Sanders driving with even less grace than usual. Hepton asked about George Villiers.

'We've scoured the FO building. No trace of him. There are guards outside his flat, but he hasn't been back there either. He does own a house somewhere in Scotland, but I think it unlikely he'd go there, although we're keeping an eye on it. No, he's vanished. But don't worry. If he pops his head up from the trenches, we'll have him.' He grinned at them.

Jilly gripped the back of the passenger seat and pulled herself forward. Sanders flinched instinctively.

'This is serious, you imbecile,' she said.

Then she sat back again, bathing in Sanders' silence. Hepton patted her knee affectionately and she winked at him. It had been a performance, but that wasn't to say she hadn't meant it.

As they neared Park Lane, Hepton decided that their destination must be the Achilles Hotel again, but they continued past it, then snaked left into Curzon Street. The Cavalier pulled abruptly into the side of the road and stopped. Someone opened the rear door from outside.

'Go with him,' Sanders ordered, sounding not a little petulant. Hepton and Jilly got out of the car, and the man who had been holding open the door now closed it. He was much the same age as Sanders, and dressed only a little less well.

'If you'll follow me,' he said as Sanders drove off. Then he took them up to and through the imposing doors of the Security Service's main headquarters.

There were six of them seated around an oval table of antique design but modern construction. When they had made themselves comfortable, the man at the head of the table called out, 'Thank you,' and the door was closed from the outside by one of two security men. Jilly and Hepton sat together, their section of the table blank and highly polished. In front of the others – three men and one woman (who had smiled conspiratorially towards Jilly, but not at Hepton) – were brown files and differing quantities of paper: typed reports, minutes, even a photograph or two. The man at the head of the table ran a hand over his face, as though checking the closeness of his morning shave.

'It's good of you to come,' he began. 'My name is Sir Laurence Strong.' He was in his seventies, but his physique still matched his name, and he had a head of thick silvered hair. Nor did he appear to require spectacles, though in these days of contact lenses it was impossible to tell for sure. He introduced himself as 'Sir' not out of any wish to impress, but because it was a fact. 'This,' he continued, gesturing towards the woman, 'is my personal assistant, Louisa Marchant.' She smiled again, including Hepton in her compass this time. She was younger than Sir Laurence, in her early sixties perhaps. Smaller and plumper, too, with steel-rimmed glasses behind which her sharp blue eyes glistened. Sir Laurence now nodded in the direction of a man of similar age to himself. 'Allow me to introduce—' It was as far as he got.

'Blast you, Laurence, I can make my own introductions.' The man turned to Hepton and Jilly. His face was stern, as though he were late for something else of more importance. What Sanders had said was true: the two intelligence services did not get on, even at their upper echelons. 'Blake Farquharson,' the man said. Then, with a glance towards Sir Laurence, 'Not yet knighted. This is *my* assistant, Tony Poulson.' His finger was stabbing towards the man next to him, who nodded agreement. Farquharson and Poulson were like young-and-old versions of the same person: same thinning hair, same thick black-rimmed glasses, same grimly set faces and worry lines.

'Fine,' said Jilly. 'We know who you are now, but not *what* you are.'

'Of course.' This from Sir Laurence again, seeming more urbane with every moment. 'I'm director general of what you probably know as MI5.'

'Ditto MI6,' snapped Farquharson.

Jilly nodded satisfaction, trying to look less impressed than she actually felt. She knew journalists who would give their non-writing arm for the chance to sit in the same room as the heads of both intelligence services.

'So,' said Hepton, 'what can we do for you?'

'Well, for a start,' said Sir Laurence, 'bearing in mind that Miss Watson is a journalist, though with no disrespect to that estimable profession' – there were smirks at this – 'we would remind you both that you have signed the Official Secrets Act. Now, that being understood, really what we'd like is your version of events thus far.'

Jilly nodded towards the file in front of him. 'Isn't it all in there?'

He laid a proprietorial hand on the cover of the file. 'Oh yes,' he said. 'But these are . . . facts. What we'd like now are opinions, thoughts.'

'Thoughts?' She leaned forward in her chair. 'I've been doing plenty of thinking this past day, and I'll tell you what I think.' Hepton had to admire her. Coming to London had made her more assertive, not afraid to voice her opinions or to ask for other people's. She held up one finger. 'I think you don't want the American troops to pull out of Britain.' Another finger. 'I think the military is planning a coup, and I think you're going to let them do it.' A third. 'I think they're being aided by the Americans, and I think both countries are going to turn themselves into fortresses.' She paused, but no one seemed ready to refute her allegations, so she continued. 'What I'd *like* to know is how much the government knows.' The three fingers became one, pointed straight at Sir Laurence. 'How much do *you* know? The prime minister *is* still head of the Security Service, isn't that right?'

Sir Laurence took this outburst quite calmly – they all took it calmly. He cleared his throat. 'Yes,' he said, 'that much is true, Miss Watson. The PM is titular head of the Security Service. However, as for your other . . . thoughts, I'm afraid they are rather off-beam. I'll admit, though, that we had been thinking along similar lines ourselves. We've had inklings, for example, that something is simmering, and that the chefs are the chiefs of staff of our own armed forces. That much is true. A coup seemed a feasible explanation. However, it was difficult to go to the PM with what were merely inklings—'

'Especially now,' interrupted Farquharson, his voice more reasonable than before, and obviously not wishing Strong to be allowed to tell too much of the story by himself. 'What with NATO bickering, and this blasted pull-out and all. You see, the military bigwigs have been whingeing, and they've also been currying favour within Parliament, seeking out supporters, that sort of thing. In the current climate, the government wants to remain on friendly terms with the military, so anything we might say would in all likelihood be taken as paranoia or even jealousy. Though,' he added as an afterthought, 'both *those* notions are preposterous.'

Having had his say, he sat back and folded his arms. Sir Laurence continued. 'What Blake is saying is that we couldn't find many friendly ears to listen to us. Yet we *knew* something was going to happen.'

'So,' asked Hepton, 'just what *is* happening?' Jilly's notion of a coup had crossed his mind too, but he had rejected it for something a little more frightening.

There was silence in the room as eyes sought out other eyes, looking for answers. Sir Laurence spoke first.

'We aren't sure. We planted agents in some of the more important military offices – new clerical help, that sort of thing. Risky, and so far we've been able to shed no new light.'

'And meanwhile,' interrupted Farquharson, 'I've got agents abroad trying to find out what they can.'

'Including Parfit,' stated Hepton. Farquharson glowered at him.

'Yes,' he said, 'including Parfit. He's one of our best men. I hope you'll be able to meet him.'

'What does that mean?' asked Jilly, frowning incomprehension.

'It means,' said Farquharson, 'that he's on his way here. And bringing Major Dreyfuss with him. Things are getting too uncertain in the States, and we want the major out of there. Now, tell us about your meeting with Cameron Devereux . . .'

# Part IV

Theoretically, the smallest size that can be detected by spy satellites is just a few inches. Not quite enough to read the headlines on a newspaper but enough to tell what kind of newspaper you are reading. There is not a square inch of the globe that cannot be photographed or monitored in this way. Somewhere, deep in a vault in the Pentagon and its Soviet equivalent, there is a photograph which if magnified will reveal your house and the make of car you are driving away from it. Oh, and be careful what you say on your car telephone.

*Guardian*, 13 March 1987

# 25

They left the embassy compound in a van that claimed to belong to *DC Hygiene*. Dreyfuss, dressed in overalls and uneasy in the passenger seat, asked Parfit – also in overalls and driving – what the company did.

'They deliver roller towels for the toilets, that sort of thing. Gum?'

He noticed that Parfit was offering him a stick of chewing gum.

'No thanks,' he said.

'Take one,' Parfit ordered. 'Delivery men around here all seem to chew gum.'

Dreyfuss took the stick, unwrapped it and folded it into his mouth. Parfit did the same, then popped the tube back into his overall pocket. He was checking in his wing mirrors. There was a car following them, but that was okay – it was from the embassy, and would stay with them for the next few miles until they could be sure no one else was on their tail. Until then, they were due to drive around – not too fast, not too slow, just driving – as though between destinations. When Parfit was satisfied, they would head out to the airport, where another car filled with his men would be waiting, watching to see that they made it to the terminal building without incident. He had arranged for two more men to be posted inside the terminal building itself, but after that, once they had headed into the departure lounge, they were on their own.

'You seem to have plenty of men at your disposal,' Dreyfuss had said when told the plan.

'I'm using just about every member of staff the embassy has,' Parfit had replied, smiling. 'When Johnnie finds out, he'll be livid.

The embassy's going to be deserted apart from himself and a few typists. I reckon our need might be greater than his.'

Dreyfuss tried not to think about it, but found himself thinking of nothing else. His mouth was dry, and the gum wasn't helping. He wanted to return to Britain, of course he did. But somehow the more plans Parfit concocted to make sure they would do so safely, the more worried Dreyfuss became, for if these precautions were necessary, surely the danger must be necessarily as great? Yet Parfit carried no gun, no weapon of any kind. *A weak man needs a weapon*, he had once told Dreyfuss. In that case, Dreyfuss thought now, I must be weak as a deathbed grandmother. For the thought of a very large gun was all that seemed to soothe him just at the moment.

'Relax,' Parfit said; it sounded like another command. 'We're only delivery men, just driving around doing our job. We don't need to look so tense or grip the seat like that.'

Dreyfuss looked down and saw that his hands were indeed clenching either side of his seat, the knuckles white. He loosened them and folded his arms instead.

'You still look tense,' Parfit said.

'That's because I *am* tense, for Christ's sake. If I try to let my arms hang down, I just know I'll end up waving them wildly and screaming to be let out of here.'

Parfit laughed. Dreyfuss wasn't sure he had heard him laugh before, and found the sound strangely reassuring.

They drove in silence for a while, until they were crossing the Potomac River.

'We may as well take a look at the Pentagon while we're here,' said Parfit. 'After all, you *did* want to see a bit of the United States, didn't you? It said so on your application form for the *Argos* mission.'

Dreyfuss turned to him. 'You're enjoying all this,' he hissed.

'I enjoy my work, yes,' Parfit admitted. 'Sometimes I do, anyway. Haven't you ever been part of a team who had a rival team? At football, maybe, or cricket?'

'I was never very interested in sports.'

'Well,' said Parfit, unperturbed, 'try to imagine it. Here's us, and we're up against the military – people like Esterhazy.'

'You seem to forget that *I'm* military,' Dreyfuss said.

Parfit glanced towards him. 'Well, try to set that aside for a moment. So it's an us-and-them situation, and I want *us* to win the game.'

'But it isn't a game.'

'Yet in many ways it is *exactly* that. And if you forget that it's a game, you start playing the wrong way. So far, the opposition has been in a strong position, because we don't know what they're up to. But now they've started making mistakes – letting you live was only the first. People are getting suspicious, people like your friend Hepton. And to cover their mistakes, they – whoever they ultimately are – are starting to take bigger and bigger chances, which only force them further and further into the open. So yes, I *am* enjoying myself, because at last I think we've got a chance of beating them. What about you?'

'I'm delirious,' said Dreyfuss blandly, causing Parfit to laugh again, louder this time.

After another half-hour or so, Parfit decided that they should stop at a roadside café.

'I thought we were supposed to keep driving?' said Dreyfuss.

'We're still early,' replied Parfit. 'And I'd rather we spent the spare time away from the airport. Nobody's following us, so why not stop for a coffee?'

'Okay, if you say so,' Dreyfuss said.

They pulled into a parking area beside a large café proclaiming *ALL DAY ALL NIGHT BREAKFAST/BURGER*. It wasn't until Dreyfuss was studying the large, plastic-coated menu, seated beside Parfit in one of the booths by the window, that he realised this capitalised mouthful was in fact the name of the establishment.

A waitress approached, looking as well used as the dishcloth with which she wiped their table.

'What can I get you?' she asked tiredly.

'Just coffee, please,' said Parfit. Dreyfuss nodded. 'Two coffees,' Parfit corrected.

'Cream?'

Parfit nodded, and the waitress tore off a sheet from her pad, left it on their table and walked back towards the counter.

'Americans used to say "cream" and mean it,' Parfit said conversationally. 'Nowadays they almost always mean "creamer", and that's a polite way of saying "whitener", which in turn means monosodium glutamate. A long way from cream.' Dreyfuss didn't appear to be listening. 'You can't believe words any more,' Parfit continued.

Dreyfuss turned his head to look at him, then narrowed his eyes. 'What the hell are you talking about, Parfit?'

Parfit considered. 'Nothing,' he said, shrugging his shoulders.

'What exactly are we doing here?'

'I told you, killing time.'

'And I don't believe you.'

The door to the café was opening, bringing in another customer. Parfit leaned close to Dreyfuss' ear.

'Don't say anything about our leaving,' he whispered.

The man walked over towards Dreyfuss and Parfit's booth, then slid into the seat opposite them. It was Frank Stewart.

'Hello,' he said.

'Mr Stewart,' Parfit said by way of greeting.

'What's he doing here?' Dreyfuss' voice had become strained.

'Parfit thought we should meet,' said Stewart. He was admiring their uniforms. 'Nice disguise.'

'It's the only way to travel,' said Parfit.

'So what can I do for you?' said Stewart. The waitress was coming near. 'Coffee and a half-pound cheeseburger, medium rare,' he called. She nodded and started back to her counter, yelling the order through to the kitchen. Stewart shrugged. 'I'm starving,' he said.

'Yes,' said Parfit, 'I thought a little chat might be of benefit to both of us. Esterhazy's walking a very thin line.'

'Oh?'

'If you're able to keep a close watch on him, without his knowing, then you might be doing yourself a great service.'

'Keep talking,' said Stewart. He picked up a sachet of sugar, tore it open and emptied it into his mouth.

'There's not much more I can add,' said Parfit. 'I'll need a telephone number where I can contact you twenty-four hours a day.'

'You're doing this unsanctioned,' Stewart observed. 'That's a dangerous game for us both.' His eyes were interested but full of caution. He hadn't survived this long without covering every bet on the table.

'What makes you think—'

'Because,' Stewart interrupted, 'you stipulated this meeting be strictly off the books. That smacks to me of a solo outing, and I've never been keen on one-man shows.'

'This isn't exactly a one-man show,' Parfit said. 'But you're right. So far, there are more suspects than people I can rely on.'

'But you're willing to take a chance on relying on me? Why?'

'Because you want to nail Ben Esterhazy,' stated Parfit. The waitress was approaching with their order. The three mugs chinked together as she carried them.

'I can't argue with that,' Stewart said, chuckling. He stared at the burger as it was placed in front of him. 'No, sir,' he said, picking it up, 'I can't argue with that.'

Dreyfuss lifted his mug to his lips. He wasn't sure he liked the way Parfit seemed to be breaking the rules. He was certain that this meeting had been set up without the knowledge of anyone in the embassy. Sure, too, as Parfit's whispering had warned, that Stewart didn't know they were about to leave the country. Parfit was trying to have it all ways. He seemed confident that such was not only possible but entirely feasible. Yet Dreyfuss still wasn't sure of his motives or his ultimate goal.

He wasn't sure about anything any more.

They stayed long enough to finish their coffee, then left before Stewart, shaking his hand.

'Be careful out there,' he said, grease from the burger glistening on his lips.

Dreyfuss smiled but said nothing. He said nothing, in fact, the rest of the way to the airport. What was there he could say and be sure of getting a truthful answer to? Absolutely nothing.

The airport car park seemed, to Dreyfuss' eyes, to be full. An attendant told them as much, but Parfit insisted on driving around.

'Somebody's bound to be coming out,' he said. The attendant shrugged his shoulders and left them to it. Parfit knew exactly where he was going, however. He drove purposefully towards where two cars were parked side by side, their drivers reading newspapers. He blew four times on the van's horn, three short, one long, and the driver of one of the cars threw his paper onto the passenger seat, started his engine and drove off. With a certain amount of elegance, Parfit eased the van into the now vacant bay. He turned to Dreyfuss again. 'Easy when you know how,' he said. 'Right, you first.'

Dreyfuss had been told what to do. He got out, walking around to the rear of the van, where he opened the doors and pulled himself in, closing them after him. In the back of the van were two parcels, one marked 'P' and one 'D'. He opened the second package, revealing a two-piece suit, shirt, tie, socks and shoes. All in sober colours, and all in his size. He unzipped his overalls and began to change. Once he was dressed, he left the van again and got into the passenger seat of the second car, whose driver acknowledged his presence with a grunt and a 'You took your time,' before continuing with his reading.

Now Parfit went to the back of the van, reappearing less than two minutes later dressed in similar garb to Dreyfuss and looking more comfortable now that he had shed his workman's clothes. The driver saw him, folded his newspaper and got out of the car, moving to the van and climbing into the driver's side. Parfit meantime slid behind the steering wheel of the car. He watched as the driver moved off in the van, then looked left and right. Appearing satisfied, he touched Dreyfuss on the shoulder. Dreyfuss felt the touch like an electric spark, and flinched.

'Stay calm,' Parfit advised, 'for the next hour or so at least. Right, we're going in now.' He checked his watch. 'We'll go straight to Departures. Okay?'

Dreyfuss nodded and opened his door again. The car had a central-locking mechanism, and he watched as Parfit locked the driver's door and all four door locks engaged with a silent movement. Then Parfit opened the boot and brought out two small suitcases and two attaché cases. He handed one of each to Dreyfuss.

'Just some clothes, a few magazines, the usual stuff a business-man would take on a trip. Remember, we're only going to London for a couple of days. We're based in Washington—'

'At an international law firm. I remember.'

Parfit nodded. He seemed preoccupied now: perhaps he was growing just a little bit nervous himself. 'Oh,' he said, remembering something. He dug a hand into his jacket and brought out two pass-ports, one of which he handed to Dreyfuss. 'There you go, Stephen.'

Dreyfuss opened the passport. It was a brilliant fake; in fact, it was more: it was for real. A real passport, bearing a real name: Ste-phen Jackson. Occupation: solicitor. Stamped with American visas, and with evidence of holidays spent in Greece, Canada, Tunisia. Next of kin: a father, Bernard Jackson, who lived in Dundee.

'There aren't too many Bernards in Dundee,' Dreyfuss com-mented. Parfit seemed to take this criticism seriously.

'Good point,' he said. 'I'll have a word with the chaps who make these up.'

The photograph was of Dreyfuss: of course it was. They'd had it taken only yesterday, at the embassy. But a make-up artist had erased a few lines from his face, and given more hair to his forehead. The result was that the man in the picture looked a few years younger; as young as he would have been when the passport was supposedly validated.

'I'll hang on to our tickets,' said Parfit. 'Okay?'

'Fine,' said Dreyfuss, slipping the passport into his jacket pocket. There was something else in there. He brought out a wallet. Opening it, he found money in dollars and sterling, a UK driving licence and three credit cards. 'Christ,' he whispered, amazed.

Parfit tapped the cards.

'Don't run up too much of a bill. We always ask for the money back sometime.' Then, having locked the boot, he was off. Dreyfuss picked up the attaché case and suitcase and hurried after him.

## 26

Dreyfuss was impressed by the performance. Parfit had assumed the brisk but awkward walk of the busy businessman, and even his face seemed to have grown new worry lines, his eyes proclaiming a head filled with spreadsheets and data analysis. There was no doubt about it: at the law firm, Parfit was the one who looked after the accounts. More, he made sure everybody paid.

Dreyfuss was no actor, however. He watched the other travellers intently, seeking out the potential assassin or arresting officer. There were video cameras trained on every angle of the building's interior. Somewhere in the security room, someone would be watching him. He prayed they wouldn't recognise him. His photograph had been in all the newspapers, hadn't it? They were sure to spot him.

They had joined the queue at their chosen airline's London check-in desk. The people in front of them looked innocent enough: businessmen mostly, one elderly couple, two young men travelling together. The young men had short hair and wore checked shirts and denims. They didn't have much luggage, either. But it was the haircuts that worried Dreyfuss. They looked like regulation down-to-the-wood cuts, the kind only an armed forces barber could perfect. Dreyfuss knew; he'd been there.

When the crew cuts got to the front of the queue, he tried to listen in on their conversation with the smiling clerk. It all seemed normal. Small talk. They wanted smoking seats, and there seemed to be a problem about this. At last, their seat numbers having been allocated, they headed off in the direction of the departures lounge, watched by Dreyfuss.

'Stephen?'

It took a moment for him to realise that Parfit was speaking – speaking to *him*. He was Stephen Jackson. But who was Parfit again? James Pardoe? Farlow? Yes, Farlow: James Farlow.

'What is it, James?' he said. He was perspiring now, and could hear his heart thumping through his inner ear. Parfit smiled at him, his eyes warning him not to panic.

'You need to put your suitcase in here.' He pointed to a gap in the desk where a set of rollers waited to send their suitcases hurtling down towards the baggage loading area. Dreyfuss nodded embarrassedly and handed over his case. 'There aren't any window seats left,' Parfit said. 'Is that okay?'

'I don't mind where I sit,' Dreyfuss blurted. The clerk was staring at him now. Dreyfuss attempted a grin, which seemed to frighten her further.

'Fear of flying,' Parfit explained to her, accepting the two boarding cards. 'He'll be fine once we're up.'

They walked towards the departures lounge, Dreyfuss on legs made of drinking straws filled with putty, Parfit looking a little less confident than before.

'Hang on in there,' he hissed.

'I'm trying,' Dreyfuss said. He was breathing deeply, trying to calm himself. Not much longer, he was thinking. Then I'll be home. Home and dry. 'What about the agents you said would be here to cover us? I haven't seen them.'

'They wouldn't be doing their job if you could recognise them. Don't worry, they were back there near the desk.'

'But we're on our own now, aren't we?' Dreyfuss whispered noisily.

'We can manage.'

Their tickets and boarding cards were checked again, and their briefcases put onto a conveyer belt that transported them through an X-ray machine. A man in a suit, a large plastic ID badge clipped to his breast pocket, gestured for them to walk through the metal-detecting gateway, after which he ran a hand-held, more sensitive detector over them. Then his assistant – an only-too-willing assistant, Dreyfuss thought – slid his hands down each man's suit, under the jacket collar and lapels, down the back, smoothly over the trousers and up along the inside legs.

'Thank you, sir,' he said to Dreyfuss with the hint of a smile. Dreyfuss did not smile back.

'I don't know about you,' Parfit said as they picked up their cases and walked on, 'but I need a drink.'

'Count me in,' said Dreyfuss. He was feeling calmer now. The worst was over, wasn't it? Then it struck him: the last time he had flown had been on a private jet, and the time before that . . . on *Argos*. His legs lost their rigidity again.

'Do you want anything in duty-free?' asked Parfit, pointing towards the glossy spending mall. Dreyfuss shook his head. 'I can never resist the malt,' Parfit said. 'Coming?'

'I think I'll just give my face a splash of water first,' Dreyfuss said, nodding towards where a door proclaimed itself the gents' toilets.

'Fine, I'll come with you.'

'People will begin to talk,' said Dreyfuss.

Parfit looked surprised. 'You just made a joke!' he said. 'That's more like it. Now come on, and stop looking so damned worried all the time.'

Only one cubicle was in use when they entered the toilets. Parfit gestured towards it and winked, reminding Dreyfuss not to break their cover. Dreyfuss nodded and, while Parfit went to the urinals, stood in front of the gleaming row of washbasins, examining his features in the splashed mirror. He looked fairly dreadful, like some old cancer patient: face pasty grey, eyes dark, cheeks hollow, and sweat cloying his hair. Another man came in and hurried into a cubicle, slamming the door shut after him. Dreyfuss heard him unbuckling his belt.

He ran some cold water and rested his hands in it for a few moments before starting to wash his face. He felt better almost immediately. Parfit was standing behind him, zipping himself.

'Ready?'

'Just give me a minute,' Dreyfuss said. 'I'll catch you up in duty-free.'

'Well . . .' Parfit looked dubious, but a glance at his watch told him they didn't have very long before they would be boarding. He could visualise that bottle of Glenlivet sitting waiting for him . . .

The door of the first cubicle, the one that had been occupied when they came in, snapped open. A teenager came out, his face flushed, and made for the exit, his eyes to the floor.

'Wonder what he's been up to,' said Parfit with a wink. He checked his watch again. 'Don't be long,' he pleaded.

'Two minutes,' Dreyfuss said, watching in the mirror as Parfit left. Alone, he relaxed a little more. He let the water out. As it gurgled down the plughole, a man in his forties pushed open the door and entered the toilets, nodding towards Dreyfuss as he made for the urinals.

'Helluva day,' he commented, but Dreyfuss wasn't sure whether the man was talking to him or to himself. He ran more water. The man came to the basin next to him, gave his hands a quick rinse and rubbed them vigorously beneath the fan dryer. Then he left, the dryer still whirring away noisily. Dreyfuss splashed his face again, rubbing at his eyes this time, pressing fingers to sockets. He spat some water back into the basin and re-examined himself in the mirror. A toilet was flushing, and the cubicle door behind him opened. A squat man wearing spectacles and a shirt too small at the neck came waddling out. Dreyfuss smiled into the mirror, and the man seemed to smile back, but kept on coming . . .

Dreyfuss saw the cheese wire. It was twisted around the man's pudgy little hands, wads of cloth stopping it cutting into the pulpy skin. It took no more than a second for the man to hoist it over Dreyfuss' bowed head and pull tight. But in that second, Dreyfuss managed to prise his fingers between the wire and his unprotected throat, so that when the wire tightened, it cut into finger joints rather than neck. But it hurt like hell, and kept on digging, rending the tissue, sending blood trickling down Dreyfuss' right hand. He watched in horror in the mirror as his eyes began to bulge, his tongue to twitch. The man was pulling him backwards, putting him off balance. With his free hand, Dreyfuss lashed out, finding first the man's glasses, then his eyes, gouging at them. The man cried out, but the noise was all but masked by the greater noise of the cubicle finishing its flush and the dryer finishing its cycle.

When both stopped, there was an eerie silence, punctuated only by the choking sounds from Dreyfuss, the squeaking noise his shoes made as he sought purchase on the floor, and the shrill breath of the small man who was slowly but steadily murdering him. Dreyfuss' whole head felt aflame, his eyes watering, ear canals singing like the sea. His chest felt tight as a drum skin. The thought of dying in this antiseptic place was appalling.

A picture flashed in his mind: Hes Adams' fingers around his throat. The picture gave him strength, and he lashed out again, but with his left foot this time, sending it backwards with a donkey kick into the small man's knee. The man gasped in pain but did not release his grip on the wire. Dreyfuss tried again, his eyes blurrily fixed to the mirror, hypnotised by the blood that was now dripping from his hand onto his shirt. His lips were drawn back from his

teeth, the grin of a monkey. Monkeys grinned when they were terrified. This time the kick landed high on the man's soft thigh, causing
no reaction. Dreyfuss tried to cry out but couldn't. He was losing
strength, his whole body tingling with electricity. Movement was
becoming difficult. Inside his head, someone opened the door of the
furnace. He was on fire, and hell-bound. But he'd take the little bastard with him. He threw himself backwards, slamming the killer
against the hard partition edge between two cubicles. Then he
reached a hand around again. The hand was becoming numb, and it
scrabbled over the man's clothes like a tiny blind animal, finding the
crotch. He used the last of his strength to squeeze. The killer
howled.

Then, from the corner of his eye, he saw the door swing open and
Parfit enter. From then it was as if everything was happening in
slow motion. Parfit approached the man from the side and gripped
him by his furthest shoulder, pinning him against his own body
sideways on. Then he brought his arm back in a straight line and
sent it thudding towards the man, heel of palm connecting with ear.
The man's head whipped to one side and there was a horrifying
snap, as though a dog had bitten into a bone. The hold on Dreyfuss
tightened further still, then relaxed.

He realised that Parfit was holding the small man – now a dead
man – upright while he attempted to ease the cord away from Dreyfuss' throat. He did his best to help, then, suddenly released, staggered to the basin, gripping its edge with his left hand while he
stared at his crippled and bloodied right hand. He ran more water
and held the fingers beneath the cold spray. As he stared in the mirror at his purple face, the colour of a newborn baby, he felt his stomach wrench, sending a spume of vomit into the basin.

Parfit had eased the corpse to the floor. He was staring at it as
though it were something unbelievable, something out of his ken.
But the way he had dealt with the man proved to Dreyfuss that it
very much was *not* out of his ken. It was what he did, when necessary, as part of his job description.

'Are you okay?' Parfit came to the basin and examined Dreyfuss'
neck, then his bleeding hand. 'Run more cold water. Keep it under
the tap.' He went over to the corpse again. 'We need to get rid of this
bastard before somebody wants to use the facilities.'

There was only one sensible hiding place. He heaved the body
upright in one swift movement and walked with it into the furthest
cubicle, where he dumped it unceremoniously onto the pan. Closing

the cubicle door, he examined the lock. It was a simple thing, made simple so that no one could stay locked in. He brought a coin from his pocket and inserted it into the screw thread next to the 'engaged' indicator. Holding the door closed, and turning the coin in the thread, he moved the indicator from green to red: the cubicle was locked.

He allowed himself a moment's pause, then turned back to examine the rest of the interior. There were drops of blood on the floor, but they couldn't be helped. What worried him more was Dreyfuss' injured hand, and the fresh bloodstains on his shirt. He checked his watch, wondering if they could last out the time until boarding. If the body was found before then . . . or if Dreyfuss' wound was too deep . . .

'I'll be all right,' Dreyfuss said, then gagged. His throat was like fire. Hadn't he been through this before and survived?

'You've got more bloody lives than a cat,' Parfit acknowledged, smiling. Then, seriously: 'But this was my fault, and I'm sorry.'

'Don't be,' whispered Dreyfuss – the least painful way of talking. 'I'm beginning to enjoy strangulation.'

'How's the hand?'

He lifted it from beneath the water. The cuts on each joint were clean and deep. He tried flexing the fingers. Blood began to pour again.

'Fine,' he whispered. 'What do we do now?'

'What do you want to do?'

Dreyfuss thought it over. What choice was there? 'Get on the plane,' he said.

'Then that's what we'll do. But first I have to make a phone call, and this time you're coming with me.'

'What made you come back?' asked Dreyfuss.

'They'd run out of Glenlivet,' said Parfit, attempting levity. 'Now let's see that hand.' He inspected the damage. 'It's bad,' he said, 'but I don't suppose I need to tell you that, since it's so bloody obvious.'

'And bloodily obvious.'

'Another joke,' Parfit said appreciatively. 'You're tougher than I thought, Major.'

'The name's Stephen,' said Dreyfuss, 'and don't you forget it.'

They wrapped wads of toilet paper around each finger, then Parfit's handkerchief around the whole hand.

'We'll get some sticking plasters at the sky shop,' he said. 'The hand will keep bleeding, but you probably won't die before we land.

If we get ice with our drinks, we'll make up a pack with the cubes and you can press that against it. Okay?'

'Never better,' said Dreyfuss, his voice laryngitic. 'Who are we going to telephone?'

'There's only one person I can think of right now. Frank Stewart.'


The telephone was one of a row of four. Parfit brought a paper napkin from his pocket. The napkin was from the café, and on it Stewart had scrawled a telephone number.

'He's going to be a bit surprised to get a call so quickly,' said Dreyfuss.

'He's going to be absolutely furious,' Parfit said, having pressed home the digits, awaiting a response at the other end.

Dreyfuss was intrigued. But he was also full of pain, and couldn't separate the two. They'd used a packet of cotton wool and a whole box of plasters on his hand, but he could feel the blood soaking through already. They'd also bought aspirin, and he'd swallowed half a dozen. He needed a drink.

'Stewart? It's Parfit. Listen, I need some help. No questions, just help. I'll explain later. What?' Parfit listened. 'No, we're at the airport. Yes, flying out.' He held the receiver away from his ear as Stewart's stream of invective flew out. Then, as briskly as it had started, it ended. Parfit returned the receiver to his ear. 'I couldn't tell you, Stewart. It would have meant too many other people knowing about it. Anyway, the point is, we've encountered a slight problem. That problem has been dealt with in the short term, but some cleaning-up needs to be done.' He listened again. 'In the gents' toilets,' he said at last. 'International departures. Last cubicle along.' There was another pause. 'How long will it take?' He nodded and smiled. 'That's great, Stewart. What? No, he's fine. I will. Goodbye.'

He slipped the receiver back into its cradle. 'Stewart sends his love,' he said to Dreyfuss.

'But can we really trust him?' Dreyfuss asked, his throat raw like sunburn.

'From the way he was questioning you in that hospital in Sacramento, it was quite obvious he hadn't a clue what was going on.' Parfit had started walking, and Dreyfuss walked with him, his whole arm throbbing. They were nearing the long, gleaming bar of the departures lounge. Parfit kept talking as they walked. 'We're up against generals, not spooks,' he said. The barman was ready to serve them. 'Scotch on its own,' Parfit ordered. 'But bring over the ice bucket, will you?' He turned to Dreyfuss. 'What'll you have?'

'Whisky,' croaked Dreyfuss. 'A double.'

The barman nodded and moved off to fix their drinks.

'Keep talking,' said Dreyfuss. 'It might take my mind off the bleeding.'

Parfit needed no further prompting. 'There's not much more to tell. Stewart will watch Esterhazy like the proverbial hawk.' He smiled again. 'It's a bit like the old days, special relationship and all that.' The smile faded. 'Of course, we can't trust the NSA *too* far, maybe not very far at all, but Stewart . . . well, I've got a feeling about Frank Stewart.'

The drinks had arrived, and with them the ice bucket. Dreyfuss reached his left hand into the chill centre of the white plastic basin and pulled out a cluster of cubes, which he dropped into his right-hand jacket pocket, packing them around his fingers and his palm. The barman was watching him but had seen worse behaviour in Departures.

'Cheers,' said Parfit, glancing towards the toilets. 'Here's to absent friends.'

'Cheers,' said Dreyfuss, before downing his drink in two hungry gulps.

Three musical notes preceded an address over the tannoy, announcing that their flight was boarding. Parfit patted Dreyfuss' back.

'Come on,' he said. 'In-flight drinks are gratis, I believe. The first one's on me.'

Dreyfuss grimaced. 'Plenty of ice with mine,' he said, feeling the damp in his pocket and not knowing whether it was evidence of melting ice or of his warm blood soaking through the compress.

'Plenty of ice it is,' said Parfit.

# 27

Hepton had the idea that everyone knew more than they were telling. Fair enough, he thought: probably *he* knew more than he was telling, too. And it was with this in mind that he asked Jilly if she knew of any restaurants where the public telephone was out of sight of the dining area, and preferably close to the toilets. They were sitting in the Curzon Street building, drinking tea and waiting for Sanders to come and pick them up. The spy chiefs had thanked them for attending the meeting, and had hoped there would be no need to meet again.

'I'll second that,' Jilly had said.

'I suppose I can think of a few,' she said now. 'Why do you want to know?'

'I want to make a telephone call, but I don't want Sanders knowing about it. For one thing, I don't trust him. For another, I don't want him to know who I'm telephoning. Everyone who gets involved in this thing seems to be in danger.'

'Who *are* you going to telephone?'

'Nick Christopher.'

'Your friend at the base?'

'Yes. Don't ask why, not yet. Are any of these restaurants close to here?'

'One's fairly close.' She was rising to the challenge. 'It's Italian. There's a wall phone downstairs, just next to the kitchen and the toilets. All the tables are upstairs. Would that do?'

'Perfect. All I'd need you to do is keep Sanders occupied while I'm downstairs.'

She smiled archly. 'If I know Sanders, that shouldn't be difficult.'

There was a knock on the door of the room, and Sanders' head appeared. 'Sorry I'm late,' he said. 'Another job.'

'Well, you *should* be sorry,' Jilly said, sounding peeved. She rose from her chair. 'Just for that, Sanders, lunch is on you.'

He shrugged his shoulders. 'Anything to oblige.'

'Good,' said Jilly, taking his arm. 'There's this little Italian place off Regent Street . . .'

Hepton, marvelling, followed.

Jilly had judged things perfectly. Sanders was keen to get on in his career, and slightly in awe of his superiors. He also felt a little aggrieved at having been left out of the top-level meeting, and his attention was total as, seated at a corner table in the restaurant, Jilly began to tell him all about it. He wanted to know every detail, and she was only too willing to tell. Soon, with a few tantalising lies thrown in to make the mixture even more intriguing, she had him hooked, a child to her fairy tale. They had just finished the first course. Hepton had ordered a veal dish to follow, though he hated veal on principle.

'That dish is very special, sir,' the waiter had informed him, pointing it out on the menu. 'You see, it says there it takes thirty minutes to cook.'

It did indeed warn of this, which was why Hepton had chosen it. He didn't want to be on the telephone downstairs and have his food waiting for him upstairs, causing Sanders to realise that he was away from the table. He had to be sure of a gap between the first course and the main. So he had nodded, and Jilly had caught his reasoning.

'That sounds good,' she had said. 'I think I'll change my mind and have the veal instead of the chicken.' The waiter had nodded, scribbling on his pad. Then Sanders had joined in.

'Make that three veals,' he'd said, and they had all smiled.

'Excuse me a minute,' Hepton said now, lifting his napkin from his lap and dropping it onto the table. Sanders nodded, but hardly paid any attention. Jilly had started another story about the meeting. Hepton rose to his feet and walked towards the back of the restaurant. An arrowed sign told him that the toilets were downstairs, and he descended the staircase slowly, his heart thumping furiously.

The wall phone was not in use. It was a modern chrome effort, with a blue receiver. It accepted most coins, and Hepton searched in his pocket. He came out with one pound and seventy pence. He checked his watch. It had just crept past one o'clock. Good: the rate wouldn't be at its most expensive. He probably had enough. He picked up the receiver, dropped in the money and saw it register on the liquid crystal display, and dialled.

'Hello?' said a voice on the other end.

'Yes,' said Hepton, 'I'd like to speak to Nicholas Christopher, please. He works in control.'

'I'll see if I can find him. Who's calling?'

'It's his brother, Victor.'

'Hold on.' The phone went quiet.

Hepton bit his bottom lip, then changed his mind and bit his top lip instead. Someone was coming down the stairs. A fat man in shirt and tie: one of the diners from upstairs. He pushed open the door to the gents' and, once inside, started whistling the background music from the restaurant's hi-fi. Hepton turned his attention back to the amount of money he had left. The LCD was ticking down, but there was still plenty of time.

He hoped Nick Christopher would recognise the code. One night, they had gone off base to a local pub, where the landlord had informed them that there was a disco in the village hall. After a few beers, they had visited the disco, and Christopher had dragged them onto the dance floor to introduce themselves to two young women.

'I'm Nick,' he'd shouted over the music, 'and this is Vic. Nick and Vic.'

In private, that nickname – Vic – had stuck to Hepton for a few weeks, producing a smile every time as it reminded them of that night and that disco.

The receiver suddenly came to life.

'Brother Victor,' said Nick Christopher knowingly. 'I thought you were on holiday?'

'I am. Can you talk?'

'Yes.'

'I mean, is there anyone with you?'

'Well, I'm at my console.'

'So there *are* people around you?'

'Not many, but yes. Look, give me your number and I'll call you back.'

'Okay, but hurry.' Hepton recited the telephone number and put down the receiver. A good portion of his money, unused, came clanking out, and he scooped it back into his pocket. The phone started to ring. 'Yes?' he said.

'Okay, I can talk now.' Christopher's voice was not as hale and hearty as it had been in the control room.

'What's happening, Nick?'

'I don't know, Vic. It's been pretty weird here since I last saw you. Fagin asked me if I had any idea where you were. He said he needed to contact you about something. And now . . . we're moving out.'

'What?' Hepton's face creased in puzzlement.

'Moving out. The place is being closed down temporarily. Something to do with fitting a new system. I don't know, something like that anyway. So everybody's getting two weeks' R and R.'

'But what about *Zephyr*?'

'She'll be stationary. There's going to be a skeleton staff to keep an eye on things. Fagin and a few others.'

'What others?' It was beginning to fall into place now.

'I don't know. But none of us. So, anyway, why did you call?'

Hepton had almost forgotten himself. 'Oh,' he said, reminded. 'I've got a big favour to ask.'

'Name it.'

'I want you to send me a video tape of Buchan airbase. As recent as you can manage, so long as it's after the *Zephyr* malfunction.'

'You've got to be joking!'

'I'm deadly serious.'

'What the hell for? I could end up in jail for a stunt like that.'

'Look, Nick, remember what I told you about Fagin and Paul and everything?'

'Yes, I remember. But Paul's dead now, isn't he? They said you were the one who found him.'

'I was. It wasn't suicide, Nick. It just looked that way. If we're going to find his killers, I need that tape. And if you could also send one of Buchan before *Zephyr* went haywire, that would help too. This is an emergency, Nick. I mean, life and death.'

'Well, maybe, but . . . Christ, I can't just—'

'You're shutting down, right?'

'Yes.'

'So it should be easy.' Hepton thought fast. 'Stuff's being moved about, boxed up, what have you. Say a couple of video tapes go missing, it's bound to happen.'

'Okay, so I put them in my pocket – then what? Down to the local post office?'

Hepton hadn't thought about that. He didn't want to involve Sanders – or anyone else he didn't feel able to trust. But if he wanted the tapes tonight . . . And he *did* want the tapes tonight.

'Nick, do you still go to the Bull?' The Bull was the public house closest to the base. It was a brisk evening walk, and a pleasant one in the summer months.

'Not for a while.'

'Could you drop in tonight? Just for a pint?'

'And take the tapes with me?'

'That's the idea.'

'I'm not sure I can get them that soon.' Christopher paused. 'Will you be at the Bull?'

'I'll try.'

'The thing is, there's a lot of logging to be done before we shut down. I'm not sure Fagin will spare me enough time. We were working till ten last night. I was so tired afterwards, I just collapsed into bed.'

'Look, Nick, try your best, will you?'

He seemed to give this serious thought. Hepton was under no illusions: Nick was a nice enough guy, but he was no hero. Look after number one, that had always been his creed. There was an all-too-audible sigh on the line. Then he spoke.

'Okay, Martin,' he said. 'If you want cloak and dagger, you can have it. I'll be in the Bull at seven.'

'Thanks, Nick.'

'You owe me one.'

'I won't forget. See you tonight.'

Hepton put down the receiver and turned towards the stairs. Sanders was standing there, three steps up, arms folded. He had obviously heard some of the conversation.

'Where are we going?' he asked.

There was no point lying. 'Binbrook, Lincolnshire. To the *Zephyr* base. I have to meet someone there.'

'Can I ask why?'

Hepton moved past him and started upstairs, Sanders following.

'No,' he said. 'But it could mean a whole lot of brownie points for you.'

'I still need to know why we're going to Lincolnshire.'

Hepton stopped and turned to him. 'Is there a video recorder in the safe house?'

'Yes.'

'Good, because we're going to be watching some videos later on, after we come back.'

Sanders nodded. 'Why didn't you just tell me?'

Hepton fixed his eyes on those of the younger man. 'Because you worked for Villiers,' he said. 'And because for all I know, you still do.'

Sanders shrugged. 'You're entitled to your opinion,' he said. 'But like it or not, I'm coming with you tonight. What about Jilly?'

'I'd rather she didn't go with us. No real reason.'

'You think it could be dangerous?'

Hepton managed a wry smile. 'These days,' he said, 'who can tell?'


Of course, Jilly was furious. She didn't want to be left out, and the fact that Hepton wasn't telling her much about the trip only served to kindle her curiosity further.

'Damn you, Martin Hepton! You were always too secretive, that was what I hated about you!'

Her words bounced around inside his head all during the drive. In the end, she had calmed a little, thrown herself into a chair and picked up a newspaper, using it as a shield against him. No matter how pleasant the house in Marlborough Place was – and it *was* pleasant – it was still a prison, a place of detention. There were two guards to look after Jilly, but they didn't only stop people entering the house; they stopped them leaving as well. And if Jilly was nothing else, she was a free spirit. Hepton could vouch for that.

*Always too secretive. Damn you.*

Yes, he'd been secretive. He had told her about his work, but not *all* about it. There always had to be something held back, something left unsaid. And he had never talked much about himself anyway, preferring to hear Jilly talk about her own life. It was so much more lively and vibrant, so much more interesting. So much more . . . open.

'I'd still like to know,' Sanders yelled. He was driving fast, with the car radio tuned in to the closing overs of a cricket match and the windows open to let some early-evening breeze into the stifling interior. The sun was coming lower in the sky. Soon, Hepton was thinking, soon it'll start getting dark earlier . . . Except that in some places it already was getting dark earlier.

'What?' he said.

'I'd still like to know,' Sanders called, 'what's on these videos.'

'Me too,' Hepton murmured. 'Me too.'

*

They were later arriving at the Bull than Hepton had intended: traffic jams all the way out of London, and major roadworks on the road north. Even Sanders' most manic driving had been unable to make up all the time they'd lost. So it was nearly eight when they pulled into the pub's gravel car park. There were a dozen or so other cars there. Hepton gave each one a searching inspection as Sanders passed them and stopped at the furthest point into the car park, then executed a three-point turn and drove slowly past the double line of vehicles once again. Hepton looked at him and saw that Sanders was inspecting the cars as meticulously as he himself had done. Satisfied that they were all empty, he pulled up close to the car park's entrance, ready for a quick getaway.

'Here goes,' he said. 'I'm dying for a pint.'

They walked into the bar by its car park entrance. There were couples at three tables, and a group of possibly underage teenagers huddled around another. A game of darts was taking place, and three men propped up the bar, as though the activity gave their life all meaning. The barman smiled at Hepton and Sanders as they approached.

'Evening, gentlemen. What's your poison?'

'Two pints of Courage bitter,' Sanders said. He turned to Hepton. 'That okay with you?'

Hepton nodded dispiritedly. There was no sign of Nick Christopher in the spacious bar, and it was well past his designated time. Either he'd been and gone, or he wasn't coming. Had Fagin got to him? And if so, what would happen next? Everyone in this bar could be implicated, could be working for Villiers and Harry. He tried not to stare, but it wasn't easy.

Sanders was managing to look casual about the whole business. Just two men out for a drink. He raised the straight glass to his lips, gulping at the first couple of mouthfuls.

'Not a bad pint,' he said.

One of the three men nearby seemed to hear him, and turned his head.

'You from London?'

Sanders smiled pleasantly. 'Not originally. But I live there now.'

'Thought you did,' said the man, turning back to his friends. 'Beer's like piss down there,' he informed them. 'And the water, you can't drink the water. Been through seven pairs of kidneys before it gets to you, been pissed out seven times before you drink it.'

His friends wrinkled their faces and chuckled. Sanders reddened. He was trying to keep up the facade, but Hepton could see he was having trouble. His eyes had acquired a fiery tinge to them, and his free hand rubbed at his armpit, just where the holstered gun nestled.

'Cheers,' Hepton said, trying to distract him, lifting his own glass to his lips.

Sanders twitched his head towards a table and carried his glass over to it. Hepton followed closely, placing his beer on one of the mats on the highly polished tabletop. The men at the bar were sharing a joke. He couldn't help thinking they were discussing him, and he too reddened slightly at the cheeks.

'Where's your friend, then?' Sanders asked, his voice sharp, kept low only through the greatest restraint.

'I don't know,' Hepton said. 'Maybe he couldn't make it.'

Sanders shook his head. 'So what do we do now?'

'Go back to London?' Hepton offered.

Sanders stared hard at him. 'Where are these video tapes?' he asked. 'We'll just have to go fetch them.'

It was Hepton's turn to shake his head. 'That isn't possible.'

'Why not?'

'It would mean going into the lion's den.'

'Better that than sitting in this particular den.' Sanders threw a baleful glance towards the bar.

'I could try phoning him again, let him know we're here.'

Sanders considered this. 'Might be an idea,' he said.

Hepton stood up. 'Back in a second.' He took a look around but could see no sign of a telephone. He went to the bar. The barman had the same fixed smile on his face.

'Yes, sir?'

'Do you have a telephone?'

The barman shook his head theatrically. 'Not as such, no. We don't have a public telephone, but there's one behind the bar.' He reached down and lifted an aged Bakelite handset onto the counter. 'Provided it's a local call, that is.'

'Oh yes,' Hepton assured him. 'It's local. We were supposed to be meeting a friend here, but we got held up. He's probably been and gone.'

'Would that be Mr Christopher?'

Hepton stared in surprise at the man, who was fussing beneath the bar again. 'Yes,' he said.

'Ah,' said the barman, as if this explained everything. 'Mr Christopher said there'd just be the one of you. Victor, he said it would be.'

'Yes, that's me.'

'Only,' the barman continued, 'he said he couldn't stop, since things are so busy back at that spy place of his where he works. So he asked me to give you this.'

Hepton stared at the plain white plastic carrier bag. The two black video cases were visible inside.

'Dirty films,' said one of the locals. 'That's what we thought, isn't it, Gerry?'

The barman's smile broadened, and the three locals gave throaty laughs. Hepton joined them, elated.

'No,' he said. 'Not dirty films. Just tapes of a friend's wedding.'

'Including the honeymoon?' rasped the first man, causing more laughter.

Hepton had brought a ten-pound note from his pocket.

'I think this calls for a round,' he said. 'Whatever these gentlemen are having, and one for yourself.'

The barman nodded, lifting the telephone back off the bar-top, and the three locals made appreciative noises, none of which sounded like 'thank you'.

'Nothing for yourself, sir?' one of them asked Hepton as the pint glasses were being refilled.

Hepton shook his head. 'We really should be going,' he said.

They watched as he went back to his table and spoke a few words to the Londoner. Then both men left the bar without so much as a wave of the hand or a nod of the head, carrying the bag with them.

'Forgot all about his change,' the barman noted drily.

'In that case,' said the oldest of the locals, 'keep the beer coming, Gerry.'

At one of the tables by the window, where a middle-aged couple were sitting, the wife suddenly produced a portable telephone from her handbag. The man took the phone and pressed a lot of digits, then waited. Eventually he said a few words, not much more than a sentence, and in a quiet voice. Then he gave the contraption back to his wife, who replaced it in her handbag. They finished their drinks and left the pub, the woman bowing her head slightly towards the bar as she left.

'Cheerio then,' the barman called in response.

'There's a lot of queer folk about,' said one local. The others nodded agreement and went back to their drinks. The rest of the night was to come as something of an anticlimax.

## 28

Hepton considered that he had seen Sanders' driving at its absolute worst. The journey back to London, however, served to impress upon him that this was an age without absolutes. Sanders seemed seized by demons, and determined to get back to the relative safety of the city as soon as he could. The men at the Bull had angered him, that was for sure. He was used to being undermined by his superiors, but not by people he would consider his inferiors by a fairly large margin. The needle on the dashboard flickered wildly around the seventy mark on the narrower roads, and Hepton felt sick in his stomach, the beer inside him sloshing wildly. On wider roads, they hit one hundred and ten miles per hour. It was, thank God, the only thing they hit.

Hepton, however, said nothing. He too was keen to get back to the safe house. Keen to watch the video tapes and see what he might discover. It was dark when they arrived, the sky spotted with yet darker clouds. The air was growing chill, so that they had to close the car windows and put on the heater for a little while. The night became greenish-yellow as the London street lights began to shine.

'Here we are,' Sanders said as they entered St John's Wood and turned into Marlborough Place. There had been little conversation on the drive back. It struck Hepton that the two of them had nothing in common, and that if they had not been thrown together like this, they would never have chosen one another as companions.

'Hold on,' Sanders said in warning as the car approached the house. His eyes had narrowed to slits, his face close to the windscreen.

'What is it?' Hepton was looking, too, but could see nothing out of place. Sanders drove past the house without stopping. 'What is it?' Hepton repeated in a low hiss.

'Too many lights on.'

'What?'

'All the lights inside the house are on. So is the light outside the front door, and the one to the side of the garage. It even looks as though there might be lights on in the garden.'

'So?' Hepton didn't want to think about what Sanders might be implying.

'So, something's wrong.' He pulled the car in to the kerb and stopped, shutting off the engine and killing the lights.

'What are we going to do? Just wait here? Jilly's in there! We can't—'

But Sanders was staring at the number plate of the car parked in front of them. The car itself was a Vauxhall Cavalier like his. He seemed not to have heard Hepton's outburst.

'Funny,' he said. 'That's Thommo's car.'

'Thommo? Who's Thommo?'

'The other lot. MI5. He's one of their . . . well, men.' He stared at Hepton, his face draining of colour. 'We better go in, but slowly. Keep with me.'

They opened the car doors and closed them – as Sanders instructed – quietly. Sanders was already pulling his gun from its holster as they approached the house. Hepton was frantic now. What had happened? There was no one to meet them at the front door, no guard. Sanders pushed open the door. There were voices coming from within, though muted. Everyone was being very quiet indeed. Then someone came into the hall, saw them, and turned his head back into the living room.

'Sir,' he called. 'Visitors.'

Another man, balding but not yet middle-aged, his moustache thickly black, popped his head into the hall, stared at Hepton and Sanders, then lifted his eyes towards the ceiling and gave a great groan of relief.

'Sanders, you bastard. Thank God. I thought they'd got you.'

Sanders was slipping his pistol back beneath his arm. He had become very businesslike, his voice like something lifted from cold storage.

'Fill me in,' he said.

The man looked from Sanders to Hepton, then back to Sanders. Sanders turned towards Hepton, who knew what he was going to say and cut in first.

'I'm not leaving. I've got a right to hear it too.' He looked at the man. 'Is Jilly all right?'

'She's not here,' the man said levelly. 'They've taken her with them, I suppose.'

'What about Bentley and Castle?' asked Sanders.

'Dead,' said the man. 'A neat job, clean. One knifed in the back, the other done with a garrotte.'

*Neat, clean.* Hepton was thinking of only one person: Harry. Sanders seemed to have read his mind, and nodded towards him before turning again to the man.

'All right, Thommo. I need details.'

'When you weren't here, I had to contact your department.'

'I appreciate that. Has anyone arrived?'

'Not yet. We only got here ourselves quarter of an hour ago.'

'Did you get anything on tape?'

'That's how we knew. No voices, though, apart from the woman's.'

'Jilly,' Hepton said. His voice was close to cracking.

'So if your surveillance team heard it all,' Sanders said, his tone accusatory, 'how come everyone had gone before you got here?'

'Surveillance is just that, Sanders. They called us, we came. All told, it took us about five minutes. But by then . . .' He shrugged his shoulders.

'This is a mess,' Sanders said, rubbing his temples.

'Jilly,' Hepton repeated. Sanders put an arm around him.

'Go sit down,' he ordered, 'I'll fix something to drink.'

Hepton began to move towards the living room.

'Not in there,' the man said. 'That's where we took the bodies.'

Sanders nodded. 'Go upstairs, Martin. I'll bring a drink up to you.'

Hepton felt beaten, utterly beaten, for the first time in what seemed an age. Harry had won, Villiers had won, they'd all won. And he had lost. He nodded his head and began to climb the stairs. Sanders and the other man – Thommo – were speaking together in hushed tones before he had reached the first-floor landing. He caught a few phrases.

'Clean-up party . . . how did they know? . . . tapes . . . phone call . . .'

Tapes! Hepton looked down and saw that he was clutching the carrier bag to his body. He ran his fingers over it. He still had the tapes. He walked across the landing, but instead of going into his own room, he entered what had been Jilly's. She had been reading:

there was a paperback lying open, face down, on the bed. It was one of the titles from the living room shelves, a modern romance. On her bedside cabinet sat a cup half full of tea. Hepton touched it; there was still a hint of warmth to it.

He had no doubts at all about who had taken Jilly. He even thought he knew why: as a warning to him, a personal warning not to go any further. They had to be desperate. They must know that it was not only Hepton's battle now; that others were involved. Yes, they *had* to know that. And yet they still wanted to scare him off. Why? Because of what he thought he knew, that portion of the secret he had not yet revealed to anyone? Whatever the answer, it was clear that they still saw him as a threat.

That thought gave him heart.

What was more, the sooner he solved the final riddles, the sooner he might be reunited with Jilly. But he had to be careful. Her life was in *their* hands now, in Harry's hands. He had to be very careful indeed. And sitting here wasn't going to do anybody any good. He needed a TV monitor and a video recorder. Ideally, he needed two monitors and two recorders – good recorders at that, with a freeze-frame facility that actually froze the frame, and didn't make it twitch or smear. A hard image, that was what he needed.

He realised that he wasn't going to go to pieces; that the worst was over. He felt calm and controlled. God knows why, but he did.

There was a knock at the door, and it opened. 'Oh, there you are.' Sanders entered, carrying a bottle of whisky under his arm and a crystal glass in each hand. Hepton shook his head.

'That's not what I need,' he said. 'What I really need is a TV lab. Your surveillance personnel probably have one. Get me there, then I'll show you what's on these.' He slapped the tapes.

Sanders studied him, to ascertain whether he might be suffering from shock or something similar. All he saw was determination and a mind ready for work.

'I'll call in,' he said. 'I think I know just the place.'

'One question,' said Hepton. 'How did they know about *this* place?'

Sanders shook his head. 'I wish to God I knew.'

## 29

It was after midnight, but the man they had summoned back from his bed and his wife to this cold building in the middle of a bleak industrial estate near Notting Hill seemed not to mind.

'No, really,' he said. 'This is what makes it all worthwhile.'

'I hope you're right,' said Hepton. The man had introduced himself as Graeme Izzard. Thommo had assured them that he was the best 'pictures' man in the business.

'I work mainly for Special Branch,' Izzard told Hepton. 'Serious Crime, that sort of thing. You know, someone walks into a building society and shoots dead a teller. They capture the whole thing on camera, but the image is too blurred to be recognisable. I clean it up until it's sharp from arsehole to breakfast time. Which reminds me . . .' He looked at his watch, then turned to Sanders. 'There's an all-night caff, just up the road and turn right. You can't miss it. There'll be about a dozen cabs outside. It's where the drivers go for their break. Get us, let's think, something hot, a sausage sandwich, something like that. Plus some cold sandwiches for later, corned beef or salami. And tell Alfie, the man behind the counter, that Izzard says he's to give you a flask of tea. Got that?'

Sanders looked devastated. He had been demoted to tea boy by a man if anything a year or two younger than himself, with straggly shoulder-length hair and a T-shirt advertising a heavy-metal band. This was the third blow of the evening.

Hepton's first impression of Izzard had been similarly coloured by his youth – he looked no more than twenty-six or twenty-seven – and his clothing. He had a London accent, too, harshly grained, the sort of voice heard at market stalls and football matches. But there was no doubt that he had a certain swagger that told you not to muck him about or underestimate him.

He offered Sanders a five-pound note from a wad pulled from his jeans pocket, but Sanders shook his head and stumbled away, still shell-shocked. Izzard watched the door close behind him.

'Stuck-up sod,' he said. 'I hate bloody SIS. Mind you, the other lot are no better. Give me Scotland Yard every time. Their heads aren't in the clouds. A bit more down-to-earth, you know?'

Hepton nodded, unable to think of any reply. Izzard had brought them into a large warehouse of modern corrugated construction. There were crates neatly stacked against one of the high walls, but this was no ordinary warehouse. Much of the floor space was taken up by another, smaller building of more solid, prefabricated construction. Izzard went to the door of this smaller building and unlocked it. An alarm sounded, and he switched on the lights before finding another key on his heavy chain and turning it in the alarm box, cancelling the ringing. He looked satisfied. They were in a small antechamber. On another door was a numerical keypad and a tiny keyhole. Izzard pushed five digits and turned a slender key in the lock, and the door clicked open.

Inside this room, there was an air-conditioned chill. Izzard swung an arm around proudly. 'The lab,' he said.

Hepton, used to technical labs, nodded, impressed. There was hardware aplenty: computers, monitors, video cameras, recorders, a huge studio-style machine for editing and splicing film, projectors, and workbenches covered in all manner of electrical instruments, bits of chopped film, broken-open cassette cases. The place was a mess, evidence that a lot of work was done here.

'All this Russian-doll stuff, a box within a box within a box, it's really to cut down vibration from outside more than anything,' Izzard explained. He bounced on the floor in his Dr Martens shoes. 'Decoupled from the rest of the building,' he said proudly. 'That was my design, actually.'

'This is incredible,' said Hepton. He had been attracted to the computers, and stood over one now. He frowned. 'I don't recognise—'

'That's my design, too,' said Izzard, running a finger over the keyboard. 'We do our own software and, in this case, hardware. It's just a number-cruncher, really. Do you know about computers?'

'I work in a tracking station,' said Hepton.

Izzard looked impressed and pleased. His face became more

boyish than ever. 'You track satellites?' Hepton nodded. 'I love all that stuff. Signals intelligence, comms intelligence.'

'That's what's on these tapes,' said Hepton, brandishing the bag. Izzard looked like a child offered sweets.

'Yes?' he said, reaching out a hand. 'Well then, let's put them on the machine and take a look.' His tone became more serious. 'What is it that you want exactly?'

'I want to examine the pictures,' Hepton said, following Izzard to one of the benches. 'Side by side if possible.'

'Very possible.'

'And then maybe concentrate on a few shots.'

'I can put them side by side on the same screen.' Izzard turned to him. 'If you like.' Hepton smiled and nodded.

Izzard brought the tapes out of the bag. There was a note inside one of the boxes. *You owe me a beer, Vic!* He handed it to Hepton, then turned his attention to the tapes themselves.

'Hmm,' he said. 'High-resolution tape, and plenty of it.' Even Hepton could see that there was a good deal of tape on each spool: perhaps as much as a couple of hours' worth. Yes, he owed Nick Christopher a beer.

He noticed that he had rested his hand on a small modem. He tapped it.

'Ever done any hacking?' he asked.

Izzard's face lit up again. 'Yes, years ago. I used to love it. What about you?'

'I've done a little.'

'I got into a couple of big companies' systems,' Izzard said, warming to his tale. 'Left messages there for the staff. Stuff like: "Do you know what your wife's up to right this second?" Childish, but still a lot of fun.'

Hepton smiled. 'Wasn't it difficult working out the code words?'

'Hellish difficult, yes.' Izzard had put down the tapes. 'Typing in everything from aardvark to zygote.'

He went to a large steel cupboard and opened it. There were bits and pieces of equipment arranged along the shelves inside. He found what he was looking for and brought it out, closing the door again. It was a small black box, the size of one of Nick Christopher's crossword dictionaries. Built into its top surface was what looked like an old-fashioned LED pocket calculator.

'It was difficult,' Izzard said proudly, 'until I made this.' He handed Hepton the box. Hepton examined it, but without success. The several home-made switches and push-buttons were unmarked.

'I give up,' he said. 'What is it?'

'It's another number-cruncher of sorts,' Izzard explained, pleased that Hepton hadn't known. 'Some of the companies use long numerical codes, and those were the worst to crack. All I needed to do was plug this box into my modem and it did all the work for me.'

'Ingenious,' said Hepton, examining the box more carefully.

'No,' said Izzard, 'what's *really* ingenious is that I cooked up a chip that put the other computer on hold while *my* computer was pumping the code numbers into it.'

Hepton saw the implications at once. 'So you didn't need to sign off and try again every time you got the code wrong?'

Izzard nodded his head vigorously, then gave a childish, high-pitched laugh.

'Brilliant,' said Hepton. 'I hope you took out a patent on it.'

'No,' said Izzard, calming a little. 'But I sold the idea to the military for fifteen thousand pounds.' He lifted the black box out of Hepton's hand and returned it to its cupboard. 'God knows what they wanted it for,' he said with finality.

As he closed the cupboard, a buzzer sounded. 'That'll be our spy,' said Izzard, 'wishing to come into the cold.' He pressed a button on the wall, and the door clicked open again, admitting Sanders.

'Cheery lot, those cab drivers,' Sanders said grumpily. He was carrying a cardboard box. Hepton could smell the waft of fried sausage coming from within it, and realised he was hungry.

Izzard seemed to know what he was thinking. 'Never work on an empty tum,' he said, making for the box.


As the work continued, becoming ever more painstaking, Sanders fell asleep perched on a stool, his head and arms resting on a bench top. Izzard, however, seemed to grow more awake as the night progressed, while Hepton, though not feeling tired, began to feel disoriented, even hallucinatory for a few strange minutes.

Having examined the two tapes, they ran them side by side, and then started freeze-framing particular shots, shots of similar buildings taken from similar angles. On the top left corner of each was an hour-and-minute counter, and they used this to align the two tapes temporally, checking differences in light and in the quality of the shadows cast by the evening sun. Izzard never seemed satisfied, and would run a section again, sharpening the focus, enlarging a shot onscreen: this enlarging process was again of his own design and the unit he operated his own construction.

'I haven't perfected it yet,' he admitted, though the results were, to Hepton's eyes, impressive enough.

At four o'clock, Izzard suggested they pause for breakfast. Sanders was snoring, so they left him to his sleep and went outside. Birds were chirping hesitantly in the distance, and a few early cars and lorries were on the road. After the cool of the lab, the morning seemed already oppressively warm. Izzard walked with hands in pockets.

'I think I can see it,' he said.

'What?' Hepton asked, still coming out of his brief hallucinatory stage.

'What it is you've been looking for. I can see it now.' Izzard turned to him. 'They're not the same place, are they?'

Hepton smiled. 'No,' he said. 'They're not.' He was pleased that Izzard could see it, too. If he could see it, then everybody could see it. It wasn't just in Hepton's mind. 'I should have realised right back at the beginning,' he explained. 'One day I was watching Buchan and it got dark at a certain time. Then *Zephyr* was got at, and suddenly it was starting to get dark earlier at Buchan.'

'Except that it wasn't Buchan,' Izzard noted.

'That's right,' said Hepton. 'That's what this is all about. Someone doesn't want us to see what's *really* going on at Buchan. So instead they've rigged a lookalike.'

'A mock-up.'

'Yes. But a very good mock-up. A bit too good.'

'How do you mean?'

'I think it must be a real airbase, but not one of the other ones the USAF has been using. We've been watching all of those at one time or other. It must be RAF.'

'Excuse my ignorance, but if all you do all day is watch these pictures, wouldn't someone *notice* that it wasn't Buchan?'

'Not really,' said Hepton. 'For one thing, our remit wasn't to watch the bases so much as watch their perimeters for protesters.'

'Weird,' said Izzard. 'Not so long ago, they were protesting about the Americans *being* here. Now they're protesting about them *going*.'

'Besides,' Hepton continued, 'we mostly examine still photos, and still aerial photos look much the same. We would be checking for things that were *different*, not things that looked the same. We're only technicians, remember. We're not spies.'

Izzard nodded, deep in thought but enjoying himself.

'This base, the one they're using, it's south of Buchan?'

'Yes, someplace where it gets dark earlier than it does in Scotland at this time of year; somewhere down here.'

'There are plenty to choose from.'

'Not very many would fit the bill. It should be easy to find which one it is.'

'This begs two rather large questions: why, and how?'

They had reached the café. There were no taxis outside now. Shifts had either ended or not yet begun. The glare of strip lighting made Hepton squint as they pushed through the door. A small, sweating man was standing behind the counter, wiping it down with a rag. He looked up as they entered.

'This is a late one for you, Graeme,' he said to Izzard.

'I wouldn't mind, Alfie, but the overtime rate is diabolical. Give us two of your special breakfasts, will you?'

'Coming up. Where's my flask?'

Izzard opened his arms in apology. 'Sorry, Alfie. I forgot. It's back at the lab.'

'Well, never mind. Do you want any tea?'

'Coffee for me, black and sweet. What about you, Martin?'

'Black, no sugar, please,' said Hepton.

The man nodded and started to work.

'How and why,' said Hepton. 'Yes, you're right. But we're very close to answering both. I can feel it. I can almost answer the "how" right now, though it's only guesswork.'

'Go ahead.' They had seated themselves on padded benches either side of a Formica-topped table. Hepton rested his elbows on the table, hands supporting his head as he thought things through.

'Well,' he said. 'A shuttle, the *Argos*—'

'The one that crashed?'

'Yes, the one that crashed. It was up there launching a communications satellite. Except the satellite wasn't just your normal COM-INT satellite, it was an intercept.'

'An intercept?'

'Yes. Its purpose was to lock on to *Zephyr*. While it was locking on, *Zephyr*'s transmissions went haywire. But nobody minded that, because as long as the transmissions returned eventually, everyone would put it down to a glitch, nothing more. Some top brass from the military were on site when it all happened, just to check that the operation went smoothly. It did, more or less. Except I noticed how pleased they were looking, and one other person, a friend of mine, caught a hint of the interference. They murdered him and wiped his disk.'

Izzard whistled softly. Hepton paused, then continued.

'So what do we have? We have *Zephyr* apparently back to normal, except that it isn't, not quite. Because whenever we lock on to one particular spot – Buchan – the other satellite breaks in and transmits its own pictures to *Zephyr* before they're transmitted to the ground station.'

Izzard was shaking his head. 'This is too big for me,' he said. 'I'm used to bank robbers and spies, not conspiracies in space.'

'Conspiracy is right. The Americans and the British are in on it for a start. But the governments don't seem to know, only the generals.'

The door opened and a well-dressed man came into the café. Hepton glanced up at him, but was too intent on his story to pay him much attention. The man slid into the booth next to theirs, so that his back was to Izzard's back. Alfie was still in the kitchen, his frying pan sizzling.

'Only the generals,' Izzard repeated. 'So whatever's happening, what can we do about it?'

'I really don't know. We could persuade Whitehall that something's going on, but the suits in Curzon Street didn't seem to think it would produce much joy. What we need is proof, absolute proof.'

'Well, you've got that, haven't you? I mean, the tapes?'

'But what do they prove? Not *what's* happening, only that something *is*.'

'So go to Buchan. Take a look for yourself.'

'Yes,' said Hepton. 'Yes, maybe you're right.'

The newcomer swivelled on his bench so that he was facing their booth. Hepton glared at him, realising that he had heard every word. The man looked pale, tired. Not a killer, not just at the moment.

'Mr Izzard generally *is* right,' he said.

Izzard's head cracked round at the sound of the voice. Then his face broke into a grin.

'Why don't you join us?' he said. The man got up and did so. Izzard was still grinning. 'Once,' he said to Hepton, 'I went to lunch and came back to the lab, and I'd been in there ten minutes before I realised this sneaky sod was in there too. Just sitting, out of my line of vision, and absolutely still. A professional voyeur, that's what you are.'

The man took the remark as a compliment. He was holding out a hand to Hepton, who was wondering now where he had heard his voice before.

'Parfit,' the man said by way of introduction. 'We've spoken on the telephone. You must be Martin Hepton. They told me you'd come to see Izzard. And since Graeme spends more time in this establishment than in his lab, I thought I'd try here first.'

Hepton shook the proffered hand, a look of disbelief on his face.

'Parfit?' he said. 'Christ, when did you get back?'

'A couple of hours ago.'

'Is Dreyfuss with you?'

'Well, the safe house didn't appear to be safe any longer, so I've booked us into a hotel. He's resting there.'

'Does he know . . .?'

'About Miss Watson?' Parfit's face darkened. 'No. We were in a bit of a skirmish at the American end. Major Dreyfuss was injured. He lost some blood.' He saw the shocked look on Hepton's face. 'He's fine, really. I had a doctor patch him up. Believe it or not, there was one on the plane. There we were halfway over the Atlantic, and this poor chap was stitching a couple of the major's fingers. Quite exciting really. I didn't judge him fit enough, however, to take the news of Miss Watson's abduction. In fact, I *was* wondering . . .?'

'If I'd tell him?'

'Something like that. No real hurry. I'd like to be filled in first on what's so exciting about these mysterious tapes.'

Hepton looked to Izzard, who spoke. 'No problem there,' he said. 'We'll show you.' Alfie was approaching with two large plates. Izzard smacked his lips. 'Just as soon as we've had breakfast, eh?'


When he had seen what they had, Parfit was in no doubt about what had to be done.

'I'll send some men to Buchan, see what they can come up with. Not a lot, I shouldn't think. Security's bound to be tight. We'll also check on the other airbases south of there, see if we can find out which one they're using as a mock-up.'

He made the phone calls from the lab. Izzard sat on a high stool, pinching the bridge of his nose between his fingers and yawning: the night had finally caught up with him. Sanders was wide awake, however, and looking ready to impress Parfit, if such were possible. He'd still been sleeping when they'd arrived back at the lab, but had been shocked into wakefulness by the sound of his superior's voice, only then to feel acute embarrassment at having allowed Hepton and Izzard out of doors without his knowing about it.

Hepton had passed his own nadir and felt numb but not sleepy. He listened to the efficient phone calls with an appraising ear. Parfit didn't waste a single word, and his instructions were as foolproof as seemed possible. When he had finished, he replaced the receiver and turned to the room.

'Well, that's as much as we can do from here. Thanks, Graeme. Can we offer you a lift?'

But Izzard shook his head, in the middle of a protracted yawn, and gestured with an arm. 'I'm only five minutes' walk away,' he said.

Parfit nodded and turned his attention to Hepton. 'I think you'd better come back to the hotel with me,' he said. 'I can't think of anywhere safer to keep you, and you can see Major Dreyfuss.'

'That'll be fun,' Hepton said in an unemotional voice. Then: 'Where's the hotel anyway?'

'Only the best,' said Parfit. 'What better cover is there than an expensive West End hotel?'

'But not on Park Lane?' Hepton asked, growing uneasy.

Parfit caught his tone. 'Just off it,' he said. 'Why?'

'Because Cam Devereux's in the Achilles.'

'Ah.' Parfit nodded his understanding. 'Don't worry, we're in the Bellevue. Two streets back from the Achilles. Not so expensive either.' He turned to Sanders, who all but stood to attention. 'You can go home, too, Sanders. Get some rest. But I'll want your report on my desk by ten o'clock.'

'Yes, sir.'

Hepton knew Sanders would get precious little sleep: he'd work through the morning to perfect his report and buff it to a conspicuous sheen. He was a company man all right. Hepton shook hands with Izzard.

'Thanks for your help,' he said.

'Any time,' said Izzard, easing himself off the stool. 'But try to make it daylight hours, okay?'

'Okay,' said Hepton, with the glimmer of a smile. Then, to Parfit: 'Let's go see Mike Dreyfuss.'


'Wait a second,' said Hepton, checking from the car window. 'This isn't the way to Park Lane.'

'A slight detour,' Parfit said. 'It won't take long.'

They were in a maze of elegant town houses, somewhere in the midst of unimaginable wealth, otherwise known as Belgravia. The car pulled in to the kerb. The streets were silent; there was little to remind Hepton that he was living in the dangerous tail-end of the twentieth century. But there were subtle hints: alarm boxes above most of the tightly shut doors, a latticework of metal bars across a basement window. Little Fort Knoxes all in a row . . .

'Here we are,' said Parfit.

'Where?'

They were standing at the bottom of a short flight of stairs leading to a doorway. To the side of the door were a dozen nameplates, evidence that the house had been divided up into apartments. Hepton turned at the sound of a car door opening. The vehicle had been there when they'd arrived, but he'd spotted no signs of life. Now two men emerged. One stayed by the car while the other came to the steps, climbed them, and turned keys in the door, opening it. Coming back down the steps, he handed the keys to Parfit.

'Thank you,' said Parfit. The man returned to the car. Both men got in. Hepton realised that they were keeping guard.

'What is this place?' he asked.

'This is George Villiers' home,' Parfit explained. 'Come on, let's take a look.'

The reception hall was huge and elegant. There was some mail on a marble table. Parfit browsed through it, finding nothing of interest. They took the near-silent elevator to the third floor, where Parfit opened one of two doors on the landing. The nameplate had been removed.

'Why are we here?' asked Hepton. He breathed in the stagnant air of the long hallway. Parfit walked noiselessly towards the far door and pushed it open. A lounge, leading on to further rooms: dining room, a small study, and past this the bedroom. The apartment seemed to be a series of conjoined rooms, shaped in a 'U' around the hallway. Hepton repeated his question, but Parfit appeared intent on his surroundings, as though planning to make an offer on the vacant property.

'He didn't own this, you know,' he mused. 'I thought he did, but he didn't. It was supposed to be an inheritance. That was the story.'

'Who does own it then?'

Parfit smiled at Hepton, his eyes hooded and intelligent as a crow's. But instead of answering, he walked on from one room to another. Hepton caught him up as he was beginning to speak again.

'I never liked him. I was against his recruitment from the start.'

'Why didn't you stop him then?'

Parfit's smile this time was bitter. 'It wasn't up to me,' he said. 'I really had no say in things.' His eyes sought Hepton's. 'All I do is clear up the mess. Treatment rather than prevention, you see.' Hepton could feel the man's irritation. It filled the room and threatened to burst from it. 'My superiors recruited him, not me. Blake Farquharson recruited him. Well, he had his reasons, I suppose.' The emotion was melting away again, or rather was being shovelled back into some hidden cellar. But still there.

Why, Hepton wondered, was he being shown this side of Parfit, a man he barely knew?

Parfit walked on, through the study and into the bedroom. The bed was narrow, the room small and airless. There were no ornaments, nothing to brighten it or make it more than just a place for resting.

Resting and waiting. Hepton could imagine Villiers lying here at night, nothing distracting him from his thoughts, and his thoughts filled with death, glory, deceit.

There was a piece of card on the bed's one pillow. Hepton lifted it and turned it over: *SORRY YOU COULDN'T MAKE IT TO THE BURIAL*. The message was printed. Parfit read it, then took the card from Hepton and slipped it into his pocket.

Hepton started opening drawers, flicking through books in the study. He didn't doubt that some team specialised in such things had been through the apartment before him. But perhaps he knew what he was looking for better than they did. There were few clues, however. He switched on Villiers' word processor, only to find that what disks there were had been wiped clean, or had been empty to begin with.

*Coffin . . . burial.* The words rang in his head, growing loud, dissonant. He was wasting his time here. Why had they come?

They were leaving the apartment when it dawned on him. He remembered the book well. It had been one of the first he had ever read . . . well, the first without pictures in it. A bear was terrorising an isolated village. The backwoodsman hunted it. He tracked it to its lair, but found the lair empty. The man was fascinated by the cave, examined every inch of it. Then found the bear and killed it. Yes, Hepton remembered. He remembered, too, the way Harry had come to his flat in Louth and waited for him there.

The hunter gains strength and insight from the lair of his victim. Parfit was a hunter. And he had brought Hepton here because he wanted him to be a hunter too.

Satisfied, both men headed to Park Lane.

# 30

If Dreyfuss took the news of Jilly's abduction better than they had expected, it could probably be put down to a mixture of painkilling drugs and jet lag. His right hand was heavily bandaged up to and past the wrist, and he lay on the hotel bed with his good arm falling across his face, shielding his eyes from the light.

He mumbled something.

'What's that, Mike?' Parfit asked. Dreyfuss took his arm away from his eyes and angled his head up so as to look right into Parfit's face.

'I said,' he spat, 'we've got to kill them. It's the only way. They're killing us; we've got to kill them.' Then he flung his arm across his eyes again and let his head fall back onto the bed.

Parfit stared at Hepton worriedly. Dreyfuss was exhausted, doped and shocked. It was a lethal cocktail. Hepton understood and gave a reassuring nod.

But in his heart, he agreed with Dreyfuss. The scent of Villiers was still in his nose.

Dreyfuss turned onto his side, letting his damaged hand fall onto the bedcovers, where it lay. He was drifting back to sleep again, looking much older than Hepton remembered him: older, sad and angry at the same time. Well, if half of what Parfit had related on the drive over here was true, Dreyfuss had been to hell and back. Hepton had the feeling that he too might have to visit hell before this was all over. A little part of him was looking forward to it.

'Get some sleep, Mike,' Parfit said. 'We'll see you later.'

Hepton was to share with Parfit.

'My room's got twin beds anyway,' Parfit explained, 'and it saves paying for another single. God knows, my expenses on this are big enough already. The accounting department is going to want my head on a block.'

'How do you explain away a four-star hotel?' Hepton asked.

Parfit shrugged. 'Well, there don't seem to be any safe houses any more, and the first place they'd think of looking after that is seedy anonymous hotels. This place isn't exactly seedy.'

'But anonymous?'

'Well, let's just say it's discreet.'

'One thing worries me,' Hepton said, watching Parfit opening the door to their room. 'How is it they keep being able to find us?'

'Search me,' said Parfit, pushing the door wide. The room was large, and Hepton didn't mind sharing. It was seven o'clock, and outside, the morning's traffic jams were building up nicely. Work was beginning for the day, and Parfit suggested they rest till noon.

'Suits me,' said Hepton. 'But listen, did I tell you about the clever little transmitter Harry planted on me?'

'No,' said Parfit, sounding uninterested.

'Maybe they're using something similar to keep tabs on us.' Hepton was becoming excited.

'Maybe,' Parfit said, his voice dull with drowsiness.

Hepton saw that he was making no impression on the man, absolutely none. He went to the door and peered out into the empty hallway.

'No guards?' he asked.

'No,' said Parfit, slipping off his shoes. 'No guards. Now that they've got Miss Watson, I shouldn't think you're in much danger. They'll try using her as a lever first. Sleep tight.' In trousers, bare feet and shirt open at the neck, he fell onto the furthest bed and turned his face away.

Hepton sat on the edge of his own bed. He lay back, resting his hands behind his head. His mind still surged with energy. The heavy curtains were only half closed, giving enough light to see by. He examined the ceiling, its ornate mouldings. He tried to empty his mind of thoughts, but they swam around like fish in a tank, this way and that, passing each other, almost touching, then darting away. He closed his eyes, but that just made his whole head swim. What was he doing? They had Jilly: how was he supposed to sleep?

He thought of Cam Devereux, only two streets away. Those scared, haunted eyes, the hollow voice. The man had been hiding something. But what? Hepton replayed the scene: the hotel bar, the pianist playing to a table of women, Devereux's hard American inflections as he told his story. Of how the stranger had come to the *Argos* control room, set himself up at a console and . . .

Why do that? Why put him at a console in the main control room, with the full knowledge of the controllers? Drawing attention to the very man who was to be *Argos*'s executioner. It didn't make sense. Surely if he'd needed to be on base at all, they would have placed him somewhere away from curious eyes, in a room of his own, with his own terminal.

Yes!

Hepton swivelled his legs off the bed and stood up. Parfit was breathing heavily, already deep in slumber. Hepton went to the door and eased it open, slipping out into the corridor. He closed the door again, making sure not to dislodge the *Do Not Disturb* sign swinging from the brass knob. Then he walked silently, purposefully along the corridor and down the stairs into the main lobby. The Bellevue was no smaller than the Achilles, but made a show of being inherently more intimate. The reception clerk recognised him and made an obsequious bow from behind his desk. Hepton gave a casual wave and went to the revolving door, entering it and pushing softly. The door tumbled round until it discharged him onto the pavement and into the smells of the city: exhaust fumes and damp trees.

The same doorman as before was standing in front of the Achilles, and opened the door for Hepton as he climbed the steps. 'Good morning, sir,' he said.

'Good morning,' Hepton returned, entering the hotel.

He walked purposefully to the stairs before remembering that Devereux was on the second floor. So he crossed to the lifts instead. One was already waiting, and he stepped in. What was Devereux's room number again? He had forgotten, but remembered the room itself, along towards the end of the corridor, past the ice dispenser and the shoeshine machine. The lift cranked its way upwards, jolted to a stop and opened. Hepton stepped into the dimly lit corridor and turned right. Past the ice machine . . . the drinks dispenser . . . the polisher . . .

Yes, this was it: 227. A couple came out of the room opposite, talking about the breakfast they were about to eat. They glanced back at Hepton, who stood hesitating outside Devereux's door, then went on their way.

Hepton was about to knock on the door when he saw that it wasn't properly closed. There was the slightest of gaps, but he couldn't see into the room. Suddenly a sickening sensation hit him in the pit of his stomach. He leaned back into the corridor, brought up his foot and kicked open the door with the heel of his shoe. The room was dark, a crack of daylight coming through the closed drapes. And there was a funny sweet smell, like the gas he'd been given once as a child in the dentist's chair. He found the light switch and flipped it. Devereux was in bed, naked. Another figure, fully dressed, was crouched over him, holding a hypodermic syringe into his upper arm. The face had jerked upwards to look at Hepton.

One side of it was scarred by long white water blisters, edged with redness.

It was Harry.

'Oh Christ . . .' Hepton whispered, the hair prickling on his neck.

Harry's lips twisted into a delinquent smirk as she looked down at the prone body and saw that the syringe was empty. She retracted it, then seemed to examine Devereux's blank face before turning her attention to Hepton. But by then it was too late. Hepton had grabbed the door handle and pulled the door tightly shut. He locked both hands around the handle. He had her now. He had trapped Harry! He looked up and down the corridor, but it was empty. Still, soon someone would appear from a room, ready for breakfast, and he would order them to telephone Parfit. The main thing was—

'Hello, Martin.' The voice was faint, lacking any trace of emotion or feeling. Hepton resisted the temptation to place his ear against the door, the better to hear her words. He remembered Jilly's flat, the bullets splintering past him through the wood panelling. 'Long time no see,' Harry continued. 'I've just been tidying up a little.'

His voice was firm. 'Where's Jilly?'

'You should be dead by now. You know that, don't you? You've turned into a real challenge, Martin. I enjoy a challenge. I'll enjoy killing you.'

'I asked where Jilly was.'

'Does it matter? We've got her. If you want her alive, quit now.'

'Quit what?'

Her laughter was as cruel a sound as Hepton had heard. 'Just quit,' she said. 'You know what I mean.'

He looked around him again. There was still no one in the hallway. His arms were aching from holding the door closed, yet Harry had not yet attempted to open it.

'You didn't have to do that,' he said.

'Do what?'

'Murder Devereux.'

'Orders,' she said. 'That's all.'

'Orders from Villiers?'

'Ah, you know about Villiers. Yes, I'd forgotten that. Stupid man. He should have been more careful. But no, not Villiers. These orders came from overseas. Someone's been keeping tabs on Mr Devereux, someone besides your friends and you.'

'Oh? Who?'

'It doesn't matter. But the Americans have been getting nervous, so they asked—'

'All that matters is that the coffin gets buried,' said Hepton.

His words had their effect. There was silence from behind the door.

'Too many people know now, Harry,' he went on. 'Too many for even you to be able to shut them all up. You can't bury it.'

She laughed again. 'I don't see anyone stopping us. I see a lot of mice chasing their own tails and squeaking, only no one's paying attention to them because no one *wants* to pay attention to them. Because what *we're* doing is for the best.'

'Who's we, though? You and Villiers? The chiefs of staff? Who?'

'Bigger than that, Martin. Much, much bigger. Coffin.'

'But what does that mean?'

'It's an acronym, of course. You know how the armed forces and the bureaucrats love acronyms.'

An acronym: the letters standing for other words. 'What's it an acronym for? I never was much use at crosswords.' He realised that she'd hooked him. He was interested, despite himself. But her voice had become faint, as though she were moving away from the door, forcing him to bring his head closer.

'I'm going to kill you, Martin,' she said, 'the way I should have done right at the start in your flat. Don't think I didn't consider it. I could have put it down to a burglary. But it seemed messy at the time. It still isn't a necessity, not now we have your friend Miss Watson. But I'm going to do it anyway.' Her voice was very faint now. Hepton kept his head and body clear of the door, expecting a shot. None came. Then he heard the sound of exhausted breathing from along the corridor.

A thickset man had just reached the landing from the stairs. He was pausing at the top, trying to regain his breath. He stared along the corridor and saw Hepton.

'What do you think you are doing there?' he called. Then he started moving forward, quickly for his size. 'This is Mr Devereux's room.'

'I know,' Hepton said. The man moved towards the doorway, but Hepton gripped his arm with one hand and pulled him back, keeping the other tight on the door handle. 'There's a murderer in there,' he said.

The man's eyes widened; not in shock, Hepton realised, but in mild surprise only.

'A murderer?' The accent was difficult to place. Mediterranean? Eastern European?

'That's why I'm holding the door shut. She's still in there.'

'A she? And her victim?'

'He's in there too. Will you go for help, please?' Hepton was becoming exasperated. Who bothered to ask questions when a killer was around? But the man made no sign of moving. He seemed deep in thought. Then, his eyes on Hepton, he reached into his trouser pocket and produced a tiny gun, so dainty that it might have been a trick cigarette lighter. It might have been, but Hepton thought otherwise.

'Help has arrived,' the man said. He took two paces back from the door and pointed his gun at it. Hepton knew instinctively what was expected of him now. He released his grip on the handle, stepped back and gave the wood a mighty kick. The door flew open and the man crouched lower, still levelling the gun . . . But apart from Devereux's corpse, the room appeared empty. More than that, it *felt* empty. Hepton studied the scene. He couldn't imagine Harry hiding under the bed or in the wardrobe. The windows were double-glazed, impossible to open, so there was no escape route there. Which left only the bathroom. He looked at his new-found accomplice, who nodded in understanding. Together they walked to the bathroom door, the man pausing only quickly, expertly to check for any sign of a pulse in Devereux's wrist. There was none.

The bathroom door was slightly ajar, and Hepton glanced into the white-tiled room. A thick splash-proof curtain had been drawn across the shower. He pushed open the door and pointed to the curtain. The man aimed his pistol again, and Hepton yanked the curtain aside. The cubicle was empty. Hepton exhaled noisily and raised his eyes to the ceiling, where they stayed.

'Look,' he said. The man looked up too, and saw that the ceiling was a false one, with one small section pushed aside to reveal a dark gap.

'You think she has escaped?' the man asked in a whisper.

Hepton considered. No, the ceiling would not support a body's weight, and besides, where could it lead? Nowhere. He dashed back into the room and looked around. The wardrobe door was open now. Inside, the suits and shirts had been pushed along on their railing to allow a body to squeeze into the space. He placed his head in the wardrobe. He could smell soap: Harry's soap. He ran to the door and looked down the corridor, but there was no sign of her.

'Give me your gun,' he ordered. The man seemed startled. 'Give it to me.' He snatched the weapon from the man's hand and ran out of the room. He headed down the corridor towards the main staircase, and took the steps two at a time. There were guests in the reception area, buying newspapers, talking to the desk clerk, about to walk off breakfast. They stared at Hepton as he made for the glass doors, pushed through them and stood on the top step. The traffic below was snarled, becoming angry. The day was hazy. Still no Harry.

A moment or two later, he heard some foreign words behind him and turned to see the man barking something at the hotel's doorman. Then he walked towards Hepton, smiling, his hand held out palm upwards.

'My gun, please.' Hepton handed the pistol back, and the man slipped it into his pocket.

'That was Russian you were speaking,' Hepton said. The man ignored him.

'We had better be going,' he said.

'But a man's dead,' Hepton protested.

'Good reason for us not to be here, my friend.'

'Who are you?' Hepton asked.

'Come on.' The man gripped his arm. 'We'll take a ride.' He propelled Hepton towards a waiting black cab. Hepton hesitated, but climbed into the back of the taxi, followed by the man, who told the driver to head towards Holborn. Then he turned to Hepton. 'I'm sorry for Mr Devereux,' he said. 'But there's nothing more to be done. My name is Vitalis, and yours is . . .?'

'Martin Hepton.'

Vitalis nodded, giving no indication that he recognised the name. 'Were you a friend of Mr Devereux?'

'In a way. And you?'

'Yes. I suppose you could call me a friend.'

'A friend who carries a gun.'

Vitalis smiled, but said nothing.

'A friend who carries a gun because he fears danger,' Hepton continued. 'Because he *knows* Devereux's life is threatened.'

Vitalis shrugged.

'Who are you?' Hepton persisted.

Vitalis didn't respond. 'The time for questions is past,' he said. 'Now is a time for action.'

Hepton found himself agreeing with this.

'The assassin,' Vitalis said, 'you said it was a she.'

'A woman,' Hepton said. Vitalis nodded. 'You were his . . .' Hepton sought the correct word and found it. 'His controller. You were Devereux's controller, weren't you?'

'What makes you say that?' Vitalis' tone was amused.

Hepton nodded to himself. 'Cam told me,' he said, 'about some mysterious man at the *Argos* base. But the only way he could have known about such a person was if he had gone investigating, opening closed doors, that sort of thing. Because the mystery man would have been in a room of his own, with his own computer and everything. But why would Cam be spying? The answer's simple, isn't it?' He fixed Vitalis with his gaze. 'He *was* a spy, he was spying for *you*.'

'Bravo, Mr Hepton,' said Vitalis. 'Yes, well done.'

'And he had come to London to defect?' It was an educated guess.

'He thought his useful time was over. It happens.'

Another question was on Hepton's lips, but he swallowed it back. If Devereux were about to defect, why would the Russians keep him on so long a leash, and leave him unprotected to boot? *His useful time was over.* His useful time was over, and so he was expendable . . . Hepton stared at the driver's back. Was he too a spy? When would the killing stop?

'Where are we going?' he asked.

'Don't be alarmed. We're dropping me off near my place of work, and then the driver will take you back to your hotel.' Vitalis' eyes twinkled. 'I presume you are staying in a hotel?'

Hepton made no answer. Vitalis just nodded and smiled. He seemed amused by everything.

'I think I know you now,' he said. 'I think I know Martin Hepton. And I want to help you.'

'Why?'

Vitalis held out his hands. 'Because I am a generous man. So Devereux told you about the man he saw at the *Argos* base, the man in the storeroom that had been fitted with a computer console and a telephone?'

'Didn't I just say as much?' Hepton said, hoping to tease a little more out of this man. The traffic had cleared, and they were nearing Holborn. There wasn't much time. There were storerooms at Binbrook, too . . .

'And he told you about the telephone?'

'What about it?'

Vitalis paused to consider whether to tell or not. Hepton could feel his fists tightening. He wanted to hit this man very hard, to force something from him other than this casual chatter. To wipe the smile off his face. He looked at the driver again. The driver was looking back at him in the rear-view mirror. His eyes were hard like marbles.

'The telephone,' Vitalis began. 'Devereux was intrigued by the telephone.'

'A modem?'

'No.' He shook his head. 'It had no dial as such. You couldn't call out, you see; all anyone could do was pick up the receiver. Devereux picked up the receiver and waited.'

'And?'

'And he was connected to somewhere here in England, Mr Hepton. To some kind of listening base. To a man who called himself Fagin.'

Fagin. The line led straight to Binbrook. Hepton tried to look composed but shifted in his seat. Vitalis seemed to know the exact effect his words were having. He glanced out of the window.

'This will do,' he called to the driver, who pulled the cab in to the kerb. 'Now, my friend Mr Hepton, can I offer you breakfast?'

Hepton shook his head. 'I don't eat with strangers.'

Vitalis shook his head. 'I am not a stranger. Well, perhaps I am. But we have a common enemy, it would seem. We have our ideas as to what is going on here. But that is not so important. All my people want to do is to observe, for the sake of our own safety.' His eyes were arch. 'Do *you* know what happened, Mr Hepton?'

'No,' Hepton said, shaking his head again.

'That is a lie,' Vitalis noted objectively. 'But I will let it pass. You will have your own reasons for saying nothing. As I say, we wish only to observe and to protect our interests. Now that Mr Devereux has been terminated, I profess I am more worried than I was. It proves . . . well, something at least.' He shrugged. 'It is your affair, Mr Hepton. By which I mean it is the West's affair. Do you know a Mr Parfit?'

Hepton considered another lie, but paused so long that a lie would have been obvious.

'Yes,' he said at last.

Vitalis seemed satisfied. 'Please give him a message from me. Tell him to remember Warszawa in '87. Goodbye, Mr Hepton.'

He stepped nimbly from the cab, gave some money to the driver and was gone, walking up High Holborn with the brisk step of a man on his way to work. Hepton thought about following, but the driver was awaiting his orders. Still, he was damned if he'd let him know where he was staying.

'Green Park,' he said. He would walk from there.

# 31

It took Parfit a couple of minutes to come fully awake, and while he washed in the bathroom, he made Hepton relate his story twice more. He seemed unmoved by Devereux's murder and the near-assassination of Hepton himself, but was interested in Vitalis. He was also interested in the acronym.

'I wonder if our code-crackers can come up with anything for COFFIN?' he mused, then shook his head. 'Tell me about Vitalis again.'

'Do you know him?' Hepton asked, admitting to himself that he wasn't going to get any sympathy for his own traumas.

'I should say so. We're old adversaries. He's not so active these days, of course. His cover is a bookshop somewhere near Holborn.'

'He's a Russian spy, though,' Hepton protested.

'Yes?' Parfit didn't seem to see his point.

'And you know where he is. Why hasn't he been arrested? Deported?'

Parfit laughed. 'Because then they'd just send home some of ours. Besides, it's nice having him here. It means we can slip him the odd piece. Let him decide whether or not it's true.'

Hepton shook his head. 'The more I know, the less sense it makes. What did he mean about Warsaw in '87?'

'Oh, we were having a bit of trouble out there. The Polish secret police were cracking down a bit too heavily on our diplomats, being a bit obvious in their operations, that sort of stuff. We could have done something about it ourselves, but we passed on a message to Moscow and let the Kremlin deal with it. They slapped a few wrists, and things calmed down again.'

'So what does it mean?'

'It means we're being allowed to deal with this mess ourselves, without outside interference.'

'You think he knows what this is all about?'

'Oh, he'll have more than an inkling.' Parfit had dried his face and was now combing his hair. He looked at himself in the mirror and swept a stray strand back behind his ear. 'More than an inkling,' he repeated. 'After all, as you said yourself, Devereux was his man.' He turned to Hepton. 'Let's get Major Dreyfuss and head for my office. If they wanted rid of Devereux, you can bet a shilling they want rid of Dreyfuss too.'

'But why did they want rid of him?'

'You mean Devereux? Probably because they realised what his game was, that's all.'

Hepton stood for a moment, wondering how Parfit could take it all so rationally, so calmly. Then, aware that he was alone now, he made a dash for the door and followed the cool secret serviceman to Dreyfuss' room.


Dreyfuss was quiet during the short drive towards Westminster Bridge. Hepton sat with him in the back, while Parfit sat with the driver in the front. Parfit had a briefcase on his lap; in it was a cellnet-style telephone, with which he made a steady stream of calls. The driver paid no attention to these, busying himself with the heavy, slow-moving traffic instead. His style of driving was the antithesis of Sanders': careful, methodical, courteous. All the same, the traffic being what it was – and London drivers being what they were – he had to fall into the shunting rhythm of the cars around him, slamming the brakes on, pulling away fast, then slamming them on again. Each jolt seemed to make Dreyfuss wince. Hepton saw that he was holding his right arm with his good left hand, trying to steady it against unwanted motion.

'You should have that in a sling,' he observed. But Dreyfuss did not reply. Parfit, hearing Hepton and glancing in the rear-view mirror, saw the sheen of sweat on Dreyfuss' forehead, indicative of continuing pain.

'Take some more tablets,' he ordered.

'I'm fed up with being doped,' Dreyfuss said through bared teeth. 'I'd rather have pain and all my faculties intact than being in that bloody stupor all the time.'

'Suit yourself.' Parfit made another call.

Dreyfuss turned to Hepton.

'First Jilly. Now Cam. We're letting these people get away with murder.' He nodded his head towards the passenger seat. '*He's* not going to do anything about it. Not if it involves scandal. He's paid to cover things up, not let them get into the open.' Dreyfuss' voice was becoming conspicuously loud, but Parfit made a show of not listening. 'If we're going to do anything, Martin, it's got to be you and me.' His eyes, the pupils tiny pinpoints, were boring into Hepton's. 'You and me.'

'Yes,' Parfit commented, 'you've done so well on your own, haven't you?'

Dreyfuss made a face at him behind his back, then winked at Hepton. 'You and me,' he mouthed noiselessly, before sitting back and watching from his window.

Hepton watched from his window too, but he wasn't really seeing anything. He was thinking over what Dreyfuss had said; that, and a lot more besides . . .

## 32

Blake Farquharson was waiting for them in Parfit's office. Hepton had expected that their destination would be Whitehall and the Foreign Office. But in fact they had travelled south, past the Houses of Parliament, over Westminster Bridge and into Westminster Bridge Road. Their destination was a large office block, where passes once more had to be issued before they headed up in the lift towards Parfit's floor.

Parfit's office, too, was modern, belying his old-world appearance. The desk was cream-coloured and constructed of metal and plastic and chipboard. The chairs were made from tubular steel, their fabric a gaudy lime-green design. There was a large cabinet against one wall, protected by a steel rod and a tumbler lock. Beside it stood a smaller filing cabinet, again protected from prying eyes. The windows were covered by prodigious quantities of net curtain – to stop glass from a potential bomb blast spraying the room, as Parfit later explained. There were calendars and year-planners on two walls, and a coffee table upon which sat a teapot and three mugs, whose interiors were growing cultures not dissimilar in colour to that of the chair fabric.

And in one chair sat Blake Farquharson, though he stood when they entered.

'Hello, Parfit.'

'Good morning, Blake.' The two men shook hands warmly, like old friends after a separation. 'You've already met Martin Hepton. This . . .' Parfit gestured towards Dreyfuss, but Farquharson interrupted.

'. . . Must be Major Dreyfuss,' he said, holding out his hand.

Dreyfuss stared at it, but kept his own by his side. Then Farquharson noticed the bandage and brought his outstretched hand up to his mouth, using it to shield an embarrassed cough.

'We had a spot of bother,' Parfit explained. He had gone to his desk and was sifting through the mass of paperwork awaiting him. He read the top sheets thoroughly, while the rest of the room kept an awkward silence. Dreyfuss had grabbed one of the chairs and was trying to make himself comfortable. Hepton preferred to stand, and went to the window. Parfit put down the sheets. 'Sanders' report,' he stated.

'Yes,' said Farquharson, 'I read it while I was waiting. I'm not sure about Sanders. He's keen, but . . .'

'That's his problem,' Hepton muttered.

'What's that?' Farquharson barked.

Hepton turned to him. 'Your Sanders,' he said. 'He's all enthusiasm, no brains. I'll give you an example.'

'Please do,' Farquharson said slyly.

'Okay, when we went to talk to Cam Devereux – who died this morning, by the way, not that you'll lose much sleep over *that* small fact – the doorman at the Achilles told us we couldn't park where we'd parked. Sanders flashed some kind of ID, which the doorman studied.'

'Yes? Is that all?'

'No,' said Hepton. 'I went back to the hotel this morning. I tried to catch a killer, and a Soviet agent helped me.'

Farquharson's eyes opened wide, and he looked to Parfit for confirmation.

'Vitalis,' Parfit said in a neutral voice. Farquharson nodded.

'And this Vitalis,' Hepton continued, getting to his point, 'stopped on the way out of the hotel to have a few words with the doorman; a few words in Russian.'

'Is that so?' Farquharson looked to Parfit again. 'That's a useful piece of information.'

But Parfit shook his head. 'We've known about the doorman for a while.'

'Well, Sanders obviously didn't know about him,' Hepton said, his voice increasing by a decibel or two. 'Besides which, I've been thinking over what Mike was saying in the car.' At the sound of his name, Dreyfuss became attentive. 'He was saying,' Hepton continued, 'that you seem to know a lot but aren't prepared to do anything about it. It strikes me that he hit the nail firmly on the head. You

know about Vitalis but don't do anything about him; you know
about the doorman at the Achilles but don't do anything about *him*.
And now you know almost everything there is to know about this
COFFIN business: it's to do with satellites, and Buchan airbase,
and Major Villiers, and Harry, and General Esterhazy, and most
probably my boss Fagin. But' – he began to space his words for
effect – 'you're not doing one damned thing about it.' He paused,
and noticed how loud his voice had become. Dreyfuss was smiling
encouragement at him and applauded silently as he finished.

Farquharson didn't like being shouted at. His cheekbones were
veined with blood, his voice tremulous. 'Well then, let me tell you a
few things, Mr Hepton,' he said. 'We need proof, solid hard factual
proof. Because RAF stations and tracking stations and their like
are out of our jurisdiction. In fact, there's precious little that *isn't*
out of our jurisdiction. The intelligence services have no formal
powers. We have to work with Special Branch, and they're not convinced so far by what we've told them. We can't get Number Ten to
listen to us, because frankly the PM has been got at by military
advisors and MoD officials. Our agents in the field have found nothing, so there's precious little we can do at this moment. Except wait.'

'What?' Hepton was yelling now. Yelling out all his fear and frustration, all the last few days of madness and murder. 'Wait for them
to pick us off? Look, whatever this COFFIN is, it's been buried. How
do we find something once it's buried? We don't. The longer we sit
here, the more chance they've got of getting away with whatever it
is they're getting away with while we sit here!'

'Bravo!' Dreyfuss called. He was smiling grimly.

'Who told you the coffin was buried?' Parfit asked in a purposely
quiet voice.

'What?' Hepton asked.

'Who told you?'

'Harry did. Well, sort of. She certainly didn't deny it.'

'And you believed her?'

'Why would she lie? She was going to kill me.'

'But she didn't.' Hepton began to see Parfit's point. 'Now answer
me another question: why is the *Zephyr* ground station being temporarily decommissioned?'

Hepton pondered this. He gave up and shrugged his shoulders.

'I'll tell you,' said Parfit. 'Or rather, I'll tell you *my* interpretation. The coffin *isn't* buried yet – not quite. But they know we're
getting close. They'll put a ring of steel around Buchan, but they

can't stop *Zephyr* spying on them from space. That's why they went
to an extraordinary amount of effort to nobble it. But because we're
closing in, they want to make doubly sure, so they're sending the
sky-watchers home until the burial's complete. That means there's
still time for an exhumation.'

'Fine,' said Dreyfuss coolly. 'So what do we do?'

Parfit turned to Farquharson, his eyes asking the same question.

'We wait.' Farquharson saw that Hepton was about to protest
and hurried on. 'We wait until we see what information comes back
from Buchan. If there's enough to present to the PM, then I'll
arrange a meeting.'

'And if there isn't?' There seemed no ready answer to Hepton's
question. He repeated it.

Farquharson looked to Parfit, but Parfit's face was a blank.

'We've got video tapes,' Hepton continued. 'Don't *they* count as
evidence?'

'They indicate that something's going on,' said Parfit quietly, 'not
what that something is.'

'You mean they're not enough?'

'What do you think?'

Hepton considered. The tapes suddenly seemed very small in
comparison to the scale of the conspiracy.

Dreyfuss was shaking his head. 'You're going to let them get
away with it,' he said bluntly.

Farquharson slapped the desk. 'Get away with what exactly? We
don't know what's happening, do we?'

But Dreyfuss only smiled, as if to say: *I've got a damn good idea.*

# 33

The first report arrived just after they'd eaten a lunch of sandwiches and tea. The tea came in disposable beakers, which was a relief to Hepton, who had feared the offer of one of the mouldy mugs. He was finishing his last cheese sandwich when the telephone rang. Parfit, himself still chewing, picked up the receiver.

'Yes?' he said. He listened, his eyes fixed to the wall in front of him. 'Is that everything?' he said finally. 'Thank you.' He replaced the receiver in its cradle and swallowed some tea.

'Well?' asked Farquharson.

'That was our man in Buchan. He's been past the base. Heavily guarded, and not very subtly. He stopped to ask why, and was told that there had been anonymous threats concerning the pull-out. He says there *is* a pull-out taking place, but there's also a lot of work going on. He thought perhaps they were busy dismantling something.'

'Dismantling something?' Farquharson repeated. 'What sort of thing?'

Parfit shrugged his shoulders. 'He couldn't be sure that it was dismantling.'

'So it could be building work then?' said Hepton.

'Building work?' Farquharson sounded sceptical. 'But that would be noticeable, wouldn't it?'

'Not if it was underground,' said Hepton. 'As in "burial".'

'That's the impression I get,' Parfit agreed. 'They've got to be building something underground.'

'Such as?'

He shrugged again. 'If we knew what COFFIN stood for, we might get an answer.'

'So,' Dreyfuss said, pointing at Farquharson, '*are* you going to go see the PM?'

Farquharson was flustered. 'What with?' he exclaimed.

Dreyfuss got to his feet. 'With everything you've got. It all adds up to quite something, after all, doesn't it? Drag the PM up to Buchan if you have to, but do *something*!'

Farquharson looked to Parfit, but saw in him no ally ready to leap to his defence. He examined his trouser legs thoughtfully and picked a thread from one. 'Very well,' he said. 'I'll do what I can. May I use your phone?'

'Be my guest,' said Parfit.

Farquharson picked up the receiver and punched out a few numbers. 'Hello,' he said, 'it's Blake Farquharson here. Any chance of a word with the chief? Yes, I'm afraid it *is* urgent. Urgent as in very.'


Hepton and Dreyfuss were given leave to visit the canteen, situated in the building's basement.

'I'll get someone to show you where it is,' said Parfit.

'We'll find it,' Dreyfuss snarled. But he calmed almost immediately and apologised. 'I'd just like Martin and me to have a little time to ourselves, to talk about, well, Jilly. Is that okay?'

Parfit looked cowed. 'I'm sorry,' he said, 'if it seems we're not doing enough to locate and free her. I admit it's needle-in-a-haystack stuff, but we *are* trying. Try to relax a little. I'll join you shortly.'

'No rush.'

Whether irony was intended or not, Parfit caught some in Dreyfuss' words. No rush indeed. Farquharson had gone off to Downing Street. The prime minister had agreed to give him a ten-minute interview, starting at quarter past four, which barely gave him time to gather together the relevant details and assimilate them. Still, actually gathering the details was a job for Farquharson's PA, Tony Poulson. Poulson would be panicking right about now, and the thought pleased Parfit greatly. What Farquharson saw in the man was quite beyond him. He had even instigated his own highly furtive investigation of Poulson's past and private life, but with precious little success: the man was as clean as a nun's conscience. But then how clean was that?

He sat behind his desk, wondering if he should have insisted on accompanying Farquharson to Number Ten. He stared at his door, thinking of Dreyfuss and Hepton. Pity the canteen wasn't bugged, but no member of staff would have stood for it . . .

Parfit was a patient man, but also a man who enjoyed the occasional slice of action. He had, for instance, thoroughly enjoyed breaking the man's neck at the airport in DC. He hoped one day to enjoy killing Harry. But it had to be sanctioned. Given that sanction, he was ready to fall on Villiers, Harry and the rest with the most extreme prejudice he could muster. A nod from the PM, that was all he craved right now. His men were ready to act. He'd arranged for Special Branch to turn a temporary blind eye. And he had the necessary tools of his profession to hand. A nod was all he needed. But he doubted he'd get it. All the same . . .

He went to the door and locked it, then crossed to the large cabinet, worked the combination and drew the steel rod out from its resting place. Pulling the cabinet open, he revealed his small but lethal arsenal. Pride of place went to his two preferred handguns, a Walther PPK and a Browning nine-millimetre pistol, the latter's magazine already engaged, thirteen rounds ready for the firing: unlucky for some. He tested its weight. Both guns had been stripped, oiled, checked and rechecked since last use. He put them back and examined the other firearm, a Heckler & Koch MP5 sub-machine gun. Several years before, Parfit had accepted a challenge from an SAS captain to spend some time with the regiment's Counter Revolutionary Warfare Unit as they played out a close-quarters scenario in what had become known as the Killing House. This was a closed environment in which they had to imagine three terrorists were holding a hostage. The captain's summary of Parfit's performance had been frank: 'That was fucking awful. You killed each and every one of them, the hostage included.' But then that had been Parfit's intention, since his job usually entailed tidiness of the most rigorous kind.

Still, he had liked the feel of the MP5s used by the unit, and had acquired one, its serial number removed. Now he touched its barrel, thinking of Harry. Did he hate her so much because he saw so much of himself in her? It was a question he would rather not answer. He lifted the MP5 fluidly to his shoulder and took imaginary aim at the office door.

'Hello, Harry,' he whispered.


There were no windows in the canteen, and the air conditioning was working flat out just trying to dissipate the smells of cooking, of hot fat and baked beans. Sad murals the colour of mud played over the walls, while afterthoughts such as room dividers and pot plants merely added to the institutional feel of the whole. Hepton and Dreyfuss were the only inhabitants. They had been given cold stares and lukewarm tea by one of the canteen staff.

'Too late for food,' she'd snapped.

'Thank God for that,' Dreyfuss had added in an undertone as she poured tea from a huge tin pot. The tea was the same colour as the wall decoration, which gave Hepton an idea as to the mural's genesis.

They sat at the only table not to have been wiped and stacked with four upended chairs. The table came from the same family, it seemed, as Parfit's desk upstairs: cream plastic and chipboard. This was a sad country, Hepton thought, a stupid country. But it still didn't deserve to be handed over to Villiers and Harry.

'It's not a coup,' Dreyfuss stated. 'A coup would be simpler, more out in the open.'

'Maybe the Yanks want to annex us?'

Dreyfuss shook his head. 'They did that a long time ago. It's just that nobody noticed. No . . . I don't know.' He threw up his hands. 'And neither do that lot upstairs. There's only one way to find out.'

'How?' Hepton was sure they were working along similar lines of thought. Dreyfuss' answer confirmed it.

'Your little tracking station.'

Hepton nodded. It made sense, didn't it? The only way Villiers and his crew could keep an eye on the Buchan operation was to use Binbrook. He thought about what the Russian Vitalis had told him. That Cam Devereux had found another room in the *Argos* base. There could be another room at Binbrook, too, a whole series of rooms, fitted with computers and screens showing what *Zephyr* was *really* seeing. Now that he considered it, he realised that there *were* portions of Binbrook that were off-limits to personnel. Locked doors: someone had called them storage areas, someone else had said they were disused and awaiting redecoration. Those locked doors might well be hiding a small, dedicated tracking station. A box within a box, like Izzard's. And if such were the case, there would probably be someone there to watch: someone like Fagin, of course, but perhaps also Villiers himself. And where Villiers was, Jilly might be . . .

'What are you suggesting?' he asked.

'I'm suggesting . . .' Dreyfuss brought his head closer to Hepton's. His eyes burned with something other than drugged or drugless pain, 'that we do something other than sitting around here on our arses. There isn't much time. I'm not saying that we go barging in there, but is everyone on the base in on this COFFIN thing? I think the answer is a definite no, or they wouldn't be moving them out. Okay, so there's the chance that you' – his finger made a circle in the air – 'could move freely inside the base. As far as they're aware, you've been on holiday. So just tell them you've come back early.'

'What about you?'

'Me?' Dreyfuss considered this. 'Do you know how they got me from Washington airport to the embassy? In a crate. After that, a car boot will come as something of a luxury.'

'A car boot?'

He nodded slowly. 'Of course,' he said, 'there is a snag. First, we need a car. We could hire one, I suppose. I've got all sorts of false documents and credit cards on me.'

'What about Parfit? Are you suggesting we do this without him?'

'That's exactly what I'm suggesting.'

'But why?'

'Because I don't trust him. I don't trust anyone in this whole thing who hasn't been hurt. You've been hurt, I've been hurt, and right now someone could be hurting Jilly. You've seen how Farquharson operates. He's scared of COFFIN. He's not going to do anything.'

'We don't know that.' But Hepton's voice betrayed his feelings. The time for action had come. He knew his way around the Binbrook base, and Dreyfuss was right: alone, he might stand a good chance of gaining entry. Once inside, he could . . .

'I could tap into their intercept,' he said.

'What?'

It was becoming quite lucid now. Somehow he'd known all along that this moment would come. The moment when he could put his skill to the test. A moment of challenge.

'I could tap into their intercept,' he repeated. Dreyfuss listened hungrily. 'I'm sure I could. I could screw up their entire system.'

'But won't there be alarms? Protection circuits? That sort of thing?'

Hepton nodded. 'Oh yes,' he said. 'There'll be codes. Entry codes. We'd have to crack them.'

'That could take for ever.'

This time he shook his head. 'I've got a friend,' he said, 'and he's got a little box . . .'

Dreyfuss thought things through. Gain entry to the camp, gain entry to the control room, break into the spoiler satellite . . . Hepton could work on that, while he, Dreyfuss, could look for Jilly. And for Villiers. A lot of ghosts were crying out for revenge. So were a few of the living.

'Right,' he said. 'If you think it's worth a try, I say we leave now, this second. Before Parfit and his boss have a chance to hold us back. I get the feeling somebody's been holding us back all the way along. Like bloody fish on a line. Allow us a bit of play, then reel us back in. Seeing what we know, how far we'll swim. Hoping we'll tire, so that we're easy to land . . .'

But Hepton wasn't listening. He was watching a young man who had entered the canteen and was studying one of the snack-vending machines at the far end of the room. He waved a hand, but it wasn't necessary. He had already been recognised. The man, smiling, approached their table.

'Hello again,' he said. 'I didn't think I'd be seeing you so soon.'

Hepton motioned towards the man and turned to Dreyfuss. 'Let me,' he said, 'introduce you to Mr Sanders. Sanders, this is Major Mike Dreyfuss.'

'How do you do?' The two men nodded. Dreyfuss was looking to Hepton for guidance.

'Sanders here,' Hepton explained, 'is a marvellous driver. He has a very fine Vauxhall Cavalier.'

Now Dreyfuss saw what he was getting at. His smile when he turned back towards Sanders was rapacious.

'Is that right?' he said. 'A Cavalier?'

'Yes,' said Sanders, pleased at their interest but unsure just *why* they were interested. 'It's parked in the garage downstairs.'

# 34

Later, Sanders was able to reflect that that was the moment, really, when he lost his job. Because he didn't see what they were getting at. Because he told them about the modified engine, modified for speed. Because when Major Dreyfuss asked to see the car, he didn't check with Mr Parfit. Because he accompanied them past the security guard and down to the parking bays. Because he turned his back on them to open the door of the Cavalier . . .

And then woke up with a sore head and the drip of oil on his face. Staring up at the underside of a car and realising he had been knocked unconscious and hidden beneath the vehicle in the bay next to his. His bay, which was by then conspicuously empty.

The walk he took back upstairs – walking because it was slower than taking the lift, and he wished to defer the inevitable – was funereal. Yet necessary. There was no way he could hide what had happened. He had to tell Mr Parfit.

He was breathless when he reached Parfit's floor, and realised with some surprise that he had just walked up eight flights of stairs. He remembered none of it.

He knocked on Parfit's door.

'Yes?'

He turned the handle and entered. Parfit was seated behind his desk, his hand poised on the telephone as though expecting a call.

'Ah, Sanders,' he said. 'Come in. If it's about your report, I really haven't had a proper chance to read it yet, but I'm sure it's . . .'

He stopped short. There was oil in Sanders' hair, and the boy looked deathly pale, looked, indeed, beaten about a bit. Then it dawned.

'Oh my God,' he said. 'Where are they?'

'They've taken the car, sir. The Cavalier.'

'Get me another car!' Parfit had already picked up the receiver and was dialling. 'Hello?' he said. 'Let me speak to Detective Inspector Frazer.' He put his hand over the mouthpiece and spoke to Sanders. 'We've got to find them before they leave London.' He removed his hand. 'Hello, Craig? Parfit here. Yes, long time no see. I want a favour. A very important one. Can you get your lads to keep their eyes peeled for a red Vauxhall Cavalier.' He asked Sanders for the registration, and then repeated it down the line. 'Thanks, Craig. Goodbye.' He stared hard at Sanders. 'I thought I told you to get us a car!'

'Yes, sir.' Sanders dashed out of the room, holding his neck where the fist had chopped down on it.

When the door was closed, Parfit took a deep breath and stared at his cabinet. It was time. He was about to rise from his chair when the telephone rang. He picked it up without thinking.

'Parfit?' said the voice. 'Blake here.'

'Blake.' Parfit's heartiness was bluff, and nothing but.

'I've had my say, but the PM reckons it's too amorphous – actual words, "too bloody vague". We're to gather a bit more intelligence before we can act.'

'It may be too late by then.' Parfit was thinking: it may be too late right *now*. The cabinet beckoned.

'Nevertheless, those are the orders from on high.'

'Since when did that stop us, Blake?'

'I don't know what you mean,' Farquharson said, his tone full of meaning. It was time to tell him.

'Dreyfuss and Hepton have left us, headed who knows where.'

The silence on the line was as piercing as any scream. There was a cough of static before Farquharson's too-calm voice said, 'What will they try to do?'

'That's what I'm wondering myself, Blake. I'd say they're capable of trying anything, and I do mean anything.'

'Oh my God.'

'So, PM or no PM, it looks as though there is no alternative. No point in my hanging around here either, so I'm going out into the field.' Parfit paused. 'With your permission.'

Blake Farquharson knew what 'going out into the field' meant in Parfit's terms. He thought quickly but hard. But then, as Parfit had said, there was no alternative.

'Of course,' he said. 'You must do what you think fit.'

'Thank you, Blake.'

'But promise me one thing.'

'Yes?'

'Keep it as low-key as possible.'

'Trust me, Blake.'

'What if you don't find them?'

'Oh, I think I'll find them. I've got a sneaking suspicion I know exactly where they'll be headed.'

He put the receiver down. Then picked it up immediately.

'Get me Downing Street, please.' He waited for the connection to be made. 'Hello? Ah, hello. This is Tony Poulson, assistant to Blake Farquharson. I believe Blake had a meeting with the PM scheduled for this afternoon. I was just wondering—'

'Haven't you been told?' The voice on the other end of the line was curt to the point of rudeness. 'Your boss took ill.'

'Took ill?'

'Had to call off. After the bloody lengths we went to to find ten minutes for him in the PM's schedule. No one is amused, Mr Poulson. Good day.' And the line went dead.

Parfit's smile was part vindication, part acceptance of the betrayal. Farquharson had never intended keeping his appointment. It was a delaying tactic, as had been so much of the game thus far. Parfit had run a check on the lease on Villiers' apartment. The route to ownership had been circuitous, cleverly so, keeping one name as far away from prying eyes as possible. The name had been Farquharson's. He owned the flat, as he owned its former occupant.

Well, nothing could be done about that now. He could leave Farquharson for the moment. For now, he had better things to do. He didn't doubt that Hepton and Dreyfuss would be making for Binbrook, and that if they actually got there, they would inflict at least some damage, perhaps even enough damage. He phoned Frazer again.

'Craig?' he said. 'Cancel that request, will you? If your lads see the car, let me know about it. But don't apprehend.'

The larger the web had grown, the smaller its circumference had become, almost in defiance of the physical laws. Not that laws meant much any more. Parfit put down the receiver and went to the cabinet. There was, as always, no real alternative.

# 35

Graeme Izzard didn't seem surprised to see Hepton, and greeted him like an old friend. Hepton had ordered Dreyfuss to stop the red Cavalier beside the taxis outside Alfie's café. Inside, Izzard was tucking into the all-day breakfast.

'Morning,' he said by way of greeting.

'It's late afternoon, in case you hadn't noticed,' Dreyfuss commented. Hepton and Izzard shared a conspiratorial smile: for Izzard, it was the start of the day.

'What can I do for you?' Izzard asked, his mind more on the tussle he was having with a particularly tough slice of middle bacon.

'It's about your little device,' Hepton began, 'the one you showed me last night.'

'Which one? I seem to remember I showed you hundreds.'

'Yes, but you kept this one in a cupboard. A relic of your hacking days . . .'

Thirty minutes later, Dreyfuss and Hepton left the industrial estate, Hepton driving and Dreyfuss clutching a small black box topped with an old calculator fascia. An unmarked police car was idling near the entrance to the estate. Five minutes later, the call went through to Parfit.

It was past six o'clock when Hepton drove up to the security barrier of the tracking station. A change of shifts was taking place. A young, unsmiling man – a stranger to Hepton – was being replaced by Bert, who had been at the station as long as anyone. Hepton sounded his horn, but Bert, not recognising the car, came out of the hut to check. Seeing who it was, he broke into a gap-toothed grin.

'Mr Hepton sir. I thought you'd gone off on holiday.'

'I was called back. Something about the place shutting down for a while. I've got to collect my things.'

'Ah, yes, shutting down. As from tomorrow, so they tell me. Mind you, *I'll* still be here. You always need security.' Hepton nodded agreement. Bert was giving the car's paintwork a cursory examination. 'I see you've been buying yourself a new car, Mr Hepton.'

'No, it's on loan. I had a little mishap with the Renault.'

'I'm sorry to hear that.' Bert was walking around to the back of the car. Hepton watched him in the wing mirror.

'Anything the matter?' he called.

'Should there be, Mr Hepton?'

'No,' he said, laughing. *Just don't look in the boot.*

'Yes, sir, a very nice car this. Hired, did you say?'

'No, it's a friend's.'

'I suppose I should log it in,' Bert said. He had finished his tour and was returning to the driver's-side window. 'All cars are supposed to be logged, aren't they?'

Hepton shrugged. 'I suppose so,' he said casually.

'Then again,' Bert reasoned, 'if you're only coming in to pick up some stuff . . .'

'That's all.'

'And you've just borrowed this car . . . well, I suppose it hardly matters, does it?'

'Whatever you think, Bert. So long as it won't get you into trouble.'

'Well then, I'll just go and raise the barrier.'

'Thanks, Bert.' Hepton thought of something. 'Oh, Bert?'

'Yes, Mr Hepton?'

'That security man, the one who just clocked off. He's new, isn't he?'

'Started yesterday. His name's Ken. Quiet bloke, keeps himself to himself. But he seems to like the job.'

'Right.' Hepton seemed satisfied with this, so Bert walked away from the car and towards his office, where a moment later he pushed the button that raised the barrier, allowing Hepton into the compound. Hepton gave a wave as he drove in, making for the other side of the administration building. There were plenty of parking spaces in front of the block, but he wanted to be far away from prying eyes. Thankfully, a few cars had parked at the rear, in a sort of courtyard enclosed by a picket fence, a hedge and an emergency generator, itself surrounded by high iron railings. Hepton did not drive to the furthest corner: there were no other vehicles there to provide cover. Instead, he made for the busiest point, where two cars had parked a bay apart, with another car a little distance in front of them. He manoeuvred the Cavalier into the narrow space between the two cars and turned off the engine. Yes, the new security man on the gate liked his job . . . They were moving their own men into the base. Slowly but surely, COFFIN was taking over.

He opened the driver's-side door as far as it would go without denting the car next to him and squeezed out, then closed the door again but did not lock it. He wasn't planning on staying long, and their leave-taking might have to be rapid. Unlocking a door took time, time they might not have.

He looked around. The place was quiet. There was a security camera trained on the back of the admin block and on the path that led towards the control building, but no camera, he knew for a fact, covered this rear car park. He unlocked the boot.

Dreyfuss blinked into the light and quickly, silently, pulled himself out of his foetal position. While Hepton relocked the boot, Dreyfuss did some limbering exercises. The boot had been a tight squeeze, and he was thankful he'd only needed to be in it for the last mile of the drive. He shook his arms loose of any stiffness and straightened his clothes.

'I thought your pal at the gate was going to ask to see inside,' he said.

'To be honest,' answered Hepton, 'so did I. But I already had a story ready about the boot being jammed shut.'

'Very likely,' Dreyfuss said. He was taking deep breaths.

'Okay,' Hepton said. He pointed towards the meandering line of paving slabs, cracked and showing tufts of wild grass. 'That's the path we take. There's a camera trained on it beginning and end, so look relaxed. Pretend I've just arrived on base and bumped into you.'

'Fine,' Dreyfuss replied.

They set off, Dreyfuss with his hands in his pockets and seeming to listen intently to what Hepton was saying, not that Hepton was saying very much other than reminding him of the layout of the tracking station's interior. At the end of the path stood a hefty-looking steel door, and on the wall next to it a numerical keypad, topped by yet another video camera. Hepton tried to look nonchalant as he pressed home the combination 52339, then waited. There was a ca-chunk as the several locks on the door disengaged. He gave it a push, and they entered a sort of antechamber. Against one wall stood what looked like a clocking-in system, but instead of identifier cards, Dreyfuss saw that each slot held a plastic-coated name badge, and beside each name a photograph. Hepton reached for his own badge and tagged it to his trouser pocket. Dreyfuss took the first badge he saw and did likewise. He had been informed: *Some guys clip them to their shirts, others to their trousers. If we tag them to our trouser pockets, there's less chance of someone noticing that you're not the face on the ID.*

He had also been warned about the wall opposite this one, which was made of glass. Behind it, in a small room filled with video screens, sat another security guard. Hepton waved to the guard, who smiled and waved back, then pushed on through the interior door, Dreyfuss following mutely. Now they were in a long corridor, and walking briskly. Dreyfuss felt a kind of complete terror overtake him. They were getting deeper and deeper into this, almost too deep to facilitate any hope of escape. Hepton misread his companion's fear.

'Don't worry,' he said. 'I reckon that with the shutdown, and the change of staff, nobody's going to think a new face suspicious. In fact, we couldn't have picked a better day, all things considered. The only thing that bothers me is that there *are* so many new faces, all of them probably connected to COFFIN. That guard back there, for instance. I've never seen him before in my life.'

Dreyfuss nodded his head. 'So what if he checks up on us?' He was trying to walk at the same pace as Hepton, but it was difficult not to fall a step or two behind and let him take the lead. After all, Dreyfuss had little idea where they were going. But he had to *look* as though he knew. He stared at the floor, matching his footsteps with those of his guide, and so concentrating grew less frightened and less nervous.

After a moment, he realised that Hepton hadn't answered his question. The silence was answer enough in itself. Any check, and they'd be doomed. Suddenly a voice sounded behind them, and both men froze.

'Hey! Martin! Hold on!' They turned slowly towards the voice. A man was approaching them, grinning. 'Martin, what are you doing back?'

'Hello, Nick.' This was what they hadn't wanted, but could hardly hope to avoid: close contact with someone who knew Hepton well.

'Did you get the tapes?' Nick Christopher asked.

'Yes, thanks,' answered Hepton.

Dreyfuss' good hand rested momentarily on Hepton's arm. 'I'll see you later,' he said, smiling towards Nick Christopher before moving off down the corridor. Christopher stared after him.

'Who was that?'

'Some new guy,' said Hepton.

'I get the feeling I've seen him somewhere before.'

'Oh?' Hepton was staring at Dreyfuss' back too, wondering where he was headed. Their plan, hatched on the way here, now seemed woefully inadequate and as full of holes as a disassembled circuit board. But then even on the way here it had seemed so. He turned to Christopher. 'Going to the control room?'

'Yes.'

'Me too. Come on.' They started down another corridor, away from Dreyfuss.

'But what are you doing back here? What was all that with the tapes?'

'I'll tell you later. Is Fagin about?'

'Somewhere, yes. Why?'

'I just need my console for an hour or so, and I'd rather he didn't know about it.'

'What are you going to do?'

'Nick.' Hepton came to a stop, gripping Christopher's shoulder. 'Remember Paul Vincent?'

'Of course.'

'He was murdered. If I can get on my computer for an hour, I think I can catch his killers. But I need your help.'

Christopher stared at him as though Hepton were mad. But Hepton's look was that of a sane man, a scared man, a man doing what he had to.

'What do you want me to do?'

'I want you to protect me. Try not to let anybody interfere with the computer.'

'No problem. But can't you tell me why?'

'Remember when you were younger, when you played with computers for fun rather than for work?' Christopher nodded. 'Did you ever do any hacking?'

Now Christopher smiled. 'Sure, everybody tried it at some time or other.'

Hepton nodded. 'That's what I'm going to attempt now. I'm going to try the scariest piece of hacking you'll ever see.'

Nick Christopher's face lit up. 'All right!' he said. 'Let's go.'

They were nearing their destination. Hepton needed to know what lay ahead. 'Have the new controllers arrived?' he asked.

'The skeleton staff? Yeah, most of them. And a few of the old gang have already left.'

Hepton nodded. 'And you don't know where Fagin is?'

'No idea.'

The storerooms that weren't really storerooms, he thought. It was perfect: as long as he was there, keeping an eye on his satellite, he was free to go to work. He pushed open a final set of doors.

The large central control room was chaotic. Some people were tidying their desks, some were monitoring *Zephyr*. There was a holiday mood in the air, jokes and laughter. Furniture was being moved, consoles dismantled or serviced. A few of the new faces looked at Hepton curiously as he moved past them. He tried to smile and nod affably. Well, he was already in the lion's cage; he might as well stick his head in a gaping mouth . . .

He passed Paul Vincent's desk. It was being dismantled. The computer had already been taken away. He touched the desktop with one finger, then walked to his own console, pulled the chair out and sat down. There was a fine layer of dust on the screen, and he wiped it with the palm of his hand before switching on. A few of the original crew, the genuine crew, saw him and called over. He waved back.

'Just in to tidy up a bit,' he explained. Any one of them could be in on it, could be part of the COFFIN conspiracy. He had to move quickly. But then he knew all the moves, didn't he? He'd been working them out for what seemed like days. He made the link with *Zephyr*'s onboard computer and checked its co-ordinates. It was just about right. Very soon now, within the next hour, it would be over Buchan. That gave him a little time to crack the access code. He already had two passwords he reckoned to be likely candidates – COFFIN and ARGOS. Then he'd let the computer work on the numerical sequence, if one existed, going through random combinations until it found the right one.

He pulled from his pocket Izzard's black box. If he remembered the instructions correctly, it would help save time. And time above all was precious. At any moment, he might be discovered. The new faces around him might twist suddenly with hate, guns pulled from pockets. Fagin might appear, or Villiers, or Harry. He didn't know how long he had. He only prayed it was time enough.

# 36

Dreyfuss walked slowly along this corridor and that. Two men walked past him carrying large holdalls. They smiled, assuming him to be one of the replacement crew perhaps. He smiled back and kept walking. A door was open, allowing him a view of an empty office. The desk had been cleared, but there was a clipboard lying on top of it. He darted into the room and darted out again, carrying the clipboard now. He held it against his chest, keeping his injured hand in his pocket. The hand had stopped giving him pain. Now, it just throbbed. Nobody seemed to be paying him much notice. He hoped Hepton was all right. Dreyfuss' part in the plan was more nebulous. He had to find Jilly, supposing they were keeping her here. It was an outside chance, though, wasn't it? Still, Hepton had told him about the disused stores. It was as good a place as any to look.

'Mr Fulton?' There was a man walking towards him. 'Mr Fulton?' he repeated. He was trying to examine Dreyfuss' name tag.

Dreyfuss looked down at it and saw that *Peter Fulton* was indeed typed there, with an indecipherable signature scrawled beneath. The small photograph was of a man younger than Dreyfuss, the hair fairer, and wearing glasses.

'Not a very good likeness,' the man noted.

Dreyfuss smiled, trying to look younger than his years. 'It was taken a while ago,' he said. He pointed to his eyes. 'And the contact lenses make a difference.'

The man thought for a moment, then nodded. 'Quite so,' he said. He gestured along the corridor with his arm. 'The guard on the main door told me you'd arrived. Shall we go?'

'Of course.' Go where? Dreyfuss was thinking. And who the hell was he supposed to be anyway? It would be just his luck if this Peter Fulton were crucial to the running of the station. They'd be asking him questions he couldn't possibly hope to answer.

'Everybody's ready,' the man said. Dreyfuss groaned silently. 'When did you arrive?'

'Oh, not long ago.'

The man nodded, seeming satisfied. He looked as though he had other things on his mind, which was fine by Dreyfuss. They walked through one set of doors, then another. At least they were progressing into uncharted territory. Dreyfuss checked each door they passed with his eyes, not sure what clues he might be given to Jilly's whereabouts: a scream perhaps, or a muffled cry? Guards outside the door?

They came to a security door. There were numbers on its handle, and the man pressed three of these before turning the handle itself. In this new corridor, things were quieter, cooler. There was a slow hum of air conditioning, the low sounds of distant voices. They came to a final door, and the man opened it, gesturing for Dreyfuss to precede him into the room. A very attractive young woman sat on a chair, watching a bank of TV screens, switching between surveillance of one part of the base and another. One side of her face was heavily made up.

The door closed solidly behind Dreyfuss, and when he turned, the man was pointing a Beretta pistol directly at his chest.

'The guard was right,' he told the woman, who had risen to her feet. 'Someone did take Peter Fulton's pass, unaware that Fulton flew off on holiday yesterday.' Dreyfuss' heart sank. 'I recognised him as soon as I saw him,' the man continued. 'Major Michael Dreyfuss, isn't it?'

'At your service,' Dreyfuss said softly. 'And you are . . .?'

'Didn't I say?' The man had come round to stand beside the woman. He bowed his head slightly, but the pistol never wavered. 'I'm George Villiers; you may have heard of me. And this is Harry.'

On hearing Dreyfuss' identity, a keen look had come into Harry's eyes. She examined him as though he were some rare species, some rare and *endangered* species.

'Where's Jilly?' Dreyfuss asked, his voice as brittle as a thread of ice.

Villiers ignored him. 'Harry,' he said, 'Major Dreyfuss came into the station with another man. I went and took a look at the main door just to be sure, and I was right – guess whose pass is missing all of a sudden?'

'Whose?' Her voice was soft and feminine.

'Martin Hepton's.'

The laugh was cavernous beyond her slender frame. She went to the desk and lifted an attaché case onto its surface. The locks clicked, and she pulled the case open. Inside was the most lethal-looking handgun Dreyfuss had ever seen. It resembled a heavily modified target pistol, with a long shining silver barrel. There was a sight in another compartment of the case's moulded interior, and she fixed this along the pistol. Then she closed the case again and brought a plastic carrier bag out from the bottom drawer of the desk, placing it over her left hand, which was now grasped around the carved butt of the gun. It didn't quite look as though she were merely carrying an empty bag, but the gun was sufficiently disguised. She touched the fingers of one hand to the scald marks on her face. Finally, wordlessly, and on silent feet, she walked to the door, opened it and left, closing it behind her.

Dreyfuss looked at Villiers, who appeared impressed by the performance. 'Where's Jilly?' he repeated.

'She's safe. For the moment. Why don't we sit down? I'm sure there are questions you want to ask. We have a little time until Harry returns. Fire away.'

Dreyfuss sat on the chair Harry had been using. Villiers, however, remained standing, leaning against the far wall next to another door.

'Okay,' said Dreyfuss. 'What's COFFIN?'

'An easy one to start with. Very well, let's take COFFIN's lid off.' Villiers smiled at his own joke, but Dreyfuss remained unmoved. Villiers' face lost its humour. 'COFFIN, Major Dreyfuss, stands for Combined Forces International Network. It has an interesting history. I myself was unaware of it until quite recently. By then, COFFIN had decided it needed a few agents in the field, people who couldn't be traced back to it. People, in other words, outwith the armed forces. Eventually they came to me, and were able to introduce me to Harry. Really, she's the more . . .' he seemed to search for the right word, '*professional* of the two of us. But I'm afraid we're very lowly figures, comparatively speaking.

'COFFIN came about by accident,' he continued. 'You see, generals don't always agree with their governments, and they command more respect from their men than do politicians. Well, a lot of generals – from the United States, the other NATO countries, even a few of the non-aligned states – got together and found that they had a good deal in common. More in common, in fact, than they did with their own countries' leaders. So they started to swap information, intelligence, that sort of thing, all very informally, very *sub rosa*. That seemed to work to everyone's advantage, so they started trading all kinds of things.'

'What kinds of things?'

'Oh, tactics, armaments, maybe even a few men for certain special missions. Of course, no one ever questioned orders, and so no one ever knew that the generals were doing more and more off their own bat, without anyone else knowing about it outside the forces themselves.'

Dreyfuss whistled, trying to sound impressed. Damn it, he *was* impressed, 'But how could you hope to keep something like that secret?'

'Easily enough,' said Villiers, warming to his subject. 'For one thing, who did they have to hide it from? A few men from the MoD and the more investigative of our journalistic profession. But the thing was so big – *is* so big – that virtually no one can see it! That's its beauty.'

'Then why the need for a burial?'

'Look around you, Major Dreyfuss.' George Villiers paced the floor like an actor of old. This was his big soliloquy, and he knew it, but to Dreyfuss he was all amateur dramatics. Amateur dramatics or no, he still held the Beretta. And while he held the gun, Dreyfuss could do little but listen.

'American defence strategy is forward-thinking,' Villiers was saying, 'forward meaning Europe, so as to prevent war on American soil. The American generals weren't happy about the enforced pull-out. It's all down to trust, and they weren't about to trust a civilian Britain not under the US umbrella. Anything might happen. We all might become bloody Europeans, and it's a short step from there to Euro-communism. They decided it wasn't *right*. So it was decided that a base was needed, an underground base, away from prying eyes. RAF Buchan was chosen as the intended site. It has a surveillance system, a few dozen staff and even a couple of silos.'

'Silos?'

'Nuclear silos, Major. Built when Britain was expecting to play host to American missiles.'

Dreyfuss' throat was suddenly very dry. 'Are there missiles, too?'

Villiers nodded eagerly. 'Yes,' he said. 'Isn't that amazing?'

'It's impossible.'

'Oh no, I assure you that it is *fact*. The missiles were already here. Instead of dismantling them, our cousins merely moved them around, stripping off a bit here and a bit there, then rebuilding new missiles from pieces of the old. Simplicity itself. After all, they already had more missiles here than anyone knew about.'

'But why do you need silos?'

'For the first strike.'

'What?' Dreyfuss' head spun.

'Buchan is merely the UK base. There are others dotted all over Europe. They are the centres of attack for a series of forthcoming coups, apparently by the armed forces of each country, but in reality by COFFIN. Soon after that, we launch the missiles.'

'But why, for God's sake?'

Villiers laughed. 'I took you for an intelligent man, Major. Think about it. Can you see Eastern Europe accepting such a series of coups so close to their borders and – if you'll excuse the pun – their satellites? No, they'll be forced to attack. But they'll be too late. *We'll* have hit them first!'

'This is mad.'

'No, it is completely sane, Major.'

'You're saying nobody's *noticed* any of this?'

'Buchan is isolated, as are the other chosen bases. The fact that the troops were pulling out gave the perfect cover for some excavation and building work. There was already a small underground chamber there, to protect the systems against nuclear attack. We disguised a building programme as a dismantling programme. The Scots are a wonderful nation, Major. They keep themselves to themselves, and so long as no one's interfering with them, they're happy to turn a blind eye to most things.'

Dreyfuss nodded. 'But,' he said, 'you couldn't hope to hide the construction work from the skies?'

'Exactly. Which is where *Zephyr* came in. I must say, the generals proposed a simple but ingenious idea. Tap into the surveillance satellite, and you can transmit anything you like. So that's what they did.'

'But I was on the shuttle that launched the pirate satellite.' It was a comment, nothing more. Dreyfuss was still looking for a chance to wrest the gun away from this insane man.

'Indeed you were,' Villiers said, smiling again. 'There was little that could be done about that. The mission had been planned for ages. The US pull-out was supposed to be amicable. To have suddenly announced that a Briton was no longer to go up in the shuttle would have been more than a mite suspicious.'

'More suspicious than blowing the shuttle up?' Dreyfuss felt queasy now, thinking of how heartlessly the crew of *Argos* had been dispatched.

'Yes.' Villiers seemed surprised by the question. 'I mean, shuttles do crash, don't they? Anyway, the generals made *Zephyr* work for them, rather than against them, which is a brilliant strategy. Of course, having decided that a Briton must go up, COFFIN had to be sure that the least capable member of the shortlist was chosen.' He was really enjoying himself now. He waved the gun across Dreyfuss' body, then up and down from head to toes. 'So there was the least risk of your seeing anything suspicious and reporting those suspicions back to Earth before the crash-landing. It all worked well enough, except that you survived the landing. At first, everyone thought you had amnesia, and decided to allow you a lease of life. And by the time General Esterhazy realised what a threat you really were, it was too late. You'd gone. And now here you are.'

'Yes, here I am.' Dreyfuss shook his head. 'I still don't understand, though. The ground crew, the technicians who worked on the *Argos* satellite, they must have *known* its purpose.'

'Why should they?' Villiers opened his arms for a second: not long enough for Dreyfuss to consider charging him, but enough to give him hope of a later opportunity. 'They built to a military design. They didn't need to know what that design's intention ultimately was, and' – Villiers stressed his final words – 'they just followed orders, the way they'd been taught.' He stared at the screens for a moment, then pointed to one. 'Look,' he said, 'there's your friend Hepton now. He's in the control room.'

Dreyfuss looked. Hepton was seated at his console, unaware of the camera trained on his sector of the room.

'Won't be long now till Harry finds him,' Villiers said. His face took on a glaze of sincerity. 'But what you really must try to understand,' he continued, 'is that COFFIN is operating for the greater good. It's *defence* we're talking about.'

'It's more like murder we're talking about,' Dreyfuss growled.

Villiers' gun hand twitched. 'The greater good,' he repeated, robotically. Dreyfuss remembered then what Parfit had said about Villiers: a cold-blooded killer with a history of instability. He tried to calm himself. The last thing he wanted to do right this second was die.

'Well, if that's what you believe,' he said evenly.

'We *do*, Major Dreyfuss. Believe me, we do.' Villiers paused, seeming to drink in his own sense of power. 'Any more questions?' he asked. Dreyfuss shook his head. 'Then if you'll follow me, or rather, *precede* me through here . . .' He lifted his left arm to unbolt another door.

Dreyfuss stood, taking a final look at the surveillance screen. He had no way of letting Hepton know Harry was on her way. 'Where are we going?' he asked.

'I thought you wanted to find Miss Watson?' said Villiers. 'Besides, you haven't seen half of what we're doing here. Not nearly half.'

Then he pulled open the door to another world.

## 37

It had all gone smoothly at first. Hepton had done a spot of hacking in his time, and the process still intrigued and enthralled him. Once, he had found himself hacking into a company's computer at the same time as another hacker. They had exchanged greetings before the other hacker identified himself as a member of the Chaos Club in West Germany; he was hacking from the Ruhr Valley into a computer system in Milton Keynes. Contact with the Chaos Club had taught Hepton much about hacking, and for a time he'd been hooked. But after a while, personnel records and medical files ceased to hold their one-time interest, and he'd given the sport up.

Like cycling, however, you never forgot the 'how'. Having accessed the *Zephyr* onboard computer, he found that COFFIN 762 was the code to unlock the interface between the two satellites, or rather between their two computers. The code was simple enough: COF-FIN hadn't been expecting anyone to attempt an access, or to have the knowledge so to do. Otherwise they would not have been so unimaginative with the password, and they would surely have used a less simplistic numerical combination. Izzard's black box had done its job, finding the number sequence in a space of minutes.

Nick Christopher was watching over Hepton's shoulder, inter-ested and excited but trying to look unimpressed so as not to draw undue attention to the console.

But meantime, Hepton was stuck. He'd got this far, but progress-ing any further seemed an impossibility, for there was a further code to be gleaned, and he had run out of ideas.

*What is your name?*
*COFFIN*

*Thank you, COFFIN. Please wait.*
-------------------------------------------------------
-------------------------------------------------------
*What is your identifier number?*
762
*Identifier number accepted. Welcome to interphase control at 19:45
hours. You have fifteen minutes online remaining before engagement
of protection circuitry. Do you wish to access:*
1. *Classification?*
2. *Interlock?*
3. *Transmission?*
4. *Quit?*

Hepton wasn't sure, but had taken a chance on Interlock, pressing the number 2 on his keyboard.

*Interlock control required. State access password.*

And that was where he had so far drawn the blank. He was in,
but he wasn't in. He could speak to the damned computer, but it
wouldn't do what he wanted until he'd found the password. COFFIN
had already been used, so it wouldn't be anything similar. He had
an idea.

*ZEPHYR*

*Incorrect password. Please try again.*

He sat there staring at the screen. If not ZEPHYR, then what?

'Try *Argos*,' Nick Christopher suggested. Hepton typed in the
letters.

*Incorrect password. Please try again.*

Hepton snarled, then typed in *FUCK YOU* and pressed the keyboard's return button.

*Fuck you too, 762*, came the onscreen reply.

'I hate computers with an inbuilt sense of humour,' Christopher
commented. Then he touched Hepton's shoulder. Hepton looked up
and saw that a security guard had entered the room. The guard
stopped and held a murmured conversation with one of the new controllers. Hepton didn't like this one bit. He reached around the side
of the computer screen and turned the brightness and contrast knobs
as low as they would go, blacking out the screen. Then he turned to
Christopher. The guard was looking in their direction now.

'Does that guard know you?' Hepton whispered.

'I've seen him around,' Nick said, trying hard not to sound
nervous.

'Yes, but has he seen *you* around?'

'We've nodded to one another in the corridor.'

'Does he know your name?'

Nick shrugged. 'I don't think so. We're not *that* close.'

Hepton's hand went to his trousers and unclipped the ID badge, slipping it into the pocket. 'Do you have a name badge?' he whispered. As well as the official ID, some of the staff owned larger, rectangular badges made from stiffened card and boasting name only. These had been given out at the beginning of the *Zephyr* project, a stopgap until the proper IDs had been made. But Nick had held onto his, finding its inverted mistake – *CHRISTOPHER NICHOLAS* – amusing. He reached into his shirt pocket now, brought out the badge and laid it in the palm of Hepton's hand. Pretending to fuss with his keyboard, Hepton attached the badge prominently to his own shirt.

A moment later, the guard confronted them.

'Yes?' Hepton asked imperiously. The guard stared at the name tag, then at Nick, whose face he recognised. He seemed confused, shook his head.

'Nothing, sorry,' he said, moving away again. Hepton watched from the corner of his eye as the guard said a few reassuring words to the controller, then left the room. He sighed and turned the screen back on. He was still no further forward. He stared upwards, seeking inspiration, and found himself gazing into the single black lens of a video camera, angled into the room from one corner.

'Shit!' he said. 'I forgot about that.'

'About what?'

'That camera.' Its red light was on, too. There was no doubt about it: it was beaming his picture back to security. Perhaps he had even less time than he had thought. He stared around the room. Two controllers were laughing over a photo in the newspaper . . .

Newspaper!

'Nick,' he said, 'do you still do those crosswords?'

'Yes, why?' Nick Christopher sounded scared: he had an inkling now that this was all very serious after all.

'Got a thesaurus?'

'Sure. Stay there.' As if Hepton were going to leave! A moment later, he returned with a large paperback book.

'Look up zephyr for me,' Hepton ordered.

Christopher started flipping through pages. 'Why zephyr?' he asked.

'Because I don't suppose Argos will be in there, and we've already used coffin.'

'Okay.' Christopher had found zephyr in the index, and now sought the correct section. 'Three-five-two,' he said to himself. 'Right, here we are.' He held open the book, his hands tense, as though he might at any moment tear the pages in half.

'Start at the top,' commanded Hepton.

'"Breeze",' Christopher read.

Hepton typed the word in: incorrect.

'"Breath of air".'

Hepton was dubious, but typed it anyway: incorrect.

'Next,' he said.

'"Waft", "whiff", "puff", "gust" . . .'

Hepton entered all four individually: incorrect.

'Damn this thing!' he cursed.

One of the older operatives came up to the console.

'Hi, Martin,' he said. 'What happened to the holiday?'

'Just clearing things up, Gary,' Hepton said, his grin as tight as a rictus.

Gary took a look at the screen.

'It's a game,' said Christopher grimly. Gary sensed that he wasn't wanted.

'That's nice,' he said, moving away. Hepton watched him go.

'Next,' he said.

Christopher had lost his place. There was a pause while he found it.

'Next!' Hepton hissed.

'Jesus, Martin, I'm doing my best. Hold on, here we are. "Capful of wind".'

Hepton stared at him, saw he was serious and shook his head. Then tapped the letters in anyway. Incorrect.

'"Light breeze", "fresh breeze", "stiff breeze",' Christopher concluded, closing the book with a thump.

'That's it?' Hepton asked.

'That's it.'

'Okay.' Hepton thought hard, seeking another way.

'What about a dictionary?' Christopher suggested.

Hepton nodded vigorously, then, while the large red book was being fetched, rubbed at his aching temples. Time was rushing by. Soon he would run out of his online allocation, and the satellite's computer would warn its guardians that someone was attempting to tamper with it. They would try to shut him down right then . . . that was supposing security didn't get to him first.

'Here you go.'

Hepton took the book. There was a mark on the cover where Nick's palm had left some sweat.

'What are you looking for?' Christopher asked.

'Straws to clutch at,' muttered Hepton. He turned to the back and found zephyr. '"The west wind",' he read aloud, '"gentle breeze, the god of the west wind".' He closed the dictionary and handed it back, then turned to his keyboard. The west wind. Well, what the hell. He started to type.

*WEST WIND.* Then the return key.

There was a pause, and he held his breath, then:

*Incorrect password. Please try again.*

Nick Christopher cursed quietly, but Hepton was staring at the screen. There had been a pause, a very slight pause, before the computer had responded. As though it were checking . . . As though it weren't sure. He typed again, his fingers solid on each plastic key.

*WESTWIND.* This time with no space. Then the return.

There was another pause, if anything longer than the first, then the screen kicked into life.

*Welcome to interlock option on interphase. Do you wish to:*

*1. Change interlock coding?*

*2. Enter interlock program?*

*3. Check interlock co-ordinates?*

*4. Oversee interlock?*

*5. Disengage interlock?*

Nick Christopher sucked in air and leaned lower towards the screen. 'You've done it!' he gasped.

Hepton almost leapt out of his chair, but gripped its arms with his hands instead. Yes, he was in! He was right there in the nerve centre of the American satellite! He wondered if someone somewhere in a tracking station in the US was watching a screen and beginning to worry. He hoped so. Because he was going to give them a show.

Christopher slapped his back. 'You clever sod,' he whispered, his voice trembling. 'You've actually done it.'

'Now watch this,' said Hepton. But Nick's attention had switched to something else. He was looking over towards the far door, his antennae twitching.

'She's new,' he said. 'Must be part of the skeleton crew. A bit tasty for a skeleton, though. No, wait a second, I've seen her before . . .'

Hepton, curious, looked up for a moment from his screen and saw Harry standing just inside the far door, holding it open as her eyes swept the room. She seemed to be carrying a plastic bag.

He froze momentarily, watching her. 'She's the one who's been trying to kill me,' he stated, his voice cool. Then he concentrated on the screen again. Any second now she would see him. And she would kill him. But he had so little time left anyway, so little time to crack the whole COFFIN thing wide open. And what a foul stench he'd release. So rotten and pungent that no one could ignore it any longer. It didn't matter if he died right here and now, just so long as he wrecked their plans.

'Hello, Martin.'

She was in front of him, standing on the other side of the console, her head and shoulders visible above the monitor, the rest of her body hidden from his view. He didn't glance up from the screen. Instead, with quiet pressure from his left index finger, he pressed the number 2.

*ENTER INTERLOCK PROGRAM*

A message flashed onto the screen: *WARNING! INTERPHASE USER TIME NOW UP. INFORMING CONTROL OF THIS TRANSACTION. PRESS RETURN TO CONTINUE. YOU ARE NOW BEING MONITORED BY CONTROL.*

Monitored by control: that meant someone would now be watching his every move, ready to negate it if they could. (Harry in front of him! Don't think about her!) He had to finish this quickly, but without allowing them to work out just what he was up to. (Harry standing right there, a rustling of plastic. The carrier bag.) It wouldn't be easy.

'Hello, Martin,' she said again. 'Bring your hands where I can see them.' And this time he did look up. He couldn't help himself. He gazed towards her dark glassy eyes. And found himself staring down the barrel of a gun, so close that he could swear he could see the bullet resting at the end of the long, long chamber.

Then the gun seemed to speak. 'Goodbye, Martin.'

## 38

'What the hell is this?'

Villiers had ushered Dreyfuss into a series of rooms, separated by glass wall dividers. The rooms were packed with electronics Dreyfuss didn't – couldn't – recognise. It wasn't like in the old movies he'd seen, banks of flashing lights and huge rolls of tape rotating on their mainframe computer spools. It wasn't even like *Argos* mission control. It was cool and peaceful, and the machines made a low, soothing sound, while six dot matrix printers disgorged their data and a row of six television monitors showed a mixture of satellite pictures and computer graphics. DAT machines recorded without apparent end the digital transmissions from . . . well, wherever. Telemetry? Satellite waves? Computer language? Dreyfuss thought all three were possible. COFFIN seemed to have limitless access and limitless funds. But then COFFIN was potentially the largest army the world had ever seen.

And in a corner of this most impressive of the rooms sat Jilly.

Surrounded by state-of-the-art hardware, her captors had chosen a good old-fashioned method of securing her: rope bands looping around her body and the chair-back, and around her wrists; an adhesive gag for her mouth. Except that on closer inspection, Dreyfuss saw that the bands were made of thin plastic strips, secured by metal clips. Unbreakable, and painful to fight and chafe against. He ran to the chair and placed his hands on her shoulders. Her eyes were wild with surprise at seeing him, and she tried to speak, mouthing her frustration against the restraining pad.

'Are you okay?' he asked awkwardly, no other more sensible words coming to mind. She nodded briskly.

A man in a white coat was standing over one of the recording machines, checking line levels. He seemed relieved to see Villiers.

'Thank God!' he snapped. 'I'm a scientist, you know, not a bloody gaoler.'

Villiers ignored the outburst. 'This is Major Dreyfuss,' he said. 'And Major Dreyfuss, this' – pointing his gun hand at the man – 'is Henry Fagin, head of this . . . establishment.'

'A bloody pawn more like,' Fagin muttered, loud enough to be heard. He was still bent over his machines, moving from one to the next like a commander inspecting his troops.

'What *is* this place?' Dreyfuss said, looking around him. One hand still rested on Jilly's shoulder, kneading the skin gently, calming her.

The reply came from Fagin. 'It's a listening post. Off-limits to *Zephyr* personnel. They don't even know it's here. Officially, it's an offshoot of Menwith Hill.'

'Menwith Hill?'

'Yes. That's an NSA operation, American personnel. The job is SIGINT, signals intelligence, picking up all sorts of information while it's in transit.' He gave a sly glance in Dreyfuss' direction. 'Nothing's safe any more, not if it's being transmitted. It still gets from A to B, of course.'

'But on the way it's listened to?'

Fagin slapped one of the machines proudly. 'And copied. You name it: telephone conversations, rocket telemetry. Here, take a listen.' He flipped a switch and a stream of noise started issuing from the speakers set into the walls. 'Know what that is?' he asked, his face opening into a smirk. 'Computers talking to one another. Satellite computers.' He pointed earthwards. 'The ground asks *Zephyr* for close-ups of RAF Buchan.' His finger jerked skywards. '*Zephyr* transmits this request to the other satellite, which then sends it live shots of a base in Wales, made to look like Buchan.' He pointed downwards again. '*Zephyr* then sends these pictures to the ground. It's quite easy if you think about it.'

'You're forgetting, Fagin,' interrupted Villiers, 'Major Dreyfuss doesn't *need* to think about it. He was there when the satellite was launched.'

'And when the crew were murdered,' said Dreyfuss coldly. Villiers just shrugged.

'A US branch decision. What could we do?'

'I'll tell you what you *did* do, though,' said Dreyfuss, remembering Hepton's story. 'You killed a man called Paul Vincent, you tried to murder Martin Hepton, you murdered Cam Devereux, and God knows, that may only be the tip of the dagger.'

Villiers shrugged again but seemed, if anything, pleased by Dreyfuss' catalogue. He glanced at one of four clocks on the wall, each one set for a different time zone.

'Harry should have disposed of Mr Hepton by now.'

On hearing this, Jilly screamed behind her gag, her face purple with effort. Villiers was delighted by this effect and lifted his head to laugh. But a choking sound from Fagin cut him off.

'What is it?' he asked.

Fagin was studying one of the computer screens. He pressed a few buttons, then studied the screen again. 'There's a fifteen-minute access alarm on the interface,' he explained quietly. 'And it's just gone off.' He turned to Villiers, his eyes twinkling with humour. 'Somebody's trying to out-sting our own little sting.'

'Can you stop it?' Villiers sounded wary.

'Oh yes. Every time the intruder makes a move, I'll just order the computer to make another. A bit like chess. Strange, though. He's in, but he's not doing anything.'

As Villiers peered at the computer screen, Dreyfuss knew he had to make his own move. But Villiers wasn't his target: Fagin was. Fagin could wreck everything. He *had* to take him out. He threw himself forward and grabbed the scientist, pulling him to himself as a shield, then backed away. Villiers was already aiming his gun, undecided whether to risk the shot.

Fagin saw his hesitation. 'For God's sake,' he pleaded.

Villiers stared at him, then at Dreyfuss. Finally he brought his gun arm down, but then angled it away from Dreyfuss and his prisoner and began raising it again. Directly at Jilly's head.

'I think,' he said stonily, 'this is what's called an impasse. Except that you, Major, can do nothing with your hostage except hide behind him. While I, on the other hand, won't hesitate to shoot mine.'

And to prove it, he turned his head away from Dreyfuss towards Jilly, taking aim and beginning to squeeze the trigger.

'No!' Dreyfuss pushed Fagin aside and started forward again. But he was too far away from Villiers, far too far away. The gun moved in an easy sweep until it was pointed directly at him. The explosion in such a confined space was deafening, but the impact in Dreyfuss' chest was silent. He felt himself propelled backwards with great force, until, with a new and sickening sound of shattering glass, he slammed into and through one of the dividing walls.

Shards sparkled in his hair as he lay on the floor, a red stain spreading rapidly across his shirt. Villiers examined him through the sizeable hole in the glass wall, seemingly content, then turned back into the room. Fagin looked ghostly white, smoothing strands of hair back across his gleaming pate. And Jilly Watson . . . well, she was staring at Dreyfuss' still body with wide, tear-brimming eyes and horror carved into her cheekbones. Seeing this, Villiers smiled at her with a face that seemed to be transfigured before her very eyes, becoming quite mad and more dangerous, even, than ever.

But now Villiers' attention was drawn to Fagin. 'Don't just stand there!' he roared. 'Get to work! Let's see who stops Martin Hepton first: you with your computer, or Harry with her gun.'

There was chaos in the control room. Some of the men had risen from their consoles to stare wide-eyed at Harry, and more especially, at the gun she was pointing in Hepton's face. A few onlookers, caught between one desk and another, had frozen where they stood, while others had slipped out of the room. Harry didn't appear to see any of this. She had eyes only for Hepton. He was still seated at his computer but had taken his hands off the keyboard and placed them either side of it. His left hand rested on the desktop, his right hand on Nick Christopher's heavy dictionary.

'I can't believe,' Harry was saying, 'you thought you could just walk in here.'

'Why not?' said Hepton. 'You did, after all.'

She didn't seem particularly angry or vengeful or confident or nervous. She seemed . . . relaxed. A job was a job, and this was just another one. Hepton took pleasure in the scars across her face, the result of his boiling water.

'Now look,' Nick Christopher said from somewhere behind Hepton's shoulder. 'You can't just come in here waving a bloody gun—'

'Don't waste your breath, Nick,' said Hepton. His fingers had closed around the book under his right hand.

'That's right,' Harry said. 'Don't waste your breath.'

Hepton swallowed hard. He had one last card. 'I was sorry to learn about your mother,' he said.

Harry's eyes widened, then narrowed to slits. 'What?'

'Your mother,' Hepton repeated casually. 'I was sorry to learn that she committed suicide. Something to do with your father, wasn't it?'

'Shut up.'

'He was in the army, wasn't he? I find that odd, you see.' He paused.

'You find *what* odd?'

'That you should end up working for the military, working for everything your father stood for. Yet he was so brutal to your mother, to Harriet.'

'Shut up!'

'That was why you left home, wasn't it? Did the old drunkard like to give you a beating too, eh?'

It was enough. Harry's teeth were bared in absolute, mindless hate. She swung back the pistol and whipped it across Hepton's face. As it connected, he brought up his left hand and gripped Harry's pistol hand, *her* left hand, angling the gun away from him, while his right hand, now clutching the dictionary, swiped at her head, connecting heavily. The gun went off, its deadly charge hammering home into a computer screen, which sparked once before starting to smoke.

Hepton rose from his chair and placed one foot on the seat, using it as a springboard to launch himself over the desk, the computer, the monitor screen, landing heavily on Harry. His left hand still clutched her gun arm, while his right flexed and sent a clenched fist hard into her face. The contact was satisfying. She gasped, writhing beneath his weight. He could feel blood trickling down his cheek from where the pistol barrel had hit him. Then Harry's knee connected with his groin, and he felt searing pain. He retched, but held fast to her arm, and punched her again, in the mouth this time. But she was wrenching free of him, kicking out, and scrabbling with her free hand towards his face, his hair, his eyes . . .

Her nails were like tools as they raked down his already bloodied cheek, digging into flesh. He cried out and pulled away from her hand. She used the moment to kick again with her full weight, sending him flying into a desk. People were pouring from the room, not about to lend a hand. Even Nick Christopher seemed rooted to the spot, his eyes on the pistol. The pistol she was raising again, aiming. Blood dripped from Hepton's face onto the stone floor. His skin felt on fire. He prepared himself for a final assault, while four feet away Harry stood, blood flowing from nose and mouth, her trigger finger squeezing . . .

'Bastard,' she screeched. 'No more!'

'Harry!'

She froze at the sound of the voice. Her gun still trained on Hepton, her eyes peered towards the far door, where another gun was trained on *her*.

'Parfit!' she spat, arcing the pistol towards the door. But too late: Parfit's bullet hit home with a wet sound like an overripe peach hitting a wall. An inky pink spray covered Hepton as Harry fell back, her head crashing against a computer screen, cracking it, then her body sliding floorwards in a clumsy, ungainly mess. And there she lay, the gun still in her hand, but like nothing so much as a toy now, a rag doll with too little stuffing. Inelegant, and not at all tidy.

There were shouts, panic, pandemonium. Parfit didn't care, didn't bother identifying himself. He walked over to Hepton.

'Have you finished?' he asked. His eyes strayed momentarily to the corpse.

'What?' Hepton was still in shock, still reeling from a great feeling of being *alive*.

'Whatever it is that you're doing here.'

'Oh.' He was jolted back to the present. 'No,' he said, 'not quite.'

'Then get on with it.' Parfit looked around. 'Where's Dreyfuss?'

'He's gone off to look for Jilly.'

'Right.' Parfit handed him a clean handkerchief. 'Here, mop some of that blood off your face.' As he stalked off, Nick Christopher slumped weeping into a swivel chair, covering sticky red face with sticky red hands. Hepton looked towards Parfit's retreating figure.

'What took you so long?' he called with a grin, before walking back around the row of consoles to his own screen, where, numbly but fixedly, he began to go to work. 'Nick,' he said, 'I need your help.'

Nick Christopher rubbed at his eyes. His voice was hollow. 'What do you want me to do?'

Hepton pointed to the computer console next to his own. 'Get that thing up and running. Do you remember that TV satellite we hacked into a couple of months back, so we could get the porn channel?'

'Yes.' Christopher looked uncomprehending.

'Good, get me back into it, will you?'

Fagin stared at the screen. Villiers was growing ever more agitated beside him.

'What's happening?' he snarled.

'Nothing's happening,' said Fagin. 'Absolutely nothing.'

'Then Harry must have found him!' Villiers said.

'I don't think so,' Fagin answered. 'Look.'

He was pointing towards the screen. Numerical sequences were appearing, rows and rows of numbers.

'What are those?'

'I don't know,' said Fagin simply. 'Perhaps he's trying to confuse us.'

'What do you mean?'

'I mean,' Fagin explained, 'maybe he's using these to throw us off the scent of what he's *really* doing.'

'You mean you don't know? I thought you were supposed to be an expert?'

'In some things, yes. But when it comes to hacking, I think Martin Hepton might just have the edge.' Fagin's smile had a hint of pride about it. Villiers grabbed him and shook him.

'So shut it down,' he yelled. 'Close the whole thing down.'

Fagin did not resist. Instead he waited until Villiers had stopped shaking him. 'I can't do that,' he said. 'All we can do is wait for him to make his move – his *real* move.' Then he sat down in front of the screen, a grandmaster awaiting his opponent's opening gambit.


The room was empty now, with the exception of two live bodies and one very cold one. Hepton was in a chair on castors. Once Nick had tapped into the television satellite, he used this chair to wheel himself quickly between the two computer terminals – his own, locked into the *Argos* satellite and, consequently, into *Zephyr*; and the TV satellite. He worked fast and expertly, so that even Nick Christopher had trouble deciding what he was doing. Hepton was happy to explain.

'I'm going to marry these two bastards,' he said. 'I'm going to take over the TV satellite and lock it into *Zephyr*, then disconnect *Zephyr* from *Argos*. Resulting in . . .'

Nick Christopher saw it all now, and broke into a wide, devilish grin. 'You can't do that,' he said. 'Do you know—'

'Of course I know. I know what it'll do. What's more,' smiling too, he turned to glance at his friend, 'I really think I can do it.'


'What's happening now?' Villiers was frantic. What had happened to Harry? Why hadn't she disposed of Hepton?

Fagin rubbed his temples. He was too old for this, too old for

Hepton's tricks. 'He's doing *something*,' he said. 'But I don't quite know what . . .' His fingers worked slowly, methodically, on the keyboard, trying to cancel whatever Hepton was doing. Then it dawned on him. His voice became a whisper. 'He's using two terminals.'

'What?'

'He's using two terminals at the same time.'

'So open a second terminal! Now!' Villiers pushed Fagin against the console. Fagin reached to a second computer and started coding in. 'Perhaps there's still time,' Villiers said.

'Yes, perhaps,' agreed Fagin.

Jilly, however, saw what they could not. One of the monitor screens had burst into life. And instead of the aerial views she had become used to, she was watching a nature programme. The scene looked very much like Africa. Parched earth, creatures gathering around a drying pool of water. Then a voice.

'Quickly, the animals learn that old enmities must be put aside, for now at least. Water is necessary for their survival, so they gather around, forgetting that they are enemies, knowing only that life is their priority. Hunters and hunted sip side by side . . .'

Villiers and Fagin turned slowly, disbelievingly, towards the TV monitor. For that was, unmistakably, where the sound was coming from. Stuck to the top of it was a large piece of Dymo tape, on which was printed *ZEPHYR: LIVE PICTURES*.

Fagin began to laugh. 'I see what he's done now!' he roared hysterically. 'I see!'

'What?' screeched Villiers. 'What?'

'Look,' said Fagin, pointing to the screen. The wildlife programme had vanished, to be replaced by sharply focused pictures of Buchan, the camera homing in on the building work, the underground silos, the tips of the missiles themselves. Villiers opened his mouth in horror.

There was a deferential cough at the open door.

'Good evening, Villiers,' said Parfit, his gun extremely steady in his hand.

# 39

The screens began to jump around 8.15. Hepton's intention was always to wreck the interface, not merely snip the connection. The estimated viewing figures of seven and a half million, however, came as a bonus. For in linking up the satellites, he had projected the shots of what was really happening in Buchan to a Europe-wide audience. While two video tapes, one master, one backup, ran, capturing the moment for posterity, satellite receiver dishes across most of Europe started to pick up a new station. Early-evening quiz shows, old movies and wildlife programmes crackled and faded and were replaced by pictures of nobody quite knew what. Some pirate station, people assumed, and many of them settled back, waiting to see if there would be any pornography on display, as the tabloid newspapers had been warning and promising. But all they got until nightfall was pictures of a building site. At least, they mostly assumed it was a building site. Except that one repeated shot showed what looked to be a large and ugly missile, resting nose up in its near-finished silo . . .

The plug had been well and truly pulled on COFFIN.

Villiers and Fagin were easily subdued, and Jilly was released. But Dreyfuss was in a bad way. Parfit felt an uncomfortable moment of sentiment: one second the pleasure of terminating Harry; the next the grief of seeing the blood-soaked shirt and feeling the fading pulse. How many lives could a man have? Dreyfuss had used up a fair quota already, but Parfit was grimly determined that he deserved yet another. He staunched the wound as best he could and waited for the ambulance.

Jilly buried her face in Hepton's shoulder and let the tears come. They were tears of frustration rather than relief. Hepton, his work finished, didn't know what his own tears were. But he let them fall all the same.

# 40

General Colin Mathieson-Briggs was sitting in his office when the men from Special Branch arrived. He knew why they had come, and had prepared himself for the moment, his tie knotted tightly so that his head remained erect.

General Jack Holliday was not, however, to be found in his office. Like Mathieson-Briggs, he had been on site at Binbrook the day they had infiltrated *Zephyr*. He had timed the whole process. From initial interference to complete locking-on had taken just under four minutes. Not long enough for anyone to notice any mischief, surely? There had been risks, of course, but they were not so great as the risk of leaving Britain defenceless and dependent on unreliable European allies for future safety . . .

His wife found him dead in the woods near their country estate. Holliday had gone shooting with his dog, a young Weimaraner. She discovered him slumped against a tree, his head taken clean off, the dog anxiously licking and cajoling the corpse's hands and neck, its whiskers shiny crimson.

In France, Germany, Spain, Greece, Turkey, Finland, arrests were happening. And in the United States, too. Parfit had called Frank Stewart and given him the go-ahead to move in on General Ben Esterhazy and others, including, at the Pentagon, General William Colt. But without any apparent fuss or urgency: it had been decreed that the whole COFFIN affair was to be kept hidden from the world at large. In London, an anxious Home Secretary signed more D-notices in the space of an evening than in the rest of his term of office put together. It was all for the best.

Though Parfit had the devil of a job convincing Hepton, Dreyfuss and Jilly Watson of this. They were gathered around Dreyfuss' bed, a good old-fashioned English hospital bed in a good old-fashioned (albeit private) English hospital. Dreyfuss was recovering slowly, but convincingly, though it seemed to him he'd been through all this one time too many.

'So what did we accomplish?' he asked.

Parfit shrugged. 'What we set out to achieve,' he answered.

'So it just gets hushed up?' yelled Jilly.

Parfit knew of her fiery reputation and was at pains not to test it too far.

'The guilty will be punished,' he said.

'But not publicly!'

'Does it matter?'

'Yes, I think it does.' She was out of her chair now, stalking towards the window.

'I *could* remind you . . .' Parfit began.

'. . . That we've signed the Official Secrets Act,' Jilly finished for him. 'I know.' She sighed. 'But it's so bloody unfair, after what we've been through.'

'Jilly.' The voice of reason was Dreyfuss'. 'As Parfit says, does it matter? We've won.'

Jilly's arm snapped out towards Parfit. '*They've* won,' she said. '*He's* won. Not us, Mickey. Not any of us.' Her eyes went to Hepton, silent still in his chair, thoughtful, looking tired and numbed. 'Martin?' she coaxed.

He seemed to come awake. 'What?'

'What do *you* think?'

'I think satellite TV'll never be the same again.' Then he laughed, the others joining in. 'And I think I need a holiday.'

'That shouldn't present a problem,' said Parfit, checking his watch. 'I'm sorry, I've really got to go now. I have an appointment in London.'

'Getting your back slapped?' Jilly couldn't resist asking.

'Not quite,' he said. 'Can I offer anyone a lift?'

'Yes please,' said Hepton. He looked over towards Jilly, who paused, but finally shook her head.

'I think I'll stick around here for a little while,' she said. She gave a hint of a smile in Dreyfuss' direction, and he returned it.

'Fine,' said Hepton, meaning it. Parfit glanced at him.

'Shall we go?'

'Yes,' said Hepton, 'let's go.'

As the car – yet another black Ford Sierra – sped towards London, Parfit revealed the nature of his appointment.

'I'm seeing our friend Vitalis,' he said. 'Having dinner with him, actually, just to let him know what happened. He did the same for me after the Polish thing.'

'Will you tell him everything?' Hepton asked, staring at the passing scenery.

Parfit thought this over. 'Probably not,' he said. 'Almost certainly not. It doesn't matter, so long as he's told a little of it and doesn't have to find out for himself.'

'The special relationship,' Hepton said quietly to himself, musing. Then he asked the question that had been bothering him for days. 'How come COFFIN always knew where to find us?'

The question seemed to surprise Parfit. He raised his eyebrows and puckered his mouth. Then he shook his head with slow deliberation.

'It could have just been Villiers, I suppose,' he said casually.

'Or it could have been someone in *your* organisation. It could even have been you, Parfit, couldn't it?'

Parfit's eyes were on the road ahead.

'It could have been you,' Hepton repeated, enjoying this deliberate train of thought, 'because you wanted to get Harry. And because you wanted Harry, you were only too willing to set us up as bait. Catchable bait.'

Now Parfit barked out a laugh, though with a slight, noticeable edge to the sound.

'It's an intriguing thought,' he said. He was on the point of adding something, but he had already given away enough confidences. It would reflect badly on the Service if people found out that Blake Farquharson was in COFFIN up to his mottled neck. There had to be a quiet demise for Farquharson. An accident, perhaps, or heart failure. These things could be arranged. Parfit was, after all, an expert in damage limitation. He couldn't tell Hepton and he couldn't tell Vitalis. He couldn't even tell Frank Stewart, who was so looking forward to being there when Ben Esterhazy was arrested. No, it had to be the Department's secret . . . for the moment. The Department's secret that Blake Farquharson, head of the Secret Intelligence Service, had been a traitor at the highest level; a traitor not to his country so much as, in Parfit's mind, to his calling. He hadn't visited the PM that day; he had called from a public telephone kiosk and made his apologies. And he had been ever ready to slip information to

George Villiers – his protégé of sorts – and to Harry; as much information as was necessary. God might know why he'd done it; Parfit didn't.

He squinted ahead into the sunshine. The sky was blue, peppered with tiny high-level clouds. If the sky was blue, how come space was black? He could always ask Hepton. There was a lot he should ask Hepton, but this probably wasn't the time.

Blake Farquharson carried only one case as he left his home. A small case, the kind one might use on an overnight trip. Not that he was going on an overnight trip. He was fleeing for ever. He had some money in a confidential account, tucked away on a Caribbean island. They would find him eventually. But that didn't matter. All that mattered was that it shouldn't happen here, at home, in England.

The streets seemed quiet. He looked up and down for a taxi, and was elated to see one turn the corner in his direction. Its orange light was on, too, proclaiming it for hire. He waved an arm, and the taxi signalled, pulled into the kerb and stopped.

'Heathrow,' Farquharson ordered, getting in.

'Of course,' said the driver, his voice oddly inflected.

The taxi started off, and Farquharson stared at the driver. He looked familiar. In the rear-view mirror, the man's dark eyes wrinkled with pleasure.

'Yes,' he said, 'you do know me, Mr Farquharson. At least, I think you do. My name is Vitalis. You are about to leave the country. Probably for some warm climate. But might I suggest a slightly cooler one? Somewhere your old friends won't find you? At any rate, let us talk.'

Farquharson stared out of the window. The taxi was not travelling fast. He wrapped his fingers around the door handle and tried it, but it was locked. Vitalis was still smiling at him. Farquharson rested his back against the seat and closed his eyes. Slowly they filled with tears.

# About the Author

**Ian Rankin** is the multi-million copy worldwide bestseller of over thirty novels and creator of John Rebus. His books have been translated into thirty-six languages and have been adapted for radio, the stage and the screen. Rankin is the recipient of four Crime Writers' Association Dagger Awards, including the Diamond Dagger, the UK's most prestigious award for crime fiction. In the United States, he has won the celebrated Edgar Award and been shortlisted for the Anthony Award. In Europe, he has won Denmark's Palle Rosenkrantz Prize, the French Grand Prix du Roman Noir and the German Deutscher Krimipreis. He is the recipient of honorary degrees from universities across the UK, is a Fellow of The Royal Society of Edinburgh and a Fellow of The Royal Society of Literature, and has received an OBE for his services to literature.